"Sweeping portrayal of the lives of five Sierra Leonean women . . . Forna's work sheds light on the history of a long-struggling nation." —*Publishers Weekly*

"An intimate portrait of the evolution of one West African community . . . Highly recommended." —*Library Journal*

"Forna's prose, reminiscent of consummate stylists such as Jean Rhys, becomes condensed and palpitating, each word doing triple duty." —Maxine Swain, *Bookforum*

"Sweeping, heartbreaking . . . the eloquently rendered oral histories that emerge . . . are suffused with joy, sadness, longing, madness, denial, defiance, and wry bitterness. . . . Fate lets you down, Forna suggests. People let you down. God lets you down. And in the end, you have a reservoir of memories, enough to feed a wellspring of stories." —*The Seattle Times*

"A literary diamond, a bloody ruby, leaving the reader elbow-deep in a treasure trove and heady with guilty delight at what has been discovered . . . Staggering first novel . . . This is a work of literature that reached as deeply into the being of a white male Anglo-Saxon card-carrying bloke as, I dare say, it would touch the heart of any woman, any African, Inuit, bond trader, or raving banshee . . . Lovingly honed stories . . . Forna is destined for the shortlist of all the literary prizes on offer with this beautiful book, not because she has revitalized the fading art of storytelling but because, for me at least, she has rekindled the dying embers of a much more precious art—that of listening." —*The Evening Standard*

"A dazzling storyteller, Aminatta Forna vividly evokes the daily lives of African women and their brave attempts to alter their destiny." —*Books Quarterly*

"A wonderfully ambitious novel written from the inside, opening up a particular society and delving deeply into the hearts, histories, and minds of women . . . Loss is a thread running through the novel, especially the loss of mothers; so too is the spirit world, which hovers around the material one. . . . The women's triumphs and tragedies are played out within a society in transition over the better part of a century: colonialism, independence, and the horrors of civil war are so subtly and deftly woven into the stories that it takes a while to realize that major national shifts have taken place. . . . Inspired storytelling and beautifully crafted prose . . . This is [Forna's] first novel, but it is too sophisticated to read like one." —*The Guardian*

"Unfolding in Forna's vivid, graceful prose like the bolts of brightly colored cloth sold in Aunty Asana's fabric store, the aunts' stories are filled with the plangent uncertainty of lives lived at the mercy of external events . . . The act of survival is a triumph in such circumstances, and the act of storytelling both a small private rebellion and a duty . . . Forna's tender, haunting novel is a celebration of the enduring power of such private narratives." —*The Sunday Telegraph*

"A writer of startling talent, as readers of her harrowing and brilliant memoir, *The Devil That Danced on the Water*, will attest . . . [*Ancestor Stones*] is written in a sumptuous prose that makes it a delight to read. Virtually every page contains breathtaking descriptions . . . The writing is luminous. . . . *Ancestor Stones* may be a novel, but it is not, I think, a work of fiction. The intimate and sometimes terrible stories it relates may have necessitated such disguise, but every word rings true. . . . *Ancestor Stones* has a purpose at once modest and grand: to record the history of a country through the stories of four half-sisters. . . . The book leaves an impression of immense joyfulness, a sense of delight and wonder. Conveying the human spirit's irrepressible love of life is the triumph of this magical book."—*The Daily Telegraph*

"Extraordinary, and vibrant with sadness and joy . . . [*Ancestor Stones*] spans generations, gloriously illuminating the lives and dreams of four very striking women. . . . Forna beautifully describes the chafing confines and glorious freedoms of lives whose rich continuity is being gradually rent asunder, as Africa's political situation becomes increasingly fraught." —*The Daily Mail*

Praise for *The Devil That Danced on the Water*:

"A masterpiece that makes sense of senselessness. . . . We could place [Forna's] memoir of Sierra Leone alongside Nega Mezlekia's *Notes from the Hyena's Belly*, about Ethiopia, or Rian Malan's *My Traitor's Heart*, about South Africa. . . . An original work made out of necessity."
—Lorraine Adams, *The Washington Post Book World*

"Populated with vibrant characters . . . At once impassioned, lucid, and understandably enraged, *The Devil That Danced on the Water* illuminates the troubled, tragic history of a country and a continent. . . . [Forna] re-creates the sights, smells, and sounds, the daily pleasures and unthinkable horrors of her childhood." —Francine Prose, *O: The Oprah Magazine*

"Reminiscent of Isabel Allende's *The House of the Spirits*, Forna's work is a powerfully and elegantly written mix of complex history, riveting memoir, and damning exposé." —*Publishers Weekly*

"A shining example of what autobiography can be: harrowing, illuminating, and thoughtful . . . [Forna's] filmic language, descriptive metaphors, and closer observations of the natural and human landscape of her childhood can take your breath away and then leave you feeling punched in the gut." —*USA Today*

"Poignant and passionate . . . [In] this moving memoir, Forna brings her family to life . . . [and] discovers the story of an entire nation's demise. . . . How lucky the reader who sees it through her eyes." —*People*

"[A] lucid, exacting memoir . . . indelible." —*The New Yorker*

ANCESTOR STONES

Aminatta Forna

GROVE PRESS
New York

First published in Great Britain in 2006 by
Bloomsbury Publishing Plc, London

Family tree designed by Jennifer Newlin Bell

This edition is published by special arrangement with
Bloomsbury Publishing Plc.

Printed in the United States of America

FIRST PAPERBACK EDITION

Library of Congress Cataloging-in-Publication Data

Forna, Aminatta.
    Ancestor stones / Aminatta Forna.
        p. cm.
    ISBN-10: 0-8021-4321-0
    ISBN-13: 978-0-8021-4321-1
    1. Sisters—West Africa—Fiction. 2. Coffee plantations—West Africa—
Fiction. 3. West Africa—Fiction. I. Title.
PR6106.O766A84 2006
813'.6—dc22   2006047708

Grove Press
an imprint of Grove/Atlantic, Inc.
841 Broadway
New York, NY 10003

Distributed by Publishers Group West

www.groveatlantic.com

07 08 09 10 11 12   10 9 8 7 6 5 4 3 2 1

For Yabome, *oya ka mi*

CONTENTS

KHOLFA FAMILY TREE

KHOLIFA FAMILY TREE

1	2	3	4	5
Namina	Isatta	Sakie	Jeneba	Sallay

Alusani   2 daughters   MARIAMA

Pa Momoh Kabia = ASANA = Osman Iscandari
(2)   (1)

Alpha   Kadie = Anguman Kamara

Adama

Gibril Umaru Kholifa
=

6 Tenkamu 7 Balia 8 Koloneh 9 Memgo 10 Saffie 11 Mamusu

Idrissa Ibrahim HAWA = Tejani Jamboria Soulay

2 sons Lansana (Okurgba)

Ambrose Horton Williams = SERAH

Ambrose jr. Ya Ya jr.

Malaika Sessay = Ya Ya

ABIE

Butterflies

I see her sometimes, usually when I least expect it: a reminder of her. In the bow of a lip: an outline a blind man could trace with his fingertips. The curve of the continent in the sweep of a skull, in the soft moulding of a profile. A man on a bus. Sitting alone. Tall above the slumped bodies of the other passengers: a surviving lily in a bowl of wilting flowers. For several seconds I gazed up at him. He never looked my way. The bus moved off over the bridge and I watched it go. And for a moment I felt it, the tightening in my guts, the drifting melancholy – the return of a forgotten nostalgia.

On Sunday mornings I have seen her in the shape of a thousand butterflies winging their way down the Old Kent Road, where only hours before razor-cut youths stumbled out of doorways and bare-legged, barefoot girls walked home – holding on to their handbags and high heels. The butterflies' dark heads were crowned with turbans, their bright robes like great iridescent wings billowed in the gusts of air from the passing traffic. In twos and threes they came together to form a colourful cloud, a great host of butterflies winging their way through the grey walls of the city to spiritual pastures: to the People of Destiny Mission, to the Temple of Christ, to Our Lady's Church of Everlasting Hope.

What do they pray for, I wonder? Held captive by fate and history in this dark country.

For some miracle, a pair of ruby slippers? A click of the heels, a spinning tornado to whisk them up and set them down again in a place far, far away – beneath a burning amber sun.

PROLOGUE

I

Abie, 2003

The Women's Gardens

London, July 2003.

IT BEGAN WITH A LETTER, as stories sometimes do. A letter that arrived one day three winters ago, bearing a stamp with a black and white kingfisher, the damp chill of the outside air, and the postmark of a place from which no letter had arrived for a decade or more. A country that seemed to have disappeared, returned to an earlier time, like the great unfilled spaces on old maps where once map makers drew illustrations of mythical beasts and untold riches. But of course the truth is this story began centuries ago, when horsemen descended to the plains from a lost kingdom called Futa Djallon, long before Europe's map makers turned their minds to the niggling problem of how to fill those blank spaces.

A story comes to mind. A story I have known for years, it seems, though I have no memory now of who it was who told it to me.

Five hundred years ago, a caravel flying the colours of the King of Portugal rounded the curve of the continent. She had become becalmed somewhere around the Cape Verde Islands, and run low on stocks, food and water. When finally the winds took pity on her, they blew her south-east towards the coast, where the captain sighted a series of natural harbours and weighed anchor. The sailors, stooped with hunger, curly haired from scurvy, rowed ashore, dragged themselves through shallow water and on up the sand where they entered the shade of the trees. And there they stood and gazed about themselves in disbelief. Imagine! Dangling in front of their faces: succulent mangoes, bursts of starfruit, avocados the size of a man's head. While from the ends of their elegant stalks pineapples nodded encouragingly, sweet potatoes and yams peeped from the earth, and great hands of bananas reached down to them. The sailors thought they had found no less a place than the Garden of Eden.

And for a time that's what Europeans thought Africa was. Paradise.

The last time I thought about that story was a week after the letter came. By then I had left London – the city I now call home – to retrace the letter's route to the place from where it had come and beyond. I was standing in a forest just like the one the sailors had stumbled into. And I remembered how in the early morning I used to watch my grandmothers, my grandfather's wives, leave their houses and make their way, down the same path upon which I was standing, towards their gardens. One by one each woman parted from her companions and went to her own plot, whose boundaries were marked by an abandoned termite hill, a fallen tree, an upright boulder. There, among the giant irokos, the sapeles and the silk-cotton trees of the forest, she tended the guavas, pawpaws and roseapples she had planted there. Then she weeded her yams and cassava where they grew in the soft, dark earth and watered the pineapple plant that marked the centre of her plot.

I thought of the sailors' story. And for a long time, I thought it was just that. A story. About how Europeans discovered us and we stopped being a blank space on a map. But months later, after the letter arrived and I traced its arc and came to land with a soft thud in an enchanted forest, and after I had listened to all the stories contained in this book and written them down for you, that one story came back to me. And I realised the story was really about something else. It was about different ways of seeing. The sailors were blind to the signs, incapable of seeing the pattern or logic, just because it was different to their own. And the African way of seeing: arcane, invisible yet visible, apparent to those who belong.

The sailors saw what they took to be nature's abundance and stole from the women's gardens. They thought they had found

Eden, and perhaps they had. But it was an Eden created not by the hand of God, but the hands of women.

The letter that brought me back to Africa came from my cousin Alpha. I didn't recognise his hand on the envelope: he had never written to me before. Alpha had once been a teacher, but in those changed days he made his living composing letters for other people. People who took their place opposite him one by one, clutching a scrap of paper bearing the address of an overseas relative or else the business card of some European traveller, unwittingly exchanged in a moment of good humour for a lifetime of another person's hopes. Alpha conveyed greetings, prayed for the recipient's health, invoked the memory of the dead, and wrote hereby merely to inform them of the sender's situation, the dislocations and hardships of the war. Sought their help in solving their many difficulties. By God's grace. Thanking them in advance.

And then he swivelled the letter around to face his customer, for their perusal and signature. They nodded, feigning comprehension. And signed with a knitted brow and a wobbling hand the letters of their name learned by heart. Or else they pushed a thumb on to the opened ink pad, and left a purple thumbprint like a flower on the bottom of the page.

My own letter was written on a single side of paper taken from a school exercise book. No crossing out, no misspellings – suggesting it had been drafted beforehand and carefully copied out. Alpha's signature was at the bottom of the page. Alpha Kholifa, plainly executed without flourishes, a simple statement. He used our grandfather's name, the same as mine, so there could be no mistake. The other thing I noticed, only after I had read the letter through, was the absence of a post-office box address. Knowingly, he had denied me the opportunity to write back with ready excuses, to enclose a cheque bloated with guilty zeros.

The letter contained not a single request or plea. The sum of it was held within two short sentences.

'The coffee plantation at Rofathane is yours. It is there.'

O yi di. In our language: it is there. Alpha had written to me in

English, but the words, the sensibility, was African. In our country a person might enquire of another after the health of a third. And the respondent, wishing to convey that the individual was less than well, requiring the help of God or man, might reply: '*O yi di.*' He is there. She is there. The coffee plantation at Rofathane is yours. It is there.

He did not ask me to come back. He willed it.

The letter finished in the conventional manner. Alpha enquired after my husband, whom he had met once, the last time I went back. We had taken the children, to be seen and admired by family and friends, though they – the children, that is – were too small then to have any memory of the visit. I remember my aunts called my husband the Portuguese One, the *potho*, which has become my people's word for any European. After those sailors who landed and kept coming back. Named the country. Set up trading posts. Bred bronze-coloured Pedros and Marias. And disappeared leaving scattered words as remnants of their stay. *Oporto. Porto. Potho.* The tip of the tongue pushed against the back of the teeth, a soft sound. Over the years the word had moulded itself to the shape of an African mouth. It did not matter to them – my aunts – that my husband was, in fact, a Scot.

The morning after the letter arrived I woke to a feeling, which I mistook at first for the chill that follows the end of a warm dream. A sense of apprehension, of an undertaking ahead. Every year for years I had told my Aunt Serah I was coming home. But every year Aunt Serah told me to wait. 'Come at Christmas. When things have settled down.' I knew I had left it long enough. A spectator, I had watched on my television screen images of my country bloodied and bruised. The burned out façade of the department store where we bought mango ice cream on Saturdays. Corpses rolling in the surf of the beach where we picnicked on Sundays, where I rolled for hours in those very waves. A father with his two sons dodging sniper bullets on a street I travelled every Monday morning on my way to school. Peace had been declared and yet the war was far from over. It was like witnessing, from a distance, somebody you know being set upon by thieves in the street. And afterwards, seeing them stagger, still punch drunk, hands outstretched as they fumble for their scattered possessions. Or else, shocked into stillness, gazing around themselves as if in wonder, searching for comfort in the faces of strangers.

What would you do? You would go to them.

I sat up and shook my husband's shoulder – my Portuguese Scottish husband – and I told him I was going away for a while.

And so there I was, standing in the forest among the women's gardens, remembering my grandmothers. Beyond the trees their daughters were waiting for me. Four aunts. Asana, daughter of Ya Namina, my grandfather's senior wife: a magnificent hauteur flowed like river water from the mother's veins through the daughter's. Gentle Mary, from whom foolish children ran in fright, but who braided my hair, cared for me like I was her own and talked of the sea and the stars. Hawa, whose face wore the same expression I remembered from my childhood – of disappointment already foretold. Not even a smile to greet me. Enough of her. And Serah, belly sister of my father, who spoke to me in a way no other adult ever had – as though I might one day become her equal.

They were the ones whose presence filled the background to my childhood. Not my only aunts, by any means, rather my husband-less aunts. Asana, widow. Mary, spinster. Serah, divorcee. The fate of Hawa's husband had never been quite clear, it remained something of a mystery. I had heard some of their stories before, though I didn't remember who had told me or when. As a child I had spent my evenings at home doing schoolwork, or trying to get a picture on the black and white TV, as a teenager I'd lain in my room fiddling with my yellow transistor radio, waiting for my favourite tunes. Without men of their own to occupy them these four aunts had always been frequent visitors to my father's house until he left to take up a series of appointments overseas and I followed in his slipstream to university.

Coming back, I thought about my aunts and all the things that had never been spoken. And I saw them for what they were, the mirror image of the things that go unsaid: all the things that go unasked.

The stories gathered here belong to them, though now they

belong to me too, given to me to do with as I wish. Just as they gave me their father's coffee plantation. Stories that started in one place and ended in another. Worn smooth and polished as pebbles from countless retellings. So that afterwards I thought maybe they had been planning it, waiting to tell me for a long time.

That day I walked away from the waiting women, into the trees and towards the water: the same river that further on curled around the houses, so the village lay within its embrace like a woman in the crook of her lover's arm. Either side of the path the shadows huddled. Sharp grasses reached out to scratch my bare ankles. A caterpillar descended on an invisible filament to twirl in front of my face, as if surveying me from every angle before hoisting itself upwards through the air. A sucker smeared my face with something sticky and unknown. I paused to wipe my cheek in front of a tall tree with waxy, elliptical leaves. Along the branches hung sleeping bats, like hundreds of swaddled babies. As I watched, a single bat shifted, unfurled a wing and enfolded its body ever more tightly. For a moment a single eye gleamed at me from within the darkness.

Here and there scarlet berries danced against the green. I reached through the cobwebs, careful of the stinging tree-ants, and plucked a pair. I pressed a fingernail into the flesh of a berry and held it to my nose. Coffee. The lost groves. All this had once been great avenues of trees.

And for a moment I found myself in a place that was neither the past nor the present, neither real nor unreal. *Rothoron*, my aunts called it. Probably you have been there yourself, whoever you are and wherever in the world you are reading this. *Rothoron*, the gossamer bridge suspended between sleep and wakefulness.

In that place, for a moment, I heard them. I believe I did. A child's laugh, teasing and triumphant, crowning some moment of glory over a friend. The sound of feet, of bare soles, flat African feet pat-patting the earth. A humming – of women singing as they worked. But then again, perhaps it was just the call of a crane flying overhead, the flapping of wings and the drone of the insects in the forest. I stood still, straining for the sound of their voices, but the layers of years in between us were too many.

I passed through the ruined groves of the coffee plantation that by then was mine. Not in law, not by rights. Customary law would probably deem it to belong to Alpha, Asana's son. But it was mine if I wished, simply because I was the last person with the power to do anything with it.

Down by the water, under the gaze of a solitary kingfisher, a group of boys were bathing. At the sight of me they stopped their play in order better to observe my progress, which they did with solemn expressions, kwashiorkor bellies puffed out in front of them like pompous old men, sniffing airily through snot-encrusted nostrils. I smiled. And when they smiled back, which they did suddenly, they displayed rows of perfect teeth. One boy leaned with his arm across his brother's shoulder, his eyes reclining crescents above his grin, and on the helix of his ear the cartilage formed a small point in exactly the same place as it does on my son's ear. I had bent and kissed that very place as he lay sleeping next to his sister, before I left to catch my early morning flight.

And later, inside my grandfather's house, I pushed open the shutters of a window, finely latticed with woodworm. The plaster of the window sill was flaking, like dried skin. The clay beneath was reddish, tender looking. In the empty room stood the tangled metal wreck of what was once a four-poster bed. I remembered how it was when my grandfather lived and I came here as a child on visits from the city on the coast where my father worked. Then I sat bewildered and terrified before him, until somebody – a grandmother, an aunt – picked me up and carried me away. It was only the fact that my father was the most successful of his sons, though still only the younger son of a junior wife, that made him deign to have me in his presence at all.

In the corner a stack of chests once stood, of ascending size from top to bottom. Gone now. Fleetingly I imagined the treasures I might have found inside. Pieces of faded indigo fabric. Embroidered gowns crackling with ancient starch. Letters on onion-skin parchment. Leather-bound journals. Memories rendered into words. But, no. For here the past survives in the scent of a coffee bean, a person's history is captured in the shape of an ear, and those most precious memories are hidden in the safest place of all. Safe from fire or floods or war. In stories. Stories remembered, until they are ready to be told. Or perhaps simply ready to be heard.

And it is women's work, this guarding of stories, like the tending of gardens. And as I go out to them, my aunts, silhouetted where they sit in the silver light of early dusk, I remember the women returning home at nightfall from their plots among the trees.

And I wonder what they would think if they came here now, those hapless port drinkers. Of all the glorious gifts the forest had to offer – fresh coffee.

SEEDS

2

Asana, 1926

Shadows of the Moon

HALI! WHAT STORY SHALL I tell? The story of how it really was, or the one you want to hear? I shall start with my name, but that is not so easy as you think. I have been known by many names. Not the way you are thinking. You people change your name the way you change your hairstyle. One day braids. Next day hot-comb. You marry and take a stranger's family name in place of your own. A *potho* name, no less. But us, we never change the names that tell the world who we are. The names we are called by, yes. These ones may change.

I had another name once, before I had even seen the light of this world. My name was Yankay, the firstborn.

Sakoma: the month of emptiness. The women were making ready, whitewashing their houses, plastering façades streaked by the rain and stained with mould. Soon the doors of every home would be thrown open. Soft, new rice to eat instead of bulgur and mangoes. The hungry season was nearly over.

My mother's hands were dipped in white, her face and arms flecked. That was how she was always able to remember I was born the week of the last rainfall before the dry season began. I had an appetite, she used to say, such an appetite because I was born at the start of the feast. That day she worked and felt her insides convulse. Pain seeped into her limbs, trickling out of her centre like juice from a lemon. With her right hand she went on smoothing the plaster in arcs like rainbows. The fingers of her left hand she began to click.

I was the firstborn of my father. Not my mother. My mother was a praying wife. My father inherited her from his uncle. After she was widowed she could have returned to her own people as the other wives did. But she stayed and chose a new husband from the younger brothers. She chose my father. It goes without saying that she must have admired him. Not because he had life, was vigorous with ambition, though he had and was those things. But because she didn't stay a praying wife for long. Within a year she had conceived.

My mother was my father's first wife. Well, it's true there was one other praying wife before her, but that one went when my father brought my mother into the house. My mother's status was high, you see. She had been the wife of a chief. The other woman had lived long enough. She wanted to be mistress in her own house. So she packed her baskets and walked back to her own village where she had sons.

So there was my mother, plastering her house. Alone and painting, no need for anyone else. This is the way she was. When the job was complete she laid the block of wood on the steps of the house and set off to the birth attendant's hut. By the time she reached the end of the village she was clicking fast. Both hands. It was early morning. The women were sweeping their compounds and the front of their houses. Dust devils danced across the ground. They looked up when they heard the sound of her fingers. Mine was an auspicious birth: my father was already a big man. Every woman who was already a mother laid down her broom and walked. Their fingers picked up her rhythm, until ten, fifteen, twenty women clicked their fingers as one.

I wanted to come to this world, to the place where things happen, I didn't want to stay where I was. I always had big eyes for this world and I was born with them open. My mother never feared for me. There are some children – you can tell the ones – born with a hunger for life. I was in such a hurry my mother didn't even have time to drink the infusion of lemon tree leaves. I was born, to the chorus of their fingers, like the sound of crickets announcing the rain.

Afterwards the midwife prepared to bind my mother's stomach. But my mother kept on clicking her fingers. The midwife pressed ten fingertips into her stomach. Shook her head. Click. Click. My mother asked for some of the tea, and they poured the cool liquid into her mouth. She arched her back. Click. Push. Click.

My brother slid into this world: small, still and silent. At first, they thought he'd gone with the leaves. My mother cradled him and called for him to come back. That was when she took my name away from me and gave it to him. If only he would come back, she promised, he would be the firstborn. She traced his features with her fingers. The baby opened his eyes, black eyes. He stared back at her. And he decided he wanted her. That was how it all began. This thing between him and me. Because his first deed in this world was to take from me what was mine.

We were twins. People thought we were lucky. They used to touch our heads as we passed by. Tap, tap. Stall holders called out to us: 'Eh, *bari*!' Twin! And they offered us delicacies to taste and gave our mother their best price without the bother of haggling. Women bending over their cooking pots lifted the lids and called us over. One month after our birth, our mother made an offering at the house of the twins: chicken eggs and palm wine, foods the spirits like to eat.

When I had three teeth my brother still sucked with his gums. My mother gave me a wooden spoon and a bowl of rice pap. I followed her wherever she went, holding my spoon. One day she sat on her stool and I leaned against her knees. A duck passed us with tiny ducklings trailing in her wake, like porpoises following a fishing boat. Wherever the mother duck walked her babies followed, attached to her by an invisible thread. She stroked my hair: 'So who is my duckling?' she asked. Me, I would have cried, if I had known how to speak. She bent down and caught a baby duck in cupped hands; she let me stroke the downy feathers before she released it. The duckling raced, wings flapping, towards its mother. I laughed. But when I saw my brother on my mother's lap, still suckling with his old man's gums, stroking her breast and squeezing milk from her nipple, I felt jealous. I wasn't so pleased to be her baby duck any more.

The women who had witnessed my birth called me Nurr too – because I was the true firstborn, because they had already left the chamber when my brother arrived and didn't hear my mother make him her promise. They thought maybe I would return. Because that's what the first child often does. They had forgotten that my mother had children before, when she was married to another man. That happened in another place. They could only see what was before their own eyes. So they called me Nurr, a thing to be discarded, slung on the heap. That's how people thought then. The bodies of children who wasted their mother's tears they threw on the rubbish mound outside the town. Nobody would bury such spirits next to their very own relatives under the flamboyant trees.

I could walk first and even carry him. My brother barely bothered to learn to use his own legs; he knew I was there to bear his weight. One day our father informed his uncles that he had decided to leave the place where we lived to start a plantation. The land was there, you see. And so we left to found our own village. Outside the town, beyond the ring of light and into the elephant grass we went. I trailed my hands across the towering stalks, as thick as bamboo poles, grazing the tips of my fingers. And then we entered the darkness. High above us the monkeys cavorted and screamed our names. The crows laughed at our foolishness; a woodpecker darted ahead of us, rapping out a warning as it went; orchids dripped nectar on to us and it slid down the backs of our necks; we skirted great boulders and waded across pools of black water as the path closed up behind us. I looked up the dizzying trunks of the trees stretching far, far into the sky. I tried to see the sun.

Single file, we went. At the front the snake man with a long stick and a pair of dogs. After him my father and the diviner who led him to the new land. My mother walked a respectful distance behind them. My father had new wives by then. They walked behind my mother. I'll tell you the rest of their names when the time comes, not now. Then I had eyes only for my mother. The youngest of the wives I walked alongside. She was a few years older than me – just a sprouting seedling wife. By this time I could carry nearly half a bushel of rice. We followed behind the others and shared a load. Behind us came *karabom*, my grandmother who had left her own house to follow her daughter to this new place.

Our belongings were carried on the heads of five indentured men. Every day my father sat in the courtroom listening to the disputes of men who laid down two coins to place their grievances before the elders. People respected him; he became chief advisor to the *obai*. Many of the men brought before the court were debtors. Sometimes my father agreed to clear their debts himself. And in return he took their sons from them, to labour for him until the day their fathers redeemed them. Whenever that day came.

The men toted giant baskets of clothes, a woven cage of guineafowl, a pair of piglets with their feet bound together, our great iron cooking-pots, sacks of rice, salt, groundnuts and the chest that held my father's fortune in silver shillings – the Queen's money – with metal locks crafted by Fula locksmiths. Last of all came my father's iron-framed four-poster bed, carried aloft by eight extra men. Past the main foot road, the path narrowed. The bed couldn't pass. The men widened the track, slashing at the trees on either side. Progress was slow. My father decided we must press on. A few times I turned my head and each time the bed was further and further behind us. Eventually it disappeared from my view, behind the twisted bends, the giant trunks and curtain of ropes. It arrived in our new home three days after us.

My brother walked along beside me. I was young but I knew things. I knew I was glad to be leaving the old place and the old women. My mother and father called us by the names the diviner had chosen for us: Alusani and Asana. As the sun rose Alusani fell behind. I urged him, but I couldn't carry him. The bearers with their loads balanced upon their heads followed us with straight backs, their eyes fixed upon the horizon. Alusani trailed so far behind he became tangled in the feet of the first man. Our mother worried he was not strong enough to make the journey. So I walked on alone, under the weight of my load while Alusani rocked and slept under the canopy of the *maka* reserved for my father.

The sky turned to violet and the trees on the horizon dark blue. The planes of our faces faded and disappeared. After some time the path broadened again; the shadows of the trees grew skimpy. I smelled wood smoke: a scattering of houses and some tents in the centre of a clearing. We changed our clothes and sat down to wait while a messenger ran ahead. In a short time the headman came hurrying out of his house and knelt before my father. One knee on the ground. Hands clasped across his thigh. I listened to him explain everything was ready. He would accompany us to the place himself in the new light. And so we accepted his hospitality. I was tired and hungry, yet I was excited, too. I rested on my haunches and I watched as each man and woman came before my father and bent down to touch his feet. And I wondered who they were.

Like a mouse's tail the path narrowed and came to an end. I rode on my father's shoulders. Better than the hammock, I thought. There in the clearing stood four houses, so new the thatch was still green. Behind them flowed pale green waters, laced by mangroves, embroidered with water lilies: a river like a woman's sleeve.

The place was known only as Mathaka. Pa Thaka, a fisherman who lived there alone without a woman of his own, cooked and washed for himself. The people thought it was a joke. Behind his back they called him a woman. My father gave our home a new name: Rofathane, resting place.

We were the descendents of swordsmen who came from the North. Holy men and warriors led by a queen who blew in with the harmattan on horseback from Futa Djallon, dreaming of an empire that stretched from the desert to the sea. They never reached the sea. The horses shied and started. Their legs buckled and they toppled over. After a while the people realised they were stranded. They couldn't return to their homeland, so instead they settled where they found themselves. They were rice eaters. The grains they had brought with them they planted. In time their empire vanished, and another arose.

Rofathane, my father told me, had another meaning: oasis. Our new home was an oasis in the forest.

My mother told us our father was to become a coffee grower. She said this while she showed me how to grind the beans we had brought with us to make coffee for my grandmother. The beans were really for planting in rows on land that was being burned and brushed by the people from the houses in the clearing. These people had been given to our father by the *obai*, because he had helped him win the chieftaincy elections. And so they came to work by day, sometimes sleeping overnight, men and women side by side under thatched canopies. As the days passed the giant iroko trees crashed down one by one, great stumps wrenched out of the earth like a giant's teeth. The land was burned and in the morning, when the fires had died down, I went out to look. I imagined the red earth beneath the blackened charcoal, as tender and new as the skin under the scabs of dried blood I picked at on my knee.

Soon after we arrived, other people followed: a blacksmith, a carpenter, a herbalist, extra hands to plant the beans we had brought, fingers to pluck the ones that would grow. A big man casts a long shadow and many people build their lives in the shade.

Until the first harvest arrived my mother allowed nobody but *karabom* to drink the dark liquid made from the beans. It became my job to make her coffee, to grind the beans first with a pestle and mortar, mix the powder with some of the water which bubbled all day on top of the three-stone fire at the back of the house. I poured the liquid into a small bowl and sweetened it with honey. Then I would carry her coffee to her, to the place where she liked to sit at the front of her daughter's new house.

The house had the best position in the whole village: at a right angle to my father's house, next to the mosque and within earshot of the people who gathered to exchange news after prayers. From the verandah she could watch the comings and goings at the meeting house, too. Together she and I sat and waited for the grounds to settle.

At those times, in the very early morning, she told me things nobody else knew. These weren't the stories I heard her tell to the other women at the back of the house where they sat on stools in the evenings, their profiles warmed by the yellow light from the palm oil lamps. I remember the sound of their laughter: I thought of it as back-of-house laughter, different from the submerged giggles and half-smiles hidden behind hands at the front of the house.

Once I laughed with them. My grandmother told a story – something about a woman who began to cook for another man while her husband was away. When she had finished, there followed a moment of silence. Next to her, my father's third wife snorted and laughed, and the laughter passed from woman to woman like an improvised melody. Though I didn't understand the story, I opened my mouth wide and laughed along with them. The music stopped. Somebody sucked her teeth. My *karabom* aimed a piece of charcoal at me and it hit me just above the eyebrow.

You, I remember how you talked to your children. You asked them: 'Do you want this or that?' 'Coca-cola or Fanta?' 'Front seat or back?' You drove them around in a big four-wheel as though they were born with no legs. You let them push away the food everybody else was eating and you asked the cooks: 'What else is there in the kitchen?' And I heard the way your children answered you. As though the world was upside down, and you were the child, they the adults.

When I was a child I was told my voice smelled of fish. By the time I was allowed to speak I had forgotten how. That is how it was. The way we were raised to be who we are.

Karabom said: 'Never say "good morning" until you have washed yourself.' Yet the day I crossed her path in silence because I had not yet been to the stream she swore at me for my insolence. People who grew thin and died were being eaten away inside by witches, she told me on another day. I stared at the necklaces of loose skin around her neck, the empty flaps that hung to her waist. Even her ear lobes drooped; the holes where her gold earrings hung had stretched so I could see right through them. *Karabom* told me of witches who lured children with gifts of eggs and meat, only to suck their blood and steal their hearts, until one day all you saw running around was the empty flesh.

She pointed to the weaver birds darting in and out of their nests suspended from the branches of a tree, in perfectly spaced rows, as though some hand had hung them there. And she told me the birds were the souls of all the children who had died. *Karabom*'s lips were black, and when she spoke I could see her teeth gleaming against her dark, tattooed gums. I thought her lips and gums were black because she drank so much coffee.

In the sky the moon faded against the growing blue. There were men whose skins were luminous as the pale shadows of the moon when it dances across bare flesh, she said. Men who sailed their houses across the sea and who were so thin because they ate only fish and drank sea water. When she was my age people told stories of captured children who sailed with them across the sea and were fed to a powerful demon. Men from faraway villages stole the children in exchange for unearthly possessions.

'Stay away from the footpaths.' The air whistled in her nostrils and her breath carried the odour of decay, as though her body had become nothing more than a vessel for a mouldering spirit. 'Only an outsider clings to the path. And run away from strangers. If they come in good faith they'll reach the village and make their business known.'

After a while my mother would come and tap me on the shoulder. I wanted to ask her whether the stories were true. But my mother was always so busy. Too busy to listen. Busy in my father's house counting little piles of stones: how many trees we had planted, how much the first harvest might yield, how rich we would surely become. When she cooked, my mother served my grandmother first – always, except when my father ate with us. I was brought up not to question my elders, so I kept the stories to myself. But I wasn't frightened. To tell you the truth I didn't believe them. Not so much as you might think. I knew people made up stories to tell children so that we would behave the way they wanted us to.

Hali, but I remember the day I saw one of the moon-shadow men with my own eyes.

I was swift. My mother used me as her messenger. I would run the whole distance – sometimes to the fields, to the herbalist when one of us was ill, to the headman at the next village, it didn't matter – and I would deliver the message, repeat the reply once, twice and run back. Look at you, so busy writing everything down on pieces of paper. Scraps of paper to lose or put away in a cupboard to grow mildew. Nobody ever bothered to teach me to write. They didn't need to. Instead I taught myself never to forget. When I was a girl, I could run. And I can still remember. Those times when my mother required an answer urgently she spat on the warm earth by her feet. The saliva began to shrivel at once, like a slug thrown on a fire. I would set off knowing I had to be back before the dark patch was gone.

This day, I remember, Alusani begged to come with me. I knew he would slow me down, but I agreed anyway. We walked in the shade of the coffee trees and entered the forest. Soon we passed the boulder marking the boundary to the village. We stayed away from the path. As we went we played a game we had played many times before. We made up riddles for the Trickster, in case he bounced down from one of the trees and refused to allow us on our way.

'How do you carry water?' I asked Alusani.

'In a fishing net!' He was quick as that. Then it was his turn to ask a question: 'What do you pour on a fire to put it out?'

I knew that one, I didn't need to think. I replied straight away: 'Oil!' This was how we always began, posing the easy ones first. The next riddle was one I had been saving. I was certain Alusani would never guess the answer. 'What do you give a thirsty stranger to drink?'

I marched ahead, swinging my arms, certain of my victory. Behind me Alusani walked on. I knew he was puzzling over my riddle. One moment we were playing a game, the next I saw what I saw and I stopped breathing. I grasped Alusani's arm. And I swear, if I hadn't pulled my brother back he might have walked right into the man – right into the man whose skin was as white as day.

The moon-shadow man didn't see us. We slipped between the roots of a cotton tree and we hid ourselves there, as though we were hiding in our mother's skirts. We waited and we watched. All I could hear was the singing of birds, sounds of the forest. The moon-shadow man moved about the clearing, in and out of the streams of light, appearing and disappearing before our eyes. I imagined that if I only dared to reach out I could put my hand right through him. People said the Trickster could make himself invisible. But even though I was just a child I did not believe the Trickster was more than a story.

I wanted to whisper to Alusani, but my mouth was dry. I dared not close my eyes even to blink. I turned to Alusani. I felt my own eyes round with fear, but I saw Alusani's eyes quick and bright as he watched that man.

The man who was made of moon shadows was surrounded by boxes. Boxes made of sticks and bound with wire. They lay scattered on the forest floor. First I had eyes only for the strange man: the way his massive feet crushed the foliage beneath them; his hands the size of palm fronds. He was gathering up the boxes, stacking them one on top of the other. Sometimes he paused, wiped his face against his sleeve, another time he used a cloth. Once he stood and gazed up at the sky. While he worked, we watched him. The air was filled with birdsong, the sound of a thousand birds. And I saw that the boxes were not boxes, but cages. And birds were imprisoned inside those cages: sunbirds whose feathers shimmered like oil across the surface of water, bright blue flycatchers, dark-throated warblers, palm swifts as small as your thumb, doves vividly plumed as parrots, and in one cage an owl's black-rimmed eyes watching us from inside a white face.

I seized Alusani's hand and we crept out from between the roots of the tree. We tried to be quiet, but the fear refused to be bound and scattered suddenly. And so we ran. I didn't see him. I didn't dare turn around. At first I didn't even hear him, my heart thrummed in my ears. I felt him. I felt the moon-shadow man look up, begin to come after us. I scraped my shin on a fallen log; my footsteps crashed through the undergrowth; cobwebs snatched at my face as I dragged Alusani after me. But in the end we were helpless as beetles at the mercy of a cat.

He didn't touch us, Alusani and I.

He stepped in front of us.

We stopped. We did not move.

We waited.

I looked at him and beyond him, for a way past. He crouched down; he put his hand into the folds of his trousers. From his outstretched hand he offered us a gift. At first I was transfixed by those luminous eyes, such a colour: the colour of water. When I did look down I saw in his hand a peeled egg. The man reached into his pocket and brought out a packet, of paper instead of leaf. He opened it and sprinkled a little of what was inside on to the top of the egg. Salt. Just salt. The man held it out in front of him and uttered a sound like the noise a donkey makes – though not so loud as that. Still, it caused me to jump backwards. He pulled his lips back and showed us his huge teeth: 'Hee-ah,' he said, 'hee-ah!'

I tried to warn Alusani. But he was less fearful than I, although I had never once thought so before. He reached out his fingers and he took the egg from the moon-shadow man.

It has been such a long time. In all that time I never spoke to anybody about what happened that day. Except now. Except to you.

Sometimes, when I used to remember, when I thought back to the beginning of what happened next, there was only one thing of which I was sure. That everything started with the man whose skin was like the shadows of the moon. The man who was busy filling cages with the souls of children.

My mother beat me for failing to deliver her message. I returned to her empty-handed long after the spit had dried on the ground. Worst of all I had taken Alusani with me into the bush. My brother tried to beg for me, but my mother was deaf, her anger like a whirlwind inside her skull, going round and round, her mouth pursed and tight as though someone had sewn it shut and pulled the thread.

Maybe in time, when I had acquired some wisdom, I would have come to laugh at my childish fantasies. Perhaps I would have thrown away the memory of the moon-shadow man along with all the other unimportant thoughts I never bothered to cherish. Maybe. Who is there that knows the answer? As it was I came to hold myself responsible, to believe what happened next came as a punishment. I took Alusani there. Alusani took the egg and I could not stop him. The memory stayed with me for ever.

Alusani began to visit the place of the spirits.

It was dawn. I ran to fetch my grandmother. I did not bow my head or greet her respectfully first. There was no time for it, no time for her to be angry either. She followed me to where Alusani lay on the cot we shared. His eyes rolled backwards into his skull. His back was arched, his body vibrated like a plucked string. *Karabom* heated water to prepare a poultice. My mother held Alusani on her lap and massaged his limbs until his joints unlocked and the light came back into his eyes. In time he drifted into a deep sleep.

In those days there were those people who had 'four eyes' – two to see the human world and two eyes on the backs of their faces, eyes that can see beyond what is here. People said twins had four eyes. Ours was a spirit so powerful it required two bodies. Sent by the ancestors, they said. Only, I didn't have four eyes. I never saw a devil or a spirit or a ghost, though there were times I was afraid I might.

At night I pressed my ear against the inside wall of the house, imagining I could hear the spirits of the dead trapped in the space between the inside and the outside wall. That's how we built our houses in those days: with two walls and two doors. The doorways were offset – to confuse spirits who wanted to come back inside into the warm. The blacksmith's uncle died: a dried-out old man with a wheezing cough and a voice like a cracked flute. My mother and grandmother went to cry at his funeral. Late that night I listened for him, for the sound of his woman's voice calling from the other side. And I pictured his sightless ghost wandering from house to house, trying its luck, banging into the walls and groping for the door.

Maybe Alusani really did have the gift. To this day I can't tell you. I only know that once he started to visit the underworld he kept going back. Pa Yamba, the diviner, went into a trance and followed him as far as he could into the land of dreams. But Alusani was going further, he was crossing to the land of spirits, where he had been befriended by a man and a woman – a husband and a wife. The woman, especially, liked Alusani. Trapped in the land of dreams, Pa Yamba couldn't get close enough to see who she might be.

The whispers rustled through the houses, like wind through the tops of the trees. People came to wait outside our compound bringing gifts: bowls of white kola nuts, embroidered cloths, leather pouches of precious salt. Maybe Alusani's spirit woman had something to tell. Or maybe she planned to give him special powers. That happened a lot. People befriended by spirits used their knowledge to amass great wealth. Others could see into the future or hold conversations with the dead. At mealtimes my mother fed Alusani from her own plate and she passed his chores to me.

When he saw the attention he received, Alusani began to repeat demands from the spirits: rice bread, sugar cane, sweet potato cakes, steamed coco yams and eggs. Everyone knows you shouldn't give eggs to a child, it spoils them. But my mother and grandmother were very afraid. They preferred to go without themselves than to upset the ancestors who might send a cloud of locusts or a bush fire. After three rainy seasons our coffee trees had reached twice the height of a man. In two more seasons the beans would be ready to pick.

Slowly Alusani became the opposite of himself. Where once he had been fine to look at and sweet-natured, now he was bloated and angry. The expression on his face was as bitter as the coffee grounds themselves and when he spoke his voice was sour with sarcasm. As often as I could I stayed away from him. Down among the groves I wandered between the rows of coffee trees growing side by side with the banana trees. I imagined my brother and I were like these trees, growing together but not the same at all.

My brother acted like a warlord. At supper he complained the soup was too peppery, so I left my place to fetch fresh lime for him. The sack in the storeroom was empty; I ran to the lime tree in the garden at the back of the house but by the time I returned he complained the soup had cooled. My brother looked at me with scorn. As though I was his servant. Day after day my dislike for him grew. I hated my mother, who had given away my birthright. And I was angry with my grandmother who ordered the cooks to prepare sweetmeats for my brother, and no longer let me sit with her when I brought her coffee in the morning.

Maybe today we would guess Alusani had a tumour growing inside his head like a kola nut, and take him to the Chinese doctors at the hospital. But people didn't know these things then. People believed there was a reason for everything. Nothing happens for nothing, that's what they said then, and still do say.

Alusani complained of a headache. I didn't care. He said he wanted to lie down. As he turned away I saw his face had a look that was sly, one eyelid drooped. My mother told me to run and fetch the herbalist, have her bring her pan of herbs. Afterwards I sat on the step outside while the woman did her work. I watched the people arriving for prayers and leaving. Twice. Maybe three times, even. I waited there a long time, in case I was needed to run another errand. When I heard my mother call my name I jumped up and went inside, swaying in the sudden darkness. My mother sat on the side of the cot, stroking her son's face. I had never seen her cry, but now I did. *Karabom* sat at the other end of the bed, holding my brother's feet in her hands. My mother beckoned me to sit down and I did so. I bent my head down, and felt Alusani's breath against my cheek, and waited. He spoke. I could barely hear him.

'Brine', he said.

And, though it took me time, I understood. The answer to the last riddle. What do you give a thirsty stranger to drink? Brine. Then Alusani closed his eyes.

My brother was dead. What else do you want to know? That's how it happened.

How you look at me so?

You've guessed, guessed it didn't happen that way at all. Well then, you are right. You're cleverer than I thought. Yes, it is just wishful thinking. I wish there had been no fire between us the day Alusani died. Alusani complained of a headache, that much is true. And his eye, the sly look – that is true, too. But he died alone in the afternoon while I went about my errands and my mother counted stones in my father's parlour. He went to sleep and never got up again.

We buried Alusani in a treeless plot on the outskirts of the graveyard. That same day I won my mother back. Every season, when she cooked the first pot of new rice, my mother had taken a knife and scored a line inside the lid of the wooden chest where she kept her most precious belongings. As we grew up she stopped bothering to count our anniversaries. Now the fear began to spread like a shadow at dusk. Alusani would return for me – because our spirit was cleaved in two.

What can I tell you? That she fed me treats, the way she had with Alusani? Or that she let me sleep in her bed on those nights when my father went to visit her co-wives? Maybe she allowed me to abandon my chores while she kept me by her side and let me pass the days playing childish games. I wish it had been that way. But the fear tainted her like dye dropped into water. Alusani, who had been her beloved, now became the very being she most dreaded. Determined not to let him have his way, she fought him for possession of me.

Pa Yamba fashioned talismans, coated them with saliva and betel nut juice, and dangled them from my neck and around my waist. I stood in his hut. It was dark and feverishly hot. Vapours from the fire filled the air, burning my lungs. At our house I saw my mother on her knees scratching a hole in the floor with her bare hands and she placed the amulet Pa Yamba had given her in the dark space. But in the morning the fear was back, more monstrous than before. I can't tell you the times we waded across the stream to the opposite bank where the diviner lived. My mother begged him to conjure ever more powerful charms. But it was never enough. She had become the man who has convinced himself that his neighbour is out to steal his goat and builds a thousand fences around it.

We were standing in the market when my mother overheard a conversation between two women. One, a tray of smoked fish balanced on her head, claimed a *moriman* had rid her of a troublesome rival who would have put her out of business. My mother did not care what these women thought of her, the wife of a big man, and interrupted their talk. But the fish seller was flattered and answered my mother's questions. The *moriman* had instructed her to sweep up her rival's footsteps and to bring the dust. This was what she told us. And so in the amber light of evening we searched the corners of the house until we found one of Alusani's footprints. I cried easily to see the shape of his foot in the earth. I wanted my mother to comfort me, but her face was flat and she went about the business briskly. The next morning she woke me early to walk to the town where the *moriman* lived. And there I knelt and watched all that remained of Alusani go up in flames.

And so it went for months. How many magic men I could not count. One splashed a liquid in my eyes that stung for a long time – to stop me from seeing Alusani and wanting to go to him. There were times I had a powerful medicine made from boiled roots rubbed all over my limbs. The *moriman* said it would deter wicked spirits. People believed these things then. My mother believed them, too. I did not. I was miserable. I smelled like rice left in the pot for days, slimy and sour. I was ashamed.

My mother was the senior wife. There was a time when I was so pleased with myself that I was the daughter of the most important of the wives. She paid the workers their wages and held the keys to the store; she ordered the provisions and hired the servants; it was she who had the authority to decide which of the women should cook for my father, or travel with him when he went away on business. I found there was nobody to help me. My grandmother shared her daughter's fears. Even my father would not confront my mother, for she was older than him in years.

★　　★　　★

I was sitting outside our house on a stool with my tray on the ground before me, preparing *ogere* to sell in the market, wrapping the balls of fermented sesame seeds in leaves and tying the packages with raffia. I used to make the *ogere* myself, standing over the pot, stirring the seeds which boiled for the whole day. Then I would spread them out on rice bags and lay heavy rocks on top of them. After three days, I pounded the fermenting seeds into a paste with my pestle and mortar.

Ogere tastes good, but you know how bad it smells. That's why we never cook it inside the house. Always on the three-stone fire in the yard. At that time it seemed a good job for me. I smelled so bad anyway.

Those days my chest felt bruised. I was growing breasts, though I didn't know it. Your uncle saw me. And he knew what he saw. And he stopped and talked to me nicely for a while. I watched him walk away, swinging his prayer beads in his hand, his body outlined by the wind beneath his white gown, and I let my imagination follow him down the street. I saw the power of his shoulders, the strength of his arms and the narrowness of his waist. I did not notice the weakness in the line of his jaw. The next day he came back with a gift: a bowl of scented roseapples. He ate one, and afterwards he handed me an apple and had me eat it. But with every bite I took all I tasted was the raw *ogere*, it overpowered the sweet fruit and made me nauseous. Your uncle appeared not to notice. I saw a man who was kind to me, and I saw the way to free myself from my mother. I ran from the smoke straight into the fire.

There's not much more to tell. It's a true story. You never knew my name was Yankay, the firstborn. That I was once a twin. That I had a brother Alusani, the other half of my soul. Or that I grew jealous of him and longed for my mother to look at me, without knowing what it was I wished for. And how I watched a man with skin like the shadows of the moon collecting the souls of lost children in the forest.

One day you married one of these men and brought him home. As soon as I saw him so close I could not help myself. I reached out my hand and I touched his skin. And it was warm, so warm – not cold like sea water. But I made you ashamed and afterwards I heard you whispering, making apologies for me you thought I was too deaf to hear.

Maybe I acted like a fool – and you can call me that if you like. I don't care because, you see, for one moment I was she, that girl again and I wanted to run to your moon-shadow man and beg him: 'Tell me where Alusani is? Tell me which one of the birds flying in the sky is my brother?'

3

Mariama, 1931

Stones

I REMEMBER HOW IT was when I danced with my mother. Sometimes I close my eyes and drift as though I am going to sleep. But I am not asleep. I am remembering a time when I was still a baby, before I knew how to talk or even walk.

Whirling. Whirling. Round and around. Don't feel dizzy. Eyes closed. Nose between shoulder blades. Lips against soft skin. Breathe the scent of her. We dance. Me on her back. We want to go on for ever. This is how we dance on nights we go together to the women's place – the secret place where women meet.

Supper eaten, mama binds me to her back. Holding me squashed against her breasts, bends over, twists my body round her own. On her back now. I know better than to fall off. Cling to her with my thighs, my fists. She drapes the cloth across my buttocks, holds it in her teeth. Ties two ends tight round her waist. Hitches the other corners up under her armpits – a knot above her breasts.

I'm part of her. Feel her flesh, muscles, sinews – walking, working, out in the plantation pruning trees. Feel her heart quicken and slow. I know who scares her. I know whom she loves. When my father passes she stiffens, drawing air into her nostrils – like an oribi we saw drinking at the river – and quivering beneath the stillness of her skin. We carry food to the workers at the plantation. She unwraps the pots, ladles soup on rice. Men come forward. Pa Foday, he comes close. '*Momo*', he says. Thank

34

you. Feel the creak of the cloth against her ribs as she catches her breath.

Evening time we slip away. Slip away to the secret bush. Walking quickly. Past houses, past gardens. Into the groves. She walks like a queen. Or like a woman on her way to meet a lover. Where the path from the rice fields meets the path from the stream, see the gap in the trees? See the cotton tree high above the rest? That's where we're headed. We follow an invisible path. No one can follow us.

Women are already here. So many women. Talking. Talking women's business, they call it. We don't care to talk. Not so very much. We wait to dance. When the talk is finished the drums start, the singing. And the dancing. We dance for the elders and the younger women, too. Whirling, whirling. Round and around. Round and around we go.

We dance until the light comes up and dances too, across a horizon flat and empty as a stage. And then we walk quickly back to the village, collecting sticks of firewood as we go.

Then I learned to talk. She stopped taking me with her. I might repeat secrets told, women's special secrets. Wait, she said, until your turn comes. That was one time.

Then there was another time. The time when the dancing stopped. And when I said her name, a space opened up that I could fall into. Silence. Silence after her name. Silence where the music used to be. Once women bound their hands to drum all night. Afterwards they met in secret, real secret. Silent secret. Away from the eyes of men. Away from Haidera. But when they tried to dance, they couldn't. The steps were gone. They had followed my mother when she went away.

I used to read the things written about us. These weren't the books the nuns approved of. One book was by a Very Famous Author. Oh, all the writing on the back said how good this book was. This famous man lived in our country for a short time and then he wrote a story that would make sure nobody ever wanted to come here. A story about a man who arrived on these shores and lost his faith.

Many years later I read another book by the same writer, about a woman who has to choose between her god and the man she loves. When I read that book I felt a pain, like I had been stabbed in my side. I felt this woman's terrible choice as if it was my own. Because I remembered my mother and how she was forced to deny her own faith.

A woman has no religion. Have you heard people say that here? A woman has no religion. And maybe it's true. We change our faith to marry and worship to please our husbands. But it was not always so.

In those days they were always coming to convert us. The Muslims from the North, the Christians from the South. We deserted our gods. But nobody wrote stories about that. Instead they congratulated themselves on how many souls they had saved. My own soul was saved twice. But my mother. My mother would not yield. And to this day nobody has ever come to me and said she was noble and righteous to do so.

We did not have a house of our own. No. We slept in a back room of my father's house. Small, not so light, one window. It looked out on to the alleyway where old men came to smoke. The tobacco smelled like burning flowers. Not such a quiet room either. There was the women's cooking circle behind us, too. Odours of simmering *plasass*, the scent of tobacco and talking, old men's voices and women's voices. Hush!

A plain room. But mama tried to make it into something pretty: striped country cloths on the floor, cloth dyed red with camwood on the walls. Lattice shutters over the windows. In the corner the box with her things in it, the things she brought when she came here.

1931. Yes, it was 1931. We didn't count years in those days. That came later. Who was to say where to begin? What year was the first? So we began in many places: the Year the New Chief Came Out of Seclusion; the Year We Came to this Place; the Year the River Rose and Snatched Away Houses in Old Rofathane; the Year the First Coffee Beans Ripened. The Year of the Locust

Disaster. That had been the year before. The villagers lit fires between the rows of trees and draped fishing nets over the branches to protect the beans. I was young. I thought a locust was some kind of fish that swam through the air. In the morning the trees were saved; there were crisp locusts scattered across the land and the air filled with their odour.

Yes, we remembered years by the things that happened. Important things.

So why do I say 1931? I'll tell you. Because that was the year of Haidera. That much I know. I read it in a book by a professor of history. An English professor, but who wrote our history, if you understand me. And he said Haidera came in 1931. So I said to myself, well then that is the year of my mother's story too. The man who wrote that book, he did not think much of Haidera. A fanatic. That's what he wrote in his book. That Haidera was a fanatic. He said not so many people followed Haidera. But he was wrong. There were many people who loved Haidera Kontorfili.

That year was also the Year My Teeth Fell Out. A warm evening in the dry season. My sisters were out, walking round the houses with their age mates. Arms encircling waists. Calling greetings to the people sitting at the front of their houses. 'I pray good evening, aunty.' 'Good evening, uncle.' 'How are you?' '*Thanto a Kuru.*' I thank God. 'Remember me to your mother.' 'Yes, aunty.' Or else they were sitting by the river, whispering into other girls' ears. I was the youngest, too young to go with them. The one who called me, he returned. And the next one too who would have been another sister. Two children missing in between, like the space in my row of teeth.

I lay at home licking my gums. That day I told my mother I was sick and she gave me mimosa tea to drink. I sipped air in with my tea, through the gap in my mouth. The tea blistered my gums, already rough from sucking green mangoes with Bobbio, the Boy with No Voice. Lying in the fields sucking green mangoes. That's what I did the day before. But I don't tell such things to mama. I let my eyes follow her. I like to watch my mother. To me she is beautiful.

Today, as on other days, this is what she does:

She goes to the box and feels among the layers of clothes. She takes a tin, a tin wrapped up in red poplin, stitched with cowrie shells and leather-bound *sassa*. Fearful amulets to protect what's inside. There is writing on the side. It says: 'Woodbines'. Just so you know. For myself, I only knew that later. On the floor she folds her legs beside her and empties the cigarette cup. Pebbles and stones tumble on to the floor, she spreads them out with a hand like a fan.

There are seventeen of them. This I know. Because sometimes when I am left alone I go to the chest and take them out for myself. I empty them into my palm, feel their weight, listen to the noise they make, like they are talking to each other. Or to me. A pinkish pebble, curved in one place, flat on the other and inside dark and glistening like a sliced plum. A big one, flat and grey with a dimple that fits my thumb, just so. A dark stone, shaped just like a cigar and veined too, like a tobacco leaf. I hold it to my lips and copy the men outside. A cream-coloured pebble, with pale lines intersecting across its length and width: paths and a crossroads. A translucent crystal. A triangular stone, dusty like chalk. A black moon-rock. There are others. Ah, my favourite: white, five-sided, smooth as my skin, but rippled as the sand on the windward side of a dune.

Alone in her room, except for me, my mother talks to the stones. Yes, she does, and often. But first she gathers them up in her hands and throws them in the air like a celebration. She holds out her right hand and catches some, leaving others to fall. She counts them two by two. One, two. One, two. This is how she goes. And sometimes: one. She puts the single stone at the end of the line. She casts and counts and casts and counts. Two rows of stones. The road to life and the road to death. All the time she murmurs soft sounds. I know these sounds by heart. The cadence of her voice, the rhythm and sequence of the vowels, the placing of the consonants. Though not the words they make.

On Green Mango Day mama beckons me over. 'See this here, Mariama,' she says. 'Here again on the road to life,' I push my face in close. A small, plain stone the colour of sand. 'Maybe a brother for you. What do you say?' She lets her hand rest on my hair. I like it. I stay. But I have nothing to say. I don't care for the look of the stone so much. She takes her hand away, folds it up in her lap with the other one. Now she's talking to the stones. Telling them this week's news. The important things that have happened to us.

Oh, she saw her clothes float away down the river. It was in a dream: a rainbow-coloured river of clothes. The brown hen hatched a deformed chick. It had no eyes. It died. A burial two houses away. My bellyache.

I'm happy. A little guilty. But the pleasure of hearing her tell the stones about me is sweeter.

Searching the stones for patterns and combinations, the answers to questions. What does she want? I don't know, cannot imagine. Because I have everything I want right here. Right here. My sisters will be back soon. Now I'm sleeping with my head resting on her thigh. The sound of her chanting, like a lullaby.

In our room late at night she made snuff. Good snuff, they said. She ground the tobacco leaves, mixed the brown dust with cloves and *lubi* from palm nuts. The cloves were what made it special. One time I stole some of her snuff. Took a pinch in my fingers, and then swallowed it quickly when she walked back into the room. My head spun. Not like when we used to dance. I felt sick and nearly fainted. Oh, so this is what snuff is, I thought. What person would want that?

But people did. Every week or so we carried a jar of snuff to Madam Bah who sold it to the customers who visited her shop. She sat there, arm resting on the window frame of her front room, merchandise piled up behind her, outlined against the darkness. Matches, cigarettes. She opened up the tins and sold them one by one. 'One stick or two? Tuppence each.' Baking soda. Balls of black soap. Imported needles. On the table next to her, a wooden cabinet with a dented fly-screen. Inside, squares of deep-fried dough under muslin and sugar cane and snuff. Not a real shop. But the closest we had.

Madam Bah was an only wife but it didn't seem to bother her at all. And she was the only woman who didn't have a vegetable garden where she had to go weeding and watering garden eggs and yams all day. Madam Bah bought all her food in the market or from other women. Also she was the only person we called madam. Sometimes I thought this was because she was a shopkeeper. So she deserved to be called madam. Then I thought it was maybe because Ma Bah sounded funny. She travelled and brought Dutch Wax prints, Brillian, shirting, beads and 'shine shine' trinkets from far off places. Whenever word was that Madam Bah had come back from a trip my father's wives stood in line to see what she had brought.

So here we come. With our snuff to sell. I stand with my nose over the window-sill shop counter. But first my mother wants to see a piece of Dutch Wax. And Madam Bah does not get up, but rocks back on her stool and stretches her arm out to reach the cloth. My mother slides her palm over the slippery surface of the cloth. She asks questions. The width? Yes, and the length? Good quality? Top quality, nods Madam Bah. She bats at a fly with her fan and it falls on to the counter, upside down, spinning. Madam Bah does not hold the cloth up so my mother can compliment the pattern. Always the conversations end the same way. My mother says: 'Maybe next time.' And Madam Bah says: 'Yes, next time. Next time there will be more choice. You'll see.'

Mama's mother died of a swelling sickness back in the days of the old. Long before I was born. My mother had no brothers. When my father saw her she was visiting an aunt in the old place. She left her own people a long way behind when she married him. All the money she had of her own came from the sale of our snuff, which Madam Bah kept in her big jar and dispensed directly into the open palms of her customers or poured into the little glass phials and silver snuff-boxes they brought with them. From our room my mother sold snuff to the younger women, who slipped in between chores and smeared the dark dust above their back teeth. My sisters pinched me and told me not to tell. Nobody, especially Ya Namina. The younger wives were among our best customers.

Madam Bah gives me a piece of fried dough to eat. She leans out of her window and strokes my cheek. And smiles a small smile, with her head on one side. And she looks at me like this. 'Such a shame,' she says to my mother. 'If she had been a boy . . .' Then she takes a pinch of snuff. Sneezes. Clears her throat. Wipes her eyes with the back of her hand.

Mama says: 'It's a fine one,' in a voice that expects to be corrected.

There is Bobbio. Sitting by a pillar in the shade of the awning. Wearing his grimy duster coat. Ashy legs. From a distance he looks like an old man. Bobbio is always somewhere, hanging around the meeting house, sitting on the edge of somebody's verandah watching them talk or eat, a forgotten guest. Sometimes, when I go outside to pee in the night, I see him. Standing silent in the shadows of a house not his own. Nobody knew what was the matter with Bobbio. Why he had No Voice. He lived with his grandmother, the birth attendant, who said he was born in Daruth. The way she said it made it sound like everybody in that town was the same way. I imagined a town of silent people, moving noiselessly about.

But other people whispered that Bobbio was slow because his mother conceived him while she was still breastfeeding her last child.

I liked Bobbio. Though he sometimes did things that made children chase him and grown-ups shoo him away. He banged his chest with his fist. Then he'd slap you with the back of his hand. Whap! Hard like that. Bobbio was strong. People became annoyed. But I understood. *Me, me,* he was saying when he hit himself. *You, you.* Trying to start a conversation. They thought he was stupid. Bobbio couldn't speak. But he wasn't deaf and dumb. Bobbio could hear. And he understood what we were saying.

In his hands Bobbio holds a string of raffia. He loops it round the little finger and thumb of each hand. And again around his index fingers so it looks like a pair of crosses. He loops the string again around his third finger, once more over his little fingers. And in a trice he slips his two index fingers through the web, turns his hands inside out and holds them up. The string had transformed into an angular crane in mid-flight. I run and reach for it. Bobbio is older than me and taller than me.

'Show me, show me!'

Madam Bah laughs at this. Her laugh is loud and empty. Just a bigger version of her smile. 'Maybe they'll marry,' I hear her say. A crease appears on my mother's brow. And she opens her mouth and takes a breath and presses her lips together. Madam Bah doesn't see. She's counting money on her lap, below the counter.

We sit on the stoop, Bobbio and I. Sitting on the stoop watching the world. We do this a lot, on different stoops. Sometimes here. Sometimes my father's house. Sometimes the house where Ya Namina's mother sits all day and doesn't mind us. What I like about Bobbio is his silence. Everybody else talks too much. We sit a while. I tie the string in knots and Bobbio takes it from me and begins again. This time slowly.

Against the glare of the sky the outlines of the houses begin to wobble. At this time of day the village is empty. Pools of rice spread out to dry in the sun. Rows of raffia stiffening and bleaching. But no people, for they are down in the fields and in the coffee grove. Only the elders are here, sitting in a row on the bamboo bench on the other side of the square from the meeting house. The old women sit on their porches. Everybody sits and waits for the day to end and the people to come back.

Behind me Madam Bah is talking. Still. While she counts out the money.

A man with woman trouble: 'Don't ask me. I mind my own business. But they say now he's gone. Gone to fetch her back.'

Sucking her teeth, a new stranger in the village: 'I hear he plans to stay. Well, we'll see.'

The prayer meeting. Madam Bah's husband the Fula carried news of this one from the town. He goes there on business. I try to imagine it. Imagine the town. And the Fula in it doing business. Running around in his white djellaba and baggy trousers. I cannot. I have never been to the town. I don't know what business is. Though sometimes he does it with my father. My father says Fulas are honest because they believe that one penny of profit dishonestly made means they will lose the whole fortune. Me, I don't think Madam Bah believes that. But then she's not a real Fula. Just married to one.

It's a big prayer meeting this time.

'The Fula says there are so many people in town for this thing. Some all the way from Kabala. It's going to be one big wahallah!'

'Will you go?'

'The Fula says we should. But I said: "Bo, leave me." Let him go. I've too much to do already.' And Madam Bah exhales so that her shoulders sag. She leans forward and beckons my mother close. Like she has a secret to tell her. And she takes my mother's hands in hers and slips some coins soundlessly across. My mother knots the coins into a corner of her *lappa*.

She reaches a hand out behind her. Already moving away. Confident that I will catch it. And I do.

'So that's that.'

'Until next time.'

I wave to Bobbio.

My Face.

Let me tell you about My Face. That day, at Madam Bah's shop, I didn't know about it. Nobody teased me. Not Bobbio. Not even the other children. We had no mirrors. We didn't look at our reflections in the streams, the way they show us in films, kneeling down to stare at our features rippling in the water. We only knew ourselves by the reactions of other people. People might turn to look at you because you were so beautiful. Or because you were disfigured.

Madam Bah had a consignment of mirrors. Small squares of glass – some already chipped – with silvered backs. She let me hold one. In no time children crowded around, trying to see their own faces. The shopkeeper had known what she was doing – letting us play with one of the precious mirrors – because in no time the grown-ups came over to see what the commotion was about.

First I was too pleased just to see my own reflection. I turned this way. My reflection turned the other. I smiled, she smiled right back at me. It wasn't long before we were poking out our tongues and pulling faces at each other. The mirror was passed from hand to hand. Everyone took one turn and then another. This time I winked. Right eye. Left eye. Right eye. Left eye. Left eye. I wiped the smeared surface of the mirror. Left Eye. I looked again. I stared at myself for a long time, until somebody snatched the mirror away. I put my hand up to my face and touched it. Traced my features, conjuring through fingertips the image still in my mind – my eye stretching down towards my mouth, lower lid pulled open. Exposed pink. A face made of wet clay somebody had dragged their fingers through.

At bedtime my mama rubbed her nose against my face. Nose to nose. Right eye. Left eye. The sloping eye and the straight. I was a happy child. Later I wondered what she made of it. For a long time I tried so hard to remember. What did she wish for when she spoke to the stones? When she asked them things. Did she ever ask them to make it right?

Haidera. Haidera. Haider Spider. Haidera Kontorfili.

Haidera Kontorfili said he could turn the sun into the moon and the moon into the sun. He could tell whether an unbroken egg would hatch a rooster or a hen. Every living creature knew his name. Whoever did not obey the rules of Annabi would one day be put to death. Unmarried women were Black Dogs. One day fire would come like rain and plague, would strike the unbeliever down.

He told us we should not fear the Europeans or pay the *potho*'s taxes. And of all the things Haidera said, it was this last one that brought the trouble down upon his head.

We are to go to the prayer meeting. The preparations take two days. Mutton roasted. Yams baked. Whole fishes fried. Ginger pulped for ginger beer. Black-eyed beans skinned, mashed, wrapped in banana leaves for *oleleh*. Sleeping mats, country cloths, canvas tents. A stove to boil water for coffee. The men haul sacks of rice and cut down great hands of bananas and plantains. I chase after high-stepping hens, push them into a basket, from where they protest in indignant tones.

The town is no more than the headquarters of one of the country's poorest provinces. And yet I fear becoming lost. Noise pounding my ears, dust dry in my throat, air too hot to breathe. Looking this way and that. We huddle together, suddenly diminished. The streets are wide as rivers. The houses have rooms built one on top of the other. I watch as people walk up outside-staircases. They look as though they are stepping through the air. Walking on air. Why doesn't someone build a staircase all the way up to the sky, I ask myself? To find out what is really there.

We cross the street at the roundabout: cracked concrete covered in yellow grass gone to seed. Two men heave a handcart, one pushing, one pulling. Their naked muscles glisten and flash with sweat. A man with a monkey on a chain. It lurches forward, startling me – a tiny, wizened, old man's face and a baby's cry. Hawkers selling food. A man standing next to a barrel of water. A tin cup dangles on a string. My father calls him over. 'Sssss!' We wait while the man lugs the heavy barrel over. It takes a little time. My father drinks first and then the rest of us, one after the other.

In the main square a hundred families jostle for space. Men in inky-black robes stroll through the crowds or stand in pairs around the perimeter. One of them greets my father and directs us. We settle, light fires, spread mats, erect screens and awnings. The sun is high, our shadows like small pools of black wax. In the shade of the canopies we rest, we wait.

I am sure I am too excited to sleep. I put my head in my mother's lap, breathe. I feel her stroking my hair, her fingers rustle when she touches the rim of my ear. Dream fragments float past behind my eyes. A bird woven out of string. Crows that shift shape into black-clad men. Staircases leading from cloud to cloud. And I sink through air as heavy as water, as if weighed down by sodden wings.

I am woken by a sound like a buffalo's roar. All around me people are standing, getting to their feet. I scramble up, crane my neck. Nothing. I am too close to the ground.

'Haidera! Haidera!'

Now I see him. Standing high up above the crowd on a platform: a man whose robes billow around him, even more full than those of my father, but plain, entirely unadorned. He wears a white turban. Around his neck an amulet swings on a leather cord.

'Allahu Akbar!'

'Akbar Allahu!'

People bow down, snatch handfuls of sand from the ground, rubbing their hands one over the other as though in water. Ahead I see my father wipe his hands across his face. He bows, kneels. My mother next to me, she does the same. I keep my eyes fixed upon my father as we pray under Haidera's command: standing, bending, kneeling, stretching our necks like herons to touch our foreheads to the ground. The movements, the pattern, the rhythm, they are just like a dance.

Now we stop praying and listen to Haidera, whose voice is as thin and high as a bird's, and like a bird's it floats across the air so that even the people at the back can hear. He doesn't speak the way we do, but with an accent from somewhere else.

'I Am the Man Sent to All Worshippers in the Name of God to Tell You the Prophecies of Muhammad. My Song is Alla, Alla.'

Haidera talks. The sun arcs across the sky. It is hard to sit still so long. People cheer when he warns of false Mohammedans who come to trick us and take our money. They cheer again when he promises to stop them and to kill any who refuse to leave. The black-clad Shekunas carry sticks and short swords. I don't doubt what he says is true. He tells us the terrible things that await those who do not follow Annabi. For them the rivers will drain into the soil, the rice harvest fail. His bird's voice rises to a shriek, like the call of a peacock.

'Those Who Will Be Saved Are Only the True Muslims.'

I touch my mama's sleeve. She is wearing her best gown and she is beautiful. I pull her finger. I ask her if we are to Be Saved. Yes, she tells me and slides her hand out from beneath mine, strokes the back of my hand lightly.

I turn my head this way and that to look at the people listening to the preacher. People who come to Be Saved. People who have come to Be Healed, because that is what they say Haidera can do. There are families like ours, men with their wives and children. Here and there a lame leg stiffly extended; a gaunt figure propped up by the shoulders; a child's inert frame wrapped in blankets; eyes that are opaque and unblinking. At the back are the beggars. Some have limbs that are missing. Others have limbs that are too big or too small. Some have limbs that are falling off. And there are poor people, who sit on the dry earth with none of the comforts we have brought with us: lined faces, scant clothing, lean and scarred bodies.

A way off: four people. Different from everyone else. Legs straight, hands clasped behind their backs. Standing when everyone else is sitting. And when the time comes to pray they alone do not kneel. Short-sleeved shirts and short trousers. Red round caps. Court Messengers who work for the *pothos*. There is one who comes to our village sometimes. The people greet him, but rarely invite him to eat. Sometimes my father calls for my mother to serve him a meal and I help her carry it out to where he sits on a stool outside the meeting house. He talks to my father and leaves again soon after. The Black White Man, they call him.

Out in front my father nods. There are sins Haidera has seen here with his own eyes. Big eyes, with lines above and beneath. 'Promiscuousness.' Drawing the word out, turning it into four words. Prom. Isc. Uous. Ness! His mouth snaps shut on the end of the word, the tongue disappears with a flick like a tail into a hole. My father bobs his head. 'Slander.' Bob, goes my father's head again. 'Blasphemy.' Bob. 'Greed.' Bob. 'Envy.' Bob, bob. And my father looks around him now. His chin lifted slightly. 'Gambling, cheating.' My father nods firmly. 'Usury.' This time he doesn't nod. 'Excessive polygamy.' The preacher's voice whistles, sibilant, trembling. Something shifts in the air.

Ya Namina, of course; Ya Isatta Numokho; Sakie, my own mother; Ya Jeneba and Ya Sallay Kamara, Tenkamu, whose family name I never knew. Memso and Saffie, who are still young and under the tutelage of Ya Namina. My father's wives are gathered around him with the exception of two who are new mothers. They have returned to their families and are not expected back until the children are weaned, two years from now. We are all here. My father sits at the head of us.

But I don't have time to think any more about that. A ripple runs through the mass of people near the platform. The crowd splits apart. A man stumbles forward like a shipwrecked sailor thrown up on the sand. In his hands he holds a carved wooden statue. Other people follow. Each holding a figure, sometimes more than one. They lay them down in front of the platform. A mound rises. Some people turn and bow to Haidera. One man prostrates himself, the whole length of his person pressed to the ground, and stays there until two of the Shekunas heave him up by the arms. The crowd roars as each new supplicant comes forward.

Up on tiptoe I can see Haidera pacing back and forth. Now his disciples are taking carvings from people and throwing them on the pile. I can barely hear what he is saying. He gesticulates, points up at the sky with his left hand, his voice rises and falls. A few words carry above the noise of the crowd. He is talking about Blasphemy and Native Idols. The preacher bites into his lip, emphasises the word Native, the way he did when he talked about Promiscuousness. As though it were something Rancid.

From behind, a shout. I swivel round. A man dashes out of one of the houses around the square. In one hand he is holding a small soapstone figure, the ones the farmers bury in the fields when they plant the first seed. In the other hand he clutches a string of beads. He is wheeling around like a kite in the sky, like a crazy man. Now two more are rapping on the door of another house. No answer. They push at the door, which opens easily. In and out. More men join in. Not Shekunas. Those ones watch but do nothing. Ordinary men. Forcing their way into shops and homes, whooping every time they find an old god to confiscate.

Whose houses they are I cannot tell you, because nobody dares to utter a challenge. The mob tears around the square and down an empty side street, out of view. There are sounds: the rush of feet, splintering wood, the echo of voices.

The fire blazes into the night. Nobody goes near it. You might think it was a stinking cesspool instead of a warm fire on a cool, bright night. A night when the stars have come out to watch the earth. Nobody warms their hands. Nobody borrows a brand for their cooking fire. Nobody pushes a yam into the embers. Instead men with long sticks poke around in the ashes. And where they find a statue or a figure that has survived the heat, they set about smashing it into powder.

Some pieces went missing. I don't know.

I know it was after Haidera. But how long after, this I cannot tell you – a day, a month, a year; these measures of time change constantly when you are a child. Sometimes a day is longer than a year. Sometimes a month is shorter than an hour. I wish I could remember.

Mama stopped making snuff.

My sisters and I tried to make the snuff instead. We searched for the pestle and mortar and ground the tobacco, *lubi*, cloves. Mama lay on the bed, a distracted presence. Did not watch us or answer our questions. She had lain there many days. Only sometimes she rose, went to her box and pulled out her possessions, sat on the floor surrounded by strewn clothing. Other times she slept. We took over her duties, cooking and carrying the food down to the plantation workers. We told nobody, except Pa Foday. We said she suffered from the fever, though it was not the time of year. Between us no mention was made of it; we dared not look at each other. Instead we shared out the tasks, uncomplaining. For once, no bickering.

But the snuff gave us away. We did not have our mother's special knowledge of the precise amounts, the balance between the ingredients. I carried it to Madam Bah, who coughed for a long time, then stepped out from behind her counter and followed me to our room. We, my mother's daughters, waited outside. After a short while Madam Bah went to Ya Namina's house next to the mosque, and together they returned and went into mama's room.

From that day we ate our meals in Ya Namina's house.

Mama was sick. Nobody could heal her. So she went in search of a cure of her own. The door to her room left standing open. Dressed only in an old gown. Hair uncovered and loose, standing out at every angle, like the dolls we made with sticks and goats' hair. She rose from her bed and walked out of the village.

When a person dies our people cry and sing. The drums sound. The house is home to many visitors. When my mother went away there was silence. My father's house was still. The silence slid down the mud walls. Great drops stretching slowly from the eaves, smothering the thoughts that hung in the air. It clotted every crevice. It rose in the back of my throat when I tried to ask about my mother, and threatened to make me retch. It filled the house until we could no longer open our mouths for fear of drowning in it.

My father, in order to avoid being drowned, went away on business with his sixth wife.

And this same time was when the dancing stopped. The steps followed mama when she walked out of the village. She went, leaving behind everything, even her name. So I wrapped it in longing and kept it for her.

Clouds spread over the sky. Overripe fruit drops from the trees at night and morning brings the smell of wet earth and the sweet stink of rotting flesh. The river is dammed. The water rises. After dark, house-children – black-eyed geckoes – feast on swarms of mosquitoes.

I was sharing a plate of rice with my sisters at the back of Ya Namina's house when mama's ghost walked back into the village. Three people saw her with their own eyes. Salia Bangura and his woman had argued and he was late that morning. She walked past them both without a word of greeting. The alpha was shaving with a piece of broken mirror on the steps of the mosque. Over his shoulder he saw the figure of a woman, dripping with dew. Afterwards he pointed at the shattered glass, dropped in fright. Old man Bangura, spoiling for a fight he could win, began an argument over whether a ghost would possess a reflection. Nobody could agree. What they did agree on was this: spirit or mortal man, it walked straight up the main road towards our father's house.

We heard them shout and dropped our plate. We ran with greasy mouths and fingers. But by the time we reached the place where the three of them stood with open mouths, she had vanished.

The next time I see her for myself.

Up the river mangroves crowd the banks. There we like to dive into the muddy waters and pull oysters from the tangled roots. Below, the river spreads out, glistening green, weed streaming just below the surface like a witch's hair. Here boulders are scattered across the sand, black pearls at a Tuareg woman's throat. It is morning, raining. Drops of rain splash on to the water, as though on to a scalding pan. Steam rises from the bottomless below. Insects race along the surface of the water, escaping on pinpoint feet. It was once my favourite place. I used to come here and dig fish out of the mud, fish with no fins and bulging eyes.

At first I don't notice her, standing half hidden in the shadows on the sharp line where the trees meet the river, in front of the abandoned fishing hut. Her hair is scattered about her shoulders in tangled ropes. Her dress is tattered, torn at the neck so it hangs down like a flap of skin. One breast is naked, tilted up, pointing at the sky. She is watching me.

I climb down from the rock, slowly. Afraid of startling her. She is so very still.

'Mama,' I cry. I start to run. She jerks slightly. Takes a step towards me, extending clasped hands, like she is begging me for something, imploring me. 'Mama,' I run faster, I catch my foot on a rock. She steps into the sunlight.

That day some boys from the village on the opposite bank had crossed to set some traps on our side. Now they see her.

'Hai! Hai!' One of them bends to pick up a stone.

'Leave her alone!' But I'm too late. Like a hounded stray my mother cowers, starts to back off. She is gone before the stone hits the branch of a nearby tree. A shower of splintering bark and leaves. I race to the boy nearest me and push him in the chest. Hard with the heels of my hands.

'She's a crazy woman,' he touches his temple and laughs loudly, 'Craz-y. Let her go from here.'

I run after her. I run behind the fisherman's hut. She is nowhere. Inside the hut a tree grows through the middle, out through the roofless roof. The mud is crumbling away from the walls, leaving wooden poles exposed like ribs. Inside there is a place on the floor, like the warm spot underfoot where a chicken has roosted for a while.

Pa Foday: he brought my mother back. As soon he came back from the plantation and heard the news. Without even a lamp, he searched all night until he found her. I remember that night because of the dry thunder. The lightning lit up the sky as bright as day. I prayed it would help Pa Foday.

And it did. He walked into the village leading her gently. And my mother walked behind him as though she had only just learned how, as though the soles of her feet were tender as a newborn's and had never touched the ground.

Pans of boiling water. Balls of soap. Comb. Clarified palm oil. Fresh clothes. Under the supervision of Ya Namina the two junior wives entered and left the chamber where they kept my mother. We waited outside like we had the time before. Later I heard them whispering to each other at the back of the house. But when they saw me hovering close by they stopped talking. They stood up and walked away, gathering their *lappas* around them, as if to cover their indiscretion. Little hurried steps. Shuffle, shuffle.

I crept up to the back of the house. I took a stool and placed it beneath the window. I braced myself when it creaked under my weight. Half up. Half down. On one leg. In the room at the end of the house I heard Ya Namina and my father talking. I thought maybe I would creep along the wall to listen. But I wanted to see my mother. I pressed my sloping eye against the crack between the plaster and the window shutter.

Still to this day I can picture her, so clearly I could keep her there for ever. They had shaved her head. What else to do? Hair so badly matted it shattered the teeth of the comb. They threw the locks on the fire. Days later I found a singed lock lying in the ashes. I stole it, hid it in a crevice in the rocks – at the place Bobbio and I once hung out eating green mangoes. A long time ago.

Alone in her room, she was dancing. No faltering footsteps, no baby gait. Body curved like a palm tree yielding to the embrace of the wind. One foot crossing the other. Crossing the other. Arms extended. Chin lifted. Head tilted: naked, shaved head. Fingers fanned backwards. Turning a perfect arc. Round and around.

Round and around.

In the end Bobbio, the Boy with No Voice, was the only person who dared to break the silence.

Early evening. The light, heavy with dust, hovered between day and night. I sat on the three-legged stool at the back of the house, filling oil lamps. I looked up to find Bobbio standing close by. Watching me in silence, unblinking. Like a house-child. Like he could see into my soul. That was a thing about Bobbio, I remember. He could hold anybody's gaze. For him there was nothing to it. Even after they looked away, he just carried on gazing at the back of their head. People learned to avoid catching his eye for fear of inadvertently starting a staring match. In fact, people often pretended Bobbio wasn't there at all. I knew what it was now to have eyes slide over you, like greasy eggs in a pan.

Bobbio led me by the hand. Down to the river bank. Made me stand on the jagged rocks, pressing my shoulders down with balled fists. Then he stared at the ground, concentrating. He began to stamp and kick, like a cricket hopping about on smouldering grass, pick up stones and throw them over his shoulder. He flung a pebble at the water. It bounced once and sank.

I had never seen Bobbio act this way. Flecks of foam flew from the corners of his mouth. A shiver trickled down my back, a trail of goosebumps in its wake. People said a *krifi* called Tang Bra lived here. Boatmen told tales of an invisible weight in the back of their boats. The mud dragging at their poles. Nobody came to this place at night.

Slowly the tension came alive, stirring in my belly like roiling eels. I got up to go. Bobbio grabbed my hand. It was nearly dark. Leaning over me Bobbio looked like his own shadow.

Bobbio is standing very close to me. His breathing is loud. I don't know what he wants. He lets go of my left hand and takes up my right. Turns it over. Palms slide across one another. Something warm, heavy, drops. I am confused, it feels familiar. I squeeze my eyes closed. Feel the weight in my hand. A surface smooth as skin. One, two, three four five. I open my eyes. Strain to see in the nearly-night. There it is. Rippled like the sand on the windward side of a desert dune. A white, five-sided stone.

Now it is I who seizes Bobbio. 'Where did you get it? Who gave it to you?' I force him to look at me. I know he understands. He returns my hands to me, waves at me to sit down. Like a spectator at a masquerade I watch while Bobbio tells his story.

And here it is. Together with the little I knew for myself:

The Shekunas forced people to forsake the old gods, learn Arabic and pray in the new way. There were bonfires in every town and village. People were afraid. They carried their prayer mats to the fields, dropped to their knees and touched their noses to the ground every time a stranger approached.

In the first few months that followed the meeting my father became suddenly more devout. Yes, I remember that. I thought little of it. I thought little of anything in those days. Where before he left his wives to their own devotions, during that time he demanded their presence in the mosque every Friday. I wore a head veil and accompanied my mother. We sat at the back of the mosque among the other women. Ya Namina, she took to accompanying him there every day. So did the two youngest wives, keen to demonstrate their obedience.

Any activity Haidera said was *haram*, our father forbade. No more drinking palm wine in the village. *Haram*. Instead the old men sat out near the fields late at night passing the gourd from one to the other and wandered back towards the houses on unsteady legs at dawn. All matters connected with the old religion: charms, even the beads mothers hung around the waists of little children. *Haram*. Offerings of cakes and kola nuts at the graves of the dead. *Haram*. Dancing, drumming. *Haram*. The secret gatherings of women. *Haram! Haram!*

It was our usual habit, on those nights when it was our mother's turn to be visited by our father, to sleep in the house of Ya Jeneba and Ya Sallay. For those three nights we shared mats with their children. It was during one of those times, while he wandered through the darkness, that Bobbio saw them.

A man striding. A woman pleading. Please. Please. Bobbio marches with matchstick straight legs and arms. Begs with a sideways bent body and clasped fingers. Points at me. Cradles an invisible baby in his arms. *Your mother.* My mother and my father. In the night. *Your father is very angry.* Hooded eyes, a rigid mouth. Now a sorrowful face. *Your mother is crying.* Bobbio follows them. At a distance. Ducking in and out of shadows. Down to the river.

I wish Bobbio could speak. I wonder what they are saying to each other. Bobbio stares at me silently. *Your mother.* Yes? My mother. Bobbio looks around. Points beyond the trees in the direction of the houses. Something about the village? Our house? *No! No!* Madam Bah's shop! Now, I am certain. The snuff. Of course. My father found out about us making snuff. Not good, but not so very bad. I let the air out of my chest.

Bobbio shakes his head. Shoulders droop. For several moments we are silent, gazing at each other. My friend drops to his knees, mimes a person praying. The mosque. Praying in the mosque. *Your mother.* My mother is a Muslim? Shakes his head vigorously and waves a finger. *Not.* My mother is not a Muslim? Shakes his head despondently. Shrugs. *Your mother is not a good Muslim.*

That evening my father had interrupted my mother in her room, as she read her fortune in the stones. My mother never looked for trouble, perhaps that's why she wasn't more careful. She never believed trouble might look for her. But at that time my father was in the grip of a fever, determined to end all the superstitions that marked us out as half-hearted Muslims. He demanded her stones.

My mother pleaded. Crawling towards him, trying to touch his feet. I watched Bobbio grovel on the ground, holding illusory garments around imaginary breasts. Reaching out to touch invisible feet. O mama! I felt my heart pounding. My father stepped smartly back, refused to allow her to abase herself. Now Bobbio was up, chest out. He pulled her up. Bobbio grabbed me and held me against him. I felt myself go limp, just as my mother had. He threw up his arm. Scattered the stones to the stars.

Bobbio could see in the dark, almost. He noted where the stones had fallen. When my mother and father had gone he went closer, inspected the stones lying on the ground. Saw they were different to the ordinary river pebbles. He slipped back into the shadows. Left them there. That was all.

A dark rock the shape of a man's cigar. A broken pebble, open like a split plum. A stone with a dimple that fitted my thumb. A twinkling crystal. A pale three-cornered stone. I won't say I found them quickly. Not at all. Bobbio helped me. But even then, there were some I never found, whose faces I did not remember as well as I imagined.

The Ancestors, she called them. Her murmured chant, once engraved upon my brain, now suddenly was gone. The effort of remembering turned into a great rock. Then, when I finally abandoned the effort, the words appeared, like a sculpture carved out of sandstone. And now I recognise them for what they are.

Names.

The name of my mother's mother. Of my grandmother. Of my great-grandmother and her mother. The women who went before. The women who made me. Each stone chosen and given in memory of a woman to her daughter. So that their spirits would be recalled each time the stone was held, warmed by a human hand, and cast on the ground to ask for help. And as the names emerged from the shadows, I saw how my father had destroyed my mother.

Mama returned. She stayed for a while. Then one day she left again. Danced on the outskirts of villages where superstitious villagers, thinking she was possessed by the spirit of some siren, left food out for her. Nearer the town they chased her away with sticks and stones. Once, twice, maybe three times, she returned, but the restlessness was too great. She could not stay. Each time Pa Foday brought her back. Eventually the time came when she went away for good.

As for Haidera Kontorfili, the authority of the Shekunas grew ever greater. He began to tell the world that the rule of the *pothos* was at an end. So the Europeans sent soldiers to arrest Haidera. The preacher swore he would never surrender. The Shekunas lay in wait on the opposite side of a bridge and killed the first man who tried to cross: a white man. Soon after, reinforcements arrived armed with guns.

Haidera was killed in battle, they said. The hyenas feasted on his body. The order went out: taxes to be collected and defaulters punished. But Haidera's followers claimed their leader had used his magic powers to evade his captors. He had transformed himself into a deer and galloped away.

4

Hawa, 1939

Fish

MY LIFE WASN'T SUPPOSED to be like this. But a lot of things happened to me that weren't my fault. If things had been different, I could have been like you. Listen to what I am trying to tell you. The truth. The way it really was.

I never had luck. Not like other people. Yet I stand by and watch other people win all the time. Two days ago my neighbour came back with banknotes flapping out of his pocket, the new ones, not even the old ones. He had bought a lotto ticket and won. Later he came with soft drinks and beer for everybody in the compound. By the time I arrived there the others had already helped themselves. My own one was flat, but I drank it just to show willing.

People with bad thoughts were always taking my luck away. I was still a girl, I was gutting fish – slitting open the bellies with a sharp knife, pulling the gleaming dark mass from within. The fish were fresh, some still alive. Under the table cats darted in and out of our legs, snatching at the pieces that fell. One moment I was concentrating on my work, the next I felt a sharp pain in my foot that made me cry out loud. A dirty white cat stared up at me with cold blue eyes. Somebody tried to shoo it away. The cat clung to the ground with its claws. We waved our arms. It hissed back at us. One of the women, braver than the rest, threw a knife which clattered on to the ground. The cat jumped up on to the wall of the house and away. Later the same women would not look me in the face. They all knew it, you see. When a cat bites you, it's a sure sign somebody out there is trying to change your luck for the worse.

When I was a child I was always being blamed, blamed for everything. It was easy to make me the scapegoat because I had nobody to defend me. So in time I found ways to make my own luck.

I remember a time of happiness.

On the first day of fishing the women gathered with their nets at dawn on the edge of the village. Then there was not one among them who dared to begin without her. Yet she took her time, always. Dressed with great care. Oiled her scalp between the partings of her hair. A bracelet dangled from her wrists, around her throat a necklace of red and white beads. And when she was ready she would call for me to fetch her fishing net down from the hook on the wall. Then she walked, with deliberate steps, down past the houses towards the stream. Never breaking her stride. When they saw her they ceased their chatter and followed her.

In those days she was my father's favourite wife. She alone. If anyone tells you any different, they're lying. This was the reason they waited for her. They knew she had my father's ear. Whatever medicine the Tuntun had placed around the river would have been lifted. The day she collected her net and walked to the river – for all the women in the village that was the most assured sign.

At the waterside she tucked the trailing cloth of her *lappa* into the waist and shook out her net. I ran forward and picked up the end – so it didn't drag across the ground. I walked behind her as she waded in. When the water reached her waist she gripped the bamboo hoop firmly in both hands. I let go of the tail, and watched it swim after her.

The way she walked – no concession to the rising water. The cloth around her waist swelled with air, and for a moment dragged behind her like a giant snail shell. Her breasts bobbed on the surface and her movements were as fluid as the water itself. Below the surface the outline of her body shifted into thousands of shapes. For a brief moment the sun caught her profile. She didn't turn once. It was as though she were entirely alone.

The shallows turned to churning mud in the rush that followed.

The women slipped and scrambled down the bank into the water like buffalo on a collapsing cliff. They jostled for the prize spots close to the bank or else midstream, where the weed grew densely along a sand spit and the fish liked to conceal themselves in the shadows. The slow ones were left to drag the bottom of the river, scooping water and fish into the open mouths of their nets.

Almost out of sight my mother walked on, between the banks of mangrove, heedless of the presence of water snakes and crabs. The boughs of the trees growing on opposite banks formed a bower over her head.

She kept flowers in her house. My father teased her for it, but she loved them, even the yellow blooms from the coco yams and the pale orange okra blossom that grew in everybody's garden. She picked them and put them in water. He built her a house opposite his own; he only had to look across to see her every day. That was where I lived as a small child with my two elder brothers. When he visited he insisted that she shared his food with him. Sat down next to him, like an equal, and ate from the same dish.

I remember the sound of my father clapping his hands loudly and me running quickly to stand in front of them both. I bowed my head. '*Eh bo!* Will you look at this child. Taller with every day. How about a song for us? What songs do you know?' My father was sitting with his legs crossed, wearing a loose-fitting green gown with a trail of embroidery down the front.

I was nervous and I felt my face growing big and hot. I thrust out my chest and pushed my shoulders so far back I felt my shoulder blades touch each other behind my back. I began a song we children sang down at the fields when we were scaring birds from the crops. We would sing across to each other, high up on our platforms above the fields. It was a song known to anyone who had ever been a child.

My father clapped, picking up the rhythm, and joined in with the reply. I remember how surprised I was at that. It was strange to think of my own father as a child and that once there were people who could tell him what to do.

And yet I noticed things about my father. Outside he had a stern face, which did not care to smile. He built the mosque and was inside it five times every day. He walked quickly. And people hurried around him, offering greetings, showing respect. A sober man. Yet I saw my mother do things nobody else did. He used to lie with his feet in her lap while she massaged them, pulling at his toes gently one by one. And I saw her hit him with a fan! Across his face, as though she were slapping him with the back of her hand, but using her fan instead. She touched him only lightly. Still, I had never seen anybody touch my father. For a long time I couldn't remember what happened next. Maybe I had made myself forget. And then I realised the reason I couldn't remember was that nothing happened. She hit him with her fan. Laughter. The conversation between them carried on.

That evening my mother sang the next part. Where my father's voice was heavy and rich, like the smell of the best coffee beans, my mother's was high and clear as an empty sky.

Then it was over. My father laughed and clapped again. He called me to sit by his side while he ate. I never could cross my legs properly, I don't know why. My thighs ached and I was unable to take my eyes off his plate. Guineafowl stewed with honey and whole lemons. It was not a dish the other wives cooked. I hadn't eaten. My stomach groaned loudly. My father laughed and his body shook. He held out a morsel of guineafowl in his fingers, and I reached up to take it from him. Then I remembered my mother. I hesitated. Hunger had prevented me thinking properly. Perhaps my father would consider me greedy. I glanced up at my mother, saw her slight smile, the way she inclined her head towards me. And I knew I had done well.

That day, or maybe it was another time, my mother fetched the small seven-stringed guitar she owned. Lately, since I have been thinking about her, I have wondered where she learned to play such a thing. I have never seen a woman play one before or since, only the travelling players on market days.

She sang a song for my father. It was a Madingo song about love. Not a love song. You couldn't really call it that. I knew it off by heart:

Quarrels end,
But words once uttered never die.
Lovers part,
But love lives on.
Marriages end,
But hearts survive.

You leave your mother's breast,
For your father's side,
And why should this be so?
Because love forever changes.

When from her father's house,
A girl goes to a man,
We see the same again,
Love's constant changes.

And when into the night she slips away,
To her lover's arms,
The same rule applies, my friend:
Love's inconstancy.

My father laughed again, a different laugh this time. My mother sent to me to go and find my brothers. The sound of her voice wrapped itself around me and followed me out into the darkness of the compound where the words broke free and floated up to the stars.

Of course my mother was not a slave. What man would treat a slave that way? Do you ask a slave advice and talk to them about how to run your affairs? Do you listen to what they have to say and then go away and do what they tell you? My mother even had a girl of her own to help her. Does a slave have a servant? So stupid. Some people were jealous of her, that's all. Because he brought her gifts. If he went away – on those occasions when he couldn't take her with him – he never once forgot to bring her something back.

The fan – that was a present. It was the shape of a kola leaf, like an upside down heart, finely woven in different colours. Another time he gave her a real gold nugget. And when he came back from Guinea he brought her an almond tree in a pot. The tree was in flower and she had it placed next to the open window of her bedroom, so she could enjoy the scent all through the night.

He chose her name himself. Tenkamu. I don't know what it was before. It isn't important. My mother was sent here by her parents to stay with relatives who lived in the village. My father saw her and he liked her. Maybe it's true he held the mortgage on the family lands. Some people say they sent her here deliberately, in the hope that she might catch his eye. That's just loose talk.

The truth is Pa Yamba was the one who noticed her first. When he went to speak to my father, he didn't realise the younger man had already decided in his own head to marry her. Pa Yamba wanted her for himself. He had a temper, he dared to challenge my father. But my father was firm. He told the older man to look for a woman of his own; this one was spoken for. *Ten ka mu*. Look for your own. That was what her name meant. Look for your own woman.

Pa Yamba thought people were laughing at him every time they called her by that name. Sometimes they were. He thought my father owed him more than that, because it was Pa Yamba who had led us to this place. In all the years that passed he still had no wife of his own. He followed her with those eyes, eyes as flat and still as the bottom of a pond in the dry season.

My father's house had two wings. My father's room was in one wing and it had two doors: one reached from the inside of the house and another that opened straight out on to the verandah. Anybody who had business with my father waited beyond the outside door. I'd see Pa Yamba there among the people who arrived every day with claims of being distantly related, hoping for a donation. I'd watch him watching her.

I knew the other wives bad-mouthed my mother behind her back. They did not care that I heard them. That's the way our people are. If it suits them they'll not let the presence of a child constrain their tongues, though they should know better. When I was growing up I heard the things they said: calling her the 'Madingo', talking about how my father had never paid a bride price for her, saying she was given away for nothing like the bruised fruit at the end of market day. They were stupid women. I knew it couldn't be true. But still somewhere inside I felt the shame burning like a coal in my belly, making me sweat with anger.

For the most part my mother behaved as though those women were not part of her existence. She did not share their cooking, or send me across to borrow ginger or salt. She turned her face away and got on with her own life. And soon I learned from her. I acted the way she did; I learned to look through them as though they were made of water instead of flesh and blood. And I plugged my ears with imaginary mud so I couldn't hear the things they said.

Still, their narrowed eyes and twisted mouths surfaced in my dreams and their spiteful words seeped through the mud.

Finda the servant told me my mother was the only one of the wives my father had chosen for himself. 'Except for the third wife and he soon tired of her. She only lived to dance. In the end she danced so fast all the thoughts flew out of her mouth.'

All the rest of the wives were chosen by Ya Namina. After my father brought my mother into the house, Ya Namina went out and found more wives. She didn't like a wife she couldn't control. Always she and my mother were polite to each other, but when Ya Namina spoke, sometimes in her voice there was something metallic inside, like a vein of iron running below the surface of the earth.

Ya Isatta, my father's second wife, had no children and so she always took Ya Namina's part – forever fearful she would be sent back to be a burden on her own family. Ya Jeneba and Ya Sallay, everybody knew these two sisters were really married to each other. Ya Sallay was sent to live with her older sister. They were so happy living in that house together, Ya Sallay married my father just so as to avoid being sent away to a husband of her own. They kept to themselves. The younger wives: Balia, Koloneh, Memso, Saffie – well, they were just Ya Namina's housemaids.

Do you know the meaning of the word in our language *ores*? *Ores*. It means co-wife. The women who share your husband with you. The women with whom you take turns to cook. The women you give whatever is leftover in your own pot. The women who are the other mothers of your children, who suckle your baby when your own milk has dried up or unexpectedly soured.

But the word has another meaning, too. Do you know it? No? Then let me tell you.

It means rival.

My mother was the sixth wife. She was tall – for a woman – almost as tall as my father. And she could even have been as strong as him. I know now she wasn't so very beautiful, because people tell me I look like her. Her mouth was big, with perhaps too many teeth. But she was *bathe*, the favourite.

Yes, I dreamed about her the other week. She's back in my thoughts again. For a few days afterwards I was able to see her face in front of my eyes – like a photograph. I never owned a picture of her. All of this was before the shop with the Kodak sign painted on its shutters opened in the town. For two days following the dream I saw her clearly. But then her features smudged. Sometimes I would be able to recall one thing, say her eyes: whites so clear, like moons against the dark night of her irises and her skin. There it is. You can picture a person easily, no trouble – right up to the time when you try to remember their face. Ah, then you can sit and stare at the wall all day if you like. Until you give up. And suddenly there they are, as clearly as if they were standing before you.

That was the way I remembered my mother: on the morning of the festival, standing in her room before it was properly day, silhouetted against a cold, new light.

Back then Pray Day was overtaking all the festival days. To meet the new year everybody swept their houses and Ya Namina ordered the servants to clean out my father's house from top to bottom. Three of my mother's co-wives came hurrying back from visiting their families, looking healthy and still plump for ones who had fasted all month.

The cooking began days in advance. Then it wasn't straightforward as it is now, no radio announcements from Mecca to tell you the moon was really hovering in the sky, only you couldn't see it because of the dust or the clouds. No. We waited until we saw it ourselves, even though that meant we sometimes began to cook too early, the food spoiled and we all fasted for an extra day or two; sometimes we began to cook too late and the feast wasn't ready in time.

There were roasted meats and special dishes baked with coconut milk and spices. I was young and didn't fast; even so the smell made my mouth water. On the morning of Pray Day everyone answered the first call to prayers and afterwards we would carry dishes of whatever food we had prepared as gifts from house to house.

But that was not the reason we all looked forward to the festival. In our house my father presented each of his wives with a costume specially for the day. The new clothes were delivered the evening before, ready for the last day of the fast.

That year my mother spent the whole of the day preparing herself. Finda worked on her hair for all of the morning: plaits so fine it was as though each comprised of no more than six hairs. These she wove, three by three, into thicker braids and then again, until my mother's head was covered in shining coils decorated here and there with tiny pale cowrie shells. In the afternoon she sat for two hours with the ends of her fingers resting in bowls of *lali* until the tips turned red. She sent me out to pick a new loofah from the tree, and I found a fine one. On the way home I held it close to my ear and shook it, listening to the sound the seeds made, like trickling water. Afterwards I emptied out the seeds and carried it to my mother. In her bedroom I rubbed her back and her arms with it, smoothed her with shea butter until her skin glowed deeply as a garden egg.

We were on the front balcony watching the darkness, watching for my father's gifts to his wives to be delivered. Ibrahim and Idrissa pretended not to be interested. They were throwing the eyeless husk of a lizard at each other: dodging and ducking, laughing in their newly deep voices, forgetting that they were men. Our own garments were inside, finished by the tailor in the weeks before. I had picked out the cloth with my mother at the Fula shop. We watched as my father's retainer came out from his room. We smothered our laughter as Ibrahim walked on the outside edges of his feet and made his legs bow and tremble, bending like the old man under the weight of the packages. We followed the retainer with our eyes as he passed through the compound, visiting one house and then the next.

Our mother did not come out. Instead I carried the package to her.

'Open it, mama!' I cried.

She was sitting on the edge of her bed, shoulders hunched, feet on the floor pointing straight ahead. She looked as though she had been sleeping. I did a little jig. My mother didn't even turn to look. She seemed bored by my playful ways. The light on her skin gave a dull cast, for a moment it seemed to me she was old. She was sitting with her hands across her stomach. The air rustled in her chest like dried leaves.

'It's late now. In the morning you'll see it. Now it's time to sleep.'

But it wasn't time to sleep. The village was still awake. Out back, Finda was preparing the last of the dishes for the celebrations the next evening. My brain was whirling with excitement.

'But I want to see it now. Let me see it.' I made my voice into a whine, but with a threat. Like the noise a mosquito makes. My mother lay back and turned over, pulling the cover over her shoulders.

'Tomorrow,' she repeated. She twisted herself around to look at me over her shoulder, smiled at me in a way that made me feel less bad. 'Send Finda for me.'

In the morning the air was cold and smelled of dust. I washed and slipped my new dress over my head. It was too long, but I had a year to grow into it. The cloth was shiny and stiff, not worn soft like my everyday clothes. I ran to find my mother.

That moment when I opened the door: in the dream, I see her

again. She is wearing her new gown, standing before the opaque light spreading through the shutters behind her. Only, in the dream we are not in the old place, but in the bedroom of the house I lived in with my husband after I was married. Everything is as it was when I lived there as a young wife, even the heavy, woven bedspread we were given as a wedding gift and the animal skins on the floor that my husband brought back from the place where he worked.

And in the dream I am thinking, how can I be married already if this is my mother, so young?

Nothing had prepared me that morning for the sight of her in that dress. A long dress, made of printed cloth from Europe, embroidered with yellow and blue thread across her breast. Sleeves that billowed out and narrowed into cuffs fastened with real buttons. When she walked the pleated skirt brushed the floor. In those days the women wore simple tunics and on special days, like when it was somebody's forty days, maybe an embroidered gown or a long skirt and *tamule* with sleeves that stopped at the elbow. I had never seen a dress such as this.

That day we bluffed better than anybody, walked in front of them all into the mosque. I felt the envy in their glances. I held my head so high. When we sat down at the back I could see my brothers in their new *bubas* practically under the alpha's nose. My father was at the front wearing an *agbada* of pure white, with a red sash over his shoulder. At the back we didn't pay much attention to the sermon; the women gossiped among each other. All talk that day was of each woman's outfit. From the outset I knew my mother's dress made the greatest impression of all. My mother was the very first to wear the new style like the Creole women in the big city.

That day! The best day of my life. The day every one of my father's wives wished she was my mother. And every one of his daughters wanted to be me. I had no fears. No cares. I did not see how life could get any better. But then my luck changed like the wind. And my life turned around completely.

★　　★　　★

There were so many of us – children of my father. And yet I had few friends among my brothers and sisters when I was growing up, only Idrissa and Ibrahim who were my belly brothers. Mariama and her sisters were gone. Ya Janeba and Ya Sallay's children kept to themselves: like their mothers they appeared not to welcome outsiders. My brothers, too, preferred their own company or that of the other young men around. And although they sometimes came and boasted to me of their exploits, we spent less and less time together.

Finda was my friend. I followed her as she went about her chores. When my brothers and I fought I ran to hide behind her. And it was she I asked the things I didn't understand, when Idrissa and Ibrahim sniggered into cupped hands but refused to tell me what was funny. Finda didn't tell me either, but she scolded them and that was good.

It was Finda I turned to when I noticed my mother growing taller.

I've told you my mother was a tall woman. And so she was. Only those days, every time I looked at her, she seemed higher than ever. Though my father was always telling me I had grown, I even began to imagine I was shrinking. I measured myself, scratching a mark on the outside wall of the house with a stick. One afternoon we were trapped by the rain, watching it fall out of the sky like sheets of glass, distorting the shapes of the houses and trees beyond, turning the ground into miniature rapids of red mud. I was helping Finda to husk groundnuts, breaking open the soft, steaming shells and peeling the thin membrane from each of the nuts.

Finda set down her pan and told me my mother was sick.

I didn't know what she meant. I asked the only question I could think of: 'Why would that make her taller?'

'Your mother isn't taller. That's just the way it looks.'

A wasting illness had stolen her appetite. And as her body drew in so it seemed to lengthen.

'When will she be better?'

'Soon. God willing.'

'Tomorrow?'

'Maybe not.'

'Next tomorrow then?'

'Soon. God willing.'

The weeks rolled past, my mother took to her bed. The house was quiet. My brothers were out all day. I sat at home and waited for my mother to get well again. Sometimes I went to her room and sat with her. The room smelled of un-aired clothing, sweat and something rotten. My mother was a black woman, but out of the sun her skin yellowed like a dried tobacco leaf. I tried to keep her company, to tell her the things that occupied my day but she seemed not to listen because too often she would laugh suddenly in the wrong place or ask a question that had nothing to do with the thing I was saying.

My father sent for a doctor. Somebody from the town. The man arrived by bicycle and carried a battered black bag, empty except for a stethoscope. Finda was displeased when he pressed the cold metal disc against my mother's breast, but she told me after that she did not protest because she knew my father had placed his faith in this man who was taking so much of his money. Under the doctor's instructions we gave her one tablet, aspirin, each day and every other day Finda rubbed her body with mentholatum from the brown glass jar the doctor brought us from the pharmacist. We waited. My mother grew thinner.

My mother was ashamed of being sick, of the sour smell that rose from her and stained the air. Finda brought star lilies and placed them in my mother's room and their thick scent mingled with the odour of sickness. As if contaminated by my mother's shame my father stopped his visits. Instead he arranged for her to visit the hospital in Kamakue. I was not allowed to go, though Finda went and my brothers too.

Idrissa described the big white building, surrounded by walls built of concrete breeze blocks and lawns of spiky grass, walkways wrapped in bougainvillaea and morning glory. I imagined my mother would be happy there, among the flowers. Of course we expected miracles. Finda was the only one who had any doubts.

The others of us – her children – imagined our mother would come home restored to the way she was before.

My brother told me how they waited many hours to see the doctor. They were sent away at the day's end with no choice but to sleep by the side of the road outside the hospital since they did not know a soul in that place. Our mother was weak and her breathing was troubling her. The dust from the road affected her greatly. Eventually a woman offered her a place to stay, though there was not room enough for Idrissa and Finda, who lay down under the eaves. In the morning they returned to resume their place in the queue. When their time came they found they did not understand the doctors' language, nor they ours. They did not have the words to explain how my mother was so changed she had become another person. The doctors looked her over, made her open her mouth, and peered into the corners of her eyes. When the examination was over an orderly was brought in to translate. The man had a wife from our parts and could speak a little of our language. The beds were full, he explained. They should come back the next week or before that if she turned much worse.

It had taken nearly three days' travelling to bring her there.

My mother sank into her bed until she merged with the bedclothes. Her spirit shrank and crept away to hide in the dark recesses of the house. For a long time things seemed to stay the way they were. My mother gently fading from life.

Two months passed. I was up early on a moist, warm morning. It had rained the night before and the ragged clouds had cleared from the sky. The sun shone strongly, patches of the ground steamed and the vapours rose up and danced in the sunlight.

Just then I forgot about that dark room and the bitter promise contained inside those walls. I felt happy. Every morning when I woke from dreaming, for a few moments I was peaceful until I remembered, and the sagging feeling returned. Once I saw Finda somewhere away from the house, standing in the street with some of her companions. They were laughing, some foolishness or other. I had walked past quickly, turning my head away. Keeping it turned even when Finda called out to me. But that day, when I noticed the rains were nearly over, I too managed to forget.

I passed my mother's almond tree at the front of the house. I was responsible for watering it. The leaves looked withered and so I forgot whatever it was I had been doing and I hurried about my neglected chore. As I returned to the same spot I noticed something about the tree. I saw it fleetingly, at first. The leaves were shaking, though the air was quite still, no wind. I saw the trunk, the branches — moving, writhing, darkly flexing like muscles on a labourer's back. I stopped where I was, afraid to go any closer. It was as though the tree were alive, trying to pull its roots up from the pot. Finda, passing by with a tray of guavas, saw it too. She screamed and it was her scream more than anything else that caused me to start. We both dropped our loads at the same time and I remember how, for a moment, I watched the beads of water and fruit race across the dust like differently sized marbles.

Remember how we used to build our chicken coops high off the ground to protect the hens from the mongoose? In another house a pair of chickens disappeared from their roosts, nothing left but bones and feathers. Not a mongoose. They always gnawed through the cane bars and carried the chickens away. No, not a mongoose. Something else.

And in yet another house something that glistened and boiled black in their cooking pot, where the remnants of a meal had disappeared. The whole compound heard the woman shriek when she raised the lid.

Ants. And ants, too, covering the almond tree, making the branches shimmer and sway before our eyes with their myriad glistening bodies and waving antennae. The two of us carried the pot to the river, it was heavy and the ants crawled up our arms and covered them with fiery bites. We lowered the tree into the water and the ants floated off, struggling on the surface of the water, drowning. Then we dragged the almond tree back to its place and trailed a ring of ash around the base.

It wasn't as though nobody had ever seen driver ants before. Or lost a chicken or two. You could tell when they were coming, the cockroaches flying ahead of the marching columns trying to save themselves. They infested the roofs of houses and dropped down from the thatch. But the talk began all the same. And the way those people talk, sideways, out of the corners of their mouths, using some words to say what they do not really mean, and other words to say the things they do. And you cannot shout at them: 'what do you mean? Say what you mean to say!' Because then they look at you as though you had let the sun get to your head. As though you were a demented dog jumping up to bark at phantoms. You have to force yourself to pretend that what is really there isn't there at all. You go on with your life.

I heard it from Idrissa first. Idrissa heard it from Finda. I found her some hours later. She was removing the laundry from the bamboo poles where it hung to dry, folding each item neatly and adding it to the pile on her head. She told me not to worry myself about it. It was just foolish talk by superstitious folk.

And I believed her. Just words. I didn't know then the damage words can do. You can't feel them, or see them. Someone opens their mouth to speak. The words are there. And then they're gone. Except of course they're not, now they're inside the other person's head, sticking to their brain. I should have remembered the line from the song my mother sang: words never die.

I know who stirred up the villagers' imaginings. My father was a Muslim. He disdained such talk. Though you would be mistaken if you thought that meant he did not believe. And even I, in my time I've seen some things that could not be explained. The *pothos* brought in laws against it, and that served to convince people all the more. For who would go to the bother of outlawing something that did not exist? And Pa Yamba, I had seen his box covered in charms and *sassa* in his back room where I sneaked in once with the other children. He still divined. Only now he lit incense, opened a Koran and chanted words in Arabic to summon the Djinna Musa.

The ants. And the chickens all the way across the other side of the village. And people asked how the ants got to be right in front of her window like that. All over the almond tree that had been my father's gift. And what about her sickness? Wasn't that what happened when you double-crossed the spirit that gave you your good luck? Or else you played at something you didn't understand? Wasn't she a Madingo? And he, who had younger wives, still so besotted with her for all that time. Not beautiful. Not so clever. Not even from a ruling family. What did she possess to make him want her? Nothing. She was only a woman. The whispers, the truth, the lies, all muddled up until everything became an accusation, in their mouths even the simplest fact sounded like a crime.

They never stopped to ask about their own envy and their own jealousy. And what about a wrinkled old man without a wife who coveted a woman who belonged to his patron? And who used to be powerful but wasn't any more. What about that? I was too young to ask the questions myself or I would have shouted out loud at them all.

I was eating a pear. I remember the taste of it. The pear was overripe, oozing juice and yet sucking the saliva out of my mouth at the same time. It tasted faintly of medicine. I was sitting on the wall outside our house. Pa Yamba had been in my mother's room for a long time. I knew my mother was dying because I had seen Saffie, the youngest of my father's wives, come back from the forest carrying a basket full of the red fruits that grow on the Christmas bush. The fruit was inedible, though birds loved it. For humans they had only one use. When you dropped the fruits in water and left them there for a while they turned the water black and we used them for dyeing things. For dyeing our garments after a death.

I was there when Pa Yamba came out of my mother's room. I saw the line of his lips, pressed together, not quite straight, a small upward curve of satisfaction. And the glow that shone out of those stagnant eyes. And the renewed sureness of his step, the impact of his heel on the dirt. The confidence of power regained. I knew just by looking at him that day that he had used my mother for his own ends.

There are some things I learned early on. When I was a child, even before I realised I had to make my own luck, one thing I worked out for myself was never to let people discover the things you knew. Keep them to yourself, because then you had the power and they did not. People will always talk loosely; they forget who is listening. In the same way I learned you must never ask a question. Because then people will guess there is something you wish to know. Keep quiet. And listen.

They said she confessed before she died.

And there was more.

So much more.

Ya Isatta's unborn children. My mother had eaten them. And it was she who had been the cause of the flu that left all our chickens lying lifeless in the dust one morning. Even lime and pepper would not revive them. The small whirlwind that spoiled the rows of trees grown from the new kind of coffee bean – that was caused by her dabbling. Pa Yamba had extracted all of these things from her before she died.

Ya Isatta said they should bring back the red water. That was the way, a long time ago, they used to discover who was up to no good. By making them drink it and the ones who proved to be witches died and that was that. And she demanded to know who would compensate her for her lost children. She said it before she saw me standing there. Afterwards she gave a kind of grunt, a noise halfway between a sniff and a snort. And then she took a great big breath, far more air than she needed. And she pushed it out through her nostrils noisily, her lips pursed together and her mouth turned down.

That moment I wished it were all true. I wished my mother had killed Ya Isatta's children. I wished Ya Isatta would carry on inhaling until she sucked her own nose into her face, followed by her lips and her teeth and everything. I imagined her face disappearing like muddy water swirling down a hole until there was just a black space where her head should have been.

Those foolish women with their okra mouths, they did not dare talk that way in front of my father.

She was buried the same day. Finda told me my father took over the arrangements himself, making sure Finda bathed and anointed the body with the proper care, hiring readers to recite verses at the burial. Afterwards at the graveside, she said, he took some crumbs of the newly dug soil and placed them on his tongue. And he mourned her as though she had been a man, for forty whole days instead of seven.

Still, a man marries expecting to lose a wife or two. Wives pass on all the time bringing new lives into the world. Nobody dresses up all in black, just the hem of a *lappa* trailed in black dye. Relatives arrive to stay in her house, lay claim to her gowns, her cooking pots, her jewellery, even her little guitar which none could play but someone could sell.

And when the week is over everything is gone. Only her children are there still to be disposed of.

Ibrahim and Idrissa, they were the lucky ones. Not so long after my mother died men appeared in the village, one a white man. They set up a table in the middle of the village next to the *barrie*. The *potho* sat behind it. The other one – a Koranko, so told the short scars that marked his cheekbones – stood next to him. The *potho* said he was the Queen's representative, recruiting soldiers to fight in a war to save the Empire. The Empire to which every one of us belonged. The pair were travelling throughout the country enlisting fighters. They had orders from the Queen that each village must nominate at least six men to the cause.

A distance from the houses more men were cutting down bamboo poles and binding them with ropes, laying palm leaves on top. In the evening we watched the same men stripped to the waist, torsos glowing in the red evening light, marching up and down in rows and swinging their arms under the command of the Koranko whose name was Saj Majoh.

Saj Majoh acted as translator for the white man. Under his command the recruits ran, jumped, lifted up logs, until he was satisfied they had the strength to become soldiers. In the evening he told the men who gathered around that they would be given as much food as they could eat and taught to march, to fire a gun and to read and write. He told them that in addition to all of this they would be paid three silver shillings every single week.

My brothers promised they would write as soon as they learned how. Nobody thought to ask how I would read their letters. They marched away, pounding the ground with such force they caused the earth to shake, singing a newly learned song at the tops of their voices. All the shouting and stamping disturbed the bats hanging in the branches of the cotton tree who loosened their claws, unfolded their wings and swirled up into the sky above the brigade of men, trailing them like an omen.

Ibrahim and Idrissa were being sent away to fight in a war, but still it made me envious to watch them go, and sad to think I was left all alone. The question nobody cared to answer was who would take care of me. My mother's family had left without taking me with them for they were poor and thought I would be better cared for in my father's house. Finda was just a servant, I was not her responsibility. Besides, I had seen how she acted around the sugar cane seller, standing with her hands on her hips, her back arched so her breasts and bottom jutted, denouncing the quality of his produce in a too, too loud voice. And I had seen the way he stood, resting on one leg with his chin pointed at her as though he relished the insults.

You know that fountain at the crossroads in the middle of town? Three pools of water and a fountain. Well, the pools are empty and the fountain doesn't work, and now the concrete is all cracked. Built for a big conference twenty years ago. All those heads of state flew in. I remember. I remember standing outside the brand new hotel, watching them arrive one by one in black limousines. The presidents and generals sitting in the back, waiting while their drivers climbed out and walked round to open the door for them. Then the driver had to close the door and walk all the way back around, start up the car and drive out. They could have just reached for the door handle. I didn't think of that then. We were so impressed. The cars were all backed up. It took some of those big men twenty minutes just to get inside the hotel. And that fountain never worked properly from the start. It was painted in the colours of the national flag. The pools of water were supposed to trickle into each other.

This is what I think about luck. Luck is like adjoining pools of water, each flowing into the other. One pool might be dry, the next pool overflowing. It's the same with luck. Some people have everything. Other people have nothing. The people who have plenty just seem to get it all, all the luck that ought by rights to belong to someone else. That's the way it was with me. Always the luck just seems to drain out of my pool and into somebody else's.

The first time I had this thought I was floating on the water in a canoe. I was on my back staring at the sky with my eyes shut, the sun a vast orange ball against a black sky. I squeezed my eyelids harder shut and watched the colours change: bursts of blue, then violet, then red, like fireworks.

Somewhere Ya Isatta was calling my name. I could not have heard her from where I was, but I knew it anyway. I knew she would be calling me to run with a message, or fetch her a cup of water, or help her search for her head-tie or prayer beads because that was all she ever did, all she ever had done since she moved into my mother's house.

When I opened my eyes the world had turned black and white, blurred, like a charcoal drawing somebody had tried to rub out. Sketched trees and mangroves, branches overhanging me black against the sky, and the grey, twisted trunk of the tree the canoe was tied to.

I sat up and stared at the water. I saw my own reflection and gazed at it for a second before the movement of the canoe in the water caused my face to wrinkle suddenly. The sun glared down on the water, but here and there, where the shadows of the trees fell, it was possible to see right down into the yellowish depths to the mud and weed growing on the bottom. A shoal of tiny fish darted past, zigzagging, flashing as their scales reflected the sunlight. I watched them go. In less than a day the fishing season would start again.

The canoe floated upstream of the dam the men had built across the water. The dam was built every year during the dry season when the water was low. When the rains came the stream swelled and the level of the water above the dam rose. The fish spawned and grew fat, trapped behind the wall of logs. On the last day the men set their traps: long, conical baskets pushed into the dam wall at intervals. They stuffed the ends with rice and the fish swam down to feed and were trapped. In the morning, at the same time as the women prepared to enter the water with their nets, the men would come down and heft the baskets out of the water. Baskets brimming with fish. Fish for the evening meal. Fried fish for breakfast. Fish for smoking in giant kilns. Fish for the days of hunger, when the river was barren as the desert.

As I stared into the water I thought about my mother. I thought about the way Pa Yamba had tricked her when she was dying and I thought of all the people who chose to believe the lies because it suited them that way. I thought about her life, now overshadowed by the manner of her death. I thought about all these things. And as I sat there – just like that, I thought of a way to turn my luck around.

I crawled out of the boat and made my way through the tangle of trees to the edge of the dam. The ground was muddy. I nearly caught my foot on roots many times. Tiny crabs hanging from the branches dropped down and clung to my clothing. I worried about the water snakes that liked to disguise themselves among the roots of trees. I pulled my *lappa* up and knotted it up around my chest and I slid into the water on the other side of the dam. I waded in until the water came up to my chest.

It wasn't easy. Especially with the first one. I was hampered by the water and my feet slid in the mud. So then I found a piece of wood and pushed it in between the edge of the basket and the logs, and in that way I levered the basket out. The water came gushing through the hole I had made, and with it dozens of the fish caught behind the logs.

Thrashing carp and smooth, whiskered catfish, curled eels, snapping tigerfish and snouted barbs; fish spotted, striped, scaly, smooth. Water and fish poured over me and almost knocked me over. I put out my hand and touched them as they swam past, stroking their sleek bodies with my fingertips. The next moment they were gone. I stood there breathing for a while, waiting to see if anybody who happened to be down by the river had noticed. But all was quiet except for the faint hum of insects and the sound of water pouring through the hole in the dam.

The rest came easily. And by the time I reached the other side the dam was beginning to break up. Small logs dislodged themselves and floated downstream after the traps and the fish. I pushed at the remaining heavy logs and they felt light. I thought probably it was too dangerous to swim back the way I had come, so I made my way up the opposite bank and crossed further upstream where the water was deeper but the river was narrower. And I walked back home through the rice fields and allowed my clothes to dry on the way.

Of course they all thought it was her. My mother – come back for revenge. Whatever else they did or did not believe, there was not a soul in the village who dared defy a ghost. And Pa Yamba made an offering to try to appease her. I laughed inside, especially when Ya Isatta began to tell me how much like my mother I was, trying to flatter me. I just bowed my head modestly and thanked her, never looking at her directly. But I could feel the big yell growing in my chest, bursting to come out. How I wanted to throw back my head and open my mouth wide and shout at her, shout at them all and tell them it was me. It was me. It was me who let the fish out.

But I knew better than that. Life hadn't been fair to me. I kept quiet. And that day I learned how to turn my luck around.

5

Serah, 1950

Woman Palava

MY MOTHER? I haven't thought about her in a long time.

My mother left.

Tried to alter her destiny. Looking back it was a brave thing to do, I suppose. Foolish, maybe. I don't know. Who did she think she was?

She was Saffie. The tenth wife. Imagine it.

A tenth wife has no status. Not much better than a servant. But sometimes it is the lowliest people who have the most courage – because they're the ones with the least to lose.

There are things I remember. I don't know if any of it makes sense. Some questions were never answered. And there were other things I made myself forget.

Well, let me see. Where do you want me to start?

My mother used to tell me how she first met Ya Namina. My mother was a young girl standing at the side of the path when Ya Namina and her entourage passed by on their way back to Rofathane. She had been at court with her husband and was returning without him. My mother was carrying a pot of water and she stepped off the side of the road to allow this woman past. Whoever she was, my mother could see she was important. Everybody around her was laden while she walked ahead un-burdened.

Ya Namina had journeyed for many miles. She beckoned the child with the water pot over. My mother lowered the heavy pot from her head, filled a cup of water and held it out to the older woman, bowing as low as she could. Bent over double like that she noticed the woman's feet: long toes, and toenails that curved at the ends and pointed downwards. Ten toes pointing at the ground.

As my mother stretched out her hand for the empty cup, the woman touched her chin, tilting her face upwards. She asked her name and what family she belonged to. That was it. Where it all began. How she became my father's next wife.

Three years later she saw the moon. Two years after that she was taken to her husband's room. Ya Isatta performed the obligations on behalf of Ya Namina, bathing her, rubbing her limbs with oil and perfume, carrying her into the room. That night my father sat on a cushion on the tapestries on the floor, counting silver coins, stringing them, through the hole in the middle of each one, into great ropes of money. My mother perched on the edge of the four-poster bed, a bed as big as a boat, and watched him until she became drowsy and fell over backwards. In the morning she woke up alone.

The next night he brought out a board hollowed out in twelve places, six on each side, and numerous small, silver beans. He beckoned her to sit opposite him, took a handful of the beans in one hand and allowed four to drop into each hollow. Afterwards he gathered up the contents of one and began to count them out. One, two, three, four. All this was done in silence. My mother gazed at him. He jabbed his forefinger at the board. She dropped her eyes. He never spoke.

Later he stood up, placed a round felt hat upon his head and left the room. My mother was a virgin. But she had been initiated and she was a married woman. She knew enough to know this was not the way it was supposed to be, though she let on to nobody. Not even Ya Isatta who called her to one side the next morning with a crafty look on her face. That was how they often spent their nights together. Playing *warri*. She became very good at it.

Of course, these were things I found out later. Ya Memso was prone to those sorts of indiscretions.

It wasn't as though nothing ever happened. My mother gave

birth to me and then to my brother. But, *warri? Warri* is a fine game. But when was a board game ever enough for a woman?

All this was many years ago, around the time people began to build square houses. All my father's wives lived in round houses. My father's house was square, it's true – it was so large. In every other respect, though, his house was built in the old way, without bricks or cement and with a thatch roof.

All the time I was growing up, corners and angles gradually replaced curves and arcs. Some people warned it was inviting trouble in through the door, making hiding places for every kind of spirit in search of a warm, dark place to nestle. The women complained the new-shaped houses were dirt traps, a nuisance to sweep, with corners full of dust and spiders' webs.

Back then my father began to draw up plans for a new house. A house with more rooms for visitors, for relatives, for new wives maybe and new children. A house with a roof of corrugated iron.

I was one of the last. The oldest children had grown up and left home. The first coffee trees had overreached their prime. New seedlings were planted every year and every year extra labourers brought in to tend the bushes. At harvest everyone, wives and children included, had to pick alongside the men in the fields. And afterwards we helped to husk the sun-baked beans, pulling away the tacky pulp with deft, skinny fingers. Raking the pale green beans out in circles on the ground, so many moons fallen from the sky.

My father was a wealthy man. No doubt about it. But everywhere glittering riches were being dug out of the earth. In the next door chieftaincy gold had been found on one family's land. Now the men were marrying wives from the ruling families, building houses, acquiring followers.

I remember where it all started:

A dry, cool morning, I watch the horizon fade, swept over by the red dust of the harmattan like a line drawn in the sand erased by the tide.

In front of us men shovel piles of sand. Others walk to and fro,

toting great blocks of baked clay. They come from the village, the
village given to my father a long time back. Some of them are the
same ones who work in the plantation. Others I have never seen
before. In the morning they arrive and depart by nightfall. Every
day for weeks now my brother and I have left our house to take up
our place opposite the site. Yaya is fascinated.

The walls of the house climb as each row of bricks is cemented
into place. The new house is being built next door to the old one,
and it is exactly the same shape, but all the dimensions are so much
bigger. Right in the middle of the dry season storm clouds sailed
over the village and unleashed a storm. Magnificent rumbles
straight from Pa Yamba's magic box. Spears of rain tearing into
the new walls of the house, washing away the foundations. Yesterday our father himself appeared to say the men must work every
day now until the house is complete. I heard the foreman try to tell
him the men needed one day off to work in their own fields. My
father's face looked as though it had just been caressed by a freezing
hand. A rigidness around the upper lip, a tugging at the corner of
the eyes. I saw it. I know these things. I am a child, versed in
reading adult faces. The foreman understands these things as well.
His nerve sputtered and died.

No problem, Pa. And he scurried away like an ant.

Today I am foreman and Yaya is the labourer. Our bricks are
baking on top of the drying rock, a great slab jutting from the earth
in front of our home where my mother dries the clothes. The
bricks are nearly ready, though the house we are building has run
into some difficulties, just like my father's house. The bricks
crumble, the mud dries out and won't stick. Today we work at
refining our recipe, squatting on our haunches over the hole where
we mix earth and water together, using a pair of sticks to swill a
slippy sliding mess.

Busy, we are. Preoccupied with problem solving. Until our
mother calls. Until it's time to do something else.

A shadow falls over us. A hand appears: palm stained red by the
earth, knuckles callused and grey. Short fingernails, ridged and
blackened. I watch the hand. It pours grey dust from a funnel of

torn paper. A moment later another hand tosses in a handful of sand. In front of my eyes our mixture transforms into something tacky. The hands take two of our bricks, smear them with the mixture, slap one on top of the other.

'Give it to me.' Yaya reaches out.

I look up. A man is smiling down at me. He has lips curved like lily petals, a tiny pink patch right in the middle of his lower lip, shining eyes, white teeth, an erratic beard. The lips uncurl and reform into a new shape, a flower spreading its petals at dawn.

'So, little brother, whose house are you building?'

'It's our house. Me and her. And our mother's house,' says Yaya, not looking up. In a small serious voice. A will-not-be-mocked voice.

But this man is not mocking us.

'Maybe when you're done there you can come and help us with this one. Eh?' The man jerks a thumb in the direction of the unfinished house, the half-a-house. His thumb curls back on itself like a wood shaving. I try the gesture out myself, experimentally. 'And what is your name, little brother?'

Yaya does not answer. He is laying bricks with a shuttered intensity.

The man watches and waits. Taking all the time in the world.

'His name is Yaya,' I say suddenly. I can't bear the silence. And: 'He's my brother. I'm bigger. He's smaller.' Because I think this man is nice – for a grown-up.

'And what about you, little sister?'

'My name is Serah Kholifa.'

'Well, Serah Kholifa. Yaya Kholifa. That's a fine house you are building. I hope that one day you people will invite me inside there to eat with you.'

Now it is I who wonders if he isn't mocking.

'Yes,' I reply. This time I use my polite voice for grown-ups.

The foreman is whistling. The man doesn't say anything. Just smiles. The foreman shouts his name – what was it? – and begins to move in our direction, to see what is going on. The man turns away. He is smiling, jogging slowly backwards on the balls of his feet. 'Don't forget me now, Serah.'

He points a finger at me. I nod. Then shake my head. Then, confused, again I nod. Yes, I promise not to forget you.

We have to clear the bricks because my mother comes with a load of clothes to dry. Only the bricks have left dirt and dust all over the drying rock. So our mother sends me to fetch water from the jar by the door. She is not pleased. And she is angry because there is cement in my hair. My braids are cemented together. She plucks at my head with sharp fingers like a chicken looking for insects in the dirt. A little way off I can see the man. He is leaning against a long-handled shovel, watching us.

Late in the afternoon I follow my mother down to the river with a new load of washing. The colour of the sun has deepened and the red dust sparkles in the air, the day has turned a hazy amber, like a piece of coloured glass tumbled by the sea. The light settles gently on our skin, the soft glow outlines our features.

Down on the rocks I help scrub the clothes clean with black soap, and I hold one end and twist one way while my mother twists the other and together we wring the water out. And afterwards Yaya and me, we bathe in the stream and watch a single, stray, green-blue, glistening bubble hovering over the river. And we practise opening our eyes underwater. And make boats out of leaves and sail ant families across the water in them.

And then I see the man again. He is coming down the path behind our mother and he passes the boy, the one who can't speak and never grew up. The man is wearing country clothes with a triangular pocket at the front of his smock. The boy is standing in the grass. And the man raises a hand and the boy raises one also. And they slap their hands together high in the air. The sound bounces off the water. And the boy laughs and the man carries on walking towards us, while the boy stands on one leg like a heron watching him.

That's all I really remember about him. That day he sat next to my mother for a short while. He asked for a piece of our soap; I saw her stand up and go to the laundry basin, unwrap it and hand it to him. And then he slipped into the water and swam with us. He let us ride on his back, and we squirmed and slid off his skin, which was as smooth as a manatee's. And then I laughed so much I took a big breath and forgot I was underwater; he held me up and squeezed me until I spewed reedy green river water back where it came from. And he said:

'Sorry, Ma,' as he handed me back to my mother. And she said:

'Come on. Yaya. Serah. Enough.' He waved at us as we walked away. And when I turned around at the last place where you could see the river, I saw him covered in lather, soaping himself with the slither of black soap.

For a long time I thought that was all it took: a shared ball of soap between a man and a woman.

But that was just the beginning. Not the whole of it. Not even the half of it.

He wasn't the usual kind of grown-up. We would talk about him in the years to come. In hushed voices. Remember when? We had gathered together fragments of the story and tried to make them fit, wedging in a little detail, filling a space with a new revelation, a sudden realisation.

We called him the Cement Man.

The Cement Man. Our name for him. Not the name she refused to call when she faced the elders: the unspoken name that circled in the air like a fly. So why, asked the elders, not too unkindly because after all this was just woman *palava*, though more serious than most – also because they knew they had her – why did she now refuse to swear?

Sometimes when I look at the past I see a swamp: cloying, dark, impenetrable. Like the mud we swilled as children building our playhouse. Mud covering everything, smeared over the detail of recollections, submerging memories. Mud you wade about in trying to locate a lost image or event. Then, usually when you least expect it, the mud throws something up: perfectly preserved as a corpse in a peat bog.

Night-time. I tumble out of my dreams and into the silence of the bedroom.

I can hear my breathing. Scared breathing. Short, breathless breaths. My eyes are open wide letting in the darkness, watching the shadowy figures scuttle to the edges of the room where they slide along the walls and slip back into the place where the wall meets the floor. Banished by wakefulness, they promise to return as soon as I close my eyes again.

I can hear my brother breathing. Open-mouthed, snuffle-nosed breathing. Still holding on to life breathing. The breathing of babies and little children, as though they can't ever get enough air.

My mother's breathing: deep-sleep breathing. Long, slow breaths. Shimmering snores suspended in the air.

Three kinds of breathing.

In my bladder, an irresistible urgency. I lie on my back, wishing the feeling away. Then I reach over and rock my brother, vigorously. I'm afraid to go to the toilet in the dark. Yaya is ashamed he still wets the bed. This is our understanding. We go together at night to the toilets behind the houses. So I don't have to cross my legs and pray until dawn. And he doesn't dream of floating on warm water and wake up in a cold, sodden bed.

We bang the door and stamp our feet, announcing our presence for the benefit of the lizards and cockroaches who lurk in the dark places and cling underneath the overhang of the hole in the floor. The hole gives way to a bottomless pit and a nameless, simmering, steadily rising tide. I squat first: knees together, ankles splayed, thighs quivering, head bent watching the steaming trickle fall into the terrifying blackness.

We march back past the banana groves. The night is cool. A huge moon dangles over the village, like an overripe fruit. The shadows are solid, sharp, small. A dog lifts its head. A nose swings our way like a weathervane, marks our progress for a while and then is tucked back beneath a tail. A lamp behind a window outlines a door and the lattice work of the shutters. Giant shapes move about inside.

We have been gone no time at all. No time at all. And yet in that time everything has changed. Something is happening in the village. Something mars the silence, rumbles beneath the stillness. It takes a moment to realise it.

Far away the sound of voices raised and bare feet pounding the ground and the flicker of torches. People! People purposefully marching. People we have never seen before.

Something is happening and we are awake to see it. Not going to miss it, not going to sleep through it like all the other somethings that happened after we had already gone to bed. Nobody will say to us: 'Oh, you were already asleep by then,' when they tell the story in the coming days. We are awake. Whatever it is we'll be the ones to tell the other children in the morning.

We hurry in the direction of our house, a pair of busybodies, to spy from the safety of our bedroom window and discover what business has brought these good folk to us in the middle of the night.

They are ahead of us. Passing our father's new house now. The smell of wet plaster carries on the breeze. The house is finished. Today the carpenter came and hung the doors: heavy, wooden doors decorated with carvings of monitor lizards – our family *tana*. The carvings are not good. The lizards look like pigs.

The people march on. We follow behind them at a discreet distance. Hearts thumping, scared breathing, not wanting to be seen. What if it is the *poro* spirit come to town? Then we should run and hide, our mother warned us one day chasing us back from the fields, 'Or he'll catch you and take you away. And I'll never see you again.' I giggled so hard as I tried to run I ended up with a stitch in my side. Then her face grew solemn. She once lost a brother that way. A little brother who had been sitting in the road when the spirit came to town. Caught unawares, by the time they heard the sound of the tortoiseshell the spirit and his dancers were already close. She was on the verandah and ran inside. The women slammed closed the windows and doors. It was too late to fetch him in. They thought he would be all right; in those days they left the very little ones. But when they came out he was gone. Into the sacred bush.

My breathing comes faster, my toes curl under me, as though my feet are afraid to touch the ground. I reach out and touch Yaya's arm.

Then again perhaps they have come from a celebration. Perhaps there will be dancing, a *bou bou* or a masquerade.

But then they would be singing. And they definitely are not singing. And nobody is improvising steps or clicking their fingers. The sound of their voices falls somewhere between a shout and a murmur.

The crowd slows. A short distance from our own house now. We are nearly home.

And now they are upon it.

They stop. In front of our house.

In front of our own house.

And we stop too.

And the first thing I feel is guilty. Guilty. A mental checklist of offences committed and undetected. As though the appearance of dozens of people in the dead of night might be something we have brought upon ourselves. For practising swear words when we are alone. For holding spitting competitions. For someone's doves we accidentally set free; they flew up into the branches of an orange tree and broadcast their freedom with thunderous coos. We didn't try to catch them. We ran away.

Then she is there standing in the frame of the door, struggling to make herself decent. Eyes small with sleep, bare shoulders luminous in the moonlight. When they see her the crowd quiets and lets one do the talking. And we stand still, trying to catch the words that flutter past like dark moths. And then we see all of them, our mother now among them. She is at the head of the crowd, but she is not leading them. Nobody lays a hand on her. I sense the invisible will that propels her forward. They move away down the street. And we run for the safety of our own house and our own beds because we know – we just know – that this is something of which we should not be part.

And he wasn't with them. I'm sure of it. Maybe he was hiding. Or had fled before he was brought in front of the court. Those people were his supporters, come to clear his name.

The sequence of things is difficult. But that must surely have come first. The people from the village came to beg. They had come to plead. But running beneath the words, the forms of deference: an insistence. They would be heard. My father would hear them. An insistence, not yet a defiance.

That's all I remember of that time.

Then came the court case.

The boy who was under the table was Soulay, younger son of Ya Koloneh. That was how it worked in those days. I mean, there are different ways of learning. You had to observe the way things were done. The boys who were chosen learned at the feet of the elders.

The elders met in the *barrie*. It was in the middle of the village right next to the well, where the women met. A round building with a tall, conical, thatch roof the shape of a witch's hat, open sided so that people going about their tasks could stop by at any time to hear what village business was being discussed there by the elders.

Whenever something important was happening we children would try to see inside. Sometimes we managed to shove our faces in between the elbows of men sitting on the periphery wall. Most times they drove us away, swatting us like flies with a long switch.

I remember playing this game. Even when it was my own mother who had been shamed and brought before the elders.

Soulay was older. He had a way about him, I remember. A way of holding his head so that it rocked back on his skinny shoulders. He used to hunch them up around his chin, so his head looked like an egg in an egg cup. His smile occupied the entire lower half of his face and showed all his teeth at once. And he could pop his cheeks louder than anyone. And spit the farthest. And once a line of ducklings followed him around for weeks, thinking he was their mother.

We met at the *karanthe* behind the mosque, feverish with curiosity. Nothing this exciting had happened since Salifu Kamara got stuck up the breadfruit tree. He'd climbed up with a long stick to get at the fruit. I don't know, but somehow he dislocated his shoulder. Everyone heard him hollering. The men ran and fetched a fishing net, urged him to leap. It took ages for him to work up the courage. Each time he seemed about to go he'd stop, shout down more instructions. To the right. To the left.

When he did jump the net wasn't taut enough. Pa Kamara slammed into the ground with such a thud the earth trembled. He broke his leg. They carried him away in the net all the way to the Kroo bone-setter in Mabass.

For ages afterwards we played that game with an old *lappa*: Pa Kamara jumping from the breadfruit tree.

That day in the *karanthe* we were as eager as the other children to hear Soulay tell his story. It makes me ashamed now to think about it. I didn't understand, I didn't understand the consequences – for her, for Yaya, for me.

She does not call his name. She denies she is faithless. And yet, when they bring out a powerful *sassa*, one from the village of the accused man – she falters.

We don't care about the accusations. We don't understand them anyway. It is the gory details we crave. What did the *sassa* look like? We want hair, horns, hoofs. And there must be something red in colour we can tell ourselves is blood. Sacrificial blood. Palm oil or betel nut. Dead things and red things.

Soulay enacts my mother's terror for us, shivering and quivering as she backed away. We watch him with glassy eyes, breathing hotly through open mouths. No shuffling. No sniffing. No nose picking or scab scratching. And afterwards we ponder the information with delighted disgust and sated bloodlust.

She refused to call the man's name.

Now she claims her confession was falsely given. The elders looked at each other and around. One peered through empty spectacle frames. Another swatted himself with an animal tail, encased at the anus point in an ivory handle. Together they looked down at her – this woman neck deep in woman trouble. How could it be so?

An afternoon, when the new house was nearly completed, my father called her and told her he wanted to bathe. She replied she would fetch water. But he shook his head. No, he said, down to the river. The two of them, together. Her husband never bathed in the stream. That was the place for children and unmarried men, men without wives and daughters.

It was the hour before darkness. The river was quiet. She agreed to his request. What else to do? In the water he stretched out, swimming off into the deep. He called to her to follow. She was nervous; reassured by his voice. A game, perhaps? His manner suggested playfulness and appealed to the part of her that was curious and eager as one who had never been favoured.

Imagine her:

Fingers pull at the sodden knot of her *lappa*, she lets it unwind and float on the surface of the water.

At first she thinks little of the firmness of his grip, the finger digging into the flesh of her arms. Her nervousness, the current. Together they swim to the other side, far from the houses. A tenth wife. Alone with this man, who is her husband. Confused. Growing less hopeful that this behaviour is the manifestation of a sudden ardour.

Can't swim. Naked. And in deep water. Points her toes downwards like a dancer – and still can't feel the bottom. Just reeds tickling her toes like a water spirit's fingers. A leaping in her guts, panic straining to be freed. And only his grip – painful on her upper arm – keeps her from taking in gulps of water. Meanwhile darkness steals across the water.

Imagine him:

A husband who feels his age. Righteous, yes. Indignant, somewhat. He wishes he'd never been told the rumours. If she had been one of the more senior wives, and discreet, the other wives might have made arrangements. Now it was already too late. And there was the man himself to consider. It went beyond what was obvious.

And so he pulls her out of sight into the darkness under the mangroves. He confronts her with what he knows, repeats the talk. She had been seen. They had been overheard. And he demands a confession, there and then. And she, with her toes pointed down and her chin tilted up, grabbing breaths as fast as she can. She confesses.

The court imposed a fine for woman damage.

The elders of the court saw this was a time to be firm, to teach a lesson to those young men who could not afford wives of their own. But they were too quick to make an example of the Cement Man.

And my father – he overplayed his hand, he underestimated his tenth wife.

We went with her. At first we moved around. We stayed with my mother's mother in her house in the town, a house built on stilts. The house of treats, where a pot of tea warmed on the sideboard all day long, where my grandmother let us play with her hair and sleep in her bed at night and gave us little sips of condensed milk. More than once our mother left us for a few days.

All the time I waited to go home. I have forgotten now the moment when the consciousness flowered. It happened out of sight, like a night bloom. Closed one day and open the next. We were never going home. I was a child. It was not for me to ask. No. You overhear a little thing here, another thing there. And some things you pick up when you are a child, you only really understand when you become an adult.

At some point I came to understand all of it: the travelling, the boarding, the buying and selling; all of this was so my mother could pay her bride price back. To free herself from our father.

A long time later I was standing underneath the cold neon light in a supermarket. Around me people were opening boxes of eggs, checking the shells for cracks. In my hand I held a box of half a dozen. A fat man with a beard dressed in blue one-piece overalls like a giant romper-suit swung into me. The carton spun upwards into the air, the eggs exited six ways. The fat man tried to catch them. He was surprisingly quick and snatched an egg out of the air. The shell broke in his hand. We were both left standing there. Bright yellow yolk and transparent mucous slid from his fingers. I found some tissues in my bag. We stared at the mess on the floor.

'Leave it,' he said. 'They'll get it.' Waved his wiped-clean hand. Stepped around the mess.

We deliberately both walked away from it and from each other in opposing directions. And as I walked away I felt a shiver, a sensation of hot and cold, of some strange suppressed panic.

I travelled away, in a direction I didn't want to go, backwards in time. For a long while the memory was gone. Only the feeling was left.

Back then we travelled east with a hot-metal smell in our nostrils, crouched on the floor of a mammy wagon, playing with tiny metal ball bearings, racing them up and down the floor. Yaya and I, we want to stand up and feel the hot, gummy wind in our faces, sit on the sides of the lorries like the young lorry boys lizard-eyed in sunglasses, who perch with their backs to the cab, and sometimes crane over to talk to the driver through the open window. And never fall or have to steady themselves with un-dignified abruptness. Even when the truck drives over a pothole. Or lurches to a stop and the women all clutch at their leaping bosoms, and at the same time check the damp wads of cash strapped below their breasts. I want to stand up and reach up to catch the passing branches who nod their approval as we speed by.

I have never even seen a truck before, but I am fearless. In a very short time we two newly superior beings snigger at the foot travellers who drop their loads and flee into the bush at the approach of her stampeding wheels and roaring engine.

At the roadside a man is selling watermelons. The truck stops and people climb down. Some of the young men light cigarettes. The woman next to us asks me to mind her bundles and trots off into the bush, hitching up her skirt as she goes. The men wander beside the road, turn their backs, as though moved to contemplate the way we have just come. I walk over to look at the fruit stacked in a pyramid taller than I am. My mother comes up behind me and buys a melon from the vendor who breaks it open for us, pushing the point of his knife into the skin and forcing the flesh apart. And we eat slices of it with our faces turned to the wind, the pale pink juice drying sticky on our chins. And save the smooth black seeds and flick them out of the moving truck one by one.

Later we pass a bus with a broken axle, sliding sideways like a crab caught on the edge of the surf. We leave it far behind as we roll on past shanty towns of scrap metal and tin into the unknown. And there we arrive coated in dust, like we have been rolled in flour and readied for frying. And when I blow my nose the snot comes out red and thick.

At night the cockroaches drop from the ceiling of the rented room. And in the morning we find them lying upside down under the beds. And I sweep them out and wonder, do they fall from the ceiling already dead? Or do they faint trying to walk upside down and bash their brains out on the floor? Behind thin cotton curtains six other cots are partitioned off like separate states. They are empty. The town keeps nocturnal hours.

In the early hours of the morning the bursts of music, the shouts and the coarse laughter steal into my dreams. I lie wedged between my brother and my mother, our bodies stuck together with sweat.

By day Yaya and I stand on the town's main street and watch rickshaws and carts bumping along the road. A truck full of men – shirtless, carrying picks and shovels – roars past, nearly knocking us down. Once in a while a shiny car glides by, scraping its suspension on the rutted road. We run alongside and try to peer through the dark glass. Try to imagine who could possess a vehicle such as that.

Eventually we stop and stand still, dizzy at the sight of so much. The people hurry past us heaving bundles, sacks and crates. People here rarely smile or greet each other. After a while I begin to notice that most of the people here are men. We walk past queues of them, arms and legs covered in cracked red mud like elephants' skin, waiting outside the Syrian diamond traders' shops. We press our noses against the windows, see men hand over leather pouches, dealers weigh little pieces of grey grit on tiny brass scales.

The view from our window looks out over pits that line the river like sores on a leper's mouth. Men in loincloths wade up to their thighs through the rusty shallows, other men dig at the sticky mud with shovels, on the banks of the river more men sift the mud and water in round trays. A vaporous sunlight glazes their shiny black ant bodies and a sour wind drifts across the houses.

One carat equals ten pounds. Two carats equals twenty pounds. A full three carats equals one hundred and ten pounds. Enough to buy a fleet of bicycles, marry, build a house of baked bricks with a zinc roof.

Our mother's bride price equalled the price of a one carat diamond. Cash only. On top of which she received a cow which was hers for the milking. Non-returnable. Two country cloths and four double lengths of waxed cotton, one dozen sticks of salt at two shillings each, cowries, rice, cocoa beans, gold and one umbrella, distributed to guests and family: all were listed by the court and added to the debt. To be repaid in full.

Our mother knew enough to know that the people who made money in the gold rush were not the miners, but the ones who sell buckets and spades. And so she buys a three-legged stand and sets herself up in business selling eggs on the roadside.

We buy our eggs for two pennies each, boil them and sell them for five pennies each. A perfect plan except that firewood is not free. Here the trees have all been pulled down to make way for the mines and railways. Firewood sells for fifteen pence a bundle in town, twelve pence a bundle on the road out of town. A dozen eggs equals twenty-four pence, plus fifteen pence firewood equals thirty-nine pence.

Twenty-one pence profit per dozen. And living costs and everything on top.

Not all the eggs are good. Some contain the pale foetuses of baby chicks, others are watery and grey. Each time this happens our profits are reduced. The eggs must be conserved. We do not eat them for lunch. We do not eat anything. We nibble kola nuts to ward off the hunger and thirst just like the men in the pits. And mother sends me on the long trek to buy firewood out of town.

And at the end of more long days than we can bear it is enough. And the end when it comes is marked only by an egg slipping through fumbling fingers and fracturing on the ground. I laugh, because for some reason I think it's funny. And because we have been fooling around Yaya laughs with me. And so I laugh all the harder to encourage him, and just because I want to. The giggles rise in my chest like bubbles of air under water. I don't notice the way Yaya's laugh hovers and bursts. Only vaguely do I hear the sound, like a whistling in the air.

My mother slaps me hard across the face.

I have forgotten what was so funny. It isn't funny any more. I bend down to try to scoop the egg up. It stares back up at me like a sorry eye, quivering with glutinous tears.

'Leave it.'

'I'm sorry, I'm sorry,' I say as many times and as quickly as I can. And again: 'I'm sorry.' Because I *am*: deeply, desperately, suddenly. Frightened faces, Yaya's and mine. No pride, no urge to sulk or seek refuge in swaggers.

'And you think that's enough,' my mother says, 'just like that? You say you're sorry?'

'But I am sorry.' My mother looks at me. Her face is empty.

'Well Serah, sometimes sorry isn't enough.'

A gecko, hanging in the crevice between the ceiling and the wall, turns its head and blinks as if in disbelief.

The next morning a line of ants trails across the floor, up the legs of the bed, across the mattress, up the wall and through the window, carrying away grains of sleep and dead skin.

My mother, curled up on her rented cot, weeps. I clutch her and cry too. I hurt her hurt. I grieve her grief. Yaya sits on the end of the bed, leans over and places his head on her legs, curls up there awkwardly grasping her calves. And the bad feeling settles itself over us like a blanket.

Hours later I sit up straight and watch my mother as she sleeps. She sleeps on her side with one arm bent beneath her head, the other stiff and straight, trapped under her body. Thinner now, the bones have crept to the surface. A web of cracks in her heels, outlined with dirt. In the dark cups beneath her eyes, a sheen of sweat and oil.

Behind her shoulder is a tiny, keloid scar with points like a star. I reach out and touch it, feel the slipperiness with my forefinger. When I was very little I used to like to stroke it while I sucked my thumb, when it was still my turn to be carried on her back. Once she told me a shooting star had fallen out of the sky and landed there. Another time she said a firefly had settled on her and forgotten to put itself out first. The last time I had asked her, a few days before, she told me it was nothing: just a spark from a lively fire.

Jagged silvery lines glimmer in the thickening gloom, across her hip bone and in the curve of her that dips from the peak of her hip down and out again towards her stomach. Some years after my brother was born she became pregnant again. She was asleep in the house; I heard the sound of her calling and ran inside. Water! Soaking the sheets, leaking through the straw mattress, dripping on to the floor where it formed tributaries and ran across the uneven floor into the corner of the room. And my mother clutching her stomach with one hand and waving at me with the other. I lurched forward, but she wasn't beckoning. She was waving me away.

'Out! Out!' And Ya Memso running in behind me. My mother's closest friend among the wives. A tiny woman, so short I once asked my mother if she had grown up yet. Ya Memso went to her, as I backed out of the door.

No more children, then. Just us two. And only many years later, when I was sitting in front of my own husband, on the far side of a table and a silence that neither of us could cross, I sat and stared into the corner of the room at the fluff, the angled shadows, the dark seam where the floor met the walls. Fatigue made my skin hurt, my teeth ache. For a few moments I gazed into that corner, forgot he was there. And the memory came back to me then. Not in a flash. Rather it fluttered down like a feather.

I stay awake and watch her until gradually the outline of her body withdraws into the darkness.

Orange robes. Bright against her skin. I notice my mother is beautiful. This is the first time I have seen her since we came back. I don't know how many months ago that was. It is harvest time. Out past the fields the rice is hanging in bundles on frames to dry. In the plantation the red coffee beans in their new red skins shimmy and shine. It makes your eyes ache to look at them for too long.

I had almost forgotten the village existed, and yet in no time I have assumed old habits, returned to the places I consider my own.

The water has closed over those weeks. Memories of our time away slipping down the sand, red mud and threadbare curtains and lizard eyes being washed away. The tide of the present rushes in to fill the space.

One difference. Our mother has no longer been with us. She left us. She didn't stay. And in that time everything has changed.

Now, from where I stand blocking the light from the door, I watch her. She looks different and the same. Oddly familiar. Like a feeling of *déjà vu*. We have embraced. A spontaneous rush forward transformed into an awkward clutching. And now we face each other from opposite sides of the room.

Not so Yaya, who sits by her feet, refuses to leave her surrounds like a dog by the warmth of a fire.

Yaya remembers nothing of the journey home. We wrapped him in all the clothes we possessed. He was shivering, his insides pouring out like brown tea and the colour leaching from his face as though his spirit were draining out. And the other passengers in the mammy wagon complained, but then said sorry. Again. Sorry, Ma. When they saw how ill the woman's son was. And might die. That would bring them bad luck, without a doubt. So they became solicitous and offered us the food they had wrapped in cloths and banana leaves, pieces of sticky sweet rice bread and pepper chicken. It was the first real food I had had in days; I crammed it into my mouth. Afterwards I felt nauseous and had to hold on to the sides of the truck. One lady who knew about herbs made the driver stop by a guava tree. She picked the leaves and made some tea for Yaya. We were let down at the footpath to the village. And somehow we stumbled the last miles home.

Tiny Ya Memso is asking far too many questions. The words jostle and barge each other on their way out of her mouth. She moves around the room, flapping her hands like a pea-hen trying to get off the ground.

Brought back, we were, as though we had been accidentally taken in the first place. Goods discovered in the bottom of the basket at home. Shoved there by a gluttonous toddler or a batty grandmother who keeps pinching things. So sorry, a mistake. Here you are. Won't happen again. Sorry, sorry.

And by now we call him the Cement Man, because we have worked out a thing or two. And so have all the other children.

They sing a song. The last line goes like this:

Bo, hide them, hide them all, O Chief,
For he is coming, the Wife Thief!

Shame bubbles up and pricks at the underneath of my skin. And the tune hangs around like the smell of smoked fish. At night I can't sleep, I hit my head to try to knock the melody out.

Patterned cloths of green and blue, waxed and beaten. The palms of her hands are stained green and blue, and the edges of her cuticles, too. Blue-green crescent moons. Now she is a business-woman, with a business making *gara* cloths. Ya Memso, as excited as a child, has already hidden hers in the bottom of the trunk where she hoards things for the day the *sabu* comes to ask about her daughters. My own is lying a thousand miles away on the other side of the room on my mother's lap.

I watch her and wish she would just go away.

In time my wish came true. This time she headed to the South. We saw her again, from time to time. Always when my father was away. She never did pay him back. She was in debt to him for the rest of her life, like the men whose lives he owned, unable to marry again until such a time as she repaid her bride price.

As for me, I no longer wanted her for my mother. I could not bear to be reminded of that awful time, I just wanted everything back the way it was before. Ya Memso treated us well. She even started a marriage box for me, with the cloth my mother brought. And gradually she added things she made herself and things she bought.

In the beginning Yaya talked about her a lot, wanting to know whether I remembered this or that. Like the way she could fold her tongue in two. The way he could and I couldn't. Once he asked me to sing a song, a lullaby. I told him he was far too old for such things. Next he wanted us to go out to the main road and find a lorry to take us south. It was foolishness.

People change as time goes by. As you change yourself. I wish she were here, so I could tell her the things I understand now that I didn't then. You look a bit like her, around the eyes. Maybe the shape of the face. Yes, an oval face – your father's. People sometimes thought she came from somewhere else.

For a long time I would not let myself think about her. The years passed. A question sat itself down on the edges of my mind. Just beyond my subconscious. Like a patient pet waiting to be noticed and allowed inside. And the question was this. Why did she refuse to swear? Why did she turn away and refuse to swear her innocence?

Well, did they or didn't they? The Tenth Wife and the Cement Man?

'Guilty,' cried the elders one, two and three. Obvious to anyone but a fool. But a time came when that wasn't enough for me. She insisted my father had threatened her. I thought about it for a long time.

She could have worn the clothes of the victim. She could have pleaded and begged. But she refused. When the moment came she saw her choices, she could not betray herself, seeing what her life would become. She told the elders she was faithful. But when the people from his village brought the *sassa* forward and demanded she vow on her own life that there was nothing, in that moment she saw the starkness of her choice.

In the game of *warri* an opponent faced with losing must sometimes sacrifice in order to win.

She didn't shrink from it, the way Soulay told us. Rather she refused it. Turned her back on one life, turned the corner to a new one. Because she had nothing left to lose.

Or so she thought.

This was what I believed for a long time. Then another day I looked again and found there was a different thought sitting in the exact same place I found the last one.

At the river, that day – the day Yaya and I swam with the Cement Man – my mother sat on the bank and watched us. And she saw in him the same thing we had seen. A man who wasn't like other grown-ups. A man with pink-splashed lips. Orchid petal lips. And she could not bring herself to swear because she knew something.

She knew that in her heart that she had wished it.

DREAMS

6

Asana, 1941

Bitter Kola

MY MOTHER TOLD ME: 'Before you are married keep both eyes open and after you are married close one eye.' But when I was young I closed my ears instead. I refused to listen to my mother. All I wanted was to get as far away from her as I could, you understand? And so I did the very opposite. I knew that in so doing I might hurt myself, but it mattered more that I hurt her.

Where to begin? I gave myself away. That's the beginning and end of the same story, the whole story, start and finish. Not to become a first wife, no. Nor even a second. I threw myself away to become some man's third wife. And would you think perhaps that man came from a ruling family, or was rich, or respected, or held an honourable position in the men's society? I would understand why you might think so.

But, no. It's true to say Osman Iscandari was none of those things.

After I married I learned a lot. I did not learn so much about men – after all, Osman Iscandari was not all men. Rather I learned about myself. I learned about us. I learned about women – how we are made into the women we become, how we shape ourselves, how we shape each other.

The day I married I rode to my husband's home on a *maka* carried by four *makamen* dressed in tunics and trousers edged with green and round felt hats with long, black tassels. They jogged barefoot. At times lifting me up over roots and stumps, at other times raising me high above their shoulders as they waded through streams. I lay back and dreamed in the silence. The *makamen* were graceful as mimes. I admired this about them as I swung under the shade of the canopy towards the border of our chiefdom: away from my home and towards a new life with my husband.

Behind me came the load bearers carrying the luxuries bought with my bride gift – a bride gift so great it was the talk of the town. That was how everyone knew that this man loved me, from the day he came to put kola. For days I begged my father – out of my mother's hearing – until I persuaded him to receive Osman. On my beloved's second visit I wore the new *tamule* and *lappa* he had sent for me. I stood behind my father's chair and gazed at him, unable to believe my own good fortune.

At the crossroads that marked the border the *makamen* lowered me to the ground. I climbed to my feet, gathering my gown up in both hands. My husband's *makamen* were waiting for me. Their uniforms were a little shabby: short trousers and striped shirts like a football team. Still, I determined not to let this bother me. Instead I settled on to the bed and arranged the folds of my yellow gown in a way I thought made me look elegant. The edges of the gown were scalloped and embroidered with butterflies. My mother thought I had made a foolish decision. Still, she would never allow anyone to say she had not sent a daughter to her husband in the proper manner. Early in the morning she had roused me to begin preparations. Kaolin from the river bank had made my complexion soft and even. Oil scented with lemon grass had been massaged into my skin and left my body gleaming. The soles of my feet buffed smooth. The edges of my hands and feet painted with henna to highlight the contrast of my palms and my soles with my skin. My teeth shone white from chewing *egboka* leaves, so bitter they numbed my tongue and left me barely able to taste a single dish of my wedding breakfast.

And when she had finished dressing me my mother placed the brocade sash over my shoulder and stepped back, nodded and left the room.

Now I smiled to myself. I imagined the expression on my

husband's face when he saw me for the first time. No longer a girl, but a woman.

I lay back, propping myself up on one elbow so that I could see where we were going. It wasn't easy to do. The *maka* rocked so vigorously from side to side. I thought nothing of it: we were on an underused path. As we neared the town the paths would broaden and the *makamen* find their stride. I tried not to think too much about how crushed my gown was becoming; I concentrated instead on the sky and the ever-changing patterns in the canopy of trees.

I was thrown out of my reverie by a sharp pain.

'Be careful!'

No reply. I tried to sit upright but my arms were pinned down by the steep sides of the hammock. The rocking and jostling persisted. I began to feel nauseous, saliva flooded my mouth. I struggled so hard I all but tipped out of the hammock. The *makamen* came to a halt and stood watching me as I tottered to the side of the path. There, in one great heave, I deposited my wedding breakfast into the undergrowth.

And so this was how I arrived at my husband's home: my wedding gown flecked with vomit and my breath sour. Not that I need have worried. My husband was not there, in his place a message to say he was away on business. Many days passed before he returned.

In the beginning I refused to see what was in front of my face. I saw a big house with many rooms. I did not notice that it was empty as a cave, with plain walls and no furniture. I ignored the chickens that ran freely through the house, dropping their chalky turds. I failed to notice the cockroaches hiding in the crack between the door frames and the mud walls, flattening their skeletons to fit into the tiny space. I did not see the way the hill at the back rose abruptly up out of the earth, engulfing the house in its long shadow. I let my eyes pass over the bitch that lay in the sun, with swollen teats and dried blood under her tail. And I mistook the silence of my two co-wives for acceptance.

They were all signs and there would be more, surfacing one by one, floating in front of me like flotsam from a shipwreck. Even when I was drowning I dismissed them all, first with foolishness, then with pride, and finally because I had put out my own eyes with hot pokers of shame.

From the beginning my face wore a happy expression and I forced myself to act the same way. When my husband returned I knew I had been right. I saw again how handsome he was: he had only to utter my name for me to shiver – a shiver that started behind my heart, trickled down my spine, crept up the back of my neck. Any time he called me I dropped whatever I was doing and ran to him. When he praised my cooking I was in ecstasy. Each morning I woke up and told myself how lucky I was. And for a long time I believed it. The bad feeling in my heart was overtaken by another feeling, a fluttering and leaping from somewhere below my belly, like a fish jumping on a hot pan.

Maybe this is something you don't want to hear. You pity us, not so? You think we don't have the same feelings as you – because of what was taken away, that we are dead down there. No desire. We come together with a man without pleasure. You see how hard it is for me to talk about these things: we are sworn to secrecy. And so we bear your contempt. But there are some things that should be said. So that you, at least, understand. Because you are our daughter. Listen.

For us it was something special: the gifts, the food – delicacies to eat whenever you want – friendships made that last for ever, singing and dancing, the company of women. For the rest of your life, wherever you are, when you are lost or alone, you may start to sing one of those songs and when you hear the voice of another woman join in the refrain – you know that woman is your sister. For all of us it was the first time we had been away from our mothers. That part was hard, even for me. I missed her.

That first night: sitting in the cold stream with the other girls, chewing on bitter herbs and waiting for the moment when your name was called. The circle of holes in the earth, filling up with blood. One by one. What you remember afterwards is not the pain.

That is forgotten, like the pain of giving birth. No, what I remember most was the sound of a blade cutting through my own flesh. Such an ordinary sound, like a cook cutting through the flap of a chicken wing.

My mother had said to me: 'When it is over you stand up and you walk.' I promised myself I would do that. I pushed a cloth hard between my thighs. My legs trembled. I gasped for air. The pain rose in waves, crashing into me. I concentrated only on one thing – walking away from that place. One step at a time. One foot in front of the other.

Twice we are made women. For the first time when we are initiated. And the second time when we go to our husband's room. With Osman there was tenderness, yes. And pleasure, too. I wanted to go to him. I longed for it.

Osman came and went a great deal leaving me with plenty of time to myself. I was waiting to conceive. Not so easy with a husband who is never there. Balia and Ngadie, my co-wives, had their own children. Balia's children had left home, except the youngest who was already able to help her with the cooking. Ngadie had two. A girl and a boy, who were so alike I could barely tell one from the other, they flitted about silent as shadows.

I began to dream of my own children who were waiting to be born. Of course I must have sons to take care of me when I was old, but most of all I longed for a daughter – a girl whose face I might look in to see my own secrets. I began to choose names, then worried it might bring bad luck. I picked leaves from the *gbono gbono* tree and stirred them into my cooking so that, with God's blessing, I might fall pregnant the next time Osman was home.

There was less to do in this place than in Rofathane. There was a well for water and only a small vegetable plot. Osman earned money working as a road inspector. The colonials were busy building roads and railways up and down the country. To the big mines and down to the coast where ships waited to carry the loads away. Osman talked a lot about his job and with pride. The new roads were built of tar and as smooth as the floors in a house.

People liked to spread their laundry out upon them to dry, as well as their rice and grain. Osman told me how he confiscated their washing, threatening to burn it, and swept the grain away.

Balia and Ngadie's daily routine did not alter to include me. I had no chores. Well, I didn't mind. Wasn't I the lucky one? I'd heard the tales of junior wives who found themselves pounding rice late into the night, minding other wives' small children, working long hours in the vegetable plot. With so little to do I spent my time on petty vanities. When I grew bored of those I began to look around me, searching for ways to distract myself.

A wasp with black and yellow-striped forelegs building a nest held me captive for a long time as I watched her rolling tiny balls of mud from the edge of a puddle and flying away with them to build a nest in the branches of a tree. Another day I noticed the funnel-shaped spiders' webs that blossomed in the grass every morning, sparkling with dew and lit by the sun. On another afternoon it was the fluttering black crest and blue feathers of a plantain eater – hopping up and down next to his nest, calling for his mate to come back. 'Kooroo kooroo ko ko ko ko.'

Gradually I began to notice other things.

Early in the morning I gazed out of my window. There was Ngadie walking towards the house from the direction of the grain store. The next morning I saw her again, and the next. I wondered what she could be doing there so early. The way she walked, with a great deliberateness, placing one foot in front of the other, like a person walking on the ridge between fields of crops. She didn't notice me watching her.

The next morning I woke before the light. I hurried down and hid behind the grain store. After a short time Ngadie passed by, eyes darting from side to side to see who was watching. I slipped in behind her, followed her along the path into the forest. She stepped off the path, I stepped quickly back into the trees opposite. Once, twice she glanced over her shoulder. I waited before I switched my hiding place and had her again within my sights. I waited and watched.

Ngadie stepped up to a tall palm tree, reached up and scored the trunk three times with the blade of the knife. Sap poured from the wound. Ngadie dipped her fingers into it and raised them to her lips. She tied a gourd to the trunk beneath the flow. From higher up she took down a second gourd and from the way she braced her body, I could tell how heavy it was. This she lifted to her lips. She raised her head and for an instant seemed to stare right at me. I held my breath. The seconds passed. She lifted the gourd a second time and I relaxed. When she lowered it I saw her upper lip was crested with foam.

In the days and weeks that followed I noticed how often Ngadie slipped away. And how when she came back she lifted her feet a fraction too high and put them down carefully.

I was pregnant. I was eating a mango. The mango dripped with yellow juice and sticky goodness. I was enjoying it so much I worked my way right down to the seed and sucked the last juice from the hairy flesh that clung there. The liquid trickled down my chin. Some of the strands became caught between my teeth and I stopped to pick them out. It was then I noticed Osman watching me. Recently I had often looked up to find his eyes upon me in this way. I was sure it was because he loved me and was proud of me. I smiled at him. To show how happy I was. Osman continued to look at me. He did not return my smile. He stood up and he walked away.

For some time Osman had not called me to his room. Because I was expecting a child, I thought. I didn't worry. One night for no particular reason I woke from a deep sleep. I lay on my back – it was difficult to sleep any other way – and I listened to the music of the raindrops dripping from the eaves of the house, striking the leaves of trees, splashing on to the ground. My eyes were closed. The noise of the rain was immense. I laid a hand on my stomach and rubbed my belly button, imagining the baby curled up inside. I was beginning to doze again when I felt the bedclothes being dragged from my body.

'Yai!' I screamed. I was being attacked by a night devil.

It wasn't a djinna. It was Osman.

'Get up!' he told me. I hastened to do as he said.

'What is it?' I asked. 'What's happening?' I tried to imagine what emergency had brought him here in the middle of the night. Osman came up close to me. Very close. He did not touch me. He sat down on the edge of the bed and was silent. I waited. My heart beat louder than the rain on the roof. It must be something very serious indeed. Then he told me to remove my clothes. I stared at him through the darkness. I wondered if I had heard correctly.

I was told a woman should never say no to her husband. 'Osman, it's late,' I began, 'and I'm sleeping.'

My husband stood up suddenly. As dark as it was I could see his features flex. He inhaled deeply. I saw the gleam of his teeth as he smiled. I relaxed a little. When he spoke his tone matched mine. 'Please don't disobey me. You promised you would be a good wife to me. Isn't that what you promised?' I was standing in front of him. He reached up and caressed my cheek.

I nodded, yes, I wanted to be a good wife. I was a good wife. But I was tired. Also, Osman was behaving so strangely.

He slid both hands down my arms until he had his hands in mine, whispering: 'Come, come, little one.' Still I protested. Osman's tone changed abruptly. 'I have only so much patience for this foolishness, Asana.'

There my protests ended. Osman's manner made me hesitate. Perhaps this was something between husbands and their wives that I did not understand.

In one way nothing happened that night, by which I mean Osman did not touch me. He made me stand in front of him until the rain stopped. He stared at my body, at my breasts, my belly, down below. The clouds passed from in front of the moon to reveal his expression. I was reminded of a time when I was a child and we came across the stiffened corpse of a dead dog. The eyes were gone. The lips were shrivelled, baring gums and teeth. We stared at it, prodding it with sticks – as fascinated as we were revolted.

My body was changing, it was true. My breasts were hard and taut. My nipples protruded. So, in time, did my belly button –

popped out like a bubble. Veins coursed like underground rivers beneath my skin. Often I found myself flushed and covered in a sheen of sweat. I did not mind. I loved my body and its little store of surprises. Every morning I oiled my stomach and polished it until it shone, dark and round as a seed pod.

The first few times, Osman stared at me, nothing more. Sometimes he made me turn away. A rustling sound, Osman's breath came thick and fast. As my pregnancy advanced he made me stand for longer. My feet swelled, I nearly unbalanced. I was shivering and naked. I begged him to let me sleep. There came a time when the tiredness overtook the fear and I sank to the floor.

'Get up!' Osman's voice was low. It occurred to me he did not want anyone to hear us.

'No, Osman. It's enough now.'

'What? Don't you answer me back. Who do you think you are? You are my wife.'

'Yes. Your wife who is pregnant – with your child. If you want your child to be born healthy then leave me alone and let me sleep.'

My tone of voice I knew was too strong. My mother had warned me of this. I had begun to feel contempt for Osman. I couldn't help myself, I added: 'Look at yourself Osman. What kind of man behaves this way?'

Osman stood over me. He reached down and seized my arm, tried to haul me to my feet. I let myself go limp. My weight was almost beyond his strength. Above me I could feel his rage massing, but I didn't care any more. Who was this man? Not the one I had married. Osman continued to tug at me as I sprawled on the floor.

An image leaped unbidden into my mind. Of the two of us in the middle of the night, fighting like children. Maybe I was on the verge of hysteria. I think probably I was. I couldn't help it. I laughed. A short, high-pitched shriek. The sound of the laugh sounded funny to my ears. I laughed again. I found I couldn't stop. Osman let go of me. Good, I thought. I started up from the floor. Then he kicked me. The blow landed on my buttock and set my whole body quivering. I fell forward on to my knees. Now I was on all fours. Before I could get up, he kicked me again at the base of my spine.

At first I was too angry and my anger made me stubborn. I clamped my mouth shut and held on to my screams. Osman grasped my hair, swung my head around and slapped me. I tried to crawl away from him, naked on my hands and knees. There was nowhere to go. Instead I crawled around the room as he aimed blows at me. His panting grew hoarse as he wore himself out on me. In the end I allowed him to win.

I let the tears flow. I begged him to stop.

And I opened my eyes.

And when they were finally open I learned a lot about my husband in a short time.

Osman Iscandari. Only son of his mother, a woman with a cat's cry for a voice who wore two strings of prayer beads wrapped in her headdress, a third looped around her wrist. Always sick. Always complaining her body was too warm or too cold. When she came to visit I saw the way she watched her son's face all day, waiting for his expression to change so she could jump up and fetch him a bowl of roasted groundnuts or a sweet potato cake or offer to rub his head. When we gathered to eat in the evening she picked out all the best pieces of meat from the stew and gave them to Osman. At night she sat on the verandah with his head in her lap, braiding his hair.

My husband had three sisters who were married and lived nearby, but in the time I had lived in that house rarely did I see them come to visit their brother. And when the youngest one of the sisters did call, I noticed the way she spoke little, only answering: 'Yes, brother,' and did not look Osman in the eye or stay to eat.

And I saw how Balia flinched when Osman raised his arm just as she bent to place a footstool underneath his feet. And I saw the way Osman smirked when he looked at her and reached slowly across himself to scratch his armpit.

Finally I noticed the way the little bitch who came to beg for scraps disappeared every time our husband was at home.

★   ★   ★

Ngadie brushed her mouth with the back of her hand and stepped back on to the path, casually – as though she had just been wandering around in the bush, in whatever ordinary way a person might wander about in the bush. She started when I called her name. I ran to catch her up. Not so easy, I held my belly with one arm and my breasts with the other.

'Wait!' I caught her arm and swung her around to face me. She glared at me.

'Let go! What's wrong with you?' She sucked her teeth: a slow, sliding sound of scorn. I did not reply. Instead I reached out and touched her face. Ngadie reared back, but I had hold of her arm. I stretched out as if to wipe a fleck of froth from the corner of her mouth. There was nothing there, but only I knew that. She was close enough for me to smell the palm wine on her breath. Her eyes held mine, yet I could see she was scanning the edges of her vision, like a dog with a stolen chicken in its jaws.

I paused. What to do next? I hadn't thought this far. I had way-laid Ngadie without knowing what it was I wanted to ask. What had I done in marrying Osman? I searched for the words and while I did so I saw the thoughts cross Ngadie's face like clouds drifting across the sky while she made up her mind what to do.

In the event Ngadie spoke first: 'So now you know. And you want to know what else there is? Isn't it?'

I nodded. I let go of her arm.

Ngadie rubbed at the place in an exaggerated sort of way. Still, she made no move to go: 'When you first arrived I looked at you. So pleased with yourself. I wondered how long it would take.' I dipped my head. 'Every time he brings one into our house he tells Balia how he is tired of us, we have no fire. Though only God and the three of us know how we came to be that way. Osman despises us. But he doesn't understand anything, he doesn't even understand the kind of man he is.'

I learned that I was not the first. There had been others.

Listening to Ngadie was like gazing at a landscape you have grown accustomed to. Only when you look at it properly you see something you had not noticed before: a termite mound like a silent sentry, a tree slowly dying, an abandoned colony of birds' nests. Ngadie and Balia, so much older. Many years had passed since the youngest of their children had been weaned.

'One of them he complained was disobedient. Told her family to come and collect her. Another one he claimed was not a virgin and that he had paid such and such amount for her bride price. Said the family let him believe it was the case. I don't know. They were quick to settle with him. The shame.' She waved a hand. Her voice was gentler now.

I was silent. Almost as an afterthought Ngadie added that she was sure Osman had other women upline who cooked for him. Otherwise there was really no reason to stay away so long.

'What am I to do?' I asked her.

Ngadie frowned and peered at me as if seeing me properly for the first time. She shrugged, her voice was brisk once more: 'What you do is up to you.' And she turned and walked away slowly down the path towards the big, empty house. Not once did she turn or look back at me.

Oh, what a fool I had been! I had stuffed my ears with straw. I had closed my eyes, refusing to see what a bad husband I was choosing for myself. I thought about my mother. What might she say? That I had been deceived by nobody but myself. The anger between us ran cold and it sprang from a place far, far back. I could not bring myself to go to her and beg.

Even in my despair I was not ready to own my mistake, I was caught in a swirling eddy, drowning, with nothing to clutch on to except my pride. I determined I would deal with Osman in my own way.

I pondered these matters as I sat on the back step. In front of me Balia's daughter caught a chicken and prepared to slit its throat with a knife. The bird was squawking, feathers fluttering. I remembered how in the village we used to wring their necks – something that had to be learned. You had to exercise a little patience, let the bird be lulled while you got a good grip. Outside the town, in a place known only as Slaughter, I had seen a Fula slay a great bull, slicing its throat with the blade as gently as if he was caressing his sweetheart.

This house I was living in contained more than one kind of hell, and I had just thought of a way to deal with one of them.

Several weeks passed. Osman came and went. When he was at home he would enter my room as he pleased and force me to play my part in his monstrous game. I offered no resistance. As the days passed Osman gradually relaxed, believing he had mastered me.

One night he fell asleep on my bed. I crept in next to him and we stayed that way until dawn.

A few days later, in the early hours of the morning, I lay awake and watched Osman. Behind the lids I could see the bulge of his eyeball, the iris trembling as he dreamed. At the corner of his mouth a bubble of spit swelled and subsided. His chest rose as he drew in shuddering breaths. In his sleep his lips curved upwards.

'Osman,' I whispered. 'Osman.' My husband jerked slightly, his mouth twitched. He turned his shoulder away. 'Wake up, Osman. Wake up.'

I let a few beats pass. Gently I shook his shoulder, taking care not to rouse him too quickly. I rocked him, whispering his name until his eyes stilled and the lids cracked open. He uttered a groan and softly sighed.

Again: 'Osman, Osman!' His eyelids opened a fraction further.

'Asana? Eh, Asana. What is it?' he mumbled, his lips struggling with the effort of forming the words, wanting to stay in the dream. The next moment his eyelids began to flutter and close as he slipped back under.

'Osman,' I said. 'Wake up and see. See what I have for you!' I groped the floor until my fingers closed around the handle of the knife. I held it up, allowing the blade to glow in the silver light. I put my lips very close to his ear, brushing the lobe. I made my voice gentle, coaxing. Osman's eyes opened. I put the blade up under his chin: the tip made a soft indentation in the flesh. 'You see what can happen, Osman? So strong but what good do your muscles do you now?' I felt his body slowly stiffen.

I laid my cheek on the pillow, let the knife down slowly and slipped it out of sight. I lay quietly. Waiting.

It happened just as I hoped. Moments later Osman sat bolt

upright. He leaped from the bed. He was naked, flailing. A little deranged, really, when I set my mind back to thinking about it. Next he bent over and peered at me closely. I let my eyes open, I gazed back at him, I reached up and stroked his cheek. 'What's the matter, husband?' I asked, as though I was greatly concerned. All the time his puzzlement grew. 'What is it, Osman? Is something the matter?' I reached up, took his hand in mine and drew him back to the bed. 'A dream, that's all. Just a dream. Go back to sleep, now.' Osman hesitated and then sat down heavily. I rolled over and pretended to sleep. After a while I felt him lie down, a long way from me, right on the other side of the bed.

From that night and for the remainder of my pregnancy Osman never touched me again. I congratulated myself heartily on my cunning. I lay back on my bed and buffed my belly with Vaseline petroleum jelly.

Osman Iscandari, I chuckled, *ng ba kerot k'bana, kere ng baye erith.* You have a big penis, but you have no balls.

My daughter arrived, as had I, at the close of the rains. Unlike me she took her time coming into this world. I bore it. After the birth my mother praised me. Nobody would ever have known a woman was giving birth in this house. At night she took the baby to her bed to let me rest, carrying her to me when she needed to feed. Still, in the hours in between I found I missed my daughter already. I could not sleep, I could not wait to hold her again. I crept into the room and lifted her from where she slumbered in the crook of my mother's body.

Kadie was named for my *karabom*, who had gone the year before. Through two rains I stayed in my mother's house while I suckled her. For hours at a time I might do nothing but gaze into my daughter's deep-water eyes, at the tiny blister on her upper lip that came from sucking; feel the way she gripped my finger with her toes when I held her feet. I examined the fine, sharp creases on the soles of those same feet and the palms of her hands. What fate, I wondered, was there awaiting her that had already been decided?

One morning unseen currents stirred the air beneath a troubled sky. A pale green glow lit the village. I sat at the front of my father's house. When I was growing up I could not imagine a world beyond this one. Change came slowly to this place. My father grew ginger now, orders from the colonials. My mother counted the money, complained about the fixed prices. She brought in extra labour to meet the demand. Above the coffee trees the hills receded in shades of grey, fading slowly into the sky. A kite spiralled down. I followed its descent through the air as gently as a leaf falling from a tree. I didn't hear my father's footfall.

'You'll be going home. As soon as your husband comes.' My father spoke in statements.

I replied: 'Perhaps, but this is my home, too.'

'*Te ting*. True. But a woman's duty is to be with her husband in his home and any day now he'll be here to take you back.' I was silent. My father waited a while before continuing. 'Of course you should make him win you again. But when he has done that you will accept him and you will go.' This is the way things were in those days. My father loved me, but for him duty came first. I could not think of running away from my marriage. I could never come home. He added gently: 'You will be missed here.'

I looked up at him, remembering how I used to ride on his shoulders, how I rode on his shoulders the day we came to this place to found the village. He spoiled me so much people called me his pet deer.

'*Teh, teh*,' he clapped his hands for Kadie, '*teh teh*.' She weaved towards him, her hand reached for the piece of sesame cake he held out. He caught her and swung her into the air, grunting with the effort it cost him.

'Yes, father.'

Sometimes I wondered how my father knew things. Only days later Osman arrived, shaking the dust out of his clothes, struggling with a cardboard suitcase of gifts: cakes of blue soap, scented hair oil, two new head-ties and many yards of the finest-grade fabric. 'Yes, yes. Come and look! All imported,' he called for everyone to hear. Some of my father's younger children and even his wives gathered around, as though Osman was a travelling salesman and not a husband come to woo his wife back. Osman flung open the suitcase and showed off each item.

I didn't mind seeing him. He was handsome, as I remembered, even sweating under the weight of the suitcase. Despite myself I smiled as I walked down the steps of the house to greet him.

Osman Iscandari. I underestimated him. Seeing him arrive at my father's house to bring me back, the sweat rolling down from his scalp, his face shining like the moon, boasting – with that stupid grin carved into his face. When I walked up the street towards that house, that empty house lying in the shadow of the earth, I had no idea of what awaited me inside.

Fourteen, fifteen maybe. Pretty enough, I'll say that. The girl scuttled forward, bending low. She began to gather up my luggage. And my, she was strong as a bush cow. The cardboard suitcase she balanced on her head while she squatted to reach for the other bundles.

I did not speak. A cousin of Balia or Ngadie? Someone's ward? A servant, even? My senior wives had not come out to meet me. A drumming in my heart, in my ears. The light receded around the edges of my vision, as though I was staring down a bat-filled tunnel. I willed myself not to look at Osman. One step at a time, one foot in front of the other. My body was shaking. The house was empty. The girl emerged from my room, she smiled and held her hands out to Kadie. I kept a firm grip of my daughter's hand. The girl's lips trembled. At that moment I caught sight of Osman mocking me, grinning at this entertainment. Not the grin of a dullard. No, rather the smirk of a hyena.

'Ah, but let me introduce you, Asana.' The voice he used was offhand. 'This is Mabinty.' Before me the girl bowed her head and dropped into a curtsey.

And that was how I met my husband's newest wife.

Osman delighted in his triumph. He did not call me to his room. When I saw that girl – humming, wandering about, toying with some new bauble, smiling stupidly even at the chickens – I recognised myself, the way I too had been.

I contemplated my position – the third wife of a man who was of a lesser family than my own, yet who treated me with contempt. Replaced by a peasant girl brought back from one of his trips – in all likelihood given to him for the price of a sack of rice.

Osman did not care that he flaunted marriage customs. One, two, three nights he was with her. And then a fourth night. I began to wonder if I would ever lie with my husband again. I wanted more children, yes. But there was something else. I was ashamed to think of it. Despite myself I was gripped by a craving I could not quell. One morning I saw Osman sitting at the front of the house waiting for Mabinty to bring his shirt. Dressed only in his trousers, slippers half on his feet, naked to the waist. I found my eyes drawn to the spirals of hair scattered across his chest, the deep ridges of his stomach in which drops of sweat glistened, the dark trail that led down from his belly button and disappeared into the waistband of his trousers. He caught me watching him and quickly I looked away.

Liquid like melted moonlight: pale, opaque, translucent. Ngadie handed me the enamel mug, hitched up her skirts and sat down on a log. The palm wine had fermented in the heat of the day. It was strong and vinegary, faintly fizzy. I took a sip, and then another, felt the trickle of warmth reach my belly. All was quiet. We were far from the house in a small clearing surrounded by palm trees: raphia palms, oil palms, coconut palms. I had already tasted the wine from all three. When I was a child I had once tried the first sap, the juice collected early in the morning. It was sweet, clear and innocent to drink. Nothing like this. I sipped again.

Ngadie had once possessed a great beauty. The traces were there in the perfect symmetry of her lips; in the gap between her front teeth considered so desirable in a woman; in the dimple on her chin that was now no more than a smudge in the soft flesh. There was delicacy, too, in the turn of her wrist as she poured the palm wine. And regret in the trembling of her fingers.

I realised, watching her, that I did not know what her face looked like when she smiled. I had never heard her laugh. I took a kola nut, split it, and passed half to her. She hesitated, her eyes held mine for a moment. Then she accepted it and thanked me.

What had become of Osman's father? I asked. Ngadie paused, the edge of the cup rested on her lower lip.

'A great man,' she replied. 'Loved by his people.' Osman had not known his father. He had been a leader who defied the *pothos* when they came crowning chiefs. Osman's father was one who resisted. 'He warned his brothers not to trust the *pothos*. He told them no white man ever gave anything without wanting more in return. They didn't listen.' The leaders seized the gifts they were offered, signing away their lands and their power with a thumbprint. In return they were given a wooden staff with a brass handle and an upholstered chair bearing the arms of the *potho* queen. As for Osman's father, the *pothos* deposed him and gave his position to a man from a rival clan. He was forced to leave his people and went to live on the other side of the land. He died. Osman grew up in his mother's family, working on the land while the sons of the new chief grew fat. Osman resented his family's poverty terribly.

Ngadie told me there were many people who believed Osman's father had been right and those people also imagined Osman had inherited his father's spirit. They waited for him to come and lead them. Osman's mother shared this belief, but the truth was, the people waited in vain. Osman did not have the stomach to be a leader. He accepted their accolades but shunned the challenge.

Balia was the daughter of one of his father's closest advisors who had joined him in exile, betrothed to Osman when they were still children. As for Ngadie, Osman had seen her beauty and wanted her for himself. Ngadie rejected his advances but Osman bided his time. The day after her father's store of seed yams burned in a fire, Osman arrived with a proposal of marriage. Her father used the bride price to rebuild his barns.

I wondered silently how Ngadie and Balia could tolerate this empty life.

Ngadie swilled the liquid in her cup and spoke as if in answer to my question: 'For me and Balia, it's over. If Osman leaves us alone – then all the better.'

In his return to form Osman made a daunting adversary. He relished my humiliation. He shamed me in public: for the way I dressed, the fashion in which I styled my hair, the expression on my face. In front of his uncles he ordered me to remove a dish of *fourah* cakes I had prepared, insisting they were not fit to serve to guests. The room fell silent. Osman's mother was quick to support her son.

'Useless girl. No good in the kitchen!' As for Ngadie and Balia, they averted their eyes when I passed. I pretended to myself it didn't matter. Osman made people think I was a bad wife, so what?

Kadie was asleep on the bed, curled and sucking her thumb. I sat on the floor and stared into the mirror. This was what I had become – a woman who existed only as what she saw reflected in the eyes of others. I was sorry for myself and sorry for the daughter I had brought to this place.

As the days passed I tried to avoid giving Osman a reason to belittle me. I spoke only when I was spoken to, I cooked several different dishes each night it was my turn to cook – chicken rolled in spices and roasted over an open fire, yams and hot-pepper soup, fried fish and cassava bread. The time came when if he deigned to taste even one of them I sighed with relief. All day I observed his face searching for signs that might alert me to his mood.

Do you see how I was becoming like all those other women – Osman's mother, his sisters, Balia, Ngadie? All I wanted to do was to avoid the pain of humiliation. Oh, how quickly that simple wish transformed into a desperation to please, so quickly I did not even see it happening in myself. My senses were numbed, I behaved like a sleepwalker. The days passed steadily, weeks turned into months. By that time I was treating Osman as a god.

Then came the morning when Osman told me I should come to his room that night. All that day, as I waited for the evening to come, I could not concentrate on the simplest task. Twice I burned the rice until Ngadie removed the pot from my hands and gently ushered me away from the cooking place. Kind Ngadie. The dish she cooked was one of Osman's favourites. That evening I claimed it as my own and watched as Osman ate two helpings, while I managed no more than a few mouthfuls. The next night and the next she did me the same kindness.

I lay in the bed with my arms down by my sides. The last time it had been so different. Before I was shy, yes – a new bride – and yet every movement was right. This time I reached across and touched him. 'I'm here,' I said.

How could I have known these things happened to men? I had been brought up to believe men were always in a state of desire. Our mothers told us to cover ourselves when we came back from bathing. In case a man should see us. There was even a plant that grew, that closed up when you touched it with your fingertips, sometimes all you had to do was breathe upon it and the tiny ferns came together and sealed like a pair of fans. *Bom mompneh runi ngang ang bek*, it was called. Cover yourself, there's a man coming. A woman's modesty and a man's desire were what made us different from each other. Yet I knew that I felt desire, even lying there next to the man I no longer loved.

That first night Osman rejected me I was wretched. I cannot tell you. Later, alone, I wept bitterly. Osman was ashamed though he would not show it. The second night I slipped out of my gown and lay naked beside him, I tried to reassure him, stroking him gently. But Osman covered his own shortcomings by blaming me, I was too forward he said. No modesty. On the third and final night, when it happened again he pointed his finger at me and called me a witch.

The next night Osman spent with Mabinty. I sat on my bed. I did not sleep. I stared into the blackness, I tried to see my future but I could see nothing. In the morning my eyes were sore from lack of sleep, I breathed deeply and walked out to the cooking place to prepare breakfast for Kadie. At the door I stopped and stared. There was Mabinty, sitting on a stool, weeping and loudly blowing her nose on her head-tie.

★ ★ ★

I lost face and regained my life, but for many years I could not see it. Nor could I see who had helped me do it.

Osman thought it was his idea to end the marriage contract and so there was no question of reclaiming the bride gift. At first I was humiliated, thrown back to my family by my husband like a no-good fish tossed back into the water.

That was the way things were for us in those days. You, I hear you talking to your friends. You have so much, but you don't even know you are alive. We had to find the answers for ourselves, to fashion them out of the thin air and seize them from the sky.

I felt I had no choice but to remain Osman's third wife, to be treated by him in any way he pleased. I was a stupid girl who jumped into her marriage with her eyes closed. Afterwards I could see nowhere to run. It took somebody else to open a door and push me out. And that person was Ngadie, once-beautiful Ngadie. In her own fate she could see the future that was waiting for me.

Later I learned to be grateful to her and to love her for what she had done. But in the beginning I was short-sighted, I could not see beyond my own shame to the great vista that stretched out in front of me.

After many years news came that Ngadie had died. For the first time I travelled back to the place where I had been a wife. Shadows still covered the house, nothing had changed. Balia greeted me with some warmth – to my surprise Mabinty, too. Mabinty now with rings of flesh around her waist and her neck. I held no ill-feeling towards her. As for Osman, who rose from his chair on the verandah to meet me, brushing pumpkin seed shells from the front of his shirt and spitting the bits out the corner of his mouth, I felt nothing. I greeted him cordially and the smile he gave me in return was surely all that remained of his blurred beauty.

Ngadie was already in the ground, fleetingly mourned – a woman insufficiently loved as a daughter, unloved as a wife.

But loved as a mother. And loved still. There were Ngadie's son and daughter. Ngadie in the male. Ngadie in the female. The him and the her, the he and the she of the woman I had known. I watched them. So alike. The only difference was the way the lines of their features had been drawn, finely traced in one, the other roughly sketched in charcoal.

On a stool at the back of the house I sat next to Ngadie's daughter, untied the corner of my *lappa* and took out a kola nut. I unwrapped the leaves, broke off a cotyledon – she accepted it in silence, turning the piece over and over in her hand. I glanced up at her, saw the teardrops gathering along the edge of her lower eyelid, waiting to fall.

'*Hush ya*,' was all I said. I laid my hand on her forearm.

I bit the kola nut and helped myself to a sip of water from the ladle at my side. The water tasted fresh and pure – it was the effect of the kola: even brackish water tasted as though it had sprung from a mountainside.

'My mother once said something about you, about how you loved kola. She said that to you even bitter kola was sweet.'

The words made no sense. One time I had split kola with Ngadie. After we had become friends. Of course it hadn't been bitter kola. There was bitter kola in the calabash containing my bride gift. Kola for the good times. Bitter kola to mark the bad.

Some days later I went home. I never returned to that place. The years slid past. I watched Kadie grow alongside the next generation of coffee trees, and I grew too. In this way slowly I found myself again. Memories of Ngadie, of her daughter's words, fell out of my mind. Not for any reason. Only because they seemed to be words spoken at a time of grief, wrongly remembered. I did not believe they held any meaning for me.

One day, I found myself passing down a street in a part of the town I had never been to before. The houses had two storeys, the streets were narrow. Two women were leaning out of the shuttered windows above me, drawing their washing in from the line that hung from one window to the next. Wisps of conversation fluttered down. The women were careless, not worrying if they were overheard.

'His tinder was wet.'

I heard the laughter that followed, coarse laughter. Shocking laughter. I walked on, the phrase wound itself after me, bringing back those awful nights – those last nights I shared with my husband when I had failed to arouse him. I remembered the state to which he had reduced me – so nervous I burned the rice.

Ngadie had offered to cook.

Three nights in a row.

His tinder was wet.

To her even bitter kola is sweet.

You see, if I hadn't become lost, I never would have walked down that street. Nor heard a woman talk about her husband's performance in that vulgar way. That started me thinking. People believe that bitter kola has the power to wet a man's tinder. Did you know that? I thought about Ngadie, of how she had offered to cook for me on those three nights and I pondered the meaning of what she had said to her daughter.

Three nights in a row.

Maybe there was a reason things happened the way they did with Osman on those three nights.

In my seat in the *poda poda* I sat with my basket of shopping on my lap, crushed by other people's bodies, all the time turning the thoughts around and around in my head, the way I examine a pawpaw before I buy it in the market.

To her even bitter kola is sweet.

And I saw that it had been Ngadie's doing.

I laughed out loud: a laugh like the one I had just heard. I laughed until the tears poured down my cheeks. At first the people around me wondered what was my problem. But they saw my joy was real, I was no crazy person. My laughter even became infectious, people began to giggle and before long the whole bus was laughing without even knowing why.

And through the people's laughter I heard another sound that came from far away: the strains of a simple melody. It grew louder and louder, filling my head, pushing out all the bad feelings, the anger, the resentment that had been locked inside for so many years. I became quiet, I listened. Though I had never heard it before, there and then I recognised it. And it was beautiful. The sound of Ngadie laughing in her grave.

7

Mariama, 1942

Kassila the Sea God

HIGH ON THE HILL, up above Old Railway Line on the road that winds down to the city. That's where I saw her. Walking with her hand on her hip. Sashaying. Like a woman who has just seen her lover coming down the street. Her felt hat was pushed back over her head, swinging by the cord around her neck. Her socks crumpled around her ankles. She placed one foot directly in front of the other. Like so. The hips swung, the hat bounced along behind her. It was her. I knew it at once. The jolt it gave me was like an electric shock, a flicker of heat across my skin that brought me out in a momentary sweat.

I tried to turn around to see her properly, but I was caught between the women on either side of me in the taxi. I felt a twinge in my neck. The pain pulled me back, as if to say – what foolishness is this?

Of course I knew it wasn't her. I never really thought it. Just the fleeting glimpse of a silhouette that reminded me of her. And as the taxi turned down King Harman Road I looked around, not to double-check exactly, but to see the disappearing figure just once more.

The other girls nicknamed her Marie Palaver. Over time a syllable slipped out unnoticed: Marie Plaba. She was troublesome. Cussed. She was my first friend. And I couldn't believe my own good fortune. To some people we were an odd couple. I could see as much reflected in Sister Anthony's smile, though she encouraged the friendship between us. She thought I was a good influence.

The mission was built on top of the old graveyard. Nobody really wanted the nuns here, or their school. But the *obai* was worried about giving offence, so he let them have a piece of land no one cared about. Outside the dormitory window you could see the outlines in the earth, like old flower beds. The trees with upturned candelabra blooms: there was only one place where they were planted in such abundance.

The new girls were always afraid. Afraid of what they had heard. Fearful of the nuns who were as pale as the dead. And had a way of looking at you, but not seeing you. Even when you were walking towards them, their eyes would just glide over you. Then at the last minute, just when you had convinced yourself you maybe didn't exist, they would greet you. For most of us it was the first time we had ever seen people like that, with eyes of coloured glass and hair like saffron threads. Well, it's true I had once seen the District Commissioner in the place where we lived. Still it was strange to be up so close to them. I didn't know how to behave exactly. When the Reverend Mother addressed me I drew my hand up to my forehead and saluted, as I had seen the Court Messengers do. Marie sniggered at that. It was the first time I noticed her.

In the dormitory where there was a shortage of beds – when they saw the world changing the local people changed too, and decided now they wanted to send their daughters to the nuns' school – some of the girls shared a single bunk lying top to toe. I lay in the crook of Marie's body, sharing a pillow, and listened to the ghost stories she made up late into the night.

Marie told me stories of women and their night-husbands; women lured away from the river bank when they went to fetch water; women who were visited by bush spirits and later gave birth to their children. Marie's mother had been a birth attendant. Once she had seen a spirit child for herself. It had two faces and four arms and legs. You could see it was part human. Born dead. It lay on the floor wrapped in an old cloth.

The school caretaker was a one-legged man. He was the only person I have ever seen like that who did not use crutches. He hopped everywhere, tall and straight, a human pogo stick. Sometimes when the wind called and the building creaked there were strange bangs and thumps. Marie said it was One-Foot Jombee, hopping through the dark on his one good leg.

I was thrilled and yet I was afraid. Afraid of the stories. And as I lay there listening to her I was afraid too that the end was near and would take with it the sound of her voice.

I would go to sleep and dream strange dreams. A palm tree with leaves of human hair. A chair made of living flesh and bones and skin that was rooted to the ground. A snake wearing a red cloth embroidered with cowrie shells. The white nuns with skin like eels' beneath their habits and long flowing hair hidden under their wimples. I dreamed I hid behind a coconut tree and watched them cast off their clothes and slip into the sea like Mammy Wata.

These visions began to enter my thoughts even when I was wide awake. Not so I thought they were actually there before my eyes. No. More like a flashing picture that appeared and just as quickly disappeared. After it I felt weakened, and that made me know it must have been the work of some kind of devil. In morning Mass I prayed to God and to the Virgin Mary, in the hope that the dreams were messages from Heaven. The answer never came, but I noticed that when I was praying the visions stayed away.

A class in Idaho had raised the money for my baptism. They chose my new name and sent it in a letter to the bishop, who came up to the school and baptised all those girls who had new names. Mary. Not so different from Mariama. As thanks I sent them back a bouquet of prayers. Twenty Our Fathers, Thirty Holy Bes, a dozen Masses and Communions, and because they had given me her name – one hundred Hail Marys. At the bottom of the letter I signed my new name with rounded letters and a long looped 'y' at the end.

Pagan babies. That's what we were. We knew our baptisms were paid for through something called the Pagan-Baby Project, only somehow we never realised we were those babies.

We were two. Marie and Mary. Mary and Marie.

In the walled gardens on the other side of the road that we tended before morning Mass and after vespers grew every kind of vegetable. We were almost entirely self-sufficient, with the exception of rice, meat, fish and palm oil which two of us were sent to the market to buy in the mornings. The school was on an island. It was quite a large island, with a small town: Tihun. And several fishing villages, a church and a boys' school. The town was a long walk, and so we went to the market in Baiama on the big island on the other side of the inlet, crossing the water in the launch along with fishwives and petty traders. At those times I would lift my chin into the wind and taste the salt. Or else I looked down at the dark shapes: the rocks, the shoals of fish, the shadow of the boat. And I would dream of Kassila, the sea god, swimming in the depths.

There were nights the sea howled like an animal in agony and the palm trees danced themselves into a frenzy. The fishermen hauled their canoes up on to the shore. And in the morning, before they set out again, muttered prayers and platitudes to Kassila, so he might make the seas still and keep them safe.

At mealtimes we ate from tin plates and drank from empty Peak milk tins. At one time we received a consignment of cutlery from a church group in America. The first day I tried to make the grains of rice stay on my fork, to cut the meat from the oxtail and winkle out the marrow. Everybody was struggling. How hungry we were when we left the dining room. So much food gone to waste on the floor. A rota was put up on the board. Every week six girls were invited to sit at Sister Monica's table. I was one of the first. Watch and copy. That was the way we learned. I held my fork upside down and piled food on the top, while all around me girls rolled tasty balls of rice and *plasass* with the tips of fingers, and popped them into their mouths.

It was the first time I saw how Europeans often liked to do things the most difficult way. The nuns preferred to carry piles of books in their arms instead of on the top of their heads, so that we were always having to run ahead to open doors for them. And once in the town I saw a white woman pushing a baby along in a pram. She was sweating and puffing, the wheels kept getting caught in the ruts and the potholes. Eventually two men ran to her assistance, hoisted the pram on their shoulders and carried it all the way back to her front door. The mother ran after them, hopping and calling, like a hen whose chick has been carried away by a hawk. And the women with their children on their backs stopped to stare at her.

I saw that woman again. Walking on the beach, all by herself, eyes streaming. Maybe it was the wind. Still, it was a strange thing to do, walk about for the sake of it. And alone, too.

Sister Eadie said that when babies are carried on their mothers' backs it makes them grow up with bow legs. But I did not think this could be true as my legs are straight.

Every day we queued for lunch, holding our plates out to the serving women who stood behind great tureens of rice and potato leaves. At that time Marie had a feud with one of the cooks, a woman with a short neck and a sly look whom everybody knew stole the food meant for the girls. Ma Cook we called her. In the morning the girls took turns helping to wash and chop the leaves. We were supposed to be assisting the kitchen staff, but this woman sat back and made us do everything. We washed and chopped furiously, even so we were almost always late for our first class.

Once Marie and I were on kitchen detail together. I tried to move a vat of palm oil from the fire by myself. The pot was too heavy and I staggered under the weight of it. Hot oil splashed on to my arms. Marie poured cool water from a jug on to my scalded skin. Ma Cook came into the room just then and accused us of wasting time. Marie told her what had happened, but Ma Cook's response was sour: '*Een mamy go born orda one.*' Her mother can have another one.

It's a coarse retort. I'd heard it before. But somehow it angered Marie greatly. She gave the woman a great shove. In turn Ma Cook slapped her around the face. A moment later the fracas brought Sister Agnes to the kitchen door, and without any questions she took Ma Cook's side. That was the way it was in those days. You couldn't answer back, you had to do as you were told. If somebody was older than you they were always right. And besides, everyone knew Marie Plaba was trouble.

Marie was put on slop duty for a week. I felt badly for her, and so every morning I collected the night-time slops from the dormitory myself and poured them down the drain, even though to do so sometimes made me retch.

Marie won her revenge the very next week. The last class of Friday was needlework. We had made samplers. God Bless this Home. Surrounded by cross-stitched borders of differently coloured threads. Sister Anthony canvassed suggestions from the class about what we should do next. Marie raised her hand.

'Let's make a present for Ma Cook's baby,' she said.

Sister Anthony asked what she meant and Marie pointed at the window. There was Ma Cook, waddling just like a woman who is about to give birth. Or like a python that has swallowed a goat. Kitchen contraband, all of it. A whole snapper strapped round her waist.

Ma Cook was given a warning and the next day she was back serving. When Marie held out her plate Ma Cook gave her an extra-large helping. I was surprised at that. Marie laughed with satisfaction. Only when we sat down and began to eat did we discover the meat had a rotten taste.

Marie told me about the soothsayer who had set up near the marketplace, who could read the future. Even the white woman had been seen visiting his place. I felt the fear already beginning to seep cold through my blood. Of course Marie wanted to go. 'Just because,' she said and shrugged her shoulders, head to one side. Just because. Just because it was something to do. Just because we were bored. Just because the sisters would be sure to disapprove. Witch doctors. Pagan antics. Satan's pastimes. So said Sister Eadie.

And so we went. I was afraid, it's true. But equally I could never have refused her.

'Try not to look so scared,' said Marie as we made our way through the marketplace. But somehow, alone, the place was different, more disorientating. The traders called attention to their wares in scornful voices. Colourful cries of red and yellow and green flew in the air above my head. The bright sun made it hard to focus. I swerved to avoid a basket of oranges and almost fell into a glistening pile of garden eggs that had transformed into a great hole that would have sucked me inside. The market was busy, full of people but only a small number of them seemed to be selling or buying. The others were busy doing nothing.

I lowered my eyes and kept them on the ground, following Marie's heels kicking up the dust in front of me.

The room was dark and thick with smells I did not recognise, not the common smells of the marketplace but desiccated, stale smells. The figure of the fortune-teller was hidden by the darkness like smoke and gradually he emerged out of it. Oh, so much is gone. I'm trying to remember. Perhaps that isn't how it was. No, perhaps it was light and the room smelled of nothing but the cardamom coffee that brewed over a metal brazier in the corner. I do remember one thing though. His mouth. A tiny child's tooth grew out of his upper gum and he had a huge lower lip that the words spilled over, to roll around the edges of the room.

And I remember that from the moment I entered that place I felt lost.

'What do you have for me?' asked the *moriman*, who wore a Western-style suit.

For once Marie was silent. We had no money. We had not thought of that.

The *moriman* busied himself, rearranging objects around him. He did not ask us to leave and we, in turn, made no move to do so. 'You belong with the white women. The ones whose husband wears black and comes to visit them once a week like a stranger.'

I had to think for a minute what he meant by that. Presently I replied: 'That's not their husband. That's Father Bernard.'

He was the priest who came to hear our confession. From the dormitory we could see him coming down the lane from the direction of the boys' school. He would grind his cigarette out in the mud before he reached the gates and enter the convent chewing on a sprig of sorrel freshly plucked from the gardens.

'Ah, so this is why they have no children of their own. What do they want with you, then?'

'We are being educated. It is a school.' said Marie, pompously.

'A school?' the man considered this for a moment, letting the word slide around his mouth for a moment or two, before it slipped over his lip.

'And they are married. The nuns. Actually. They're married to God,' added Marie.

'Ah yes. They have a spirit husband,' nodded the *moriman*. 'A very powerful spirit. One day I would like to visit this school and see these witches for myself.'

'They're not witches. They're nuns. I told you.'

The *moriman* shrugged. 'Then tell me, where did they come from and how did they get here? And what of all those things they possess? Beyond the knowledge of mortal man. Such things were not made on this earth.'

The nuns didn't have a great many possessions, still they had more than any of us. In the library were picture books and old magazines. Among the pictures of giant cities, of men in hats and women holding dogs like babies there were some I remember more than the others. Pictures of men in uniform, of aeroplanes filling the night sky like bats. A ruined city. Some years later I saw a photograph of a great cloud the shape of a cotton tree. An image of a scorched pocket watch with the time: a quarter-past eight. And another one, a strange photograph of the shadow of a man on the steps of a building, except most of the building was gone. And so was the man. Only his shadow remained. It was the first time I realised there had been a war.

'And so they are bringing you up to worship that spirit too. That's good. It is a powerful one. But, tell me, do they teach you their witchcraft? Or keep you just to work for them?'

Upon the floor he spread a few bits of metal, some nails and little pieces of scrap. From his pocket he took another piece of metal and this he rubbed between the palms of his two hands. Eyes closed, face tilted upwards, he muttered some words in another language. Not Temne or Mende or Creole. Arabic, maybe. He blew across the surface of the ground in front of him and then on to the lump of metal in his hand. Then he extended his hand, palm down, over the objects as they lay on the ground.

Before our eyes those dead pieces of scrap came alive. One by one they leaped from the floor. Flew through the air into his hand, his fingers closed around them.

It was a cheap trick. But I'm telling you now – other things happened in that dark room. Things that truly came to pass. That I can never explain. The *moriman* told us to close our eyes and to imagine the person we most wanted to see. Behind my eyelids I saw my mother and I walking together when I was very small. I smelled the scent of her, felt her squeeze my hand. 'Open your eyes and tell me what you see,' said the man. Right there behind him, I saw her. Standing in the shadows of the room. Her eyes rested on me for a moment. Then she took a backwards step and slipped through the wall.

There were no trances, no mirrors or bowls of water through which a diviner communed with the spirits as we had been led to expect. There was a piece of paper with some markings, dots. Questions. My mother's name. I looked up then, expecting to see her once more. At times he counted up the dots. One or two he circled.

A star close to me. A spirit calling my name. Sometimes I thought too much. As if in passing he told me I would never marry.

Marie was full of questions where I had ventured none. But the *moriman* made as though he was deaf. He drew and scratched on his piece of paper. Eventually he looked up.

'Somebody is blocking you.' The words made a loud noise in the sudden silence of the room.

I looked at Marie. I could feel anxiety creeping up under the skin of my back.

'You know who it is.' That's all he would say. I waited uncertainly. I wasn't sure what was supposed to happen next. 'Come and see me some other time.' And he got up and left the room.

And that was it. Marie stood up. A moment later I scrambled to my feet and followed her into the light.

I know what you're thinking. Isn't that what these diviners always do? It was part of the entrapment. To entice you back. Persuade you to part with your money or some goods you were willing to exchange for the next part of the prophecy. And maybe it was.

An hour after we returned Marie spoke out loud the very thing I had been thinking. 'Ma Cook,' she said.

We were cleaning the dormitory. Marie swept. I followed behind scooping up the dirt with two pieces of wood and throwing it into an empty margarine tub. The next time we saw Ma Cook coming towards us down the corridor Marie deliberately bumped her with her shoulder. Ma Cook opened her mouth to curse her, but Marie was there first. '*I dae nah you head*,' she said.

I dae nah you head? Well, it means, sort of: 'I'm watching you.' You could interpret it like that. And that is part of it. Really, it is a warning. A threat and a warning. You had better watch out, should anything happen to me. Or, if you like – wish me ill and ill will befall you.

I would wake up feeling neither happy nor unhappy, but with the sense that something was going to happen. The next moment I'd remember what it was. And the feeling would settle over me like a chill, as though a cloud had passed across the sun.

But after a month the feelings gradually quietened. The dreams and the visit to the market and the *moriman* all merged into one. Sometimes I really believed that I had dreamed the whole thing. And I would feel relieved. Ah, it was only a dream! Not real but an illusion. Not real but real at one and the same time. And gradually I began to live with the knowledge the same way I lived with my dreams.

The wind changed. At the end of the dry season the wind came from the north, from the desert, and blew for many weeks covering everything in fine red dust. But there were times, when for no reason whatsoever, suddenly it switched and blew straight in off the sea, breathing salt into our hair and coating our parched skin with a viscous film.

I was alone folding clothes on the bunk I shared with Marie. Folding her clothes and mine and putting them in the trunk at the bottom of the bed. Marie was on kitchen detail for the second time in a week.

There are times you know when something terrible has happened, even before anybody tells you. There is a certain stillness. Invisible currents. Strange things happen, small things. Vultures flying overhead in the direction of the sea.

A woman came running, flat-footed, past the walls of the school, clutching at the ends of her *lappa* to stop it unravelling. Her breasts swinging wildly under her blouse. I can see her still, freeze-frame her at the moment she ran past the gates of the school. These are the things that register in your subconscious. But if you ask me, when did I first realise? I would tell you it was before that. By the time I saw that woman running down the street with her head thrown back and her mouth wide open as though she were screaming, I already knew.

One-Foot Jombee hopped up to the iron gates and looked out. When he came back he was bouncing around, waving his arms. Fleetingly I wanted to laugh, to stop the clutching in my stomach. I feel bad now when I think about that. Moments later he was back at the gate again, this time accompanied by one of the kitchen women. He opened the gate and closed it behind her.

You've seen the way birds gather, landing in ones and twos and threes, until there is a whole flock where a short while ago there had been an empty patch of land. People were making their way down to the wharf like seagulls gather to greet the fishing boats as they come in. The noise from the direction of the wharf gradually thickened and swelled until it reached our ears as we sat in class. Until the nuns rose and closed the shutters telling us the sun was too bright that day.

By mid-morning Marie wasn't yet back from the market.

Lunch was late. I left the girls waiting outside the dining room and slipped away into the road. Not through the main gate, but at the back of the latrines as though I were going to the garden. By now the number of people in the lane was not so great. I joined them on their way, not quite running, not quite walking, as afraid of what was ahead of them as of being left behind.

The sea was laden with bodies. A shoal of strange fish. Those not dragged down by the currents rolled face down in the water. Except one fat woman who floated face to the sky, as serenely as a maiden bathing in a lake. Men in canoes were dragging them out one by one, until somebody had the bright idea of casting a fishing net and landing them all in to shore at once.

Marie!

I pushed through the knots of people gathered on the beach and on the quay. I felt like I was rushing through a dream too fast, waiting to fall into wakefulness. Anybody who had anybody still out there was standing staring out to sea, the water licking at their ankles. The spectators and ghoul-mongers stood up on the new wharf.

I ran down to the shore where the bodies were laid out on the sand. I searched for Marie among the faces of the dead. How ashamed I am now to remember my relief as I gazed at each body and did not recognise Marie. I passed weeping fathers, husbands, sisters, mothers, without a second thought. And after I had trawled the dead I searched through the living. I ran this way and that in the dimming light, peering into the smudged features of strangers' faces. I found her in neither place.

In time I walked back to the convent and there she was. Lying in our bed. Sister Anthony was bent over her, rubbing her chest with brandy.

Over the days that followed the corpses bobbed up like corks. People had been trapped under the hull of the boat when it capsized. Young men with cloths wrapped around their faces loaded the bodies into barrows and wheeled them up the lane, past the convent. The dead were mostly market women. The water had bleached their skin. The motion of the waves had gently stripped them of their clothing. Hungry fish had nibbled away their fingers and toes. A terrible, sickly perfume arose from the corpses; it invaded the island for many weeks to come.

Every time I heard the rumble of wheels I slipped away to stare. The other girls thought I had a sick mind. I didn't care. I was driven by the need to know. But the state of the bodies made it impossible to tell. In the end I never knew whether Ma Cook was among them. Or whether Kassila had dragged her down to the bottom to keep her there with him.

The coroner's report said it was an accident. The change in the wind had shifted the tides and so the position of the sandbank. The boatman had failed to navigate the dangerous new currents. Despite a life working on boats, he never learned to swim and had perished along with the rest. The account was assembled from the stories of the survivors, among them Marie.

And for three Fridays in a row there was no fish for lunch. Just boiled yams and roasted plantains.

The villagers gathered on the beach, on the cusp of darkness. Above me, on the broken boards and the few upright poles of the old jetty, seagulls alighted one by one. The beach was no more than forty yards long, a steeply curved semicircle of sand in the embrace of a row of fishermen's huts. People holding long tapers, silhouetted against the deepening blue of the sky, made their way to the water's edge. A ram bleated shrilly as it was led down. Food for Kassila. An hour later all I could see were a few bobbing lights on the water. And all I could hear was the final song as it faded and rose in time with the motion of the waves.

In the morning scarcely a sign that anything had happened: some bloodstains in the sand and the butt of a candle rolling in the waves.

Nothing in the coroner's report contradicted what everyone already knew. Kassila had caused the boat to capsize. The coroner was only able to tell them how he had used his powers to alter the currents. He could not tell them the reason.

But nothing happens for nothing.

And I knew. And Marie knew – we knew the reason. She had been spared and Ma Cook had perished. What other proof did we need?

I waited for Ma Cook to appear in my dreams. After a while I began to will it. But Ma Cook refused to appease me. From time to time I would become absorbed in the task of solving a maths problem or I would be weeding between the rows of wild greens in the garden, only to find myself looking up in answer to the silent call of my name. Or I would glimpse a fleeting movement out of the corner of my eye, turn and find whoever had been coming was gone. Ma Cook's spirit was taunting me, playing spiteful games. I walked all the way to Tihun and lit a candle for her in the church there. And I did that every week through the whole of Lent.

For a while Marie slept alone in our bed. The time came when we shared again. I lay in bed and listened to the wind. I could feel her breath faintly on the back of my neck, and the cough that for weeks after the accident wracked her body with spasms and caused the bed to judder. I wanted to reach behind and pull her close to me, but my arms could not reach across the space between our bodies. Ma Cook had wedged herself in between us, I imagined her there lying on her back and giggling to herself.

After heaven and earth Kuru made people. He called his angel and told him to separate the people into black and white. The angel did so. Then Kuru told the angel to bring all sorts of tools. When these were gathered in a pile in front of him, Kuru gave to the black people the plough, the hoe, the hammer and the anvil. And he sent them to live in the hills and the forests to be farmers and blacksmiths. They hoed the land and planted crops, and built themselves houses from earth and thatched them with palm leaves. To the white people he gave a compass, a ruler and a sextant. They built ships and sailed the seas. They traded and grew wealthy. Then Kuru saw that he had divided the gifts unfairly. So he gave the black people something that nobody else had. He gave them the power of divination.

The black people could have used their gift to make themselves rich, but they didn't. Instead they talked to the spirits and the ones who had gone before. They sought their advice and consulted them on what to do. This was the way they lived their lives.

I learned that story before I left the village to go to school. And I wondered at the meaning of it. Everything in those days was education, education. We wanted to learn the Europeans' ways. At first I thought the story was supposed to act as an encouragement to learn. And a warning not to be like the foolish black people who failed to use their gift to make themselves rich.

But now I don't think that at all. Now I think maybe we were so keen to copy others that in so doing we forgot who we were.

On the wall of the room in which Father Bernard held our catechism classes was a sampler by some of the senior girls. It was only a few years old, but already it had yellowed in parts and bleached in others. It was the air, you see. It caused everything to rot. The First Commandment read: 'I am the Lord your God. You shall not have strange Gods before me.'

I remember because I memorised all Ten Commandments in preparation for my First Communion. And also because I wondered for a long time whether I had broken it. *Before me* – you shall not have strange Gods *before me*. It did not say *as well as me*. Still. I worried too that I had committed a mortal sin in wishing ill upon Ma Cook. I confessed to Father Bernard. I was very much afraid. But Father Bernard assured me Ma Cook died as the result of an accident. Nobody's fault. Not the boat boy's. Not mine. Whatever the *moriman* would have me believe, Kassila did not exist. The sea god was nothing more than a story told by superstitious folk. I received no punishment save a dozen Hail Marys for going to the market without permission.

Ma Cook's spirit continued to flit in and out of the corners of rooms like a bat. Sometimes she brushed my face or played with my hair and that made me cross. I would put my hands on my hips and shout at her, daring her to come out. But of course she never did.

At my First Communion ten months later I drank the blood of Christ. And ate his flesh. The class in Idaho had sent me a box in the post. Inside was a framed print of the Virgin. Also a second-hand white dress with a label inside which read: 'Ages 8–9'. And although I was much older than this it fitted me anyway. I wore white shoes and white nylon stockings that twisted and stuck to my thighs in the heat. The last item in the box was a gilt St Christopher medal on a chain, which I slipped over my head and wore under my dress. After the ceremony all of us who had taken our First

Communion drank orange squash and ate rice bread together with Father Bernard and the nuns.

You loved that St Christopher medal when you were a baby. You used to play with it. The way it glistened and twinkled when you held it up, rotating backwards and forwards on the chain. Once you broke the chain, but we managed to fix it. I wore it for many years before and after that. The patron saint of storms, of lightning, of mariners and travellers. I thought he would easily be a match for Kassila. Then one day the Pope decided St Christopher wasn't a saint any more. Just like that. Now suddenly nobody knew for sure whether he had waded across the river carrying the Christ child upon his shoulders. Or if he had existed at all. It was just a legend, they said. And they stopped believing in him.

But what is a legend if not a story so great it has survived the retelling of countless generations?

I was on the ferry crossing from the peninsula to the city. By that time I could have afforded the first-class lounge easily, but the soft drinks were warm and the stink of the latrines filtered in through the air-conditioning system. So instead I stood on the lower deck and leaned over the barrier. The surface of the water was dark and greasy. I stared past the floating slick and my own reflection, deep down into what was below. And as I did so my medal fell out of the neck of my dress and dangled over the railing where its reflection caught in the water, flashing like a beacon.

And there, suddenly. There he was. Kassila! Rushing up out of the darkness. His hand was outstretched, great talons reaching for me. He wore a suit of tarpon scales, a crown of spines, coils of hair like jellyfish tentacles and a beard of bubbles. I knew what he had come for.

I slipped the St Christopher medal from my neck and threw it over the railing. It hung for a moment in the air before it hit the waves and began to spin slowly through the water. For a few seconds more I followed the shape, distorted now, as it drifted downwards. I imagined myself falling in after it, head first, plummeting down into the green. Sinking into the billowing darkness. The cool waters closing above me, shutting out all the heat and light and noise.

Then I saw Kassila seize the flimsy chain in his huge hand. He twisted his great body and spiralled back down below.

And only the tip of his tail cut through the surface of the water.

8

Hawa, 1955

Josephine Baker

THEY WANTED WATER. So much water! The headwoman organised us to fetch it from the stream and we carried it up in buckets on our heads. They were using up all the water from the stream near the work site. The water we brought was for them, for baths and washing. That was the first time I saw inside the compound. A boil had welled up under my eye, tight and shiny, close to bursting. I set my bucket down and felt it with my fingertips. I saw a man looking at me, who turned away when I looked back. After that they didn't want me to carry water again.

The men slept in tents instead of houses. And mostly washed themselves out of doors. All except one who came and went, who wore long trousers but spoke with a woman's voice and bathed in another tent some distance from the camp. The chief assigned three dozen men to work for them. They began collecting the mud from the bottom of the river bed. We used to creep up to watch them, two or three of us hiding behind the big boulders. The white men stood on the shelf of the river bank and watched the men from the village digging, loading pans with gravel and rocks which other men carried on their heads and dumped into wooden boxes running with water. That was where all the water was going. There were times the one with the woman's voice called for a bucket of earth to be brought over, which he spread out on a canvas cloth, inspecting the mud and rocks, crushing some and weighing the powder on a set of brass scales.

What they were looking for nobody knew, but the day they

found it – what a commotion! I was washing clothes at the stream. Ever since the men had arrived the water flowing downstream from where the work was going on was too muddy to use, so we had to walk much further upstream to a place where the water was still clear. When I heard the shouts I crept along the waterside and crouched down below the river bank.

The men in charge were behaving like children. Hugging each other, punching arms and slapping backs. The one with the woman's voice, who I now realised had breasts, they did not slap and hit, but carried on their shoulders singing a song: 'For she's a jolly good fellow.' Then they set her down and spun her around between themselves, dancing like crazy people. All the time watched by the men who did the digging, who were silent, while they waited to be told what to do next.

The white men gave everybody the rest of the day off. As they made their way back along the path to the encampment, I followed them, staying parallel to their position, blending myself into the shapes of the trees, stepping from shadow to shadow, treading lightly so as not to disturb the leaves on the forest floor. It was easy. They made a great deal of noise as they went. The path was narrow and they walked in single file. I recognised the one at the back as the same man who had sent me away that first time.

He was carrying a heavy bag on his shoulders. It caused him to walk at a slower pace than his companions. I watched as the gap between them widened. For a moment he stopped, set down his bag, and wiped his brow with a cloth. Then he blew his nose on the cloth, folded it up and carefully replaced it in his pocket. At that moment I stepped out on to the path behind him, treading on a small twig to catch his attention. Naturally, he swung round, startled to see me there.

We faced each other. He did not recognise me. The boil was gone. I told you I had been washing clothes. I had stripped to enter the water, keeping just a cloth tied around my waist. Now I was wearing only this same cloth. I saw his eyes drop from my face and move down my body, like a slow dribble of sweat. I stepped forward and picked up the bag. It was heavy, but I did not let that show. I placed it on my head. And in that way I walked in front of him, all the way to the camp and back inside.

The tents were taken down, replaced by low buildings with zinc roofs. I had a job in the camp. I worked for the man, who was called Blue by his companions or Mr Blue, like the colour. In the mornings I boiled coffee and eggs for him. He would sit outside the door in front of a table that afterwards I folded and put away, on a chair that did the same. At first I went back to the village every evening, but after some time Mr Blue said this did not suit him. And so I slept on a mat at the door of the hut. In the evenings I heated water for him to bathe and in time I learned how to pour the whisky he liked to drink and how to wash his clothes and tidy them away in his trunk. In the mornings he sat with his legs stretched out in front of him, with nothing to do but watch me work.

He did not ask me my name. Instead he told me he would call me Josephine. He said I looked like Josephine Baker. I did not know who he meant. Only that it was easier for him to remember.

I liked my new job. Mr Blue had so many possessions. His brown leather belt with a brass buckle I kept polished with animal fat. The same with his boots, of which he had two pairs. I rinsed the dead bristles from his shaving brush, and wiped the bar of soap, set them both back out on a towel the way he showed me. I plucked the hairs from his comb. Long, transparent hairs the colour of sand.

Papers covered in something I thought looked like centipede tracks. Writing. How could I have known? I had never been taught to read or sent to school. A Thermos flask that kept coffee hot the whole day long. Maps. Magazines. Books. Other things I had never laid eyes on before, whose purpose I could not imagine. On the green felt table-top: an instrument made of brass, with numbers and letters and an arrow that swung around towards the same point, wherever you directed it. A glass you could hold in your hand that made everything bigger. I stared through it at the hairs on the back of my hand, at a silverfish crawling out of his trunk. I could even see the lice swarming along the vane of a chicken feather.

In that place I saw ice for the first time in my life. A great block delivered on the back of a truck. That evening Mr Blue told me to put chunks of it in his drink and in those of the others whom he invited around to his hut before dinner. While they were eating, I took a piece of it and sat at the back of the hut, feeling the unearthly coldness, holding it in the cups of my hands to try to stop it slipping away. Afterwards my fingers felt stiff, aching like I had been wringing clothes all day.

Mr Blue found me playing with the magnifying glass. He said nothing. But watched me as I replaced it and continued wiping as I had been. From then on I carried the cloth with me whenever I went to look at Mr Blue's belongings.

Some days I watched Mr Blue. In the evenings, from the darkness outside the window while he was readying himself for sleep. He would sit down, his camp bed creaking under his weight, pull off his boots and his socks and throw them into the corner of the room. He would struggle with his braces and pull at the front of his shirt, trying to set the buttons free. His chest was covered in hair, like hog hair. Thick slabs of flesh on the sides of his body overhung his belt. He would loosen his trousers and lie down. There were times, when I was sure he was sleeping, I would creep in. The room was filled with his odour, even the walls sweated. Mr Blue slept on his back, one hand covering his penis. I stood in the darkness and listened to the sounds coming from him. Snorting as he breathed in, whistling as he breathed out. Sometimes I might stay there an hour or so. Before I went I moved his shoes, placed them neatly under his bed, picked up his shirt and vest and hung them on the peg.

One day I found some shillings and other coins in the pocket of Mr Blue's trousers. I set them aside while I worked and from time to time I glanced at the little pile of money. There was quite a lot, enough to buy half a bag of rice. When Mr Blue came back I fetched his drink and stayed there while he took his first sip. He waved his hand at me, but I didn't move. I bent in front of him, put my hand out to show him the coins.

'Master,' I said, 'look at your money I found today.'

He took the coins and pocketed them, looking at me all the while. 'Thank you, Josephine,' he said. He reached out his hand and I stretched mine out to meet his. A coin dropped into the palm of my hand.

Small Boy set a penny down on the dirt between us. From the pocket on the front of his shirt he took something gnarled and yellow and placed it next to the penny. He said I could have whichever one I wanted. I reached for the penny. Small Boy laughed. He picked up the small lump of metal and tossed it in the air.

'Take the penny. But this is worth many hundreds of pennies.'

Small Boy was the one who used to translate Mr Blue's orders for me before I learned to understand, telling me Mr Blue was asking for this or that. He taught me everything I learned in that place. Every day Small Boy told Mr Blue that he needed four pence to buy the food, when I knew that what we bought could only come to three.

He placed the yellow metal in my hand, I felt its weight for a moment, but before I could close my fingers Small Boy snatched it away again.

The chief gave permission to the prospectors to come to our place. I was there when the chief came to the camp, accompanied by only two elders. I saw what happened.

They sat outside Mr Blue's house, refused his whisky, instead I brought them cups of water. Balanced on a metal tray, the way I had learned. After a short time they stood and followed Mr Blue inside. Mr Blue was laughing a great deal as though something was very funny. The chiefs and the elders did not laugh, nor did they speak much. Instead they sat down and waited. Mr Blue called for Small Boy who came in bearing a tin box. I had seen it two nights before. It was full of money. Mr Blue walked around the back of the chief and leaned over him, putting his hands on both his shoulders. My eyes widened to see him do such a thing. But if he had taken offence, the chief did not let it show. Mr Blue asked Small Boy to open the box.

Well, to look at what was inside you would think it was more money than any of us had ever seen. And it was! All you could see was ten-shilling notes. The chief nodded and grunted. Waved for the box to be closed. Then he got up and left. Mr Blue said he would send the trunk down.

'Josie! Come, come,' he beckoned to me. I moved towards him. Mr Blue sat down on the seat vacated by the chief. He poured some whisky from the bottle into a cup and handed it to me. 'Here you are, doll. Cheers!' Touched the edge of his glass against mine and drank. I tipped the cup. The liquid burned my lips. I licked them and felt the heat transfer to my tongue. I stood holding the cup out in front of me. Mr Blue stared straight ahead of him for a few moments. He glanced my way, reached out and touched the back of my thigh, rubbing his thumb up and down. I did not move. Then he poured himself more and drank that, too.

I gave my cup to Small Boy in the place where we sat behind Mr Blue's house. Small Boy laughed as he described the trick Mr Blue had played on the chief. Placing a few ten-shilling notes on the top of the box. Underneath them nothing but two-shilling notes. It worked every time.

'Too greedy,' laughed Small Boy, tipping the liquid down his throat like a fire-eater. 'Too greedy. All of them. They trip up on their own greediness.'

Small Boy, who was the age of my uncles, arrived at the same time as the prospectors. He had travelled with them for many months, all across the country. Mornings, it was his job to shave Mr Blue, who sat in his chair with his head tipped backwards, coffee by his side, while Small Boy set to work lathering his chin and stroking the edge of the blade across Mr Blue's face. I could hear the faint rasping noise of the hairs being cut, one by one.

It happened that on certain nights the miners stayed up late drinking, playing games of cards, swapping lies and stories. When one bottle of whisky was finished Mr Blue shouted for Small Boy to fetch another from the store. Small Boy's job was to stay awake to serve them, but on this one night he fell asleep and did not hear our master calling. Mr Blue's voice became impatient:

'Where the hell is he?'

Footsteps in the dark. I reached across and shook Small Boy.

'Get up!' I whispered. 'Mr Blue is calling.'

Small Boy jumped to his feet, forcing his eyes open, wide and round as marbles: 'Yes, master. Yes, master. Here I am. See me now.'

Mr Blue waved the bottle in the air, jangled the store keys in his other hand like a bell. 'Where in the hell have you been? Can't you hear me calling you?'

'I'm sorry, master.' Small Boy reached for the bottle and took it from Mr Blue's hand. He ran to the store and returned a short time after.

'And ice. Bring ice.' The truck had not delivered ice since two weeks before.

'The ice is finished, master.'

I heard Mr Blue throw curses at Small Boy. They bounced off the walls of the houses. Silence. Small Boy made no reply.

'Dumb fuck.'

'Leave him alone, Blue. How could it be his fault?' The woman's voice, soft as a moth's coat. Another silence followed, a sort of stop–start silence. You could almost hear Mr Blue wanting to speak and thinking better of it. He told Small Boy to pour the drinks. The woman refused any more, saying she was tired. I listened as she wished them all goodnight and her footsteps faded away. Small Boy must have made a move to leave then as well, because suddenly came Mr Blue's voice:

'You stay right there!' He said he was hungry and told Small Boy to fetch something for him to eat. Of course there was nothing. The food had been cooked and eaten. What was left was for Small Boy and me. There was no fridge. Small Boy replied he would have to light a fire. 'Well do it, damnit.' Then: 'Jesus. Oh, don't be so bloody stupid. Do you think I'm serious? Bring that bottle over here.'

By now I was listening carefully from behind the hut, on the other side of the darkness. I heard Mr Blue's voice: slack, slurred and yet stitched with something hard, as he set about provoking Small Boy. The other men laughed, enjoying it. From the manner of their laughter, I could tell this was something that had happened before. He instructed Small Boy to provide some entertainment, since he could produce neither food nor ice. Small Boy replied there were no entertainers to be found in the camp either.

'Then you'd better entertain us yourself.'

Small Boy asked how he was to do so.

'Let's have a song,' said one man.

'Yes. A song,' came another and began to sing himself.

'No, no. We'll sing. He'll dance.' Mr Blue again. 'You can dance, can't you?'

'No master.'

'Oh, come on. You lot can all dance. You're born jigging around. It's in your fucking blood.'

I imagined Small Boy standing there alone in front of Mr Blue and the other men. Alone in the middle of the night, underneath the stars. I wondered what was going to happen next.

Mr Blue begin to sing and the other men joined in. I heard him order Small Boy to dance. There was a small sound. Thud. Thud. Like that, the double thud like a stone being thrown. The same sound again. And then a clatter as the stone ricocheted off something in the distance. I heard the sound of Small Boy's feet shuffling in the dirt. Of his breathing. Of the men clapping and cheering.

I stayed awake listening, for as long as I could. By the time I fell asleep Small Boy still hadn't come back.

The next morning I brought Mr Blue his second cup of coffee. His fingers trembled as he grasped the cup and raised it to his lips. The lump in the front of his throat moved as he swallowed, like a rat under a blanket. He leaned back in his chair and tilted his chin as Small Boy started to cover the bottom half of his face with lather. Sweat drops, glistening like insect eggs hung on his forehead. Small Boy jerked the leather strap tight across his forearm and stroked the blade of the razor against it. Then he stepped forward and drew the flat side of the sharpened blade across Mr Blue's cheek.

★　　★　　★

Mr Blue complained the workers were always breaking things. The excavator in the first pit that scooped up giant mouthfuls of soil and rocks: three days' work lost, he said. Just like that. Every day it was something. Shovels and hoes turned to chalk. Wooden handles snapped like dried grass stalks. Steel pick heads shattered. A sledgehammer cracked like an egg. The mining had continued through several seasons. At first Mr Blue had seemed pleased. But now he was always complaining. Always complaining. These Africans don't know how to take care of their tools, refuse to learn how to maintain machinery, he said. This to the director and his wife who came to inspect the mines.

In the clay oven Small Boy's bread made with palm wine and baking soda swelled and rose. Small Boy fashioned chicken cutlets and sweet potato croquettes and made a salad of cucumber and tomatoes, which he dressed with oil and vinegar from the store. A table was set up in the middle of the camp. The woman draped a cloth over it, and we collected together every cup, spoon, knife and plate in the place. Small Boy showed me the bottle of wine the visitors had brought and I watched as he pulled the cork out of the neck.

That morning the water pump had broken for the second time in a month, in the middle of the rainy season. The pits filled up with water and had to be bailed out by hand. There weren't enough buckets. Half the men stood around idle, watching the other half work. Overnight the rain would come down and fill the pits again.

The night was cool, but Mr Blue was twitching and sweating. Later, when the evening was through, I would watch him as he slept, hear the words he shouted. Orders. Names. That's how the words sounded, anyway. I would watch him as he tried to turn in his too-narrow bed, while outside the rain subsided only to accelerate again, revving like the truck engine or a piece of machinery.

The guests had been sitting for a long time, the canvas sagged beneath their buttocks. I had already cleared the empty salad plates. Small Boy was waiting to serve the main dish. Underneath the table

Mr Blue's knee jerked up and down. Up. Down. Up. Down. Above us dark clouds crowded together like a horde of crows under cover of the blackness. The candles on the table dipped in the breeze. Mr Blue shouted for Small Boy. Once. Twice. Small Boy was arranging and rearranging, with endless patience, a dish of cooling potatoes. Every time Mr Blue shouted he replied: 'Yes, master. Coming, master.' The third, or maybe it was the fourth time we heard Mr Blue's voice, he waved at me to begin carrying the plates through.

'At last.'

'I could eat a horse.'

'What is it about these people? Everything takes so long.'

'Every day. Every damn day. Now you know what it's like.'

Somebody cleared their throat. That was the last thing I heard before the thunder tore out of the blackness.

For me, I loved the night-time storms at the start of the rainy season. Always at the same time of night. I stood still and let the water soak my clothing until I felt it trickle down the backs of my legs. Mr Blue and the visitors scattered. Small Boy stayed with me and together we set about clearing up the remains of the meal.

I was watching a fly. Smaller than a bluebottle and silent, a sort of tawny-orange colour. It was flying back and forth in a tight square, as though it was trapped, bumping into four invisible walls. Bump. Turn. Bump. Turn. On and on. I flicked it with the end of the cloth and missed. Mr Blue came in to tell me he was leaving. A few matters to sort out with Head Office. I nodded. I thought Head Office was another white man. When I went outside I discovered that all of them were gone, including the one with the woman's voice.

Life was easy. We did not worry about our chores. Mr Blue had left without giving us any instructions. Small Boy and I slept indoors taking turns on the bed. After a few days it was as though we had lived there for ever. In the corner of the room black and yellow mould grew on the soles of Mr Blue's work boots and a greyish fur began to climb up the leather. Much later, when I picked them up to clean them, a shadow remained on the concrete floor that refused to wash away.

Mr Blue came back, his chin stubbled with white. Small Boy went to heat water and fetch the razor and brush, but Mr Blue waved him away. Instead he sat in front of the camp wireless with the headset on his ears for many hours into the night. Listening to the voices that floated on hissing, bubbling waves. The voices carried news of the strikes into the camp.

Later I heard people say those strikes were the beginning. First the strikes. Next the rebellion. Finally the end of the rule of chiefs. Maybe that's the way it was. I don't know. I only know what I saw.

The voices issued Mr Blue with instructions. Flying pickets. Wildcat strikes. Trade unionists. Troublemakers. Refuse access, they said. Mr Blue was to issue notice of an epidemic if necessary and use the excuse to seal the area.

Early the next morning Mr Blue went down to talk to the workers. Rows of faces, wiped clear of all expression, like sand after wind. The men listened to the lies spilling over Mr Blue's narrow lips: talk of quarantines and infection rates, instructions on how to avoid the spread of the pretend contagion. He gazed away above their heads at the tops of the trees as he assured them a doctor was on the way from Mile 47.

Too late! Between the wireless and the bush wire, the bush wire was the faster.

A man stepped forward and laid down his pickaxe. Others followed. A few anxious ones hopped from leg to leg, consulting the sky, not knowing what to do. But in the end they followed their brothers. Though some said: 'Sorry, master,' as they laid down their tools. I hid behind some fencing and watched as, one by one, the men turned their backs on Mr Blue. Barely a word had been spoken. I had never seen such a thing. Mr Blue stared straight ahead, not moving, not speaking, not blinking even. Refusing to watch them walk away from him. All the time his lips were set in a strange smile. He looked like a *rongsho* risen from the grave.

They passed me, they did not notice me crouching there. Their leader came first. I recognised him from the pits, he was one of the men sent to work there by the chief that first week. I remember him to this day: a tall man, with a beard like a Muslim. Well, that could have been any number of men. But he had a patch on his lower lip where the brown gave way to pink. Like a stain or a splash.

Later there was talk, scandalous talk. I was even told his name, though I don't remember it now. And I was too young then really to remember the events of which they spoke, because those things had happened years before and the man had gone away and since returned. Later, when for a short while, this man's name became known to all, people talked of some past disgrace. It concerned a woman, I know that much. A junior wife.

Morning and the sun rose over silence. The mine machines were stilled, their voices quiet. It seemed there had been no other sound for months. Now it was as if the birds and animals were shocked into a silence of their own. The silence crept outwards, out until it stifled everything, even the humming of the forest.

The silence is what I remember most. Because it was not the way we did things. The silence was something different. Before then silence was something I thought that I alone understood. I knew when not to speak, when not to let myself be heard. Silence was my friend, my twin, the other half of me. Silence was my weapon. Not a blustering gun, but an invisible spider's web.

The men did not report for work. Instead they marched to the gates of the compound. You could see the dust on the road as they came. Feel the thrumming of a hundred bare feet, like the beating of the earth's own heart. I remained out of sight, watching. A brass padlock dangled from the iron chain wrapped around the gateposts of the compound. Mr Blue stayed inside, alone, not counting Small Boy and me. The men waited without speaking. A thin, black line between the green of the trees and the red earth, like the colours of a flag.

I waited for Mr Blue to rouse himself and go down to them. Mr Blue waited by his silent radio.

Late in the afternoon the light thickened to the colour of rust.

The singing began. The men's voices carried into the compound, buoyed on the waves of silence, and poured in through the cracks around the windows of the room where Mr Blue stood. Some songs were known to me. Others were society songs I had heard but rarely. A short time passed and the men sang louder. The air began to tremble under the weight of their voices. It was as though they were calling to the thunder, which answered them, rumbling through the sky, bringing the rain.

I came and stood behind Mr Blue. The air inside his room was heavy, it stuck to the roof of my mouth, caught in my throat and muffled the sounds from outside. The rain began to come down. Needles of sound bounced off the tin roof. The windows vibrated. Mr Blue stood, hidden by the darkness, staring at the men outside who stood in ragged rows behind the man with the mark on his lip. A firm man would have gone out to talk to him, but Mr Blue was not that man. Water streamed down the glass, distorting the faces and bodies of the men beyond. Light seeped out of the day. Mr Blue and I stood and watched, until the figures merged with the darkness.

Much later I watched Mr Blue leave his room, quietly but not quiet enough. Down to the perimeter fence, where I saw him lay a trail of white powder on the inside, like a line of ash to ward off soldier ants.

The light came back and the men were there. As though they had never gone, but stood like sentinels through the night.

Mr Blue asked us to bring all the empty bottles and cans we could find. He sat on the floor filling them up with powder and nails and pieces of metal. In the afternoon he took to his camp bed with a fresh cold, rolling his aching head around on his pillow, coughing into a handkerchief. While he was asleep Small Boy slipped away and came back.

Mr Blue was a prisoner, although none of us behaved as though we knew this. Small Boy said the men were angry because now they had learned the value of the gold they were digging out of the river and up from the former rice fields. Some of the men had been panning for themselves, trading with the Syrian traders. But this was not allowed.

On top of that, across the land the tax had jumped up to twenty-five shillings. And now the authorities wanted to tax even more people. They wanted to tax the young men without wives or even homes, who already owed their labour to the chiefs, building their houses and working on their farms.

Small Boy told me the railwaymen were the ones who started with this kind of trouble. The very first time was right after the first war when the men who fought in Senegal came back to find a cup of rice that used to cost one penny now cost five pence. And bread was sixpence, but their wages were the same. That was the first time the railway stopped. Small Boy, who had then barely grown into his name let alone grown out of it, remembered the great, silent locomotives. How he followed his brothers, clambering over the roofs of the carriages, like birds on a basking hippopotamus.

In the city people accused the Syrians of hoarding food and looted the Syrian stores. By then the Syrians owned all the stores.

The next time the railways stopped it was because the black railwaymen were made to take tests but not the white ones. Governor Slater called it a 'fight to the death' and called in the troops, who came with guns. And when the railwaymen went back to work some had lost their pensions, and others their jobs, and some their lives. And everyone earned even less than before. The Railway Workers' Union was banned. But the anger didn't die. Instead it changed shape and wore a new face, with an ingratiating smile. The railway workers said: 'Yes, Sir. Yes, Missus,' and doffed their caps and punched holes in the first-class tickets of the administrators and their wives with a pointed pinkie nail.

So when the cost of a cup of rice doubled again because all the farmers turned their backs on their fields and headed east with their hoes to dig up diamonds instead of yams, the leaders of the new Artisans and Allied Workers' Union and the Transport and General Workers' Union asked for one shilling and sixpence more pay a day. The bosses offered them four pence. In the city they stoned the houses of the new African ministers, who should have supported them but didn't. Small Boy had seen the pictures in the newspapers. They soon changed their minds after their windows were broken. And last year the railwaymen went on strike again.

'Now everybody, he wants the same,' said Small Boy.

Head Office was closed. The bosses couldn't get inside. The strikers encircled the building like a noose. That was why nobody answered Mr Blue's calls on the radio. Small Boy said never mind. He had seen it all before. We only had to wait.

So we waited through that day and the next. Mr Blue lay in his bed and didn't ask for anything. I looked at him. I thought about these people who had to be carried over rivers, who fainted in the sun, drank only boiled water and slept under nets. Their skin tore like old cotton, their flesh was soft as a baby's. They were weak, but they were strong at the same time. We outnumbered them greatly and yet they ruled us.

The radio hissed and spat. Mr Blue sat bolt upright like a corpse struck by lightning.

In the empty compound Small Boy picked his teeth and hummed. Beyond the gates a centuries-old anger, pricked by a new pin, bubbled and burst.

Silence from outside. The singing had stopped. Then the blustering guns came and tore through the silence.

And that was that. Mr Blue told me he was being reassigned. He handed me my wages and five shillings' 'loyalty bonus'. I gave him my thanks.

So I packed Mr Blue's belongings while Small Boy washed the pots and cooking things, folded the camp bed, the bed roll and the chairs. Packed them all up inside six wooden boxes. Into the boxes followed the tins of lunch tongue and sardines, jars of sandwich spread, bottles of grape juice, kerosene, matches. I heated the flat iron on the fire outside and pressed Mr Blue's shirts one by one. Inside the trunk a fly's corpse dangled from a web. Stains and rings of mildew patterned the bottom of the trunk. I laid the sheets and mosquito net on top of them. Then the newly ironed clothes. Shirts. Shorts. Socks. Then everything else. Belt. Brush. Boots. Gauntlets. Helmet. Helmet case.

Outside, Small Boy scraped the razor's edge up Mr Blue's neck, slicing the head off the ingrown hairs, leaving a trail of red spots welling in the white froth, reminding me of the splashes of red on the ground outside the fence. The rain had come and washed them into the ground. Small Boy had been right. We had only to be patient. Somehow news of the strike had reached the chief who sent his messenger to alert the District Commissioner. By the time the strikers arrived the next morning DC Silk was waiting in front of the compound with his soldiers, ready to arrest the ringleaders. A few were wounded in the scuffle. The leader was badly injured and might even die. Some were taken away – to jail, said Small Boy. The others would be fined. The chief had wanted them all put in stocks.

I set to work on the desk. Rolled the maps and dropped them into long cardboard tubes. The compass I placed inside its soft pouch. Underneath a bundle of papers lay the magnifying glass. I picked it up and held it out in front of me. A ring of shimmering light appeared, dancing upon the wall. I turned to it. Just as soon as I did it shifted to the ceiling. And next to the floor. For a few moments I fancied it was a spirit's shadow. Then I realised that the movements echoed mine. A cloud passed over the sun, and suddenly it was gone. I gasped with disappointment, but only for a moment. The sun reappeared and so did the shining, dancing creature.

I begged Mr Blue not to forget me. I begged him to send for me as soon as he could. Mr Blue murmured, of course he would. But Small Boy's face told me something different. I watched them leave. I went back into the hut and sat alone on the cold floor.

In the distance, like the humming of bees, I could hear the mine machinery. I wondered who the next master would be and whether he would be as good to me as Mr Blue. I decided to wait and see.

In the meantime I unwrapped the magnifying glass from the corner of my *lappa* and held it up high, where it caught the light and began to dance for me across the naked walls.

9

Serah, 1956

Red Shoes

WELL, THERE WAS THIS one white woman. I mean she was our teacher, she was married to the District Commissioner. I think she taught, you know, just to keep herself occupied. There wasn't much to do except run the house. A lot of those types did not bring their wives, or the wives didn't want to come, or if they did they lost their minds and had to be sent home. That happened.

Once when I was growing up a District Commissioner was invited to attend a *palava* of the chiefs. It was a grand affair, the chiefs travelled in from miles. Some important land matter was to be discussed that required the Commissioner's approval. This man decided to bring his wife along, as a diversion for her – she was recently arrived in the country. At that time I was a young initiate, and our dancing opened the proceedings.

The men talked for hours. You know how it goes. And while they did so, I watched the woman. She sat with her hands on her lap, head to one side. Her glance flew from face to face, settling on each for a moment, like a bird flitting through the trees. From her expression you would imagine she was paying a great deal of attention, though it must have been entirely unintelligible. Even the chiefs were using interpreters between themselves. The time passed slowly. But the woman's face did not redden in the heat. Rather it grew pale. She was swallowing, swallowing all the time, looking in her husband's direction. He had his back turned to her, listening closely to the words his Court Messenger was whispering in his ear. He couldn't see her. I saw her eyelids flutter like a fledgling's wings, her eyeballs rolled back as though she was trying to see the inside of her own head.

Gbap! She fell off her chair.

Well, there was silence at that. Then the chiefs, the *pa'm'sum*, everybody hurried over. The chiefs began waving their fly swats around her. The woman lashed out at them. I could hear her screaming. The more they tried to help her, the more she sobbed and backed away, holding her handbag out in front of her. In the end her husband managed to calm her and lead her away, his arm around her shoulders. The whole *palava* had to be called off and reconvened at another time. Later the Court Messenger came to explain the woman was suffering from malaria. But those close enough to see what had happened said she had made up her mind that we were all cannibals. Every one of us. And that the chiefs, in their garbled tongue, were really discussing the best way to kill her.

Our teacher, Mrs Silk, was not this sort. Not at all. For a start there was the way she looked at you, straight in the eye. And she would ask you to look her in the face too, when you spoke. It got me into trouble with my grandmother, who slapped me for being so bold. But when you talked to Mrs Silk and saw the way she looked at you and smiled and nodded. Well, it made you feel good in yourself. Like you were saying something interesting. So I learned to look down at my grandmother's feet, and up into Mrs Silk's eyes.

Every morning Mrs Silk arrived at the school in her husband's car. And every morning we gathered at the windows to watch. Mrs Silk sat in her seat, making no move to get out. Her husband would climb down and walk all the way around the front of the car to open her door. And then he kissed her.

Kissed her!

On the lips!

Just like that!

In front of us all!

We'd whoop and duck down out of sight quickly, before they looked up.

What did we think? We thought: what shameless people are

these? Such behaviour in public! But secretly I had another thought, and I think some of the other girls did, too. How this man must love his wife to allow himself to act that way. Yes, Mrs Silk was very lucky. Oh, and I prayed one day I would have a husband to love me like that, too.

We used to powder our faces with chalk dust. To dampen the shine. We smuggled in hot-combs and ironed each other's hair in the dormitory at night. I wonder the teachers never seemed to ask themselves how we had curly hair one day and straight hair the next.

Hannah Williams. Now she was the first one to own a pair of shoes. Brought them back after she went to stay in the city with her Creole father, who had a job in the Government offices. I had never owned a pair in my life. And I didn't know anybody who did, although my grandmother embroidered slippers for women who were getting married. So frail, with soles made of canvas. By the end of the day they were spoiled.

Everybody wanted to walk in Hannah's shoes. Come evening she would take them out and let us take turns up and down between the bunks. One girl walked like a duck. Another fell flat on her face. Everybody cheered the ones who walked well. My turn came early on, because I was in Hannah's group of friends. I slipped the shoes on.

La i la!

It felt as though I was stuck ankle deep in river mud. I couldn't flex my feet. It was as though a great weight rested upon each one. I could barely lift them off the ground and put them back down. Still, when everybody cheered, I tell you, I was grinning like a fool.

The dormitory had a wooden floor. Hannah's shoes made a slapping sound. In the corridors of the school Mrs Silk's heels tapped out her progress to the classroom door. You could hear her swivel where the corridor divided. Kop, kap. Swivel. Kop, kap. One day I crossed the compound in Hannah's shoes and walked with them down the school corridor to see if I could make the same noise, but I could not. Hannah was upset with me for wearing her new shoes out of doors.

I yearned for a pair of shoes of my own. By this time I was staying with my grandmother in town during the school holidays, in the house we had once thought of as the house of treats. Well, I begged her. I volunteered for every errand and every chore and when I was finished, I invented new ones. I whitewashed the stones at the perimeter of our property. I even soaped and rinsed the nanny goat. No thanks. None at all, my efforts went unacknowledged. Then one day, when I was on the brink of giving up: 'Wash your face and oil your legs,' she said. '*Makone*. We're going to town.'

There were two shoe stores, two styles of shoes for girls. There was Bata Shoe Store on the main road near the police station. Further down the street, beyond the general store with the poster for Blue Band margarine was the shop selling Clarks shoes. I knew what I wanted. I wanted Clarks shoes. The styles were close, but Clarks were butter coloured and soft as skin. Bata shoes were made of an inferior leather, dark and stiff. Hannah Williams had Clarks shoes.

Clarks shoes: one pound, eighteen shillings and sixpence.

Bata shoes: one pound fifteen shillings.

I remember the prices exactly.

We went to Bata.

Well, I did not want those shoes. Not at all. So I claimed they didn't fit. I pushed my toes together and walked like a crow. I hopped up and down, as though the floor was burning. The saleswoman knitted her brow, pursed her lips and drew in her chin. She pressed at the ends of my toes with her fingertips, measured my feet a second time. Lengthways. Widthways. She brought down a second pair, then a third. Still no luck. After a while she stood back and shrugged her shoulders, turned to my grandmother and said: 'Once they are worn in the leather will soften, you'll see.'

Hali!

What did I do? I threw myself on the floor and wept. What do you *think* I did? I begged my grandmother to take me to the store where they sold Clarks shoes. My grandmother was a stern woman. In the market she sent me to the stall holders to ask their best price. Once. Twice. The traders complained to me they were barely making a profit, but always they lowered their prices. Only after the third time would she come over, exchange greetings and watch them closely while they packed her purchases.

But Bata Shoes was a shop with assistants and a ceiling fan.

She gave in so quickly, I was surprised. My tears dried on my face. And yet as we walked to Clarks Shoe Outlet she held my arm with a grip so tight I could feel the flesh squeezing through her fingers.

Once inside the store I was terrified my grandmother might change her mind. So I forced my foot inside the first pair of Clarks shoes I was given and jumped to my feet. I strode up and down like a soldier on parade. My grandmother ordered the shoes wrapped. She paid and we walked to the door. I tucked my new shoes under my arm and carried them home. I tried to keep a straight face. I tried not to do anything that might annoy my grandmother. And I tried not to think about the way the shoes had pinched slightly across the arch, and how I could feel the ends with my toes.

Lord have mercy! But those shoes gave me so much grief. Even to wear them a little each evening left me hobbling.

So I lent them to the girl who helped in the kitchen. She had broad, strong feet. Rice planter's feet. It was her job to wash us; she used to scrub our hands and the soles of our feet using blue soap and the brush with which she scoured the floor and walls. She was silent, resolute and almost impossible to please. The loan of my shoes she regarded as a singular favour. By the time I packed them in my box ready to go back to school they were a size bigger.

Sundays was the single day footwear was permitted on the school grounds. Between those times I practised walking until I was about the best in the school. At the end of that term my feet had already outgrown my shoes. Still I wore them for four more months before I was ready to give them up. I knew I'd never get another pair so soon. I simply learned to live with the pain.

Now, how did it go? It went like this:

Back to back,
Belly to belly;
I don't give a damn
'Cos I done dead already.

After dark we used to sneak away from my grandmother's house and gather outside the home of the half-Lebanese son of the garage owner, the only person in that place who owned a gramophone. It was he who used to play the Zombie Jamboree. Only certain kinds of women went to his house. Women who wore tight dresses and smoked cigarettes, who looked each other up and down and sideways beneath heavy lids and kept sullen faces, so they always looked like nothing around them was good enough. We called them High Life women.

A floating population of us lived in my grandmother's house. I really don't have any idea who some of them were, but each child arrived with a claim of kinship, no matter how fragile. Parents who were short on funds sent their children to stay. And in return, my grandmother never sent their offspring back. She raised us well, though I don't remember any active upbringing as such. No. Rather, we were like a collection of differently coloured and shaped bottles left out to collect rainwater, some half-filled, some almost empty. You learned from being around her what would earn a nod of approval or awaken a furious rage. I don't remember her ever touching us, not even when we cried. And certainly we could not imagine her young, no matter how we tried. Yet somehow she left us all with the impression, like the afterglow of a radiant dream, of having been thoroughly loved.

Still, we ran away from her when we could. First to watch the High Life women and strut to the Zombie Jamboree on our dance floor of dust, in the square of yellow light beneath the window of the garage owner's son. Later, when the Lakindo clubs started to be held among the stalls of the empty marketplace, and before the elders banned them because so many men complained their youngest wives were disappearing at night to attend the dances, we used to hide and watch the couples dancing in the dark.

We didn't celebrate birthdays. We didn't know when we had been born. Presents came occasionally, always unannounced, which made them all the sweeter. The year I turned approximately sixteen my grandmother returned from the market with a pair of red patent-leather shoes with real heels. The choice seemed so utterly unlike her in any way I wonder if later, when she looked with a different eye, she didn't disapprove of her earlier self in buying those shoes. But I guess at the time she thought they were as smart as I did.

I wore them to my graduation. And later to my first dance. In those days the dances began at four o' clock in the afternoon. Yaya and I walked the three miles from home barefoot, we washed our feet at the standpipe and clumped into the dance in our shoes. The first time was a disaster. My feet sweated in the heat. Inside the plastic shoes they slipped and slid like eels in a bucket. Our dance routine collapsed, we stumbled over each other's feet, bruises like purple and black pansies bloomed on our shins.

From then on we wore our shoes to rehearse. At the next dance we rhumba'd like professionals. And for the first time I danced with somebody other than my brother.

Janneh was five years older than me. A student at the university in the South. He had a voice the colour of deep water, tapered fingers, long legs with high calves and two scoops of muscle and flesh for his buttocks. He owned a motorbike. A motorbike! In those days few people even had bicycles, though you could hire one outside the petrol station. You couldn't actually ride away on it, though. You sat on the back and they pedalled you to your destination.

The Honda's engine was as loud as the roar of a forest beast, it drowned out my screams. My skirt was bunched up between my legs, I pressed my knees together and held on to the padded seat between us. I couldn't bring myself to touch him, to actually put my arms around his waist. Going up a hill I felt myself sliding dangerously backwards. At the last moment I reached out and grabbed Janneh's shirt, slid my arms around him. Down the other side my body was pushed against his. I felt my stomach flip. Just for a moment I pressed my nose against his shirt and breathed in. A warm, pungent smell, cloudy and pure at the same time. Like the smell of crumbled chocolate. Or new puppies.

My legs were trembling as I let myself into the house. From gripping with my thighs on to the motorbike, I told myself. Only once I was in bed did I remember Yaya, who walked all the way home alone. My brother did not dance with me for days.

The first elections were held four years before we were supposed to become independent. So the people could practise voting, I suppose. We were allowed to choose our own Prime Minister and some members of the cabinet, although the British would still tell them what to do. That way the Prime Minister could practise his new job without the burden of actually having to make any real decisions. They gave us the cow but kept hold of the tether.

The second time, though, it was for real. Janneh told me he had written a paper about the ways our constitution needed to be changed; it had been published in a newspaper. The motorbike belonged to the People's Progress Party. Janneh travelled with a cardboard box of fliers and posters strapped to the pillion seat. The posters bore a picture of the PPP's candidate, a man with a parting cut like a railway track into his hair and small, pursed lips. A week after I met Janneh, I stopped to look at one of the posters on a pillar box at the post office.

'Mouth like a goat's anus,' said the man behind me to the albino boy shining his shoes. 'Doesn't stand a chance. Tell me why they even bother coming to stand here, eh?'

The albino was silent. He flexed the shoeshine cloth and pulled it back and forward across the toe of the man's right foot. When he spoke his voice was high and light as the sound of a bamboo flute: 'They say they have candidates all over the country. Every constituency. One people. One country.'

'*Parah!*' replied the first man. 'Let them take this one back to where he came from. Give us our own sons first.'

The wind whipped our faces like a damp cloth, we flew through clouds of dust. At the sides of roads upon which no other vehicle travelled, we stopped to picnic. From high on an escarpment we watched a tornado spin across the plain below, watched people trying to outrun the gathering storm as it rumbled across the landscape, bearing down upon them like a snorting bull. Behind it the sky shone blue. And on the horizon a rainbow arced across the sky. On our way back down the dirt track crumbled and slid away under our wheels. In the next town we pasted the goat man's image over the face of the candidate for the opposing party. We handed out fliers to passers-by. At the kiosk where we stopped and Janneh treated me to my first taste of popcorn the vendor took a flier from a stack on his counter, folded it into a funnel shape and poured popcorn into it. Then he sprinkled greyish salt all over the popcorn and the goat man's crumpled features.

'Doesn't matter,' said Janneh. 'Actually, it's a fine thing. Helps spread the word. More people than ever get to hear our name.'

I asked Janneh why people said his candidate, whose name was in fact Sulaiman Bio, would not win.

'Says who?' he asked, pushing his eyebrows together.

I told him about the man at the post office.

'The decision is in the hands of the people. They know what they want. They know what is *right* for them. And they know their rights.' It was something I had heard him say before. When Janneh spoke he always sounded impressive. And yet, it seemed to me, talking to him felt like chasing butterflies. The words were beautiful, but their meaning was sometimes hard to catch.

Another day Janneh asked me if I wanted to be a returning officer. I was so flattered I said yes straight away, with no idea what I was being asked to do.

My post was a rice-weighing station in a town I had never been to before. I was given a seat behind a desk upon which were heaped piles of voting papers and a long list of names. At my feet, a metal ballot box. Two more boxes, wooden this time, were placed at one end of the room next to each other. A thin curtain suspended on a wire hung between them. The officer in charge gave me the key to the metal box and said he would be back to collect it at the end of the day.

Polling started at seven-thirty sharp! I pushed at the door of the station, which was really a shed, and the sunlight streamed in, lighting up the rice dust suspended in the air. I picked up a pile of papers and stood there in readiness.

An hour later I went back to the desk and sat down on the chair. I straightened the papers, arranging them into two neat stacks. The list of names and the pen I placed in front of me. I strolled back to the door and looked out. Two men were coming down the lane. I turned and hurried back to the desk. I watched them as they strolled past the open door without turning once. I got up and stared down the road after them.

Outside the station posters fluttered faintly in the breeze. It had rained in the night. Damp patches of ground steamed gently in the sun. The leaves on the trees shone bright as jewels. Tiny black midges danced across the puddles. A man with a rolled umbrella appeared before me. I stepped aside.

'Are you here to vote?'

'How much for a bushel?'

I smiled. I explained who I was. I was the returning officer for the elections. The rice station would be operating again tomorrow. In the meantime he could come in and vote.

'Now?' he asked.

'Today. The elections are being held today, to decide who should head the Government.' I gestured with my hand towards the polling booths. The man hesitated and then stepped inside. I continued: 'What's your name? I have to mark it on the list to say you've voted.'

The man told me his name: 'Abu.'

'Abu?'

'Yes.'

'Abu what? What is your father's name?'

'Abu Kamara.'

I traced my finger down the list. There were a lot of Kamaras. Dozens, in fact. Oddly no Abu. I checked. 'Abu, yes?' Yes. 'Do you have another name that you use? A middle name?' He said he did not. Alfred Kamara. Alhaji Kamara. Maybe this man had been to Mecca. 'Are you a Muslim?'

'I am a Muslim.'

That seemed to me to be good enough. He had a vote, I just couldn't find it. I did not want to disappoint him or lose my first client. I placed a tick next to the name Alhaji Kamara and handed him a voting form. I told him to go into the booth and select his candidate, and then to press his thumb into the purple ink pad to sign and again on to the bottom of the form, unless, that is, he knew how to write his name.

He had one question. 'Who is it I am voting for?'

'You vote for the candidate of your choice.'

'What is his name?'

'Your choice is your own. I can't tell you that.' The man stood and gazed at the paper in his hand. He moved neither forward nor back.

'So who did you vote for?' he asked. I hadn't voted. I hadn't thought about it.

'Sulaiman Bio. The people's choice.' I cited the campaign literature. 'People's Progress Party.'

'The people's choice?'

I smiled, nodding. Said it again. The people's choice. The choice of the people. That way round it sounded like a foregone conclusion. The man moved towards the booth. 'Third one down,' I added, to be helpful.

Minutes later he departed with a purple thumb and a purple stamp on the back of his hand to stop him from trying to vote again.

Later in the afternoon I kicked off my red shoes and rubbed the soles of my feet. From time to time I went to the door to try to encourage passers-by, such as there were, to come inside. Still no one came. I went back to the desk and gazed idly at the list of names. I felt like a hostess who had been snubbed by her guests.

I let my eyes run down the list. Name upon name.

Like ladder rungs.

Railway track sleepers.

Or a row of sleeping children.

Players waiting to be picked for a team.

First I stole Jeneba Turay's vote. I took it as my own. I reckoned by now she wasn't coming, whoever she was. Since I hadn't voted anywhere else I didn't see how it could possibly matter. I pressed my right thumb into the ink pad and then on to the bottom left of the voting slip.

With an hour to go before the election was over, two votes lay in the cavern of the ballot box, like visitors in an empty church. So I spent the remainder of the time filling it up: creating signatures and using up the fingers of one hand and then the other and finally each of my toes to create fictional thumb prints. At six o' clock I closed the door and waited for the box to be collected. I kept my inky hands folded behind my back while the men heaved it into the back of a van along with the others.

On the Honda I clung tight to Janneh as we raced through the towns and villages. The votes were being counted. People were dancing in the streets. We were still travelling when the moon joined the sun in the sky. On the road raindrops thudded like silver bullets into the dust. We left the bike at the side of the road and ran across the fields to shelter in a *kabanka*. And there, for the first time, we made love. Tracing trails of shivers across each other's skin with the tips of our fingers. Moving to the rhythm of the rain as the storm gathered force above us. Drowning in a smell like crumbled chocolate and newborn puppies.

In the morning we stepped out to shower ourselves clean in the rain. And lay sparkling on a bed of stones while the sun dried our skin. Though neither of us knew it, this was the last time we would be alone together. Soon after, Janneh headed back south where he became Information Officer of the National Students' Union. I graduated with honours in my West African School Certificate and won a scholarship to study in England. We tried to stay in touch, but you know how these things go. I missed him, of course. But so many things were happening in my life I could not carry on minding for too long.

After much counting and recounting the results of the first election ever to be held in our soon-to-be republic were announced. On the radio the BBC World Service described it as a mixed verdict. An opportunity missed, they said. An African election marred once again by the blight of the tribal vote. In almost every ward people had voted for members of their own ethnic group regardless, it seemed, of the qualities of other candidates.

One or two of the local newspapers, however, noted one small exception: the successful candidacy and surprise win of one Sulaiman Bio, representative of the People's Progress Party. A southerner, who had succeeded in defeating his rival candidates in an otherwise totally northern stronghold.

SECRETS

10

Hawa, 1965

The Music of Flutes

WELL, I SUPPOSE. Better I tell you than you hear it from one of the others.

Remember once you had some boyfriend you broke up with, and how you came home and refused to leave your room? You stayed inside moping, weeping, wouldn't eat. All this for a man you didn't even want. You told me you loved him, and yet it was you who refused to be with him. 'It won't work,' you cried. 'We are too different!' What does this mean? I thought to myself, this girl can have whatever she wants and still she's unhappy. Ever since then I have wondered at the world, how everything has changed and yet nothing has changed.

For me it was the other way. I had a husband, but he was not the man I loved. Everybody told me I could not have the man I wanted. Too different, they said, it won't work. And they kept repeating these words, as if they were praying for it to come true.

For weeks I couldn't get the stink of burned coffee out of my nostrils. The odour clung to my clothes, my hair, my skin; coating everything like an invisible film of shame. I didn't shed myself of it until I left the village and went to live in the town. I had been betrothed, but of course my marriage plans went up in smoke along with the plantation. The groom's family began to argue about the bride gift. Some time later another man was found for me who worked in the slaughterhouses. By then my choices were few. This man was so poor I became his only wife. I started my married life working like a servant.

Now instead of the smell of burned coffee I suffered the stench of dead animals. At night my new husband came to me. His skin smelled like an animal hide, his hands of blood, his breath of viscera. I pushed him away and told him to wash himself before he touched me. Then I would lie and listen to him out in the yard throwing water from the bucket over himself with a ladle. In the first year of our marriage he liked to whistle as he washed himself. Then he would come back to me, still whistling. But that kind of smell doesn't wash off. So I pretended to be asleep, knowing he would never dare bother me.

I can't say I either liked him or disliked him. I was prepared to live with him. To accept my fate for what it was. But always he wanted something more. My fate was no longer in my own hands. A marriage cannot be pulled apart easily as a dam in a river. When he caught me wrinkling my nose, he would tell me at least his was honest work, good work. And it was true we ate meat every day. Sometimes twice. Evenings he would arrive home with a parcel under his arm: maybe a rack of ribs, a sheep heart, a skirt of beef. If he was trying especially to please me he brought a cow foot. I'd put it in a pot with thyme, tomatoes and hot peppers. Boiled for four hours, it was tasty and tender as chicken.

There was so much meat; we had meat to spare. I wrapped up what was leftover and gave it to my other mothers, my father's wives who clasped my hands to their hearts as they thanked me. At those times I would give a small smile, incline my head slightly. Shrugging off their thanks. As if it cost me nothing to do.

And though I didn't encourage my husband I fulfilled my duties. I bore him three children. All boys. I lost two more. They were girls, and might have grown up to help me around the house. But there it is. Nothing to be done. What more could any man ask for? Each time my belly swelled, he would kneel, press his cheek against it and close his eyes. He stopped speaking for days after each of the two babies returned. Really, he was as tender and sentimental as a woman! Of course I regretted it, too. But deep down in my heart I saw it was for the best. I knew I could not stay this man's wife for long.

My third son was born with hoops of fat round his neck and his stomach. Such an appetite! I employed a pair of wet nurses and he drained them both. So I fed him myself. And what lungs! When he wanted me he screamed, his little body rigid with rage. My husband called him Lansana. But at other times, when I was alone with my son, I would brush my nose against his small one. '*Okurgba!*' I would whisper. Little warrior! My name for him. Born with the spirit of a fighter. I laid my son on the hide of an unborn calf. I knew I had borne the child who would take care of me.

After each child my husband left me alone for a while. When in time he ventured near me I told him I was too tired. At that he offered to help me with my chores. I insisted I could manage. Whoever heard of such a thing? Gradually he left me alone more often, but never quite enough.

The next child came early and nearly killed me. The doctor at the clinic smelled of tree sap, of indigo dye and starched cloths. He asked me how many children I had. 'Six,' I replied, counting them all: the living and the dead and this one.

They put a needle in my arm and sent me to sleep. In my dreams I laughed and danced to flute music as they pulled the dead baby from inside me. I woke up and wished I could sleep to dream those dreams again. I never asked whether it was a girl or a boy. After two days I went home. The months passed and I did not conceive again. I soaked bitter roots and cooked our rice in the water, my husband and I dipping our fingers into the pot to eat together. The months came and went. My breasts and my belly remained flat. At my husband's urging I went back to the clinic, to see if the doctor had other medicine, stronger than ours.

I remember how I stood and waited in front of the wooden desk while the nurse searched through the drawers for my records. Ah, yes, she said presently, pulling a brown envelope from among many others. She bent her head to read what was written there.

'Tubal ligation.' I didn't even know what the words meant.

'Your tubes have been tied. So you won't have any more children. It says here you have six already.' She pointed at the words on the paper. Six! The way she said it sounded like an accusation.

While I listened to flute music in my dreams, while they pulled the dead baby out. This is what they had done to me.

Oh, I know what you would have done in my place. You would have talked about rights and consent: small words with big meanings. But I did not know how to think that way. I did not even insist she call the doctor for me. I asked no questions. I nodded as though I knew this already, accepting her words. I turned around and went home. Who was I to argue? In my mind I thought the doctor, whose qualifications hung on the wall behind polished glass, must have known better than me.

I told myself I still had three children. I had Okurgba, my youngest. And when I told my husband, no more children, I was thinking that perhaps then he might leave me alone.

And so my life continued. It was not the life I had chosen for myself, not the life that should have been mine. But I lived it anyway.

One day I saw the woman who had my life. She passed me, followed by a servant girl carrying a stack of differently coloured cloths. She did not recognise me. Why should she? She didn't know I existed or that I had once been betrothed to her husband. I followed her to the tailor's shop where I watched the owner jump up from her seat to greet her. I stood in the shadows of the entrance, next to a pile of offcuts. I bowed my head and pretended to search among the scraps. But I need not have worried, for nobody came to serve me.

I watched how they attended to her, flattering, praising her taste, holding samples of embroidery under her chin. She ordered maybe six or seven gowns, I never heard the cost discussed once.

Above me a shelf held stacks of coloured threads. Music from a plastic radio buzzed like a swarm of bees around my head. The sound of the treadles drummed in my ears. I wanted to knock the radio and spools from the shelf, upturn the Singer sewing machines, tear up the paper patterns. I wanted to run away as far as I could. But I did none of these things.

Instead I watched this woman through the half-light of the tailor's shop. This woman living the life I should have lived. I knew I was no beauty. But I was prettier than this one. Maybe you wouldn't believe it to look at me now? But then I possessed a complexion so fresh and smooth that even a fingerprint showed upon it. I had dimples high in my cheeks, and above my elbows, in the hollow of my back above each buttock. My waist was slim, my back curved just the right amount. By contrast this woman was as black and shapeless as a midday shadow.

On her way out she passed close by me. I turned away, but still I smelled her. Cloying and sickly. I almost choked on the odour. Vanilla.

You know what people here sometimes say, that death makes saints of us all. I was thinking about that only the other day. After my mother died suddenly all her co-wives who had thought of nothing but how to usurp her began to say what a sweet tempered person she was, how kind, how generous.

When somebody dies, look at how all the women go to sit for hours in the family's front room, offering words of comfort when only the day before they bad-mouthed the lot of them. Look at the men giving money to the widows, even though they spent the last year trying to put this same man out of business. Today everybody will tell you what a good man your grandfather was. How wise, how honest. But there was a time when these people turned on us and drove us from our home. And now they pretend as if it never happened.

Of course nobody likes to speak of that time now. What's past is past, they say. Too quickly. Wanting to shut you up. Well let them try now. Because now you are here, you want to know. And now I will tell you.

It was soon after I stopped working for the European, Mr Blue.

On that morning I woke up to the sound of singing. Not the joyful sound of a wedding party. No, something angry in the distance. I stepped out of the door of our house. All around me were people running, throwing sand on the cooking fires, slamming shutters. A child was standing by the well, wailing at all the uproar. A woman ran and grasped her by the arm, dragging her along the ground, causing the child to cry even louder. She pushed the child inside the door of her house and ran off in search of her other children.

The wind was blowing in great gusts that day. It raced through the village like an omen: whipping up whorls of red dust, scattering the grain drying in the sun, rolling balls of chicken feathers down the street.

Inside the big house Ya Namina was shouting orders to the servants. One of my small brothers stood at the open back door. My father pushed a box into his hands. The box was wrapped in tattered cloths, so I knew it must be very ancient. Out of the back of the house, I watched my brother dart into fields, his legs spinning like wheels. Then suddenly he tripped. I caught my breath as I watched him stumble for a few paces until he righted himself. My father looked around, saw me standing there.

'Hawa, go with him. Help him! Run! Run!'

Out of the open door, through the banana groves, into the dappled shadows of the trees. I ran silently, not daring to shout to my brother. Just past the silk cotton tree, I caught him up. For a few seconds we ran abreast, like a pair of panicked animals. Then we turned off the path, out of sight, and dropped to the ground.

We waited. Catching our breath again. Then we climbed up to our old lookout at the top of the sapele tree from where we could see the houses. From there we watched the people marching through the village, up to our compound and the steps of my father's house. The wind picked up their voices and threw them like echoes across the treetops. To this day I remember the words:

'We have spoken. Who so denies us, he is lost.'

Then the singing turned into shouting, the shouting into a great howling. The wind joined in, shaking the branches of the tree, threatening to send us hurtling to the ground. We were frightened and slid back down the tree trunk to the forest floor.

Later in the day we waited with our backs against the tree. My brother complained he was hungry, but I did not have time for that kind of talk. I told him to dig the crickets out of their holes in the earth. He wandered around scratching at the ground and came back with a bundle wrapped up in his shirt. But we were too afraid to light a fire to roast them and so we waited with hunger growing in our bellies until we ate them raw and fell asleep.

Sometime in the night I woke abruptly. Somebody close by. I held my breath. A pangolin was watching us from a short distance away, weaving her head from side to side. Her den must have been close by. I sat up, the pangolin backed off. I could hear the caw of night birds. The air carried the smell of night blooms and rotting leaves. Somewhere close by a pod fell off a tree and split open, scattering seeds with giant-sized sounds, causing me to start. The fear settled in my bowels. I stood up, walked some small distance, propelled into the darkness by a sudden urgency.

How I wished to be at home! Safely asleep on my bed. How long we were supposed to stay out there in the forest, I had no idea.

Without realising it I was heading in the direction of the houses. Suddenly I heard voices, fleeing footfalls in the darkness. I pressed my back against a tree. The blood rushed around my head. I stood still, listening to the thud of my own heart, like the beating of a thousand bats' wings. I pushed the heel of my hand against my chest to still the sound.

Shapes. Shadows. They passed me so close I could have reached out my hand and touched them. Bodies gleaming in the moon-light. I turned and pressed my face against the tree. I stayed that way for I don't know how long, feeling the smooth bark against my cheek, wishing it was my mother's skin. I whispered her name. The wish turned into a dream. For a moment I was in her arms. Then just as quickly the dream lost its colour, and turned back into a wish. Try as I might to hold on to the comforting feeling, it slipped away. I was alone and afraid again.

The moon shone like a blind man's eye. In the dim light I saw the form of a man, coming towards me through the trees. He drew close, saw me and stopped. We stood still, gazing at each other through the grey. As I looked at him I had a strange feeling, like a scent that carries the memory of a touch, or a taste that brings a glimpse of something past. I had seen this man before. I felt sure of it. I did not move. I stood there as fleeting images formed behind my eyes. I saw the bolted gates of the miners' compound. The men standing silently beyond. The police. Twists of smoke coming out of the barrels of the guns. Red and pink stains blossoming like flowers on the wet ground. And as the memories formed and dissolved I saw him staring at me, making up his mind what to do.

You see, I believed this man was dead. The same man who even before that was once mixed up in some trouble with one of the younger wives.

So now I made up my mind that this was no mortal man but a *falang*, come back to settle old scores against the people who had murdered him. I didn't try to run away. For some reason I felt no fear. I was certain the time had come to die. In the pale light I could just make out the mark on his lip, the stain like a splash. He stepped towards me. My legs went weak. I closed my eyelids to shut out the darkness crowding in. When next I opened them I was alone again in the forest.

The rest of the night I spent with my body wrapped around the box of sacred objects entrusted to my father. I slept with my cheek resting on the lid. Inside the box was the skull of the *obai* who went before. We grow up and we are told a chief never dies. Instead his spirit flies out of the old body and into the new one. The elders keep the head of the last chief to bury with the body of the next. So the line goes on unbroken.

We slept and woke up damp with fright and dew. And when we woke up the rule of the new chief was already over.

And afterwards we heard how the rioters sang the same song all over the land. In town the pink and anxious Assistant to District Commissioner Silk gave the order to fire upon a crowd gathered around his office. Some fell. Those who didn't took off through the chiefdoms, marching upon the compounds and houses of the chiefs, lighting bonfires of paper money, throwing radios and refrigerators from the windows, chasing the chiefs' wives into the banana groves.

For days the ash and soot floated down like black rain. And that awful smell. Years later, even to make a cup of coffee for the man I was married to made my stomach churn.

The colonials held a Commission of Inquiry and blamed the disturbances on the chiefs. So they curtailed the powers of some, and others they deposed. Nobody could understand how this could be, since a chief is a chief for ever. Others said it was right. And yet others asked who had given the chiefs such power they were able to rule in defiance of their people?

Of course, the *pothos* were no fools. They knew better than to stay too long afterwards. They packed their bags, gave us back our country and whoosh – like the wind they were gone.

I met Khalil under my father's roof, where he had come to live with my family as a ward. Nearly ten years had passed since the rebellion against the chiefs. My father no longer attended court. He lived in his house in town. The day I first saw Khalil I arrived struggling with my son in my arms. Okurgba escaped and jumped in a puddle, scattering some ducklings. Khalil ran down the steps and caught him for me. After that I would see him often; sometimes as soon as I turned the corner and came into view of the house, Khalil would appear and walk alongside me.

Later people said things about me. How could I, a married woman? And him so much younger than me. Still a schoolboy. Well, that was true. Ah, but he had a way about him, I don't know. He knew things. In many ways it was as if he was the older of the two of us.

You see, I didn't know anybody who had been to school. Mariama, yes. She was sent to the missionaries because nobody knew what to do with her. Your Aunt Serah, well she was born later than me. By then things were different.

How could you possibly understand? You would jump on an aeroplane sooner than you would ride in a *poda poda*. I had never left my home. I had never even seen the sea.

Khalil described the oceans for me. Told me of lands covered in snow. Of red deserts where nothing existed but sand and rock. The sun was a great orb of burning gas, he said. The moon was the size of the earth and only looked small because it was many miles away. Even the stars, though they might look like holes in the sky, were really planets whose light reached us years after some of them had already died.

One day I came back from the market with a package of oxtail. I had left some at my own house – by that time I had a girl to help me with the cooking and the children. The remainder I brought with me.

Khalil teased me, saying oxtail was his favourite: 'I hope there's enough for me.' Of course he was only a ward, he would have to wait until my father and others had eaten.

I smiled and spoke with the same laughing tone. I wagged my finger at him: 'You wait until I count up what's left,' I said.

'How many did you get?'

I told him thirty. But then I had left two each for everybody at home. I remembered then I had forgotten about the girl, doubtless she would want to eat.

Khalil stopped walking and asked: 'So how many are left?'

I told him I would count them.

It's so simple for you. Of course I could count. But to add, subtract, multiply. To play with numbers the way you juggle balls. How do you know how to do these things unless somebody shows you? Khalil was the one who taught me. At first I was slow, embarrassed by my ignorance. But he persisted. Every day we drew numbers in the dust, subtracting, adding, then multiplying, dividing: heaps of beans, grains of rice, bowls of oranges, even the stars in the sky. And by the time we had finished I counted the number of times I thought about him in the space of an hour, I multiplied that by the number of hours in the day. And I realised I had fallen in love.

Step by step I moved into my family home. I found reasons to visit, reasons to stay over, reasons not to go home. I sent trays of food over to my husband to keep him from complaining. But I could not stop the rumours from reaching him. And when he finally sat up and looked around him, he realised that I had left.

After the rebellion a change had come over my father. Slowly at first. For days at a time he stayed shuttered up against the sun. In the darkness of his room his skin stretched until it was thin and dry as paper. The flesh moulded itself to his bones. His voice faded to a whisper.

When he had accepted my bride price my father knew he was marrying me to a man who was beneath me. The amount was so little. Like I was worthless, the last item left behind at an auction. And yet all the time I was growing up I had listened to the stories of Asana's bride price, seen the listeners' eyes grow as big as coins as the figure rolled out. She who hadn't even held on to her man.

So one day I went to ask him to pay back this small amount of money, to free me from my marriage. My face burned as I stood there in that closed, dark room, listening to him tell me of the disgrace I was bringing upon the family. I remembered how it had been when I was a child and my mother made me sing for him. The terror I had of him then. Now I listened to my father talk to me as though I were that very child. I bowed my head, reached out and touched his feet.

But at the same time as I begged my father not to disown me, different thoughts began to enter my mind. I was thinking that my father was stuck with his head in the past. Oh, yes, perhaps he had been a big man, son of a chief's daughter and a warrior, and all that. But that time was distant now. Peasants had set fire to his plantation. Dragged him from his house and set him on top of the rubbish heap, pelted him with jibes and taunts. Yes, these were the things that had happened. Never to be undone.

And as I left his room my father's new wife passed me by carrying a platter of rice. Not a young girl offered to him by a humble family hoping for his patronage. Nor the daughter of a chief. A middle-aged widow whose family were glad to be free of the burden! Brought here by Ya Namina to help care for my father.

Over the days that followed I made up my mind to ask my brothers to do what my father would not. Ibrahim and Idrissa. They were successful men now. Idrissa, an Army Major. Ibrahim a businessman with a big import–export business.

And then, as if to pre-empt my plans and prove he had never cared for me, my husband upped and left. Two days before Eid-al-Fitr. For Kabala, to where the Fula had driven their herds and work was plentiful.

Well, I moved back to my house. And after a while, when he had graduated from school, Khalil came to stay with me. I had no reason to go to my father's house any longer. And so I did not. Khalil's parents were angry and they sent his brothers to complain to my father. But I didn't care. You see, it was my own father who had exchanged me for free meat. Who was he now to criticise me for living in this way with Khalil? There were those who said I had brought shame on the family. But the truth was – we were already shamed.

Besides – and it took me a while to realise this – there was really nothing anybody could do.

I was happy, even though it was hard for us to make ends meet. We ate fish. Fish stew, fried fish, pepper soup with smoked fish – into each dish I poured the gladness inside my heart. I wrote a letter to my brother Idrissa who was stationed at his Army barracks further north. Well, Khalil wrote it. It was good to have a man who could write. And he signed my name on the bottom. Almost always my brother enclosed a little market money in with his reply. I sent Ibrahim a letter at the same time as I wrote to my eldest brother. I dictated my words to Khalil: 'This letter serves to remind you of your sister, who is always praying for your success.' Khalil signed my name at the bottom. Madam Hawa Kholifa.

Now when I look back, through my whole life, my two brothers were the only people who looked after me. Yes. Even Khalil, in the end, betrayed me.

My joy lasted three years.

The problem began when I had to send the girl back to her family. I saw the half-smiles she had begun to give Khalil. Some weeks later, after a visit home, Khalil told me his mother complained she had no grandchildren.

I said: 'Let's wait and see.' I smiled and settled against him. Khalil wrapped his arms around me.

But from that day on his mother determined to cause problems for me. The next time he returned from visiting her he repeated her words to me: 'She says you're too old.'

I saw something in his face when he said this. Something that told me he agreed with his mother. It was as though a snake had bitten my heart. Yet how could I possibly tell him the truth? I couldn't go back to the clinic to find the doctor. He had gone, closed his practice and moved to the city to make more money. Either way there could be no more children for me. No children for Khalil.

I have to tell you why I did what I did. So you understand. You make fun of me behind my back. So glum. You pull your own mouth down at the sides with your fingers. Oh, no, Aunty Hawa has always been that way, you say when your children ask what they have done. Well, I was not always this way. I had a chance to be happy once. But let me tell you how much I loved this man. I loved him so much I sacrificed my own happiness for his sake.

I found Khalil a wife. I even begged one of my brothers to give me the money for her bride price, convincing them that this was what I wanted. I complained there was too much work for me, what with the trading I did at my stall in front of the house. I needed somebody to cook and to mind the children.

Zainab. I chose her myself. Her parents were dead so that made it all the easier. I watched her for many weeks before I made up my mind to approach her. Why her? Not fussy and vain like the other girls with black-lined eyes, always slipping away on any pretext when they should have been at their chores. Chattering to each other on the street corner. You could see from Zainab's hands she was a hard worker. And for the most part she was quiet.

My problem, my mistake, was that I was always too trusting. Too ready to see the best in people. I had to learn to think differently. Sometimes when I look at my own face I see what you see. Eyes narrowed – against the glare of the real world. Smile bent out of shape. Grooves either side of my nose – worn by tears. This is what you see. But I know I didn't always look like this.

At first the arrangement seemed suited to us all. Even me, I accepted it. The girl turned out to be as hard a worker as I had hoped: she could husk a bushel of rice in a morning. And the children liked her well enough. Khalil's mother was satisfied, at least she stopped sending her complaints to my house inside her son's mouth.

One night in the early hours of the morning, I woke from dreaming about a puppy I once owned as a child. I was holding it in my arms, only the dog was purring like a cat. Listen, I said, holding it up to my mother. She bent her head, but before she could reply the dream vanished. I was alone in my room. I could feel a weight at the bottom of the bed. I didn't really believe in djinnas, none that would come visiting like that, at any rate. A rat, perhaps, or a snake. I sat up. Do you know what I saw? My neighbour's cat. It jumped off the bed, ran across the floor and leaped out of the open window, the moonlight glinting on its fur.

The air, heavy and still, parted and closed around me as I walked through the house. At the back door I slid the bolt and stood breathing deeply. A short time later I pushed the door shut. And as I did so I heard the sound of another door closing, like an echo. I made my way back the way I had come, ears cocked, treading softly. I stood outside my door, but instead of going inside I reached out, opened the door and closed it again. A moment later and sure enough out she came. Like a mouse. Scuttle, scuttle. Along the wall and into her room.

Twice a year I would return to Rofathane to visit Ya Isatta who remained there living in my mother's house. This time Zainab came to help carry the provisions. Lately there had been something. Something in the air. For one the girl's attitude had changed. The previous evening I had called for her to bring me water. She served me, tilting the bottle over the back of her hand, letting the water slide into the cup. Everyone knows this is a most insolent way to serve a person. I tried to catch Khalil's eye, but he looked at the ground. I let it pass. But it vexed me, made my scalp itch with annoyance to think about.

I was always a swift walker. I have my mother's height. Not like these girls you see swinging their buttocks and slithering the soles of their feet across the ground. Gradually I put a little distance between us. They were talking; they didn't even notice. As I drew level with a maize field, I stepped off the path and waited, hidden in the tall stems. Zainab and Khalil grew closer, I strained to hear their voices. They were speaking in murmurs. A name drifted up. Suffyan. Khalil's father. That man who thought I wasn't good enough for his son! What were they saying about him? Something about the harvest. That was six months away. I leaned forward to let the words reach my ears. Too far! I tipped forward, unbalanced and stumbled. I snatched at the maize, but the stalks snapped in my hands. I fell to the ground, landing back out on the path right in front of Zainab and Khalil. Their faces were still full of shock as Khalil helped me up and Zainab brushed my clothes. I straightened my headdress. Nobody spoke. We walked on.

In the days that followed Zainab became as lazy as an overheated sow. Twice I caught her sleeping in the middle of the day. On the bamboo bench at the back of the house, lying on her side, with her mouth open and her arm across her belly. I shook her shoulder. 'What's this?' I said. I watched her rouse herself, wipe her mouth and move off slow as an anteater. Of course she wasn't sick. Too strong for that. And anyway, if she was she would have said so soon enough.

Later, alone − I saw it. And at that moment the only thing I couldn't understand was why I had been so foolish, so blind. Why had it taken me so long?

Zainab was having a baby.

I could see it all ahead of me, plainly. Like fields of rice rolling into the distance. A mighty river winding its way through the trees. The depthless blue hovering over the thin flat line of the horizon. This woman had come to take my life away.

A sister of mine was sick, I said. Khalil did not question me, did not ask which one. I packed a box with three of my best dresses, leaving all the rest stowed in my wooden chest. I took my small, blue teapot and the money I had from my last husband hidden in a cigarette tin. Later I sang Okurgba a song, one my mother sang to me. I sang it to you sometimes when you were a child. When you would let me. When you didn't call for someone else to put you to bed, you preferred anyone to me. Probably you don't remember now. 'Why is a bump taller than a man?' goes the chorus. 'Because the bump sits on top of the man's head.' Okurgba liked to sing the reply. That night his eyes were already closed before I finished the first verse.

My son was still sleeping when I left the next morning. By the time I reached the roundabout in the centre of town a creamy dawn sky stretched over the earth like a great canopy. Some people were already waiting at the place where the buses arrived and departed, next door to the Agip petrol station. Dusty faces and feet told of the distances they had travelled. Inside the empty buses the drivers were still asleep, stretched out on the seats.

A child leading a blind man passed me once, doubled back and reached out his tiny hand. I found a few cents. So that one day fate might repay my act of kindness. 'God will bless you,' said the blind man three times, as though I had given them a fortune. I bought a pair of roasted plantains for breakfast and some oranges for later. Presently the drivers began to emerge from their vehicles. Towels slung round their necks, they disappeared to wash. On their return they climbed in behind the steering wheel and waited with the doors open.

I took the seat behind the driver, put my box under my feet. The bus did not set off until it was full, until somebody had been squeezed into every last place. The driver removed my box and stowed it on the roof. Out of sight, so I could worry about it for the rest of the journey. Still, I was glad I had the sense to sit where I did. Whole families jammed the aisles and others sat on the roof, wedged in among the sacks of rice and livestock.

Just outside the town we passed burning fields. The smoke blew straight through the open windows making my eyes smart, biting at the back of my throat, coating my tongue with a bitter taste. I thought of all that lay ahead of me. I had never been to the city on the coast. I cannot say I was afraid. No. The anger in the pit of my belly burned up all the fear. Whenever we hit a pothole, which was often, the bus bucked like a bull. The women around me squealed and covered their mouths with the backs of their hands. But I sat still, silent, thinking my own thoughts.

From time to time I gazed out of the window, saw the landscape shift from red to green, as trees and bushes grew up out of the earth. Great boulders sprang up. Once we passed a deserted quarry: black, silhouetted machines like giant insects. Ahead of us I could see hills, beyond which lay the city. Otherwise there was no traffic, just people carrying firewood, or making their way to the town. A line of ducks crossed the road in front of us, the driver braked suddenly to avoid bad luck. A man on the roof was nearly thrown off, his legs dangled next to the open window as his companions struggled to pull him back up. Oh, he was cursing and spitting. People called to him it was the ducks. Then he understood and began to laugh. Another time I might have laughed too.

The road was like a river, whose banks were lined with villages. At each stop buskers held their wares up to the windows of the bus: bananas, groundnuts boiled or roasted, jelly coconuts. I realised I was hungry already. 'Half–half,' I told the boy, who chose a coconut from the pile and sliced off the top with his machete, turning it into a scoop for me to use. I drank the milk, but the flesh was nothing more than a thin layer coating the inside of the shell. I paid the boy, subtracting half as a penalty. He fussed, but what could he do? The sound of the engine swallowed his protests and moments later we left him standing on the side of the road.

I kept my eyes fixed on the hills. But as the hours passed they only seemed to recede. Finally the bus began to wind uphill, the engine whining under the strain. The driver ordered all the cheap fare passengers off the roof and made them walk. At the brow of the first hill the rest of the passengers stood around, sucking oranges and spitting the pips into the long grass, waiting for them to catch up.

I crossed the road away from the others. Down below, here and there, single columns of smoke spiralled up above the trees. Beyond the forest I saw a river, grey and glittering, a viper winding across the plain. Further on and the viper transformed into the tree, whose branches reached upwards and outwards until they touched the sky and merged into it.

'It's so great even the birds cannot fly across it, or so they say. They drop out of the sky with exhaustion.'

It was the driver standing at my shoulder. He was gazing at the horizon.

'What is?' I asked. He looked at me, smiled and pointed at the sky, at the place where it turned from one kind of blue to another.

'The sea,' he replied. 'Is this the first time you're seeing it?' I replied that it was. 'Then you are very lucky to have done so,' he said.

As we travelled across the tops of the hills, climbing and turning, I kept catching glimpses of it. Each time I turned my head, gazing at the view until it disappeared behind the next bend. I felt light-headed, my heart lifted. For a moment I forgot my sorrows, the place I had come from. I had only one thought in my head. I had seen the sea.

When I was a little girl and I was unhappy, when my mother was angry with me or my brothers teased me, I used to hold my breath until I fainted. When I woke up I would be in my own bed. Everybody crowded round me with big, worried faces. Happy to give me whatever I asked for. In that way I could make problems go away.

How I wished I was still that girl, to be able to make bad things better so easily. I stood in the place where I stepped off the bus for a long time, summoning the courage to move. Dust and people and terrible noises swirled around me, lashing me to the ground like ropes. I wanted to hold my breath until it all went away.

The first people I asked directions answered in a language I couldn't understand. By chance the fifth person I turned to happened to be a townsmate. What luck! He carried my box on his shoulder while he showed me to the place I needed. 'Watch yourself, sister!' he told me as he set down my box.

Five days I was in that city. Five days that seemed like five months! It was already late afternoon when I arrived. I sat on my box and waited as the light dwindled. Two men playing a game of chequers on an upended crate threw glances at me in between games. In time one of them came over and asked me my business. I explained to him. I pointed at the building. He turned to his friend, who shook his head. Together they made me understand the address I had been given was the wrong one.

What was I to do? I had no relatives in the city. In those days there were no such things as hotels, and even if there were I could never have afforded to stay in such a place. I was stranded. The men seemed to understand this. One of them beckoned me to follow him. I suppose I should not have trusted a stranger so easily, but what choice had I? Besides, in those days it was different. People helped each other. Not like now. I followed him through the streets, long straight ones that soon became narrow and short. Here the houses were small and wooden, built side by side with no room in between. On the steps a woman braided another's hair by the light of an oil lamp, a man sat in front of a python skin for sale, a thin puppy licked the dirty water from the puddles. We passed piles of stinking refuse and gutters foaming with filth. Next we were in an open space with a big cotton tree, children playing with a straw ball in the dusk. And presently we reached a small house where a woman sat next to a candle on a saucer, with a child sucking at her breast. From the way they greeted each other I did not imagine the man and she were very closely related to each other.

In exchange for a sum the woman gave me a place on the floor to sleep, yams and pepper soup with skimpy shreds of meat to eat. Later I lay listening to the sound of a man and a woman arguing in the street. My nostrils were filled with the stench of the pit latrine outside my window. I lit a small stick of incense. I dreamed and woke and for a moment imagined I was somewhere else.

In the morning the landlady taught me some words to use to find my way around. But the words were not enough. I went from one place to the next, grinding the stones of the streets into dust beneath my heels, while the sweat poured off me. Each day I exchanged a little more of my money for the woman's food and a place to sleep, subtracting what I had spent from the little I had left.

All the time I felt the hope in my heart growing smaller and smaller, like the first piece of ice I held in my hand and watched melt away, until the last sliver disappeared and the enchantment was gone.

Still I persisted. You see, I had come to that city for a reason. I had to find the doctor, the one who had tied my tubes. To ask him if he might undo what he had done, so that I could bear children again. It was the only thing I could think of to stop Zainab from replacing me.

Maybe you think I was stupid to go to a city full of strangers, in search of a man whose face I couldn't even remember. Only his hands and the certificates on his wall and the smell that clung to his clothes. But as it happened, on the fourth day I passed a building and I smelled that same odour. Something like starch and indigo dye and wood resin all rolled into one. I followed it to the place it was coming from. I entered the building, somewhere I had never been before. I found myself in the waiting room of a doctor's surgery. Not the same man I had come to find, but another one with clean soft-looking hands and certificates on his wall.

Yes, the doctor told me. The operation was reversible. Not easy, but possible. Even after that there was a chance I still might not bear children. I ignored the last part of what he said. I felt the hope begin to crystallise again. I was sure after all this time I was to be rewarded with some good luck. After all, hadn't I seen the sea?

But a moment later, I felt all the same newly formed crystals of hope melt, drain away out through the ends of my fingers and the soles of my feet. He told me the cost. Six pounds!? I had never even seen so much money.

I returned home on a different bus. All the time I barely lifted my head to look at the landscape. I set my mind to thinking. I would write to my brothers. Perhaps they would help. I only had to work out how to ask them for the money in a way that meant they couldn't refuse me.

These thoughts were still chasing each other in my mind as I walked the last of the way home. Too late, I realised I had forgotten to think up something to tell Khalil about my trip to see my sister.

The house was quiet. There was my son standing outside my neighbour's house. I knelt down and stretched out my arms to him, and he ran to me, throwing himself against me. I lifted him up and held him to my chest, pushed my nose into his hair and breathed his good smell. I walked up the path.

The house was empty. No cooking smells. No children. Something strange. Where were Khalil and Zainab? I turned around and around on the same spot. Okurgba laughed as if this was a game. I set him down. I thought many things. Somebody ill? One of the children? I never imagined what was to come. I opened the door of my room. Everything was exactly as I had left it. One by one, I pushed open the doors of the other rooms. Khalil's. Zainab's. Empty. Just walls and a floor. Sleeping mats rolled up in the corner. Pegs bare. All gone.

They had left me.

The neighbour informed me of the manner of their departure. They had left my three sons with her. She relished my discomfort and the petty power her knowledge gave her, that much I could see. Watching me with gleaming eyes and a curved smile like that cat of hers. I half expected her to lick her lips as she spun the story out to see my reaction. I emptied my face, simply to deny her the satisfaction. But it came down to this: they left no forwarding address; hand in hand, they ran away like children.

When she had finished she pretended to comfort me, inviting me to sleep in her home, but I brushed her aside. I had only one question. When? I asked her. When did they go?

And she told me. Later on the same morning, the very morning that I had left for the city. At almost exactly the time I first laid eyes on the sea.

11

Mariama, 1970

Other Side of the Road

IN THE VILLAGE WHERE we lived people didn't always greet each other in the usual way. Often they just said: 'Baba?' Like that, with a question in the word. A pair of doves somehow escaped from their locked cage and flew away, and people smiled knowingly: 'Baba.' If the bucket had been left at the bottom of the well, they said the same: 'Baba.' Or if a young girl had been made love to by some man whose name she refused to call, the other men nudged each other while the women spat into the dust. 'Baba!'

When I was perhaps ten I asked Ya Sallay – who by then had become my mother: 'Who is Baba?' And she told me that she had asked the very same thing soon after she had married my father and come here herself. She was told there was once a man who went by that name. Babatunde was an unreliable type of person, the kind who would borrow something and not bring it back. This man owed money to everybody in the village, and was never ready to repay it. So his creditors decided to hold a meeting and sent a message telling him to attend. But Baba somehow got wind of the purpose of the gathering, and on that day he fled the village.

Well, the men went out looking. Even sent messages to the neighbouring villages asking after him. For days people searched the neighbourhood, and whenever they crossed paths would say to each other: 'Have you seen Baba?' And after many months and years the question became simply: 'Baba?' And then there came a time when the other began to answer in jest, as if to say, I am very well thank you: 'Tunde.'

So this man's name became detached from him and used for all sorts of other things. And in the end he stopped being whoever he had once been and became all the things they said about him.

Ya Sallay laughed when she told me this story. But I didn't laugh. Rather I worried for Babatunde. I didn't care that he was a scoundrel. I felt sorry. I wondered where he was and what had become of him. I thought about him living far away, among strangers, without his name, not knowing who he was any more.

Once I went to live among strangers and I learned what it was like to lose yourself. To feel the fragments flying off you. As if your soul has unhitched itself from your body and is flying away on a piece of string like a balloon. Lost in the clouds. You think, I only have to catch the end of the string. But though it hovers within sight, you cannot grasp it. You try and try. And then there comes a time when you are too tired. You no longer care. So you say: 'Let it go. Let me just fall down here on the soft grass and go to sleep.'

I left home on the day our new President ordered everybody to drive on the opposite side of the road. In the crowded bus there was panic, because every time we looked up a car was hurtling towards us on the same side of the road. Unwary pedestrians stepped in front of vehicles. Drivers honked their horns. Cars swerved around each other. Our driver drove too close to the verge, skimming the wooden stalls. And when the bus reached the stop we all had to climb down into the traffic, because now the passenger door was on the wrong side.

By the time I reached the quay all I could think was how glad I was to be leaving. I showed my ticket, paid for by the Christian Mission who had given me a scholarship to study in England, to the man in a buttoned uniform who stood at the end of the gangplank. As the ship sailed off into the silence, some of the passengers, the Africans who had never left home before, gathered on the deck to wave goodbye to everything we were leaving behind. The sea swelled up and the sky stretched downwards. In front of our eyes the city disappeared and the coast shrivelled into a wavy line. And all of us saw how small our country really was.

A girl on her way to the United States boasted she would soon be seeing the cowboys and indians for herself. Foolish girl! Still I said nothing because although I knew in England women no longer wore bustles and carried parasols, there were no horse-drawn carriages or steam trains, no hot-air balloons, and no white rabbits with fob watches – I could not imagine what I was going to.

In England the air was flat and colourless; sharp to breathe like broken glass. The pavements came up hard and struck the soles of my feet. The people walked fast, but spoke quietly. And skimmed past, never touching each other. Everybody went about and minded their own business. Even when they spoke to you, they seemed always to be looking at something outside the window or on the other side of the room.

In the hostel where I stayed we lived in rooms on top of each other and next to each other. Names on the doors: Bidwell, Holt, Pichette, Clowes, Schenck, Buchan, Bersvendsen, Wilkinson. And I saw that was how people lived all over the land. Like colonies of the blind. On top of each other and next to each other, but without ever seeing each other.

A girl from Ghana was assigned to help me settle in. Emma. Without her I would have been lost straight away. I liked her. I wished she had been there for longer. Maybe, if she had, things wouldn't have turned out the way they did. She would never have let it happen. Together we went shopping for warm clothes. The freezing air seeped through the fibres of my cotton clothes. Emma walked as swiftly as all the people in this place. Weaving in and out of the crowd like a needle through silk, and me a thread trailing behind her. In the shop she fingered woollen pullovers piled high on tables. Never had I laid eyes upon anything so luxurious, though the colours struck me as lifeless and dull.

'Pah! Made in Hong Kong. And look at these prices!' She wrinkled her nose, dropped the pullover as though it gave off an offensive odour and talked in a loud, loud voice. 'Come on!' She marched out past the security guard whose eyes followed her from the shadows beneath the peak of his cap.

'They think we all steal,' she told me out in the street.

'Why would they think that?' I said. To my mind nothing had happened. I didn't understand why we were suddenly standing outside the shop.

'Just the way they are. Suspicious minds.' I was silent, I didn't know what to say.

Emma watched the television news a great deal. Every evening, jumping up to change channels to listen to the same things repeated by a different person, deaf to the complaints of anybody else who happened to be in the common room. I remember pictures of an aeroplane with a bent nose, that flew faster than the speed of sound. One day everybody would travel the world in this way. The Chinese put a satellite in orbit and joined the space race. I had never known such things were happening. I watched it all with wonder. I had never even seen a television before. I thought of our new President and how the only thing he had done was order everybody to drive on the other side of the road. Then another day a jet flew into a mountain. Two days later a second one smacked down on to the runway, like a tethered bird that had tried to fly. On the news they played the last words of the co-pilot taken from the flight recorder. 'Oh! Sorry, Pete.' A moment later every single person on that plane was dead. A week later a third aeroplane did the exact same thing, only this time the people were luckier and mostly survived.

I stared at the terrible images of rescuers picking over debris. In my dreams I saw fizzing, flashing pictures like the images on the television. I saw planes bellyflop out of the sky, smash nose first into mountainsides. I wondered if the people on the ground could hear the screams of the passengers. Or even if they screamed at all. Or just said 'Oh!' And were gone.

Emma whooped with joy when a black man punched a white man so hard in a boxing match he knocked him out. In South Carolina black children were driven to school in buses with armed guards. I saw the expressions on the faces of the crowds at the boxing ring. And I saw the looks upon the faces of the white people as they threw stones at a bus-load of small children. And I saw how similar they were.

Somewhere along the line I started to become confused. Missionaries had brought me here. Given me a scholarship so at last I could qualify as a teacher. I must be grateful. Of course, I was grateful. Emma, on the other hand, didn't seem grateful at all. If anything she seemed to be angry a great deal of the time. Though once, when she was short-changed by a stall holder over a bag of plums, she laughed like it was a huge joke.

'What would my mother say?' she asked me, holding the coins up under my nose on the flat of her palm. 'She thinks an Englishman's word is his honour.' And when she saw my nonplussed face she laughed all the more until the tears welled in her eyes. 'Oh, Mary!' Shook her head and put her arm around my shoulders.

Later, how I wished I had asked her all the things I wanted to know. At the time all I cared was that she wouldn't think me stupid. I didn't even know what the questions were, the answers to which I needed so much. Just ask, people would say. But how do you know what it is you don't know? When I needed someone to tell me, Emma was gone. Back to Ghana. At the end of her sabbatical she stopped by to wish me farewell.

'Take care. Don't think you can go behaving the way the girls here do. One of our sisters was murdered like that, out alone at night. They found her body, but they never found who did it to her.' She kissed my cheek and squeezed my arm and was gone.

Alone I walked to the teacher training college. I dared not deviate from the route Emma had taught me. After classes I hurried home, nervous of the dimming light. I worked hard. I copied the words of my teachers down on to my exercise book and spent my evenings memorising them line by line. Still, in my first oral test I scored poorly. It was difficult for me. People pushed words through closed lips, made lots of 'zh, zh' sounds. I couldn't understand. I watched the television. I went out and bought a dictionary, set about learning twenty new words every day.

Other times I watched the birds squabbling on the window sill, gorging on pieces of the town's rubbish. On the other side of the thick glass I was only inches away from them. I could see how they tottered on deformed, toeless feet – useless for roosting on the branches of trees. Only good for balancing on concrete ledges and hobbling along the pavements.

At night, when the heating went off, I pulled my overcoat on to my bed and told myself how lucky I was. Outside the silent rain drifted above the houses. Half-asleep, half-awake fragments of dreams drifted through my mind: bathing among the drifting weeds; running through the rooms of Ya Jeneba and Ya Sallay's house and finding each one empty; riding in a bus that veered from one side of the road to another, the passengers screaming, the bus hurtling off the road and down the side of the hill.

Mornings I woke early, watched my breath escape from me in thick plumes taking the memory of the dreams along with it. The dampness in the air reminded me of home, but that was all. I set my feet down on the freezing lino, in the tiled chill of the bathroom I waited for the water heater to produce a thin stream of hot water. Outside the sun shone brightly, invigorating me with hope. But by the time I stepped into the street the sky was suffocated by clouds and the sun was gone, like a promise broken every day.

Evening time I sat alone in the big refectory on the ground floor of the hostel. One day the cooks served roast chicken for supper. The flesh was pale, flaccid. Kept lukewarm under bright lights. The chickens here were so much bigger than at home, but tasted less good. How I yearned for a bowl of pepper soup, prepared the way my mother used to make it when I was ill with a fever: a little lime squeezed into the broth.

Still, I was hungry. The meat slipped down my throat. Afterwards I picked up the bone in my fingers and began to chew the ends. I cracked the shaft between my molars and licked out the marrow, careful to spit out the shards, making a pile of them on the side of my plate. A girl with pale hair and skin so thin you could see the blue veins in her neck came and set her plate down opposite me. For a moment she glanced at me and just as quickly looked away. Then she slid her tray off the table and moved to another place. Afterwards I noticed the way she kept glancing across at me. As though she had seen something dreadful, that never the less compelled her gaze.

That night I gazed into the mirror in my room. So many mirrors in this country. So much glass. In shops, on the sides of cars, on the outside of buildings. Everywhere I went I saw my image reflected back at me. Everywhere except in the eyes of the people. Nobody looked me in the eye. I saw how they watched the ground as I passed, only to feel their eyes boring into my back. Except, like the girl that evening, when they didn't think I was looking. Caught out, they closed their faces and shifted their gaze as if, all the time, they had been looking at something else.

As I examined my reflection I wondered what it was she had seen. At home people did not look at my sliding face as if it was so strange. Then I remembered the time after my mother went away, and the people in the village, my father's wives – how they fell silent when they had been speaking and saw me there. And how their eyes had begun to glide over me, as if I was invisible. And here was a girl who looked at me with a scared look, so scared she could not bring herself to sit near me, but moved away.

Dear Ya Jeneba and Ya Sallay,

I have arrived in England. I have my own bed and even my own room. How happy I am to be here and for this most wonderful opportunity to expand my knowledge and to advance myself. There are so many things to learn. I am endeavouring to study hard so that you and all of my family will be proud of me.

It has been easy to settle in. I feel at home here already. The people are very friendly. Already I have made two new friends with whom I explore the town in my time away from my studies.

Please send my regards to my father, my mothers, my brothers and sisters.

Your respectful daughter,
Mary

I enclosed a portion of my scholarship money. Enough to buy two sacks of rice, plus a little left over to pay for the letter-writer to read them my words. I also sent a photograph of myself, taken soon after

I arrived. The image was badly underexposed, my face a mass of shadows. At the last minute I picked up a pebble from the side of the road and pushed it into the envelope.

I went to live among strangers. Something happened. I have never told anybody, and nobody ever asked me, except you. It was nothing like what happened to the girl Emma told me about. The truth is, I can't remember so much about it. I have some memories, a few. But when I look back to that time everything I see is like the photograph of me, a cluster of shadows. I have some memories, a very few – but they exist without clues.

Emma had left. I was alone. I moved through time, passing from day to night to day. I don't know how many weeks or months went by. The days merged into each other, except for one day. One day was different.

I went for a walk. I had been feeding the pigeons on my window sill – pieces of dried up mashed potato. Increasingly I had taken to carrying my meals up to my room. In a strange way I had become quite fond of those ugly birds. They were not at all timid. I watched them land and take off, carrying pieces of potato in their beaks and I had the sudden urge to escape from my room for a few hours. I put on my duffel coat, pulled the hood up over my head and pushed my hands in my pockets. Outside the hostel I turned right, away from the college. The pavement followed the curve of the hill. I passed a shop selling newspapers and sweets. The road was lined with plane trees, their height and great leaves reminded me a little of home. At the bottom of the hill I found myself at a place where several roads met. In the middle was a small green, a duck pond, a parade of shops: Dewhurst Butchers, a bakery, a shop selling dressmaking fabric. In the window was a dummy draped in fabric fashioned into a flowing dress. I thought perhaps of buying cloth to send home; I didn't dare go inside.

On and on. Here the houses were fewer, mostly bungalows with gardens all the way around, some with garages. In front of one house plastic toy windmills stuck into the grass turned in the wind. The whirring sound they made was the same as the call of a little black and yellow bird at home. I walked on, passing rows of mismatched allotments until there were no more houses. By now the rain was coming down. The path narrowed, my shoes slipped in the mud. Empty fields on either side, no crops but hillocks of rough grass. I pushed back my hood and felt the rain on my face, numbing my lips and my nose. I lifted my head to the sky.

The scent of rotting fruit: a plum tree had scattered its fruit across the path. I sheltered beneath it for a while. I was hungry, I picked up a plum and bit into it. The fruit was acidic and fizzed faintly on my tongue. Still it tasted good. I gathered several more, searching for the ones that hadn't been attacked by the birds. For a while I ate greedily, then I collected up more of the fruit and pushed it into my pockets to feed to the pigeons on my window sill.

More time passed, how much I don't know. I wiped my chin on my sleeve. I was cold, I decided to start back, to get back into the warm. The rain had eased off a little. On the way I passed the house with the windmills. I stopped to watch them, their red and yellow sails rotating, picking up speed as sluggish gusts of wind blew through them. I stared at the turning wheels, felt them sucking the thoughts out of my mind. One by one, the thoughts whirled away from me until they were caught by the rotating blades and spun out in all directions, across the garden and up into the air. At first I tried to catch them, but changed my mind and flew after them instead. Then I was floating up in the sky, side by side with the birds, gazing down at the shrinking dot of the town, heading far out to sea.

A child's face. At the window, framed by curtains, a child was watching me, unblinking black eyes. For several seconds I stared back. The child didn't move and neither did I. Just gazed into each other's eyes. I felt peaceful. For a moment I caught a glimpse of my own face among the reflections in the glass, my head superimposed upon the child's shoulders. The image wavered. I saw the child's eyes grow wider and its mouth open, though the sound was drowned out by the rain and the flapping of wet wings. A woman appeared behind the child. I saw her look up and take a step towards the window, pushing out her chin and drawing it back with a jolt, something like shock.

I turned away, pulled my hood back over my head. I walked fast, until I broke into a run. My heart was beating. I began to feel afraid. I worried the woman might leave her house, come after me, demand to know what I was doing. Suddenly the fear reared up, like great shadows behind me, chasing me. Faster and faster, I ran all the way to the hostel.

The next day it was cold, too cold to get out of bed. I lay there, pulling the cover over my head to block out the slow light that burned through the window. I dozed and dreamed. And in my dreams I saw sometimes the child, and sometimes the face of Bobbio my childhood friend. Another time I was snatched up by a great, black bird, carried through the air and dropped into a nest, where I lay on soft feathers, surrounded by jostling chicks. I woke up to the sound of tapping, saw a pigeon's red and yellow eye staring at me as its beak struck the glass.

The room grew dark and light again. How many times I don't know. Once somebody knocked on the door of my room. I didn't answer, I waited until they went away. It was quiet again, I was pleased at that. Silence, except for the sounds of the pigeons on my window sill, but they were my friends. Another time, another knock. Still I didn't reply; the person came in anyway. She looked a bit like one of the nuns from the boarding home, so I let her urge me out of bed and slip my duffel coat over my shoulders. I put my hands into my pockets and felt the slimy mush that lined the bottom. I wondered what it was.

Next I was in a car. The driver kept turning around to look at me, asking me questions I couldn't hear so instead I looked out of the window. A stone horse reared up from a plinth. The rider, half-risen in the saddle, stared straight at me. A man leaning out of an advertising billboard, proffering a cigarette, fixed me with his gaze. A woman beckoned me with a sideways look, raised a steaming mug of drinking chocolate. A dog's bulging, brown eyes followed my progress from the kerb.

A man asked my name. 'Mariama,' I replied. I don't know why I said that. I had been Mary for a long time. We were out of the car now and in a new place. More questions followed. I couldn't find the English words so I answered him in my own language. He spoke to the woman who had brought me. Meanwhile I sat in my chair and looked at him. There was something strange about him. I stopped listening and watched him closely; still it took me a while to put my finger on it. Then I saw: he had no teeth! No gums, no tongue. Just a black hole behind his barely moving lips.

It was dark again when I woke up. A soft bed. A hard, square patch of white light fell on to the floor like a trapdoor. Behind the glass murmuring voices, careful footsteps. I sat up and twisted my body round so I could see out of the window behind me. It must have been the early hours of the morning. The street was empty, save for a lone figure who waited at the side of the street for a bus or a taxi. I was on the second, maybe third floor of a house. I looked up and down the street, at the puddles of light below the street lamps.

The figure below me moved, the slightness of his frame told me it must be a young man or a boy. I watched him idly for a few minutes. Something about him seemed familiar, something in his walk as he sauntered between one lamp post and the next, as though he had nowhere particular to go. Briefly he stepped into one of the circles of light. I caught a glimpse of his profile. The high forehead, the shape of the skull, the upturned edges of the lips, the man below me was an African. He looked up, straight at my window. Bobbio!

Yes, it was he. Oh, how happy I was to see him. I cannot tell you. I waved. I worried about making a noise, I don't know why exactly – the place was so hushed, you know. But I knew Bobbio was there for me. All I needed was to tell him I had seen him. I tapped on the glass. Bobbio grinned at me. Waved back. Oh, Bobbio. I pressed the palm of my hand flat against the glass and I stayed like that for a long time, looking at Bobbio who clasped his hands together, held them up and looked right back at me.

I slept soundly, the bed like a big boat, bobbing on the waves of a warm, blue ocean. In the morning I jumped up and went to the window. At first I couldn't see my friend, just a line of people waiting at the bus stop, shuffling in the cold. But I never doubted he would be there. I searched the line of people. The bus arrived. The queue inched forward. Ah, there! A glimpse. Behind the woman in the blue anorak and the boy with his hands stuck in the pockets of his striped blazer: bare feet and the hem of a duster coat. Other people came and stood, blocking my view. I didn't know what Bobbio was doing or how he had found me, but none of that mattered. Bobbio was there. And while he was outside I felt safe.

I remember that time, because although it was supposed to be a bad time for me, in some ways it was a very good time. The big shadow of fear shrank and slipped away under the door. I lay there and thought of nothing at all. I forgot about what I was doing in England. I cared nothing for the passage of time, instead I watched the patterns of light on the ceiling. Sometimes I sat at the window looking for Bobbio, until somebody came to put me back to bed. At the time it felt like years were slipping by, but now I think perhaps it was only days.

'Hello dear, visitor for you,' the nurse put her head around my door. It was she who brought me my meals and made me understand I was in the college sanatorium. She tended to talk a great deal as she moved about my room, turning off the night light, rearranging the bedclothes. I had always been sure to reply politely to her enquiries, I didn't want her to think me rude. Once the doctor with no teeth had been back, but had examined me only briefly and directed all his questions away from me.

'Eating much?'

'Yes,' the woman had replied. 'Nothing wrong with her appetite.'

'Said anything?'

'Nothing I understand. They've called. Apparently somebody's on their way. Somebody who can translate.'

That afternoon a young woman followed the nurse into the room. She was black and slim, dressed in European clothes, though she moved easily in them as if she wore a simple kaftan; not at all the way I always felt: tight and trapped. She swung her hip on to the side of my bed, perched there. Leaning forward, she took one of my hands in both of hers and looked at me. I saw deep, brown eyes, tilted upwards at the corners. Buffed skin. When she smiled she showed all her teeth at once and a wrinkle appeared across the bridge of her nose. I let her hold my hand. I even smiled back at her, she seemed so kind.

'Who are you?' I asked. The woman held me in her gaze for a few moments.

'I'm Serah. Serah Kholifa. Your sister.'

Yes. It was your Aunt Serah. I didn't recognise her, so many years had passed since I had seen her. She had been just a small girl. Now she was studying in Liverpool. Oh, yes, I knew this. But the distance was great. She had written suggesting I visit during the holidays, when they came. But they were a long time in coming, I never made it. On my college registration form Serah was listed as my next of kin. That day when she arrived at the sanatorium, she had only to take one look at me to see what had to be done. She took me away from that place.

We left in a taxi. I was impressed at that, how easily she made it happen. At the gate I swung my head this way and that.

'Have you forgotten something?'

I replied I was looking for Bobbio, my friend. She frowned and the wrinkle appeared on her nose again.

'Oh, yes. I remember him.'

'He was here.' I couldn't see him any longer. 'I never asked him what he wanted.'

My sister looked at me. 'Oh, Mary,' she said. 'I expect he came to tell you something.'

And she took me in her arms and held me.

How long ago, how faraway it had all seemed. The smell of the earth. The whiteness of the sun. The way night arrives like a thing unto itself, instead of the creeping darkness that comes to steal away the sunlight. I returned home the way I departed. I stood on the deck watching the coastline widen in front of me, felt the sea breeze, the molecules of air, salt and water attaching themselves to my skin. Even the whiff of fish and oil at the dock was like a perfume. And the people! The pride in them as they looked and never looked away. For the first time in a long while I saw myself again, reflected in their eyes.

That's it, my story. Why do I tell it to you? Not so that you may feel sorry for me. No. But because that day you came home – the very first time, when you brought your new man and your babies, I saw in you a glimpse of something that brought the memories of that time back. Not in a bad way. Not in a way that hurt, but rather an echo of something I have known. I watched you then, and I have been watching you ever since. At that time you were nervous, smiling and laughing maybe too much, trying too hard in front of your husband and your children, your fingers fluttering like butterflies in front of your mouth. And the same again when you came back to us a few weeks ago. Until yesterday when you came out, for once not wearing one of those T-shirts that show your nipples, but in a gown Aunt Serah let you borrow.

And today you asked me to braid your hair. All that combing and fussing with those hair creams that have to be imported from America had become too much trouble, you told me – here, with only river water to wash your hair. So I plaited your hair, just as I did when you were a small girl, me on a stool, you sitting between my knees. And while I worked the strands I let you listen to my story.

And now I look at the change in you and I feel happy. For I know what it is to forget who you are. To feel the pieces falling away. To look for yourself and see only the stares of strangers. To search for yourself in circles until you're exhausted. And I wonder if my story means something to you. If perhaps what happened to me, little by little, isn't the same thing you felt happening to you. The very thing that brought you back home.

12

Serah, 1978

The Dream

WELL, THIS STORY IS no secret. Heaven knows, there are no secrets in this town.

Congosa! Gossip. It's what people here do all the time, because they can't be bothered to work. They stick their noses into other people's business and think they know it all, but of course they don't.

The truth is we were the envy of the whole country. Because we were the dream, did you know that? Every parent prays for a special child, and then suddenly – a whole generation of us. As though some *maleka*, some angel somewhere up above had tripped and scattered her load of blessings all at once. We were the gilded ones. We went this way and that, flying on the wings of our dreams. Me to England. Yaya first to Germany to study design and then architecture in England. We did not miss what we were leaving behind, when we kissed each other goodbye there were no tears. Only Ya Memso cried a little to see us go, but even then there were more tears of joy mixed up with the tears of sadness.

Neither of us looked back at the old, only forward to the vision of the new.

People will always say women forget the pain of childbirth, which is strange because I remember it perfectly clearly. What you do forget, utterly, is why you once loved somebody. The physical pleasures, the joy of a newborn, the disappointments, the betrayals, these things you can remember – but when love itself is gone, it vanishes without a trace. It leaves nothing behind.

When I think about Ambrose now, all I can really remember is his voice.

He had a way of speaking. He would tell me I was beautiful. 'You aah beautiful,' a long exhaled sound, like a sigh, as though he couldn't quite believe it himself. Often, when he spoke on the telephone the person at the other end didn't realise they were talking to a black man. He was particularly proud of that. And then there was the way he dressed, so stylish and so neat; when I first met him I thought he must be from Senegal or another of those French places.

There was a black American girl on our course. African American as they say now. She liked to hang around the African students, and when she talked everything was 'black this' and 'black that'. She called me sister. 'Sistah'. That's the way she said it. For some reason it made me giggle, even though I liked the way it sounded. I didn't think like her. *We* didn't think like her. We hadn't reached that place yet. To be honest, I'm not sure we ever did.

She told me I walked like a queen. I longed to be Carmen Jones. I took up smoking: Sobranie Cocktails, with gold tips and pastel-coloured papers; spent hours hot-combing my hair in the same style as Dorothy Dandridge. Later I changed and had an Afro, because by then they were all the rage. People told me I looked just like Cleopatra Jones.

Well, Ambrose certainly treated me like a queen. When we went out he would hold doors open for me to walk through. If I was carrying a parcel he would insist on taking it from me. He invited me to eat in restaurants where he called for the wine list and talked to the waiters without bothering to look at them. When the food came, those same waiters served me first, only coming to Ambrose second. And he behaved as though this was the way it should be, and I pretended I was used to it although the opposite was true. The way I was raised, only after all the men had eaten did the women sit down to share what was left. And it was the women who fetched the water and carried the heavy loads.

I loved him so much I even used to buy Ambrosia Creamed

Rice. Just for the name. Bloated, sweetened, milky grains: nothing like rice at all.

These are the things I remember. As for the rest, the years – like an army of silverfish – have eaten them away.

Some months after we met we spent a weekend in Lyme Regis. Ambrose had promised to show me Venice. 'Show you Venice,' he had said, and the words slid off his tongue. Of course I knew he had never been there, but what did it matter? The way he spoke made me believe in him. It would have been impossible for us to travel, we were overseas scholarship students, we would have needed visas. Still, for a few weeks I let myself dream about it.

In Lyme Regis a family dressed in oilskins, slick as seals, watched as I waded into the sea. Underfoot the pebbles were slippery, the water so cold it made my ankles ache; I waved to Ambrose standing in his polished brogues and sheepskin jacket on the shore. Back at the guest house, where the hall smelled of smoked fish and the sweet-sherry odour of elderly English people, I warmed my hands and feet against the clanking radiator in our room and later my feet were swollen, shiny and itching. In the mornings we lay together in bed until we heard the woman who ran the place banging on the door, insisting we let the maid in to clean the room.

That's as much as I remember about Lyme Regis. The greasy feel of the rain, the ceaseless rolling of the ocean, the metallic taste of stewed tea and the guest house owner hurrying along our love-making. I didn't know it at the time, but by then I was already pregnant.

I spent far too much money on the wedding cake. Three tiers, with a little model bride and groom on the top. The bride had ridged, yellow hair and blue dots for eyes, the groom's face was a pink splodge under a slick of black. Ambrose laughed, joking they didn't look much like us. Still I had set my heart on such a cake.

I changed my name to his. It had become the fashionable thing to do among African women, to take our husbands' names. Now, of course, your generation are all busy holding on to their fathers' names, to show how emancipated you all are. Well, then, it was the other way around. To the African way of thinking, we took our husbands' names to show how sophisticated, how Westernised we were. And most of all how different from our own mothers who kept the names they were born with all their lives.

Ya Memso wasn't happy about the marriage. She didn't think Ambrose's uncles were serious people, the way they behaved over the bride gift, you know. By all accounts my father was most exacting, because by then I was an educated woman. Ambrose's family didn't like that, not at all. They were city people, they thought they were doing us a favour. They were already vexed at having to travel all the way up to the provinces. In their view my father was a bumpkin with too many wives and far too many children.

So Ya Memso walked all the way to town and hired a letter-writer. Then she carried the letter to the post office. But she had no address for me in England. What to do? The clerk standing behind the plywood counter smiled and took her money. It was a small matter, he assured her, he would look it up. And she believed him. Went away comforted in the knowledge that the addresses of everybody in the whole world were contained within one giant ledger.

It happened that once a month the overseas students gathered at the registrar's office in the university to collect their Government grants. One such day everybody received a brown envelope with their name in the window as usual, with the exception of Ambrose and the other students from our country. At first nobody worried. Some kind of a mistake. But the next day Ambrose returned home empty-handed, and the next.

Four days later one of the students appeared in the common room with a newspaper. On an inside page was a short article, just a paragraph, and a photograph above. The picture was of a crowd gathered outside the closed doors of our own national bank building. Even given the bad quality of the picture, you could just make out the angry expressions on the faces of the waiting people, the blank looks of the security guards and, at a window of one of the upper floors, the managers looking out.

I had given up my postgraduate course once Junior was born. Now I went to work at the Lyons Coffee Shop, in order that Ambrose could finish his own studies. It was mindless work. But once I had worked out how to fill the teapots with hot water from the spout of the machine that hissed and spat without scalding myself, it suited me. I liked the drift of people, the banter among the other girls, the paper bags of teacakes we were given at the end of the day and ate for breakfast in the morning.

There was a game they played among themselves, surreptitiously, mindful of the manager who would have sacked them if he had overheard. A man would come in and they would award him points out of ten. Whoever had the highest score won a date with him. Not really, of course. But they would go on to describe the evening, where they might go, what they would wear, imagine what this man they didn't even know was like. These were their dreams. To ride with a man in a car. To be taken up town to the theatre. I thought their dreams very small indeed. To the customers I might seem the same as these girls but I told myself my destiny was far greater. I thought I was better than them.

As I rule I was not included in this game.

'What about him, then?' Jeanette said to me once, picking at a lipstick-stained strip of skin on her lower lip. But before I could reply Shona gave her a nudge:

'She can't . . . ' she hissed.

'Why ever not?' Jeanette frowned.

'Well . . .' Shona pulled a face and stretched her eyes wide, looking at Jeanette all the time. Jeanette gazed back blankly. Shona wavered, only for a moment. 'She's married!' She sounded relieved when she said that. But of course I knew this wasn't the reason. Grace played, she was married.

Shona was a stupid girl, too stupid to worry about. Another day she tried to make amends, pointing to a man on the far side of the room: 'Look, love. There's one for you.' The man, a black man, was sitting at a table in a windowless corner of the room. He was alone. On the table in front of him lay a pair of gloves and a folded newspaper. He was writing, scribbling furiously, in a notepad. I was silent, not speaking for a long time. Beside me Shona shuffled, a tickle of discomfort. 'I don't mean just because . . .'

Still I didn't answer her. I was staring at that man, feeling everything around me, the lights, the noise, grow faint. Even the sound of Shona's voice. I stepped out from behind the counter and walked across the room, without bothering to pick up a pad or collect a menu. I stood in front of the table where he was sitting, my hands by my sides, until he looked up at me.

'Hello,' I said softly. At that he stood up suddenly, pushing back his chair so that it fell over. I didn't try to catch it and neither did he. Instead we took a step towards each other.

'Hello,' said Janneh.

So that was how we found one another again. Seventeen years had passed. Janneh walked me home at the end of the shift. Night-time was coming, bringing with it the cold. I pushed my hands into the pockets of my thin coat. In England my hands and feet were always, always cold. Even in what passed for summer. Without a word Janneh removed his gloves and handed them to me, and I slipped my fingers into the warm place inside.

Janneh was working as a journalist. He was in England for a short time only, looking for a second-hand Linotype printing press. He planned to set up an independent newspaper: 'A free press, you know. One the Government can't control.' I smiled, even though what he was saying was serious. I remembered that about him, the way he punctuated his conversation with certain phrases. 'You know,' was one of them.

At home I invited Janneh to stay and eat with us. Ambrose would be back soon. So Janneh accepted and squeezed in next to me in the tiny kitchen, peeling onions while I squeezed lemons for chicken *yassa*. When he asked me my news, I told it to him, including how I came to be working at the Lyons Coffee Shop. Ambrose joined us, we fitted the extra leaf in the table in the sitting room and sat down, and for the first time I heard about the things that were happening back home.

Government ministers who built houses high on the hill. Houses with east and west wings, pillared porches and glass chandeliers. On the outside homeless people built their little *panbodies* against the high walls. The wives of these big men drove around in shining Mercedes, frequently flew out of the country with their husbands on official business, shopped and slept between Egyptian cotton sheets in smart hotels. Meanwhile the price of rice climbed higher every day. People went to withdraw their savings from the bank and found they were refused their own money. The poorest souls walked around with swollen stomachs and feverish eyes.

These were the things Janneh wrote about in his newspaper column. He discovered and published the official salaries of the Government ministers and demanded to know how they could afford to live so well. He worked late into the night, alone in his office, sometimes only returning home to change his clothes. Once he pushed open the door of his flat in the small hours to find men in safari suits and smooth-soled shoes searching through his belongings. Janneh waved his arms and shouted at them. They set upon him in a flurry of punches, winded him and broke one of his ribs. It still hurt him to breathe.

Some days later his editor had called him in. Janneh's boss was a good man, a widower with three daughters whom he loved. Janneh noticed his editor kept glancing at the framed photograph on his desk, how he never looked Janneh in the eye. He told Janneh he was working too hard, gave him a six-month sabbatical. Janneh cleared his desk, he knew he would never be able to go back.

'Thank you, that was very good indeed.' Janneh lay down his knife and fork and smiled at me. 'We need people, you know,' he continued, this time switching his gaze to Ambrose. 'Educated people, but most of all good people.'

I carried the empty plates into the kitchen and set them in the sink. I heard Ambrose offer Janneh another beer. Janneh declined, he continued talking: 'People who understand the world. People with experience. People who know what needs to be done.'

The pineapple I had bought two days before was ripe. I found a knife, sliced off the ends, then I cut diagonally into the skin. The pineapples in England were so small, I often wondered where they came from. Ambrose still hadn't spoken.

'Well, what do you say?' Janneh again, addressing him directly this time. I waited for Ambrose to say something. Something that would tell Janneh he was a person who knew how to do what was right.

'So what are you saying? I mean how exactly do you plan to go about this? Are you going to take over the Government?' Ambrose was using questions to answer questions. It was something he did to avoid giving a reply, I knew. He did it whenever we had a disagreement, especially when he knew I was right. It was a lawyer's trick. Round and round, I scored deeply into the pineapple's flesh.

'Of course not,' Janneh laughed lightly, grew serious again. 'But we need to draw the people's attention to what is happening. These guys are lining their pockets, man. Grabbing what they can while they're in office. And it's our money. Yours. Mine. Everybody's.'

'And you think they're just going to stop because you say so?' Ambrose was refusing to budge.

'Not because *I* say so. Listen, we have to get out there and inform the people. Once they know what's going on, that their future is being stolen . . . The newspaper is just the beginning. We can't take this lying down.'

I glanced up, I could just see Ambrose leaning back in his chair, Janneh was hunched over the table. Ambrose had his hands clasped across his chest. Janneh seemed to be worrying at an imaginary spot on the table surface. Ambrose was shaking his head in mock weariness. Oh, how I wanted to run over and seize him by the shoulders. To yell at him, for God's sake! I raised the knife and cut the pineapple into slices.

'Janneh, dear fellow, I don't want to disappoint you but the trouble with the black man is that he just isn't ready to govern himself yet. He hasn't learned how. And frankly, I'm not sure he's up to the job. The same thing is happening everywhere.'

'Precisely!' said Janneh, pointing his finger in the air. 'The very reason we must act now.'

Ambrose let his chair tip forward. 'Open your eyes, my friend. Look around you!' he said. 'Just name me one country, one country on that whole damned continent that has made a success of itself since the white man left and I'll join you tomorrow. But you can't, can you? And do you want me to tell you why? Because none of them have!'

And with that he leaned back again, as though the discussion was over.

All the time Ambrose was speaking I grew more and more ashamed. Dismissing Janneh as though he were a teenage hothead. I admit, I used to be impressed by his lawyerly language, the way he could handle anybody with his clever words. I carried through the pineapple, three plates and three forks. Ambrose was smiling, not showing his teeth but with the ends of his mouth turned up, still swollen with self-importance. Janneh had stopped fiddling and sat staring at his hands on the table in front of him. For a moment he looked defeated. Then he raised his head and faced Ambrose squarely. When he spoke his voice was low, the inflection contained in a single word.

'None of *us*, Ambrose. None of *us*.'

And I saw my husband shrivel up and shrink, right there before my eyes.

After Janneh had gone, Ambrose and I lay side by side on the divan, not touching, cold under the nylon quilt. Ambrose was still awake. I could tell by his breathing, and by the fact he was lying too still. That meant he was brooding.

'You know, you ought to warn that friend of yours he'll end up behind bars,' Ambrose said eventually, speaking into the dark. 'You mark my words. He's looking for trouble in the easiest place to find it. They'll lock him up and they'll throw away the key.'

And with those words he rolled away from me.

A friend of mine once was ill. I remember I went to visit her at a time when she must already have been sick. Her skin was luminous, her eyes shone, when she smiled she showed pink gums and white teeth, her hair was braided into thick plaits. In every way she appeared as beautiful as before. But the disease was eating her from within. When she brushed her teeth her gums bled. Her teeth were loose. The plaits were all that held her hair close to her scalp and when she undid them, it fell out in great clumps. She told nobody how ill she was. Gradually those closest to her noticed the changes, but they said nothing. Her flesh wasted away, her teeth fell out and she tied a cloth round her balding head. Still she refused to admit to her illness or go to the doctor and though her family, her friends, even strangers saw that she was dying, nobody said out loud what had become evident to them all.

That was the way it was with this country. Those who noticed refused to speak of it, as though they feared that to do so would make it real. Others drank and danced, partied into the night as though tomorrow was a long way away. And so it seemed as if everything was fine.

When I first arrived back all I thought about was how much I had missed it. There's a beauty about this place, one that cannot even be imagined. How small a hummingbird truly is! I sat on the verandah of our new bungalow and watched a tiny, shimmering bird flit from flower to flower before coming to land on the stamen of a scarlet hibiscus, as though it were a tree branch. Under the bird's weight, the stalk merely bowed, the petals quivered as he disappeared into the hollow. A moment later I watched him fly away, a blur of beating wings. The giant fan palm in the garden, its leaves spread out like a peacock's tail. The lustrous evening light, the colour of mother-of-pearl. These were the things I saw.

I travelled upcountry to visit my home and left money with Ya Namina to pay the doctor's bills for my father. A month later Ya Memso came to stay, bringing with her all the contents of my marriage box. I saw how round her eyes grew to see the way Ambrose and I lived, with indoor toilets and hot water pouring straight into a tub and glass windows that closed out the rain and the dust, but allowed the sun inside. The manager at the coffee shop had given me a farewell gift, a bonus on my last day. I kept it until we were on our way home to tell Ambrose. How delighted he was, hugging me and lifting me up off my feet to swing me around. He put it down as a deposit on a Volkswagen and promised he would teach me to drive.

Ambrose said there was no reason for me to work, and so I stayed at home with Junior and little Yaya, who was born soon after we returned. I enjoyed myself, why not? Though sometimes I wondered what the years of study had been for. Every morning I waved goodbye to Ambrose as he drove to his job in the Attorney-General's office where he was helping to draft new Acts of Parliament. I made friends among the wives of Ambrose's colleagues and spent my days visiting, going from house to house. I would sit in their parlours, being served cold drinks by the houseboy, eating honeyed sesame cakes and roasted groundnuts while our husbands worked late.

Hannah, my dear friend Hannah, had never married. She never did go to study in England, despite her father's connections which should have been enough to secure her a Government grant. Instead she had taken a shorthand and typing course at the Young Women's Christian Association and as it turned out was working as a legal secretary at the Attorney-General's office. In the evenings Hannah would come around and we would hide away in the bedroom I shared with Ambrose. She would try on my clothes and my shoes, which were far too big for her and afterwards we would lie on the bed giggling like schoolgirls again. 'You have found a man who really knows how to look after you!' she teased me. 'Why don't you find one for me?' And she wore my shoes to work with paper stuffed into the toes.

It bothered me that Ambrose did not take to Hannah. There were times I found myself defending her. One evening as I sat with Ambrose I suggested to him perhaps I might take a job. After a few months I had begun to find the gossiping and endless keeping company dull, I needed more to fill my days. Ambrose wouldn't hear of it.

'You're a decent woman, Serah,' he told me. 'Why do you want to be like those girls? Men don't respect them. With those tight clothes they wear and that stuff smeared on their faces.'

I bridled at that: 'You mean like Hannah?' I retorted. But Ambrose only told me not to be so ridiculous.

It occurred to me Ambrose had never objected to me working when we were in England, but I pushed the thought to the furthest place in my mind. And, if I'm honest with you, I didn't really know what I wanted. Part of me was pleased Ambrose wanted me to stay at home. Ya Memso and my father's wives, always so busy with their gardens or else harvesting coffee or taking food to the workers. Ya Namina balancing the books. My mother's hands, the stained crescents of her cuticles. Sometimes I imagined I was one of those women on television in England, with a carpet sweeper and children I fed on instant pink desserts, and a pet who dined on food that came in special tins.

So you see, this is how I was thinking when I came home. I was thinking in a small way. I had forgotten Janneh's warnings. I bought food for the table with the new money with the President's face on it, but did not notice the prices because Ambrose's salary was enough to cover our needs. At the post office I bought stamps with the same man's face on them. The world's first self-adhesive postage stamp was invented in this country. Did you know that? Some countries produced the smallpox vaccine. The atom bomb. Canned peas. Permanent press cotton. The microchip. We had flower stamps. Bird stamps. Stamps in the shape of diamonds. Country-shaped stamps. Stamps in the shape of the continent. One with a small hippopotamus who lived only in our swamps. Stamps that required no licking. Stamps with the President's face on them. Yes, we would be remembered for our stamps.

At the time I did not think things could be so bad if we had new stamps and our very own new money.

It's true there were occasional power cuts and the drainage in the city was poor, the smell sometimes drifting into the house. I planted frangipani between the fig trees, beautiful pink frangipani. I picked the blooms and floated them in bowls of water and placed them all around the house. And soon all you could smell was the scent of those flowers.

★　　★　　★

One thing I forgot to mention, I saw my mother again. I mean just that, literally – I saw her. On my way back to the city from travelling north to see Ya Memso and my father. It was at the junction of the roads heading north, south, east and west. At the time I was sure it was her, passing through the crowd. She didn't see me. So many people were gathered around the car, some selling, others simply staring. A private vehicle was still a rarity in those days. People were curious. Just as we had been, Yaya and me, that time when we went to the East with her and we travelled in a truck and chased shiny cars up and down the streets of the mining town.

My heart thumped hard inside my ribs. I told the driver to wait, got out of the car, and stepped towards her, but a woman carrying a tray of fish upon her head passed in front of me. The fish were packed into tight circles with all the care of a flower arrangement, their mouths open, pointed at the sky as though they were catching raindrops. For a few moments my view was blocked and when the way was clear again, my mother was gone. I craned my neck, searching for her among the people changing buses, but I couldn't find her again.

All the way home I wondered what I might have said to her. What kind of life was she leading? Did she even know I was back home?

Then I decided maybe it hadn't been her at all. Just a woman with the same look. Why, I probably wouldn't even recognise her now. By the time I was in front of the gates of my house I had decided I had been mistaken.

Ambrose's work kept him late at the office on many evenings. There were times when I was already asleep by the time he came home. The lawyers in his office were labouring around the clock drafting the new constitution to turn us into a republic. It was important work.

One evening he arrived home bringing a friend of his, a townsmate whom he had happened upon in the street. I don't mind telling you that from the very start there was something about this man that I didn't like. He sweated and wiped his forehead with a flannel he kept in his pocket. He wore a suit, shiny at the lapels. And shoes made from two types of leather like a Nigerian pastor. He held on to my hand for too long and pushed his face into mine, his breath was sour and the look he gave me was of hunger mixed with something knowing.

It was a Thursday, the servants' day off. I went to the fridge and fetched cold beers, poured some nuts into a dish along with some of Ambrose's favourite fried dough pieces and carried them out to where the two of them sat at the front of the house.

How this man liked to talk! And to drink. Several beers were downed, Ambrose went to fetch a bottle of Scotch and set it on the table. I watched as the man filled his glass right up to the brim. I tried to replace the bottle with a bowl of cashew nuts, but he waved at me to put it back. Time passed with no indication of when he might be leaving. We sat side by side on the settee watching him drink, until Ambrose was obliged to invite him to eat with us. I whispered into Ambrose's ear there was no food. Ambrose's erratic hours meant he had taken to eating on his way home. I ate with the children. It was too late now to start cooking.

'OK, we'll go out.' Ambrose picked up his friend's jacket just as the man poured himself a third glass of whisky.

'What? Hey! Out you say? But I am very comfortable here. This is a fine place you have.'

Ambrose apologised, explaining there was nothing to eat. His friend belched and laughed, a big laugh, fat with scorn.

'Let your woman cook some rice for us. What do you think a wife is for, my man? Or don't you know? Maybe you'd like me to tell you.' This time his laugh was harsh: a coarse, dry cough.

Well, I'm sure you can guess by now Ambrose didn't like to be mocked. Who does, after all? I would have felt better if he'd told his friend to watch how he spoke in front of me, but instead he tossed the man's jacket towards him.

'Come on. We'll get some roast meat.' He turned to leave, without looking once at me, though the set of his jaw betrayed his mood.

But his friend was too drunk to notice. I saw him clap Ambrose on the shoulder as he staggered out, heard him teasing Ambrose about what a spoiled wife I was. 'Is that what they teach you in England?'

And that laugh. 'Heh! Heh!' All the way down the lane.

I sat in the house listening to that laugh, like a bad odour, mingling with the smell of the frangipani. I went to the bathroom and took a cigarette from the packet of 555s I kept wedged behind the cabinet. Ambrose, who once used to light my cigarettes with a lighter he kept in his pocket, now forbade me to smoke.

I remember my grandmother once made a joke at my expense soon after I made her buy me a pair of new shoes, too tight because I had been in so much of a hurry to possess them. She had caught me hobbling around the house as I tried to walk in them. 'Who knows how much a pretty pair of shoes pinch, except the person wearing them?' she said, because I was always wanting something more, something that somebody else had, and this saying now fitted my predicament in more ways than one. My grandmother laughed some more.

The grass is always greener, I suppose that's the nearest saying. Or perhaps it's about appearances and how they can be deceptive. Or does it really mean be careful what you wish for? Perhaps it means whatever it needs to mean, some combination of all three. The truth is I did not care for who I was. I closed my eyes and made a wish. The wish came true. I closed my eyes and made another wish, and that came true, too. So I kept my eyes closed and kept on wishing.

Come to think about it, the old shoes were soft and made of canvas. The saying must have been invented later.

The point is, I had nobody to turn to. My grandmother had passed on years before. Even if she had still been alive what did she or Ya Memso or even my mother know of the way we lived now?

Those days Ambrose was so busy he still hadn't got around to teaching me to drive. When he found out I was riding the *poda podas* he told me I should take taxis instead. What would people think? But taxis were expensive and the truth is I liked the minibuses. I liked the rattle of the day's talk in my ears. I liked the dense scent of sweat from a hard day's work. Gradually I learned what hardships people bore by the things they joked about. A woman so fat the bus boy charged her for two places was comforted by a passenger who reassured her she would soon be as thin as everyone else. A market woman pushed her nose in the air and imitated the voice of our first lady, her friends laughed until they noticed the man on the back seat watching them through narrowed eyes, and one by one fell silent. 'We'd all run away from this place if we could,' to a girl whose fiancé had jilted her and gone to live in another country. Even through her tears, the abandoned girl agreed.

One Friday in the late afternoon I was returning home from Fula Town. I had to switch buses at the big roundabout in the centre of town near Government House, close to Ambrose's office, and I was waiting there for a *poda poda* headed west. I was thinking idle thoughts, listening to the music of the bus boys calling the different destinations, when I saw Ambrose drive towards me. What luck! I thought, perhaps he had time to quickly drop me home. I stepped off the kerb and waved, the sun was in my eyes, I shielded them with one hand and carried on waving with the other, but Ambrose didn't see me. The car, in the middle of the traffic, swept on by. Too bad. I shrugged. I stepped back on to the pavement, but just as I did I heard the slow wail of a siren starting up. A policeman raised a white gloved hand, the traffic came to a standstill. At the top of the hill the President's convoy came into view.

I looked this way and that for the car. Ambrose was on the other side of the roundabout. If I was quick I could just make it. I began to hurry over. But as I wove through the cars I saw I had been mistaken. The driver of the car was a woman. Though I couldn't see her face, I could see her hands resting on the steering wheel. And yet again the car was identical in every way to our own. I paused, I checked the number plate. No, I had not been mistaken. It was our car. So who could be driving it, if not Ambrose?

The policeman lowered his arm, the cars moved forward. The sun was behind me, reflecting off the chrome of the cars, lighting up their darkened interiors. The traffic gathered pace, the profile of the driver came into view, and briefly she turned her face towards me. It was Hannah.

At home I smoked three 555s in a row. I was angry, yes. But I felt sure there was an explanation, I just did not think it was right a man's wife should use common people's transport while her friend drove about in the man's car. I hadn't even known Hannah could drive.

I was angry, yes. Suspicious? Not so much. I did not reckon on Ambrose's reply:

'You are my wife and Hannah will never be a threat to you.' Those were his words. I stared at him, my brain felt sluggish and cold. Then it dawned on me – Ambrose was confessing to an affair.

Afterwards I realised he couldn't help himself. I don't mean about sleeping with Hannah. I mean in telling me. There had been no tears, no threats or recriminations. I hadn't even had time to think such a dreadful thought, let alone utter it. And the expression on his face: it told not of shame, or fear or even guilt.

'Now Serah,' he had said in his lawyer's tones. 'Now Serah. You must understand. This is Africa. We are in Africa now. And I am an African man. That's just the way it is.'

No, Ambrose hadn't been confessing at all. Not at all. He'd been boasting!

I heard about it all in the months that followed. Everything. The gossips made sure of that. The shop where Hannah charged new clothes and shoes to Ambrose's account, the bars they visited, and the parties Ambrose's face-wiping friend took him to. Parties where men brought girls like Hannah. Parties for men like Ambrose – men who wanted the best of both worlds.

Hannah's place was up on the hill and she was not at home when I arrived. The houseboy let me in and showed me into her tiny sitting room. A moment later I heard him at the back of the house, pounding clothes in the basin under the standpipe.

I only meant to talk to Hannah. To sort the matter out. I had even rehearsed what I was going to say, up to a point anyway. I had made a vow not to allow myself to ask details of their betrayal, I'd heard enough already. No, I would take care to talk to her as a friend, we would both behave in a dignified manner. I wasn't the first woman to find myself in this position, and I wouldn't be the last. But there was no question of allowing Hannah to continue to see Ambrose. None at all.

I smoothed my skirt and sat down in a low chair. It was some months since I'd been in Hannah's flat. I wondered what she earned and whether Ambrose was giving her money as well as gifts. The minutes passed. I stood up and wandered about a bit, going over my lines in my head. Back and forth. On the table at the other end of the room was a pile of Hannah's belongings. I caught a glimpse of a record: Orchestre Bella Bella, a Congolese band. I owned exactly the same record, except it occurred to me I hadn't seen my own copy in a while.

Outside the pounding had ceased. I heard footsteps: the click of heels on concrete. I spun around. I could hear Hannah's footfall along the exterior wall of the house. Suddenly I was unprepared. I didn't want her to see me when she passed the window. I moved and stood beside the door, where I would be ready to greet her when she came in. In my haste I brushed against an umbrella standing there, flustered now I reached out and caught it before it hit the floor. I stood with my back to the wall holding the umbrella in front of me. Outside I could hear Hannah rummaging in her bag for the keys. I tried to prop the umbrella in its place and as I did I glanced down at it.

James Smith & Sons. On New Oxford Street. I still remember the look in Ambrose's eyes when I gave it to him on his first day at the Inns of Court. He had opened it in the living room and twirled it around and around, even though I warned him it was bad luck. It was raining the morning he set off, a soft drizzle. He had clicked his heels and sung a chorus from 'Singin' in the Rain'; it was so unlike him, so endearing, I laughed and embraced him. He kissed me in return and promised to cherish it always.

The door opened.

Am I proud of what I did? At the time, no. I was angry. I wasn't proud of myself, I was miserable. Only later I became defiant. Am I proud now? Well, now you're asking. Now I'm thinking back on it. Yes, actually. I believe I am.

I hit her. Again and again. Oh, what a noise she made as she went down. She begged me to stop. But I didn't stop. I beat her the way you beat a snake, to make sure it's dead. And maybe I would have killed her if the houseboy hadn't heard the *palava* and come running. He caught my raised hand. 'Stop, Ma. I beg.' So softly, it brought me to my senses. And ever so gently he removed the umbrella from my hand.

I had spent my whole life trying not to be like my mother. I had taken the opposite path and hurried along it, all the time looking over my shoulder instead of ahead, so that I failed to see how the path curved back again in the same direction.

When a woman is thrown out by her husband, there aren't many places for her to go. Ambrose said I had humiliated him, by playing into the hands of the gossips. That might come as a surprise to your way of thinking, but it's true. In the city appearances were the thing that mattered most. I had caused us to lose face; next to that Ambrose's fidelity was unimportant. Of the two of us, it seemed, I was the one who was in the wrong.

So there. No home. No husband. No job. The first person I went to was my sister Mary. And she was there for me, just as I had been there for her once, she made space for me and my sons in her tiny room at the Catholic Mission School for the Blind, but it was clear we couldn't stay there long. What I've learned, though, is that luck likes to stay out of sight until she's needed. Ya Memso had not seen my mother for many years, since before I left to go to England. From the time I married up until that day she had held on to my mother's share of my bride price. Well, the marriage was over, so she gave it to me to rent a place until I found a job. My qualifications were good, it didn't take me long. And with the rest of the money Ambrose had given me I paid for driving lessons and in time bought a small car of my own.

So you see, in this way my poor mother, bound to my father by her own bride price, unexpectedly gave me the keys to my freedom.

And do you know what else I think? I think Ambrose was bluffing when he ordered me to leave our house, imagining I would soon beg him to take me back. He didn't know I was my mother's daughter. He didn't know I preferred to make my way alone than live with unhappiness. Yes, Ambrose was wrong about that, just as he was wrong about many things.

There was one thing he was right about, though.

A single issue of Janneh's newspaper appeared on the streets. The next day the police rounded up all the newspaper vendors and put them in prison. As for Janneh, he simply vanished. His empty car, the headlights dying, was found at a crossroads one morning. Other people disappeared, too. A nursery school teacher here. A city councillor there. A poet ordered down from his crate in the marketplace. One by one, like lights going off all across the city. People talked about a labour camp in another country where the President was a friend of our President. But it was only a rumour. Nobody had ever come back to say whether it was true or not.

As for me, the gossip-mongers soon found new victims to torture with their tongues. Tongues like leather cords, tying a woman down, cutting into her every time she tried to break free. They laughed, not knowing that the last laugh belonged to none of us. Ambrose spent his days at the Attorney-General's office drafting new laws to take away our freedom little by little. And they never even noticed, they were too busy tittle-tattling. But one day they would find out what some of us already knew. That the reality was not so brightly coloured as the dream. That the dream no longer existed, maybe had never existed. It was all just a rainbow-coloured hallucination.

And when you reached out to touch it, your hand went straight through to the other side.

13

Asana, 1985

Mambore

WHEN I WAS A CHILD *Karabom* warned me of the dangers of breaking the rules. I must be careful not to trespass in the sacred forest, she said, or the men who belonged to the secret society would snatch me and take me away and I would not see my mother for a long, long time. This was what happened to children who played truant, or who went wandering alone in forbidden places.

I heard these warnings all my life. Sometimes they came to town, the members of this fearsome order – to stir our terror in case, untended, it congealed into something resilient. Women and children ran away to hide, we were not even allowed to gaze upon them. Such was the power of the society, even the chiefs obeyed them for in times of peril it was the society we looked to for protection. For centuries people feared them even more than they came to fear the army.

Another day *Karabom* had warned me against keeping bad company. Two girls were walking home, she told me. One a girl of noble birth. The other a girl from a disreputable family, the kind of people who move from village to village like nomads. She had grown up doing as she pleased, disregarded her chores and never learned to cook. On their way they passed a place where the society men were busy in the forest. They could tell this by the tools left lying at the side of the path, among them the tortoiseshell drum they beat to warn people of their approach. The errant girl picked it up and, despite the protests of her friend, banged on it loudly, laughing wildly as she did so. Within moments they were surrounded by masked men, who carried them away deep into the forest. They were not seen for a year or more. Even the wealthy father, with all his connections, could not find his daughter or free her from the men of the secret society.

'What happened to them?' I wanted to know.

'Who?' said my grandmother, knowing perfectly well. It meant she was finished with talking.

'The girls.'

'I don't know,' said my grandmother. 'It's not important. They came back, but their chances were ruined. What man would want to marry girls like that?'

The question itched me like an insect bite for a few weeks, and then I forgot it. I was a child after all. Such was the awe in which the society was held that it was forbidden to speak of their doings, but still, there were whispers. I can tell you now the girls were not ravished, nothing like that. The society was an ancient and honourable one. But one that guarded its secrets and demanded respect. Those for whom awe proved insufficient were bound instead by its oaths of allegiance.

Remember when you were a child you used to ask so many questions? La i la! Aunty, what's this? Aunty, what's that? Your father spoiled you. Letting you talk too much. He should have used a firmer hand with you, I told him so. But your own children talk even more. Just open their mouths and say the first thing that comes into their heads, doesn't matter who else is speaking. When I tell them to be quiet, you frown at me. Oh, it's natural to be curious. How else are they supposed to learn? Aunty, you mustn't stifle their imagination. And you turn away from your elders to answer the questions of a foolish child.

But sometimes a child learns best by finding their own answers.

Look at this *lappa*. You see a piece of cloth, isn't it? Me? I see a head-tie. I see a skirt. I see a sling for a baby. I see a cloth to dry myself. I see a sheet to lay upon my bed. I see a covering for a door or a window. Or this empty tomato puree tin? You would just throw it into the rubbish, eh? But to the girl selling groundnuts here – it's a cup to measure her sales. To that woman sitting behind her stall, it's an oil lamp. To our way of thinking there are many ways of looking at the same thing.

Sometimes you think you are trapped. Either you walk one way down the road or the other. A road to the left. A road to the right. Choose, it doesn't matter which. Neither one is what you want. But sometimes, if you look very closely, you can see the path curling through the trees. Hard to see. But only because nobody has yet trodden it.

Does any of this make sense to you? You think so? That means you don't understand at all. Maybe I just have to tell you how it happened.

'No married woman ever bore a bastard.' Those words of my mother came back to me twenty years after she uttered them, soon after we buried my father.

The year was 1985. I was watching those of his wives who had outlived him still sitting on the mat. Some had even come back from their families to sit there. Not cooking. Not fetching water. Doing no work at all. Spending their days idle while the rest of us waited on them hand and foot. These women would not bear a bastard, it would be a miracle if any of them bore a child at all. Most of them were older than me. But still, we must all pretend to wait and see. They would sit there for a whole other month, while everybody else looked after them. Because this was our custom and it was a very old one. Nobody would challenge it, for fear of being called disrespectful.

Our father lived to be over a hundred years old. He had married eleven women and he was the father of some three dozen children, most of whom were believed to be his. But in the end he died alone. Out in a worker's hut, surrounded by the forest and close to the fields he had gone out to inspect. He must have felt unwell and lain there to rest. The creatures of the forest found him first. My mother, Ya Namina was away. Ya Isatta should have been in charge, but she was a weak woman and least favoured of all the wives. And since nobody bothered to tell her anything, she thought he had gone to be with one of the others.

The corpse was in an appalling state, the silence surrounding it confirming every suspicion. Still, the elders insisted my father had been dead no more than twelve hours, so like a good Muslim he could be buried the day he died.

Cloths were hung in front of the windows. Photographs of my father displayed on every surface. Two bolts of black calico purchased and transformed into mourning robes. My mother instructed the tailor on the style in order to avert disagreement. She waved away all help, for she had already buried one husband, and by that time so had I.

The day my mother made that remark about married women came soon after the birth of Alpha, my second child. I was still wearing black for my second husband, whom I mourned an entire year because I had loved him a great deal but also because it gave me more time alone. She had watched my belly with narrowed eyes, counting off the months in her head. An afternoon as I sat playing with my new son, she urged me to make myself respectable. In case there were other children waiting to come.

My mother always thought I should have become a head wife like her, to have other wives to do as you say. She could not imagine how a woman could want anything else. But I was not married to my second husband for long enough to go looking for younger wives, even if I had wanted to. My husband was a good man, but too much given to discussing politics. Mostly he argued with his friend Pa Brima, and always both men ended up standing and shouting at each other across the table. Pa Brima was always the first one to sit down. One day, though, he stayed on his feet. My husband was greatly vexed. So much so that he came home still full of anger and sometime during the night choked to death on his own opinion.

That night they had argued over whether everybody deserved a vote. One man, one vote. This was in the days before those sorts of elections. Pa Brima thought it was the most foolish thing he had ever heard. 'You take some useless youth and you give his opinion the same weight as one of the elders?' he demanded. Later he blamed himself, wept that he had killed his best friend. I remembered that argument of theirs years later, when we had elections but everybody already knew who would win. All of us with a vote, but nobody to vote for.

After a respectable period, suitors began to appear. Don't forget, this was a long time ago. I was still a woman many people considered to be attractive. I knew how to dress, how to carry myself. I knew how to keep house. I was still capable of bearing children, that much had been evidenced.

The first man told me all about his many possessions. How many pairs of shoes he possessed, how many shirts. He even owned two Western-style suits as well as many dozens of robes and embroidered tunics. Oh, and so many other things! On his fingers he ticked them off one by one. Leather-bound copy of the Koran: one. Camel hair carpets: three. Electric fans: two. Transistor radio: one. Refrigerator: one. He handed me a picture of himself standing next to the fridge. Only in the photograph the fridge was a painted one, because it had been impossible to carry the real fridge all the way to the photographer's studio. In my head I saw him one day counting me as one of his possessions. The two of us posing together for a photograph. Me, with flawless matt skin, gazing up at my husband: unblinking eyes, lips parted in a frozen smile, gleaming teeth. A perfect, painted wife.

An old man stared at me through watery eyes, squeezed my breast with trembling fingers and told me to be at his house in the morning.

The *sabu* who was representing the next suitor gave me one week to make up my mind. She had another prospective bride in mind. After three days she returned and told me to hurry up. Their number two choice was now in receipt of a rival offer.

The fourth man had dead eyes and a shadow that seemed to follow him, hovering behind his shoulder. When he sat down he was entirely still, all except for his leg, which jigged up and down as though it had a life of its own.

I turned them all down, but it seemed as though every time I answered the door another one fell over the threshold.

★   ★   ★

Ya Jeneba and Ya Sallay did not sit on the mat. They stayed only a few days and returned to the house they had continued to share in Rofathane, coming back to help with the preparations for the forty-day ceremony.

I watched how alike the two sisters had grown over the years. Throwing their heads back and clapping their hands when they laughed and they laughed easily, the same phrases, in the same lilting voice, the same gesture, wiping sweat from their foreheads with the insides of their wrists.

Their father had been counsellor to the chief of a neighbouring chieftaincy. Jeneba and Sallay were the daughters of the same wife, belly sisters. Jeneba the eldest by about thirteen years. Their mother died before Sallay was old enough to remember her. And though she was wet-nursed by another of the wives, it was Jeneba who cared for her sister. Carried her everywhere, played with her, plaited her hair, bathed her and slept with her at night – like a favourite doll. Nobody called Sallay by her name, instead they called her Baby Jeneba. Jeneba's marriage to my father was a dynastic one, agreed by the families. When the time came for Jeneba to leave for her new home, Sallay ran after the hammock bearing her sister away. She ran and ran until somebody picked her up and carried her back. She would not stay, so they tethered her to a tree by one leg like a goat. The child sat down and refused to eat or drink, or speak. Nobody had ever witnessed such stubbornness in one so young. Some wondered if she wasn't one of those children who could exist on nothing but air. Whatever, if she took no food or water she would become a spirit one way or the other. The trouble was that every time they untied her, she ran away down the path and into the trees to find her sister.

So they sent her to live with Jeneba. Such arrangements were not uncommon. When Sallay reached marriage age, the two sisters wept anew at the thought of being separated. So another solution was found. Sallay became my father's wife.

While I searched for ways to forestall my fate, my daughter seized her own destiny. She had chosen her husband: a young man from a family of bakers, softly spoken as a result of a cleft in his palate. Towards me he kept his eyes lowered, but when he looked at Kadie his gaze burned with such intensity I half expected to see my daughter swallowed up in flames. He brought her sculptures made from dough. One was fashioned as a pair of doves, another a cat curled up asleep. As his wooing grew more determined so the sculptures became more elaborate: a deer standing between the trees, a man and a woman sitting side by side, a nest of baby birds.

Kadie showed no interest in the wedding plans, was heedless of the negotiations over her bride gift. Whenever I showed her swatches of cloth she yawned and kissed me. 'Whatever you think, mother,' she said, before changing the subject back to her beloved.

One evening as I looked at my daughter, I thought for the first time how much the nature of love had changed, so much so it was almost unrecognisable.

And then I shook the thought out of my head, because I was her mother and, after all, one of us had to be practical.

The stores in the city sold cloth far superior to any in our town. I stared at the towering piles of folded cloth behind the shop owner. So many to choose from! She was wearing a heavy woven cotton of dark red, shot with gold thread and the highest headdress I had ever seen. I decided to ask her advice.

'What is the occasion?' she asked me.

I told her: my daughters wedding *ashobi*.

'Come.' She moved out from behind the counter, beckoning me over. From a glass-fronted cabinet on the other side of the room she pulled out bolts of the finest fabric I had ever seen.

'What's this?' I asked, fingering an edge. Printed on two sides, too.

'Sheku *lappa*,' she said, 'from Nigeria.'

It was a hot day, she clapped her hands for two glasses of water while we settled down to make a deal. Many dozens of yards of fabric were required to make *ashobi* outfits for everybody. In the time it took to agree a price we talked of many things. I learned how she travelled to Lagos and brought back the cloth herself. How her shop was the first of three stores she planned. Another in the North and then the South. In time, outlets in the East and West as well. Hours passed before we concluded our business, both of us delaying the time when we would arrive at an agreement and our conversation would come to an end. I decided I liked this woman. I liked her broad, flat face, which was honest – especially for a shop owner. We exchanged names and parted company, but I thought about our conversation for a long time. After the wedding I left Alpha with my mother and travelled back to the city. I was a widow. My daughter had just married. I had negotiated her bride gift well and since my husband was no longer alive, all of it came to me. Well, not exactly all of it. There was family to consider, but even once those obligations were met, a good sum remained. Enough to go into business.

Madam Turay shook her head at me: 'Pack one good dress, but wear something not so good for the journey,' she told me. I was wearing my best dress for the trip, I did not want to be shamed in the streets of Lagos.

A saltwater wind whipped our faces as the ship gathered steam. The deck tilted first to one side and then to the other, making it impossible to stand and so we stayed huddled on the floor. I stared at the sea, which from a distance had seemed so inviting but now writhed and roared like a beast. The wind sculpted the water into great white crested waves. I felt certain we would soon all be dead. I could not understand how a boat made of iron could possibly float, but I saw no creases mar the features of Madam Turay's flat face, so I told myself perhaps we would be all right. Madam Turay found us a place near the middle of the ship, close to the great chimneys where we were sheltered from the worst of it. I pitied the poor souls out there on the open deck in front of us, and I envied the paying passengers in their bunks down below. With each movement of the ship my stomach lurched, as though it had broken free and was rolling around my insides. Madam Turay lit a small stove and set about brewing us some tea. She told me to fix my eyes on the horizon. I did as she bid me and gradually I began to feel better. The horizon looked so close, I assured myself we would be there in no time at all.

Three days and nights the ship sailed. The first night I watched the sun set behind the mountains. In the morning the coast had disappeared from view. Sometimes the sun was in one place and sometimes in another, but the horizon always stayed in the same place. When night-time came the sky burned with a million stars. But the sight of them was nothing compared to the sea. *Hali!* If I tell you how the sea glowed with sparkling green lights that came from the deepest parts and lit up the sides of the ship. To see it made my hair stand on end. A woman next to me – we were almost all women there – began to weep and pray. Another burst into song. A deckhand tried to calm them, telling us these were not supernatural beings but living creatures so tiny as to be invisible, but whose tiny bodies gave off a certain electricity. He took a pebble from his pocket and cast it into the sea, and where the pebble landed a flash of lights lit up the water. She did not believe him, and I only pretended to because I appreciated his good intentions.

The next day I saw a black heron flying overhead. And then a praying mantis, weighed down by sodden wings, clinging to the railing. I put her in an empty cup until her wings dried out again. I saw the flags of a line of herring boats on the horizon. We were close to land.

All morning it took for the ship to dock, my stomach flipping like a beached fish every moment. Despite the tea, my lips were parched and flaking. The salt glistened on my skin like powdered diamonds. My clothes, which had been soaked and dried several times, were now stiff as paper. Still, my discomfort was soon forgotten as I followed Madam Turay through the streets of the city.

Lagos! It smelled quite like our city, and it looked and sounded a bit like it, too. But, oh, in every other way the difference between them was immense. Our city was a simple melody, whistled by a solitary man. Lagos was one hundred pipes, horns and drummers.

There was so much to see, I can't tell you. What I can tell you is the thing I remember most. The women! So tall and proud (and frequently hard faced), who wore their headdresses as high as the roofs of the houses.

Madam Turay worked fast and I followed at her heels, my ears, eyes and brain absorbing everything. Shop owners pulled out bolt after bolt of fabric at the wave of her hand: Dutch Wax, batiks, prints. And other fabrics, delicate to the touch: cambric, georgette, crêpe de Chine, organza, brocade. Still others I had never heard of: shantung, duchesse, bombazine. The shopkeepers who were sometimes Indians and sometimes Syrians indicated which cloths were currently in fashion among the women of Lagos. Prices were agreed with a barely perceptible nod of the head. At night we returned to the house where we stayed with four other women. Two from Ghana. One from Guinea. Another from Upper Volta. All doing the same thing we were doing. All traders. Some buying. Some selling. The Ghanaian woman showed us some samples of cloth, heavy machine-loomed cotton in green, yellow and gold. She told us we could order in any colours we desired, for she was the owner of the factory where the cloth was made.

Within two months of our return all the cloth we had bought was sold. Madam Turay was delighted. She had given me thirty *lappas*, each measuring two yards, to sell initially. She offered me a ten per cent commission, we agreed twelve. One evening I cooked and invited a number of women round to my house. After we had eaten I opened my chest, the big one my mother had once owned, and I displayed the *lappas*. For those who bought three I discounted the last. I encouraged the women to return the next week and bring a friend. Whenever a woman introduced me to a new customer she was rewarded with a discount on her next purchase.

I followed Madam Turay to Lagos and then to Accra. Four months later we went into partnership and I began to make the trips alone. The following year we opened a store right in the centre of town, close to the Agip petrol station and the place the long-distance buses arrived and departed. On the morning we raised the sign 'Kholifa Turay Cloth Merchants' there was already a sizeable crowd outside, we could only allow six inside at a time while the others waited outside, some under the shade of the awning, the ones at the back sweating in the sun.

To my house I added a two-room extension for Ansuman and Kadie, who by now were expecting their first child. And one Friday, after prayers, we moved them in together with their small amount of furniture. Ansuman brought me a gift, a dough sculpture. It was a house, with a roof and a door and windows that opened to reveal children peeping from within.

Later the same evening, long after the two had gone to bed, I sat outside on my stool at the back of the house fingering the keys on the belt around my waist, watching the patterns in the darkness, thinking about my dreams. A long time ago I learned how to read my dreams. Not in the way you're imagining, with some kind of magic, but to look at them in such a way as allowed me to read what was in my own heart.

In my dreams I lived in a house. A small house, not too big. Sometimes a round house, like the kind I was brought up in when my grandmother still lived. Whitewashed with painted shutters and a place to grow vegetables at the back. Other times a square town-house with a new wing, like this one. In my dreams I lived in this house with my children, everybody fat and smiling.

One day I noticed something about this dream, which I had had a great many times before. Something missing. I stood back and looked at my dream, the way you might look at a painting or a view. I looked everywhere, from the path leading up to the door, to the empty hammock swinging at the front of the house, I even searched the corners of the rooms. Nowhere. You see, in my dream there was no man. Just me and my house and my children.

And I knew I was as happy as I ever would be.

On the final day of my father's forty days, my mother stood alone and naked in her room, waiting for the women to come who would wash her. The house had been swept, the drapes removed from the windows, shutters opened, mirrors revealed, the pictures of my father gone, too – given away to friends and relatives as keepsakes. All but one: a photograph taken before his slow death began. It showed my father standing alone in front of his house. Whenever he was photographed, which was not often, it was alone. Always. Except for the picture of him sitting alongside the other advisers to the *obai*, the one you once showed me in a book written by an American academic who came here as a young Peace Corps. He was leaning slightly forward, unsmiling, gazing with a terrible intensity into the camera lens as though he was trying to look into the future. Either that, or he had some unspoken dislike for the photographer.

The clothes she had worn during her mourning were gone too, with the exception of one simple house dress left for her to wear. It lay across the bed behind her.

My father would be my mother's last husband. There were no brothers for her to choose a new husband from, the way she had chosen him. Maybe a cousin or a nephew could be brought in to take care of her. Maybe she would become a praying wife, join a household run by another woman. But in my heart I knew my mother would never be capable of living like that, she who had always been a head wife.

Outside, smoke from a charcoal pit drifted across the compound. the carcasses of a sheep and a goat hissed on their spits. Vats of rice bubbled on a row of three-stone fires. Women called to each other, lifted lids, passed wooden spoons from one to the other, heaved huge pots, cuffed a child here and there or clapped hands at the dogs who wove their way through the fuss. There would be prayers, then libations performed in my father's honour by members of the society, heedless of his Muslim faith.

I should not have looked in at my mother, but I did. Hidden where she couldn't see me, behind the shutter of the open window. In all my life I cannot remember having seen her naked except that one time. I had never even seen her without her hair covered.

There she stood, in the centre of the room, like a child waiting for her mother to come and dress her. Arms by her side, palms turned out, staring into the shadows. Folds of empty skin at her belly. Long, flat breasts. Her hair white and soft as the clouds.

Her lips were moving, a murmured prayer. In less than a minute the women would arrive to lead her to the stream. She knew what was coming, she'd been through it before. They would remove the last mourning dress, would wash her arms and hands, her body and her face. They would give her water to rinse and spit. They would wash away her old life and warn my father's spirit from coming back to her. For she was no longer his.

Then I realised she was not staring into the shadows, but at the portrait of my father. And though I couldn't hear what she was saying I realised she was not praying, but talking to her husband one last time. Once she gestured with her right hand and as she did, offered a glimpse of her face to me. I saw the grief and the love there. And suddenly I felt hot with shame for spying on her. I turned and walked away.

Once when I was a teenager I accompanied an aunt on an errand to another village. We passed a woman bathing alone in a stream. She acknowledged the two of us by inclining her head.

'Good morning, Ma,' I returned.

My aunt shook her head. 'Good morning, *Pa*,' she corrected.

I had heard of women like her, though I had never seen one. They were women who had become members of the men's society, not like the silly girls who banged the tortoiseshell drum – they were being punished. No, rather these were women who had already married and borne their children, women of age and wisdom, who had earned a certain kind of respect and whom the society honoured with their title. As we continued I turned my head again and again to look again at the woman, standing there up to her waist, alone in the water.

The memory of this came to me as I sat with my mother, Ya Isatta and several of my aunts, among them the one with whom I had walked from one village to the other. They were visiting to congratulate me on the success of Kholifa Turay Cloth Merchants, though in a remarkably short time the talk had turned to my continued unmarried state. My elders had turned out in force to urge me to take a husband. The store was a success, they were pleased at that, naturally. But now I would need a man to help me. I could not see why they should say this. They were telling me to give away what I had worked so hard to build up. Besides, I was happy.

Once, in the hollow of a dead tree behind our home, a wildcat gave birth to her kittens. I used to climb a nearby tree and watch them for many hours, playing outside the den while their mother caught rats and mice to bring back to them. After a few months they began to accompany her on hunting trips in the early morning. In those times she taught them to creep up on a partridge until they were inches away, to avoid the cobra's lair and to steal the eggs from the nests of birds. The seasons passed, the tree crumbled into soft powder, an aardvark dug a warren beneath it. At night sometimes, rarely, I would catch a glimpse of her and her tiny dark-skinned baby scratching at the termite hills. Another time a she-leopard and her two cubs were mobbed by monkeys on the banks of the stream; the mother fought her assailants tooth and claw, bringing down four or more and lacerating a dozen others before she retreated.

My aunts thought that I was unnatural not to want a man in my life, but to me it seemed the most natural thing in the world.

I said nothing, I watched my aunts' faces, I nodded and dreamed and at some point my mind travelled back to the day I went walking with my aunt and saw a *mambore* for the very first time.

From the day a woman joined the men's society she would be called Pa, give up her creel and learn to use a line and hook, exchange the stool at the back of the house for the hammock at the front, swap her snuff for a pipe. And she relinquished her place in the society of women.

The *mambores*. The women who lived as men.

My aunts' voices droned on like flies in the summer. I stopped listening and dreamed. I saw the house that was sometimes round and sometimes square. I saw the fat, happy children. I saw the empty hammock swaying in the early evening breeze.

And in that moment I saw something else.

I saw the hidden path curling between the trees.

My mother was ready. The women had knocked on her door and now she preceded them down to the river. She walked with her chin up, one shoulder bare where her dress had slipped. The silence blew through the gathered crowds like a breeze, people stood and watched in awe.

Women were coming from every direction, out of houses, up the path, through the crowd, women laying down their cooking spoons, women preparing to leave the fires unattended, women squeezing through the people. One, two, three. Ten, twenty, thirty. Seventy, eighty, one hundred. One by one the women fell in behind my mother, from the oldest to the youngest.

Every woman in the village. Except one, and that one was me. I let them pass. I stepped aside to join the men.

Yes, it's true. I can see you've guessed it, but don't know quite whether to believe it. Me, your own aunty. Well, you've guessed right. It was nothing dramatic. I let the men of the society come to me. I let it be known that I would consider relinquishing the birthright of womanhood in exchange for the liberty of a man. And in time they found me. After all, there are few women who would choose such a life. Naturally, there were those things I missed, mostly the company of other women. But I had made the life I dreamed of, and it suited me. I had taken my own path, neither right nor left.

After a while we heard the singing and knew it was over. When the women reappeared their mood was changed, they were dancing, shuffling their feet through the dust, swaying their bottoms. Somewhere in the centre of them all she walked alone. They had dressed her in a new costume made from a heavy blue fabric: a silk damask of four hundred threads, real damask from

Syria, double-sided with highlights of silver woven through the design.

I knew because it came from my own store, I had chosen it myself. On her shoulder she wore a sash of the same cloth, her hair was hidden inside a tall headdress. My mother, walking towards an unknown future. As beautiful as a bride on her wedding day.

CONSEQUENCES

14

Hawa, 1991

Sugar

IT HAD RAINED DURING the night, an unseasonal rain. In the morning the ground was stained in dark patches, like sweat. The light was dull, there were no shadows at all. And yet the rain had done nothing to clear the air, which was heavy and hot. I woke early, went outside to urinate and afterwards I lay on my bed, looking up at the rafters.

From somewhere in the darkness above me a drop of water fell slowly through the dense air, shattered upon a rafter and showered on to me. I didn't move. I felt the water sliding down my face. In my mind I saw the next drop, swelling and growing like a ripe breadfruit ready to drop from the tree. Instead of a drop of water I imagined a great fruit whistling through the air, smashing on the rafters and covering me in sticky flesh and juice. With that thought I pulled myself up.

There was a hole in the roof, and by the time the rains came the zinc would have rotted in a dozen more places. I told myself I must remember to tell him when he came home, so he could go and borrow a ladder from my uncle opposite and climb up there to take a look. He would know what to do. He would send into town for a hammer and nails, and some sheets of zinc. Then he would climb up there again to fix it, while I prepared him something to eat. Maybe groundnut stew, which was always his favourite with smoked catfish from the river. Or then again I would have made that to celebrate his homecoming. Maybe a bowl of pepper soup and some coco yams. Or sour sour. Or cassava leaves. There were no leaves left in my plot, I had lost them all to the locusts. I would have to go into town to the covered market, to see what I could find. I would buy only the best: the youngest, sweetest leaves.

Whenever he came home the truck dropped him off at the roundabout in town and he would walk to the house. Not sticking to the road, but in a straight line. Cutting across from one road to the next, through backyards and down the sides of the houses. His walk came from me, not his father. Of course, they taught them these things as well. How to walk in straight rows, swinging their arms and raising each leg up high, holding it there for just a moment, letting the heel drop to the ground so it sent up a little spurt of dust. Not looking this way or that. All the time with their eyes fixed straight ahead. When he came home people looked up to watch him pass. Little boys ran after him, begging to try on his cap or else placing their small feet in the prints left by his boots. Even before I saw him in the distance, I could always tell when he was on his way.

That dark morning I went out to the yard and called for the girl to get on and light the fire, while I washed. I untied my *lappa* and hung it up on the peg. I stood there for a moment and looked down at a body I no longer recognised. Loosening all over, as though I was shrinking inside. I pulled at a handful of my skin, and felt the flesh slip away from the bone. My body was nearly smooth, the hair no longer had the energy to grow. After all those years spent stripping the hair away. I soaped myself, using the last sliver of the soap my son had brought. Imperial Leather: the soap wore away until all you were left with was the label. And then I doused myself with water from the bucket, dried with the *lappa*, slipped on my plastic shoes and made my way back inside.

The girl came to inform me there was no sugar for the tea. Stood in front of me holding out the empty blue cardboard box with the red lion stamped on the cover.

'So you told me yesterday. And the day before. And the day before that,' I told her. 'Perhaps you think I'm senile, that I don't remember.'

'No, aunty.' But she didn't go away, just stood there with the box in her hand. As though I would magically fill it up again.

So I asked her: 'You think I can snap my fingers like that and make sugar for you?'

'No, aunty.' She spoke softly, especially when she was being rude. This girl could go back to her family for all I cared. If she ever became somebody's wife they'd send her back with sixpence on her head in no time at all.

' "No aunty, no aunty." ' I mimicked her. 'So what do you want me to do?'

'Maybe you can buy some when you go into town.' And she had the audacity to look me straight in the face when she spoke. Straight in my *eye*! Such insolence. I snatched the box and threw it upon the fire. You just had to watch the change come over her when Lansana was home on leave. Like a cat on heat. That sullen face suddenly all pouts and simpers. Encouraging his teasing. Brushing her breasts against him whenever she passed, hiking her skirt up round her thighs when she sat down opposite him. Then and there I promised myself I'd be rid of her before his next visit.

At breakfast the girl ate noisily. Swallowing great mouthfuls of porridge and plugging her face with hunks of bread. She'd eat me out of house and home, this one. I stood up and removed the dish, before she could finish the lot, otherwise there would be nothing left for tomorrow except carambola from the tree that hung over the wall from my neighbour's garden. And that always gave me problems with my stomach.

'Have you ironed my dress yet?' I asked her.

'You haven't given it to me,' she said with her mouth still full. Always with an answer. Too clever for her own good. I would have thrown it at her, but for the fact it was my best dress. I stepped inside to prepare myself.

I sat down in front of the mirror and creamed my face, using some of the face cream Lansana had given me. On the side of the jar along with some kind of Arabic writing was a drawing of a woman with black, black hair and eyelashes, red, red lips and white, white skin. She was holding a rose up to her face. A red rose. I dusted my face with a little talc and dabbed some perfume on my neck and between my breasts from the little bottle I kept hidden from the girl. I put it carefully back in its place behind the loose stone in the wall.

The girl came in with the dress just as I was replacing the stone. Now I'd have to find a new place for the bottle. I stood and watched her out of the corner of my eye as she laid the dress on the bed. She was making a good show of pretending not to be interested in what I was doing.

'Go count the chickens,' I told her, just to get rid of her. Go count your chickens before they hatch, I thought. She'd get a surprise soon enough when I sent her on her way. That would wipe the smirk off her face.

I slipped the top over my head. It was tight-fitting, with narrow sleeves to the elbow. I regretted then that I had sent the girl away. She might have made herself useful helping me, but it was too late for that. By the time I managed to get my head through and straighten the bodice I was damp with sweat. I stood with my legs apart while I wound the *lappa* three times around my waist and then sat back down again for a moment to catch my breath. My jewellery box was on the table in front of me. I opened it and rummaged through the odd buttons, hair clips and safety pins until I found what I was looking for. The pair of gold earrings.

I let them drop from one palm into the other. I pushed them through the holes in my ears and lifted the mirror up to my face. I turned my head from side to side, feeling the weight pulling at my lobes. The reflected light bounced from my cheekbones. I took them off and inspected them again. One of the hoops was very slightly dented. I rubbed my finger across the place, as if I might smooth it out. It didn't matter. Nobody would see. All they would notice was the size of the hoops, the quality of the gold. Eighteen carat. Twenty-four probably. Such good quality, a son buys nothing but the best for his mother.

Outside I heard my neighbour calling. I didn't answer. I stayed where I was. Let her think I wasn't at home. She'd only be coming to bother me for the four cups of rice I borrowed from her the week before. Let her wait. She had plenty of rice. I had seen inside her storeroom myself. It was full of food. The Government had warned against people who hoarded food, driving up the prices so everybody suffered.

While I waited for her to clear off, I searched for my umbrella and when the coast was clear I stepped out of the house.

I walked to town. I didn't have the money for transport. The rain was gone, replaced by the sun. I walked the whole way, carrying my umbrella aloft. When Lansana gave it to me I told him it was the widest one I had ever seen, and it was true. It provided me with a pool of shade to walk in.

With each step I felt the earrings swing against my face. Every so often I lifted my hand to my face to feel them again. I wished I'd brought the mirror with me so I could stop and look at them.

A tune came into my head and I hummed for a while as I walked. Then I remembered it was something my first husband used to whistle and I stopped. Both my first and second sons lived with him now, working in the butcher's trade. They didn't visit their mother as often as they should; I suspected him of turning them against me. But then they were as soft and foolish as him. Still, you can't throw away a bad child. They were my sons. I would always be their mother. The rest of it is up to God. Now Lansana, my Okurgba, my warrior – he'd made me proud. Followed my brother into the Army, where he had been promoted I don't know how many times. He wore stars on his shoulders and sent me gifts he paid for with his salary.

Outside the Contehs' house the awning had yet to be dismantled, though the chairs were gone. The opening of the house had been Wednesday past. I hadn't been invited. I could have gone anyway, but I chose not to. The Contehs didn't know it but I knew they whispered about me behind my back. That morning I would have liked them to see me pass, but the house was quiet. In fact, the street was empty. A thought came to me. I glanced around. I lowered the umbrella and rolled it up. I veered towards the front of the house. The thatch of banana leaves on top of the awning was already fading, the green bamboo poles that held it up had begun to blanch. Still nobody looking. I reached out and hooked the handle of the umbrella around the pole nearest to me, gave it a good yank.

I walked on. Behind me the awning lurched violently as one corner collapsed. Never looking over my shoulder, I raised the umbrella over my head, and walked on to the end of the street.

There was the petrol station where the bicycle taxis waited. I hadn't travelled that way in many months now. It wasn't such a comfortable way to travel but it was better than being on foot. Anything else was unaffordable. The price of petrol was always going up. Always going up. Nothing ever became cheaper. None of the boys leaning on their bicycles looked up as I passed. Well, I wasn't young any more.

In front of the covered market I slowed my pace a little, just to see what was on offer. I had a few things to buy, but that would have to wait until the end of the day, when the traders were willing to drop their prices just to be rid of the stuff. Other times I went to market in the early morning. The stall holders liked to treat their first customer well. Not for the customer's benefit, I should add, only because they thought it boded well for the rest of the day.

Ahead of me two women entered Asana's fabric store. I wondered whether she was in town or travelling. Who would choose such a life? No husband, no time to talk even. Always busy, working herself into the ground. Well, I suppose she didn't have any brothers. But really, she should have had more sons. I bought the cloth for my dress there the last time she was out of town. Seven yards of brocade. The girl in the shop – who did she think she was? – looked as though she was about to refuse me credit until I reminded her I was family. I passed by on the other side of the road, deciding against going in. Wait until Lansana was home and then we'd go in together.

I imagined us walking down the street. Him so broad shouldered and handsome. Many months had passed since he'd been given leave. In all that time I had not heard from him, I could only imagine what duties he was undertaking. Who knew where in the country he might be, some place without a post office. And you know, sometimes they didn't allow them to write, especially when the mission was important or secret.

Rain was threatening, a dark cloud rose up behind the mosque, though the sun still shone. The light shimmered, catching the white robes of the men gathered at the front of the building after midday prayers. Women, dressed in all manner of colours, made their way from the back door. Some people were waiting to cross the road by the roundabout, others stood about in clutches exchanging greetings at the same time as they eyed one another up and down. I slipped into the crowd, mingling, nodding to this person and that person, enjoying the looks that came my way. And sure enough presently I saw somebody I did know: the woman who was once my mother-in-law, in a manner of speaking. Remember Khalil? The one who betrayed me? His mother.

Well, I'm telling you now – it couldn't have been better. I turned away and strolled on a short distance. When I felt her close behind me, I swung around like I had suddenly remembered something.

'Aunty!' I said, as though she was the last person on earth I expected to see there.

'Hawa,' she nodded. She would have liked to move on, but I was blocking her path.

'I hope you are well?' Or some such irrelevance.

'As you see me, by God's grace.'

'And the family?' I persisted, though I noticed she made no enquiry as to my own health.

'They are all well.' She glanced over my shoulder, wanting to get away. But I was not finished yet. The thing about niceties is that there is no end to them. I asked after every member of the family by name. She took no care to elaborate on her replies. Then I mentioned Khalil's name. She looked at me directly, then. Suspicious eyes flickered over my face for a moment, until she caught sight of the earrings. I smiled and put my hand up to touch them.

'A gift from my son,' I told her.

'Very nice.' Thin lips stretched tight into a smile, a mouth like a rubber band.

'Solid gold. Twenty-four carat.' She was silent. 'Bought with his salary, you know. He is in the Army. A Major. A promotion, another one.' I wasn't sure if that was correct, but it didn't matter.

And maybe I should have stopped there. 'He'll be coming home soon. On leave.'

'Well, I am glad to see you are so well. Until next time, Hawa.' And she stepped around me, which was annoying because I had wanted to be the first one to walk away. Still, the victory was mine.

I moved off in the other direction. There were still a good number of people outside the mosque, the imam among them in a long purple coat over his robes. I raised my umbrella over my head as I turned down a side street, passing the stalls selling second-hand electrical goods and suchlike, to where the Syrian traders – Lebanese, they were called now – had their shops. Looking about me I ducked into the nearest entrance.

The man behind the counter, shouting at somebody at the back of the shop, stopped the instant he saw a finely dressed woman enter and smiled at me.

'Good day, madam,' he said. That was how impressive I looked. I moved closer to the counter, underneath the dusty glass of which lay many pieces of jewellery, mostly gold.

'How much for the gold?' I asked.

'To buy?'

'No, to sell.'

'What carat?'

'Twenty-four,' I told him. He raised his eyebrows.

'Show me.'

I slipped my earrings off and dropped them into his outstretched hand. Oh, it was a difficult thing for me to do. He weighed them in his hand, scratched the surface with a dirty thumbnail and shook his head.

'This is not twenty-four carat.'

I looked back at him. 'Eighteen then,' I said confidently. Still good.

He shook his head at that, and dropped them into a small set of scales. 'Where did these come from?'

I decided not to mention my son. Not because I had anything to hide, but because these days too many people were saying bad things about soldiers, about the things they were doing. He would try to pretend they had been looted and use that to offer me an even poorer price.

'Left to me by my mother,' I replied.

Nine carat! Can you believe it? Of course he was taking advantage, but what was I to do? I didn't bother to thank him. I took the money and put it in my purse. As soon as Lansana came home we would come back here and give that thief back his money. Redeem my earrings for the measly sum he gave me.

Outside the shop I stepped into a doorway for a few moments to adjust my headdress so that it covered my ears. A few people were still standing around by the mosque. I kept my chin high as I walked by. I could feel their eyes upon me. I looked neither to one side nor the other, but straight ahead, to the bicycle stand, and gave one of the fellows there my address. In full view of the lot of them I climbed on behind him and we rode away.

I felt the wind in my face. I sat sideways on the parcel shelf with my ankles crossed, feeling as demure as a girl out with a suitor. I felt something I had not felt for a long time.

I remembered the last time Lansana had come home, bringing with him a cassette player. He liked to listen to it all day, morning, noon and night. He took baths and changed his clothes, sometimes several times a day. Then sat back down, tapping his fingers or his foot on the floor, turning the cassette over every time one side finished. To tell the truth the noise got on my nerves: the repetitive sound of some man's voice. One evening I asked him to turn it down. I had to raise my voice over the sound of the music, if that is what you could call it. I repeated myself once, twice. The third time Lansana suddenly swung around and faced me. For a moment he looked furious, I wondered if he had been asleep, dreaming, and I had woken him up. But then his face softened and he smiled. He stood up and grasped both my hands and swung me around, and had me dance with him to that terrible music. Yes, I really did. I danced.

I would not have that feeling of joy again for years to come. After that day when I was forced to sell my earrings, I waited for Lansana as long as I could. By then the girl had gone, I saw the people fleeing all around me, I was too afraid to wait any longer. I pushed three of my dresses into a plastic bag, that was all, there was no food in the house. We followed the footpaths to the main road, passing villages emptied of people. I saw a lad I knew, a salt seller, walking in the other direction. 'Be careful, Ma,' he warned me. They were shooting northerners at the checkpoints.

When I reached there I listened carefully to the answers people ahead of me gave. My turn came, I bowed my head, I muttered the name of the same town in the South. The soldier demanded the name of the headman, he narrowed his eyes: yellow eyes, dark at the core. I supplied it, giving the name I had just overheard, and passed through. My son is a soldier, I wanted to tell him. He's in the Army. Perhaps you know him. But I dared not, I kept my head down and carried on walking.

There were no lorries. But there were more checkpoints, each time we passed through another the risk grew. So we left the road and walked through the trees, standing in the shadows whenever we heard people on the path. We were close enough to hear them, to smell them. It was impossible to tell one side from the other, soldiers from rebels, they all looked the same.

Once, a long time later, in the displacement camp, a consignment of food had arrived. All the women gathered around holding their plastic cups and measures, waiting to be given their own share. We had waited a long time for this food. But when the crates were opened there was none. A mix-up. The boxes were full of lipsticks, hundreds of them, in their gold coloured cases. The men in blue helmets immediately surrounded the vehicle and prepared for a riot. All of us had such hunger in our bellies. But a moment later they pushed back their helmets and lowered their sunglasses, to make sure what they were seeing was really true. The women rushed forward, myself among them, to snatch up these shining lipsticks. The many miles between us and our lost homes, our rotting feet, the grass and leaves with which we had tried to line our stomachs, the emptiness of the future: for a short while all was forgotten. We stood in the sun, laughing and ribbing each other, painting our mouths in vivid colours.

But all that was yet to come. For a few moments more I lifted my head up and savoured the sensation of riding on the bicycle, of people watching me from the sides of the street. We freewheeled down the main road, swerving to avoid the potholes, which somehow made it all the more enjoyable. And once we were around the corner and out of sight I tapped the fellow on the shoulder and got off the bicycle. Told him I had changed my mind and walked the rest of the way home.

When I reached the house the girl was there waiting for me, leaning against the door frame with her arms crossed. She smiled at me, lips closed – and did not stir herself to come help with my packages, but watched me as I walked towards her. She didn't move even when I was inches from her, practically nose to nose. She was grinning openly by that time. Turning my body slightly sideways, I was forced to squeeze past her.

As I did so I reached for the box of sugar cubes in my bag. I dropped it into her hand. And watched the smile fall off her face.

Some people say he is living in America, that lots of soldier boys went there. To the land that created the blue jeans and trainers and rapper singers they love so much. I must confess though, I have a daydream about him, a new one. That perhaps one day he will read my story, there will be a knock on the door and there he will be, in his uniform, with white gloves and shining buttons as smart as the day I went to see him on parade. His eyes will glow with happiness, not glitter with the unfathomable anger that seemed to possess him towards the end. And I will hold out my arms: 'Lansana,' I will say. Perhaps I will cry, I won't be able to help myself, it has been so long. And he will hug me and say something, anything, in the teasing way he did whenever he wanted to make me smile. And there I'll be, laughing and crying at the same time, as I step aside to let him in.

15

Serah, 1996

The Storm

ONCE I STOOD THOUSANDS of feet up on the edge of an escarpment, side by side with Janneh watching a storm race across the plain below. In the distance tiny figures ran ahead of the dust, dark clouds bearing down upon them. They were huddled over, clutching at their clothing, holding on to children, trying to shield themselves from the fury of the storm. In between us and those terrified souls, I could see more people, just beginning to sense the growing tempest, hurrying along, not yet caught up in its violent swirls, gazing up at the sky in an attempt to read the signs. Directly below were others still, oblivious to what was happening only a few miles away, tending their animals, watching their children at play, sitting outdoors in the sunshine.

I remember how we wanted to shout and wave and jump up and down. But instead we did nothing. We were too far away. And even if they had heard nobody would have believed us, for where they stood they could not see the omens in the sky.

Sometimes I think this is what happened in our country. Nobody heeded the warnings, nobody smelled the rain coming, or saw the lights in the sky or heard the roar of thunder, until we were all engulfed by it.

In Italy before the war in Europe, Benito Mussolini made the trains run on time. I read that once in a history book. He also wore a white uniform and a helmet with a plume on the top, and knew how to talk to people in a way that made them want to believe him.

We had a new President. A young man, who might have been a Benito Mussolini, who was handsome and finely attired in his uniform and who wore mirror sunglasses and swaggered in front of other heads of state, men in their sixties and seventies whom he appeared to despise, perhaps because they reminded him of the President he had just chased from our country. Nobody wanted to be ruled by the old, fat President and his corrupt cronies and because the new, young President cleaned up the streets and emptied the gutters of filth and spoke about democratic elections and looked so fine, the people were happy. Women sewed dresses printed with his delightful features, young men copied his mode of dress and eyewear, everyone joined in the campaign to clean up the streets. Clean up the Government. Clean up the country. People turned over their mattresses, bleached the steps in front of their houses and hosed down the walls, swept the dirt from their yards into the street from where it was miraculously removed. We were putting our house in order.

It felt good.

Some of the fat men who had financed the old President feared reprisals and left. Good riddance. Others, less high profile, stayed quiet and bided their time. Overnight it became impossible to find a single person who would admit to ever having supported the former President. The shopkeeper on the corner of the street who had voted for the party all his life gave his store a lick of paint and stencilled the new regime's slogan on his shutters. Ambrose printed up business cards and boldly offered his services to the new leaders.

The President's face in his mirror shades appeared on the front of international magazines. 'The youngest leader in the world,' said the headline. He had not even celebrated his thirtieth birthday. We were so proud of our baby-faced leader: so slim and strong, not bloated on bribes and flattery. So proud we handed him our anguish and hopes and fears to carry on those broad shoulders of his. The rest of the world looked on, smiling fondly. Or so we thought. We could not see they were really laughing at our foolishness.

In their neat and shining homes, people settled down to wait.

And waited. And waited. And just as they were beginning to wonder how much longer we might have to wait, to fear our leader was just a pretty face with a silver tongue, he was toppled by another young man with equally babyish features though he was not quite as silver-tongued. So that when, in a tarnished voice, he announced we were to have elections for the first time in many years few believed it, and many didn't hear at all because they had given up listening a long, long time ago.

A Monday. The year, 1996. I was in my late fifties.

I stood before my reflection in the mirror on my wardrobe, watching my own movements in the half-light. No electricity for three days running. The clothes I had put out the night before hung from the door: a trouser suit in pale blue linen. I discarded it and instead chose an orange-gold gown embroidered at the sleeves and around the neck. In the dimness of the morning I made up my face, applying the brushstrokes from memory: foundation, powder, lipstick, mascara. Then I slipped the gown over my head. From the shoe rack on the back of the door I chose a pair of gold shoes to match the gown, with open toes and high heels and a strap that encircled my ankle, bought from Bally of Bond Street. I slipped gold bangles on to my wrists, clasped a necklace around my neck and hooked earrings in the lobes of my ears.

Since the early hours angry sounds had rolled over the city. Sounds like thunder from the direction of the Army base on the hill. A booming and the spit and crack of lightning. But in the morning, no sign of a storm, nothing to be seen at all, only a light dew on the ground that soon transformed itself into pale, curling vapours and vanished in the heat of the day.

In the lane a single hawker called his wares outside houses that were still in darkness. Silence everywhere. No car horns, no chatter of schoolchildren. Most schools were closed for the day. The corridors and classrooms of those that remained open were empty, as parents kept their children at home. A pair of dogs scrapping, a cockerel trumpeting: these were the only sounds.

From the verandah I looked out over the street. A woman

emerged from a house and threw a pan of dirty water into the road, ducked back inside without once looking over or offering a greeting. A rumbling, growing in the distance. An Army truck loaded with soldiers rolled past the junction swiftly on out of sight.

At seven o' clock when it was light I sat down to breakfast with Yaya. The bread was stale. No point sending out for a fresh loaf, the Fula shops would certainly be shut. I spread a slice with margarine and chewed a mouthful but, though I drank a glass of water, my mouth was so dry swallowing was impossible. The hunger was gone, replaced in my stomach by a tight, hard ball. I made a cup of instant coffee with the water in the Thermos and sipped at it. Its empty, bitter taste was all I wanted.

'Are you still going?' Yaya asked me.

'Yes,' I said, but a few dry crumbs caught in my throat and through them the word came out fluttering and small. I cleared my throat and coughed.

'Yes,' again. This time the sound of my own voice convinced me a little.

We waited together in silence, not in our usual companionable silence, but a taut stillness in which every sound echoed and reverberated.

The members of the women's volunteer group had been told a car would be sent to pick us up. It never came. I wasn't surprised at that. I gave the driver twenty minutes more, then I went to the telephone and dialled the number of the next woman. The receiver hissed faintly with static, the sound of the numbers clicking through, but again and again the call failed to connect. On the other side of the room Yaya fiddled with the knob of the transistor radio. There was none of the usual morning chatter, the endless announcements of births, deaths and marriages, the wishing of luck for exams, congratulations for scholarships, jingles for Mazola oil and Eveready batteries and Bennimix baby food. The dial passed station after silent station, like empty bus stops.

The crackling again. Once, twice. This time from somewhere in the distance. Followed by the thunder of another truck. I crossed the room to look outside. Yaya called to me to stay away from the windows. I pressed my back to the wall and moved the curtain a fraction. Another truck, also full of soldiers, standing waving their guns in the air, singing songs as though they were on their way to a football match.

From the radio a single voice rang out. It made me jump. That's how nervous I was; my heart felt like a trapped animal trying to claw its way out of a cage. A woman's voice, expressionless and staccato as an untrained actress reading somebody else's lines, announced the streets were calm, the polls had opened and people were beginning to vote. The elections were under way.

But the polls couldn't be open. It was impossible.

Rofathane. The village was all but encircled by a river that was a wide stream in some places and a deep channel in others: in many ways the place I grew up was almost an island. The path to the playing fields was crossed by means of a footbridge: the slender, swaying trunk of a single palm tree that rested between one bank and the other, spanning the swirling waters.

My mother taught me to cross that bridge and at the same time she also taught me how to master my own fear.

By that time Yaya had taken my place on my mother's back, but was still too small to play with. I used to tag along behind the older children and one day followed them on their way to the playing fields. But when we reached the bridge I stopped, too frightened to go any further. Instead I stood on the opposite bank, listening to the screams and chatter fade away, watching the water rise and fall, seeing myself already plummeting down and disappearing into a whirlpool.

The next time I came to cross the bridge I was with my mother. As soon as we neared it I clung on to her hand and dug my heels into the earth. My mother was unmoved. She picked me up and set me on the bridge, holding on to me lightly from behind.

'Look straight ahead,' she told me. 'Don't look back. And never look down. I'll be right behind you.' And with that she let me go.

I dared not disobey my mother, so although my knees trembled I did as she bade me, and when in midstream I wavered she prompted me. 'One foot in front of the other. Don't think about anything else, just look where you're going.'

Urged on by her gentle certainty I summoned my courage up from the inside. And as the years went by, in this simple way I learned to have power over my own fear.

I had forgotten that time. But that morning, after I listened to the words being spoken on the radio, I walked to the gate of the yard. My mind was set, I looked straight ahead, I ignored the little knot of fear rolling around in the empty hollow of my stomach.

Yaya came with me to the gate. The look on his face told me he would have tried to persuade me to stay at home. But the look on mine told him I was determined to go. My look won. My brother put his hands on my shoulders, kissed me on each cheek and watched in silence as I started walking down the empty street.

I dug into my handbag until I found the laminated badge and pinned it to my chest. I placed one foot in front of the other, I kept my eyes fixed straight ahead, I refused to think of the danger. One street later I banged on the iron gates of Redempta's house. She was ready, waiting for me. Never doubted that I would come, she told me later. I waited a moment while she fixed her badge to her chest. We looked at each other, we laughed because fear hates the sound of laughter. And we walked on.

Had anyone else been in the streets that morning they would have seen two middle-aged women, out for a stroll in the early light. But the words pinned to our bosoms told a different story: 'Returning Officer. Presidential Elections 1996.'

One by one we collected each woman from her home, until we walked two, three abreast down the main road. At every polling station along our route we dropped off a pair of women until, once again, it was just the two of us, Redempta and I.

A great cotton tree with buttressed roots stood in the middle of the football ground in front of the schoolhouse. Beyond it, on the steps of one of the classrooms, sat a pair of soldiers. They stood when they saw us, began to move towards us. We, too, advanced at an almost identical pace, neither hurried, nor slow. Straight ahead, until we stopped and faced each other: the soldiers and their adversaries, two middle-aged women.

What did we want? We indicated our badges. Reporting for duty, it crossed my mind to say.

'It may be dangerous to be out today, there might be trouble,' said the second soldier, as if we would be so easily cowed.

'Then so be it,' I said. 'We are here to bring in the vote. Now we need to get on, this station was supposed to open an hour ago.' For some seconds nobody spoke or moved.

The soldiers were roughly the age of my two sons. I watched as the one in front of me bit his lower lip, twisted it and then suddenly dropped his gaze and stepped aside. We moved past him and into the building.

'We will stay here for your protection,' he called after us, in a voice that was hollow at the centre.

'As you please,' I replied.

My knees shook as I walked, my hands holding on to the handle of my bag were slippery. Once inside we freed the three ballot boxes from the padlock and chains that held them together and set them out in a short, neat row. Just seeing them there, squat and imposing, somehow made me feel better. In a cardboard box along with paper and pens, we found the sign that said 'Polling Station' with a big, black arrow and this we placed outside the door. From her bag Redempta unpacked her own special cheese and jam sandwiches, a flask, a can of Peak milk and two cups. I watched her smooth, placid face beneath that terrible cherry wig she wore, absorbed in the task she had set herself.

We settled down to wait.

A man pushing an icebox of soft drinks in an old pram turned the corner, saw the soldiers, thought better of it and moved on with his load. The minutes passed. Dawn had been and gone, not a bird in sight. Outside the soldiers ground one cigarette stub after another under the heels of their boots. That and the scratching of the bats in the branches of the cotton tree, the gentle unfolding and wrapping of wings around bodies, were the only sounds. I could sense my fear skirting the building, attracted by the silence, looking for a way inside.

What did I think of while we waited?

I can only tell you what I didn't think about. I did not think about whether people would come. Nor did I waste the effort on wishing the soldiers away, because I knew they were there to frighten people off. I didn't think about the trucks carrying more soldiers all over the city. I didn't think about the other polling stations, sitting in pools of silence all over the country. Nor did I think about what we would do at the end of the day. Most of all I didn't think about the fear clawing at the cracks in the windows, scuttling under the floorboards, crawling across the roof, looking for an opening.

Instead I thought about that day, a long time ago, when I sat in a rice-weighing station wearing my favourite pair of red shoes.

The smell of rice dust on a cool morning, so clean and pure. By contrast this room was sweltering and smelled of ink and sour milk. Then it had been the end of the rains, harvest time. The land had been opulent, bursting with hope and fertility. Now, halfway through harmattan, it was desiccated, a semi-desert. The sky was choked with dust. The city stank. Hope had shrivelled and crumbled away.

When people are afraid they stay indoors. They close shutters, bolt doors, hide behind the flimsy tin and cardboard walls of their huts. That day even the police stayed inside, safe behind the thick walls of their solid British-built stations. Only the madmen wandered the streets, dazed and smiling, unexpected lords of the city.

There is but one reason people would venture outside on such a day.

Women's voices as muted and soft as the music of water. I had fallen into a kind of wakeful reverie, at first the sound drifted over me as though it had escaped from my dreams. I stood up and walked across the room to the door. The standpipe was on the other side of the football ground. The women approached it up a steep, rocky path hidden between the houses, bordered by tall grass on either side. Some were carrying plastic containers and bright-coloured buckets. They were barely clad, a tank top over loose breasts, a *lappa* carelessly knotted around hips or hitched up and tucked into underwear. Theirs was hot, damp, effortful work.

One of the soldiers, leaning against a door frame, had been picking his nose and flicking the hardened snot at an empty tin. At my appearance he straightened and followed my gaze in the direction of the women. I emptied the remains of my cup of coffee on the ground, nodded at him and we stood, both of us, watching.

A young girl at the water pipe with a baby on her back looked over briefly. I waved. She hesitated, then raised her hand and waved back.

'Morning-o,' I called and she echoed my greeting before bending back to her work. I called again, to a woman in a black dress with a comb stuck into her partially braided hair. Then to a girl in an old print frock. Within moments the women had formed a cluster over the water pipe. From time to time one of them straightened and looked over in our direction. More women arrived, were beckoned over, set down their containers and joined the huddle.

Beneath their slouched bodies I could feel the alertness, the muscle and sinew quickening under the skin, as the soldiers watched the water women beneath hooded lids.

Redempta came and stood next to me. She was a big woman. I'm sorry you never knew her. She was not so tall, but wide and straight. We stood shoulder to shoulder. Redempta began to hum. I remember that, because at first I wondered what she was doing. And then quickly I realised and I joined in. It was a woman's song, one that we were taught by our elders, we used to sing it on the way to the river with our water jars and again on the way back when they were full and heavy. Perhaps the soldiers knew this, perhaps they didn't. They must have had mothers and sisters, so I guess they did. We hummed in unison and the sound of our humming carried across the empty ground to the women on the other side and gave birth to the miracle that followed.

Those that still held on to their plastic containers set them down, they began to wander over. In the lead was the woman with the baby on her back, she was dressed in an old slip that fell off her shoulders, a green cloth tied around her head. There was something slightly unusual about her, something that made you want to stare. I think it was her eyes, they were hazel instead of deep brown, she was a fair skinned woman. Too fair for most people's tastes, still I remember even then thinking that she was beautiful. I saw the caution in the tread of her feet on the ground, but nobody watching would ever have guessed it from the way she carried herself, the way all the women carried themselves, as though they had never known a day's fear.

I straightened the board with the sign on it. I went back inside to take my place. A few moments later I heard Redempta giving directions:

'Collect a voting paper. Behind the curtain, doesn't matter which one. Mark your X. One X only, against the name of the candidate of your choice. Sign your name, or make your thumbprint before you leave. Thank you.'

After the women, word went around. Within a short time a queue had formed that flowed across the playing field and looped around the cotton tree. At first people came silent, shuffling, with lowered eyes. But when they saw us going about our business, when they saw how our will had triumphed over the soldiers who now stood uselessly to one side, they raised their heads, took their voting slips and pushed their thumbs into the ink pad with a flourish.

A man with a cockerel under his arm shook my hand and offered me the bird as a gift. I told him I was just doing my duty. A woman pressed a pair of skinned oranges into my hands. This time I accepted, I handed one to Redempta and sucked the juice out of the other. I was thirsty. There were other gifts, but the greatest reward of all came those times I pushed back my chair and went to the door to stare, with wonder, at the long line of people. Once I looked over at Redempta who, at exactly the same moment, raised her head from the pile of papers she was sorting; our eyes met, she gave me a wink and the slow smile that was hers.

Through the tightly woven streets in the east of the city, west to the whitewashed villas of the wealthy, south to the fishermen at the wharf, news that people were turning out to the polls spread through the city. Until finally, it reached the northernmost point, to the Army barracks on the hill with the painted cannon in the courtyard.

Nobody heard them coming, we were too busy taking names and counting heads, filling in voting slips and making thumbprints. Maybe we were too busy telling ourselves how clever we were. Maybe we had stopped paying attention.

The truck barrelled out of a side road, straight across the open space, sending people in every direction. From the canopy at the back jumped one, two, three – a dozen or more soldiers, guns at the ready. The people didn't wait to find out what was happening. Inside the station papers fluttered up like doves as people scattered. I wanted to run after them, to shout: 'Come back!' I wanted to scream and weep to see them go like that, knowing they were gone for good.

It was for our protection, the Commanding Officer told us. Tensions were rising in the city. All the time he was speaking his eyes roamed around, gathering details. He ignored us when we thanked him and said we did not need his protection. Voting here had been peaceful. He clicked his fingers and pointed. There, two soldiers set off at a trot. There, another two, guns at the ready. There, there, there! Men raced hither and thither at his command, and when the activity came to an end, I saw they had the entire polling station surrounded.

Nothing to do then, but go back inside and wait.

Redempta and I, neither of us had a word to say to each other. We moved about the room, tidying the papers that had fluttered up in the panic, setting the chairs and the table back. When we sat down again we did not meet each other's eyes, but looked mutely at our hands. There was nothing left to do.

In the heat the minutes stretched out, one by one. I don't know how much time passed, less than an hour I would imagine although it felt like an eternity. Then came sounds of life from outside. I straightened in my chair, cocked my ear. Redempta raised her head. Together we crept over to the window.

Advancing down the lane: boys, you know the ones, always hanging around hustling for a little money here and there, offering to watch your car, playing their music too loud. They came waving palm fronds, marching in choreographed mockery of the soldiers, in formation, until they were ranged on the opposite side of the football field. For a while they threw insults across at the soldiers, such colourful words, at another time I might have closed my ears. That day I listened and I watched intently.

There was one lad, dressed in denim shorts and a ragged T-shirt. Not a ringleader. More like a younger brother or cousin, somebody on the edge of what was happening but who yearns to be at the centre. It didn't take much to imagine his short life so far. Born with legs as skinny as bamboo that refused to grow straight but were bowed out and kept him home with his mother while the other boys were out playing. But later he became good at other things: mending stereos, fooling passers-by with card games. They give him a nickname and make him feel part of the gang. Most of the time. Except on the nights they put on their dark glasses and jeans and leave their homes, arms around each other, and come back in the early morning, with sour breath, smelling of cigarettes and perfume.

This lad threaded his way through the line of his companions, found himself a vantage point and stood square to the soldiers, a rock concealed behind his back.

The soldiers were a poorly trained lot. So many young men wanted to join the military; not for the pay which was miserable and on many months was never paid at all, but for the benefits – the unofficial ones, with which they supplemented their incomes. Everybody knew about the things they did, and yet even their parents and grandparents showed them respect, afraid to do otherwise. Everyone, that is, except the street boys. They had grown up side by side with the soldier boys in the same slum. The street boys knew which taunts were the most exacting. The soldiers stiffened and bristled to hear their mothers and sisters spoken of in such a way. An intake of breath, a sucking of teeth.

And somewhere among the ranks of the soldiers the bow-legged street boy's counterpart. One-time victim, now with a gun in his hand. Unconfident, nervy, his trembling forefinger wrapped around the trigger of his weapon.

A lizard scattered suddenly, foreshadowing what was about to happen. Another barrage of insults, and the bow-legged boy brought the rock out from behind his back and flung it with all his might across the divide. It fell short, sending up a small shower of dirt. Nobody was hurt, but somebody's nerve broke. A single shot, followed by another. Two bullets skidded through the earth. The third shot brought down the bow-legged boy, sent him flying backwards, legs and arms at awkward angles, like a scarecrow caught by the wind. The cotton tree shuddered, as a thousand bats flinched.

Time paused, as if considering whether to move swiftly on or turn back and reverse what had just happened. Time moved on. Realisation descended in an instant. Anger and outrage burst forth, the street boys began to advance. More stones. A volley of shots. This time aimed at the air above their heads, there would be no more casualties. The boys retreated with their wounded companion, swearing, holding up their fists, some still managed a swagger. Retreating all the same.

The colours of the day had fled, darkness was approaching. Redempta and I sat alone in the polling station among the ballot boxes.

A truck had arrived, collected some of the soldiers and driven away again. By my best estimate six, perhaps eight men remained. The van that was supposed to collect the ballot boxes was due in the next half an hour, but who knew now whether that would happen. At some point the soldiers would have to decide what to do with us.

I listened to the blood thumping in my eardrums, my breathing growing louder as the darkness closed in. Outside I could hear the bats leaving the cotton tree, taking to the skies one by one. I could see them through the window, watch them spiral upwards, their dark shapes outlined against the silver-blue sky, stretch their wings and turn towards the sea.

I could only just make out Redempta's form in the half-light. I inched my way towards her through the gloom and whispered into her ear. She nodded briskly. We got down on to our hands and knees and crawled around, groping in the darkness until we found what we were looking for: the chain that had held the ballot boxes together. I removed my headdress, wrapping it around the chain to muffle the sounds, in case the soldiers should hear us. We sat back to back, passing the chain around and between us.

Whatever happened next we were as ready as we ever would be, we sat and held hands in the dark.

Footsteps. The door was opened, the young officer in command stood silhouetted against the sky. Behind him the cotton tree encircled by flying bats. Polling had now officially closed, he informed us. We had done our job. From this point on he would take charge of the ballot boxes.

'We are instructed not to allow these boxes to leave our sight until they are properly handed over to be counted.' Redempta's voice was steady.

He would have expected us not to give in straight away. He replied smoothly: 'Well, I am an officer of the Army. You can regard yourselves as having placed the ballot boxes in safe custody.'

'We cannot do any such thing.' I spoke up, to show we stood together. 'We are very clear about our instructions. The boxes must go to the centre to be counted.'

'Exactly. And that's where I will make sure they are delivered. Believe me.'

Liar! He would have burned them, emptied them, thrown the ballot papers in the gutter, where they would float down to the sea like paper boats.

We were silent, Redempta and I.

'Eh bo, aunty.' His voice was changed now, softer, respectful almost. 'You've done your duty. You can tell that to your grandchildren. Now let me do my own. Look how dark it is already. My men will take care of you, make sure you get home.

The streets are unsafe, nobody will come to collect these boxes tonight.'

Neither one of us answered. We both thought this last bit was true. We had been forgotten. It was just us, this man and his soldiers.

'Get up now. My men will help you.' The officer switched on his torch and directed the beam at us.

It makes me feel like laughing now to think of the sight we must have made. Two middle-aged women, dishevelled and squinting in the sudden brightness, sitting on the dusty floor of a classroom in our gowns and good shoes, holding on to our handbags. The chain that bound us together went around our waists and then through the handles of the three sealed ballot boxes. The key to the padlock was tucked down Redempta's bodice. As good as at the bottom of the ocean.

The stand-off could not last for ever, but it lasted just long enough. Minutes later, out of the darkness – the sound of an engine. Yaya! He had spent the day waiting, listening to the no-news coming from the radio, knowing the less that was said the worse things must surely be. When night arrived he collected his car keys and stepped out of the house and drove through the streets, not daring to switch on the headlights, until he reached our polling station. Together we loaded the ballot boxes into the back of the Peugeot under the sullen stares of the soldiers, and though every moment we thought that they might stop us or that some authorisation might arrive to arrest us, deep down we knew we had called their bluff. We were not street boys, but three middle-aged citizens. The truth is, once we were no longer afraid, there was nothing they could do.

At the counting centre, Redempta, Yaya and I, we handed over the boxes to a white woman wearing a T-shirt printed with the words: 'INTERNATIONAL OBSERVER' in bold letters. And after our mission was complete, we drove home through the dark, silent streets, laughing as we went.

Oh, Redempta! My dear, Redempta. She lived long enough to see how all our efforts had been wasted. Even as we sat chained to our ballot boxes, on the other side of the country people with telltale purple thumbs were having their hands sliced off, to punish them for daring to insist upon their own leader. The Army handed over power with one hand, only to seize it with the other a year later. Old enemies created new factions and joined together against a common foe, us: the women and the children and the ordinary people. The new President, who was an old man, shook his head, climbed into his waiting helicopter and disappeared into the clouds. From those same clouds a maelstrom was unleashed, and of the many lives destroyed by its rage, one was Redempta. Murdered, alongside her husband, her children and countless others, the day the rebel army stormed the city.

I had a dream. In that dream I was playing with my children in the sun, not a cloud in the sky. I looked up, and high above me I saw the ghost of Janneh. From the top of the escarpment he was waving at me and shouting, but he was too far away for me to catch the words, so I smiled and waved back at him. A cloud crossed in front of the sun, for a moment I could hardly see him, I let my hand drop back to my side. Janneh was still calling to me. But it was too late, too late! The gathering winds swept his words away and hurled them out to sea.

And from somewhere in the distance, I heard the first, faint roll of thunder.

16

Asana, 1998

The Box

FIVE MONTHS EARLIER I had woken to a dawn the colour of steel. The curious light lasted through the morning and into the day as if the sun had never risen. The land glowed in silvery shades. Here and there pools of quivering light rested upon the side of a house, on the great leaves of the vine that climbed the wall around my yard. In the middle of the day I looked up at the sky expecting to see clouds, instead I saw the sun, a white disc.

A hawk dropped out of the sky and drank from a puddle of water. A superstitious person might have made something of it, otherwise nothing else remarkable happened. My granddaughter had baked black banana bread and she brought me a piece of it on a dish with a glass of water, staying to keep me company. My appetite had waned as I had grown older, and I covered the dish with a cloth, telling her I would enjoy it later. We spoke little, content in each other's company. I liked simply to watch her liquid movements: flicking a fly with the corner of her dress, fanning her face with her hand, twirling the end of a plait. She sat on the step with one leg stretched out in front of her, the other bent, her cheek resting upon the knee, facing away from me. In the half-light of that day I gazed at the back of her neck, the soft furrow that ran from the nape of her neck down between her shoulder blades; from behind the curve of her waist belied the child she was carrying, just now beginning to show in the roundness of her stomach. With each passing week the birthmark above her navel widened and stretched.

Adama had been eleven years old when her great-grandmother died. Too young to really remember, old enough not to have forgotten. She had loved my mother fearlessly. In a way I had never been able.

When she was three, ignoring Kadie, her own mother, she strode with tiny steps up to her great-grandmother and demanded loudly to be taken to the toilet. My mother threw up her hands and stared aghast, as though she had never cared for a child in her life. Kadie quickly led the child away. But my mother had been amused. The girl called her Ya Mama and sometimes Yammy, and my mother encouraged it.

I know, it's the oldest story in the world. The fresh spirit who frees one that has been bottled too long.

She had been away when Ya Mama died. And she had appeared to accept it as children do when they have yet to learn the meaning of for ever. Years later she began a game, which she played obsessively for a while. I came to think of it as the 'remember' game.

'Remember when that bird landed on Yammy's shoulder . . .'

'Remember when I made her coffee . . .' Mud and river water, mixed together in a tin cup. My mother had been fooled into taking a hearty swig. Later, in the mornings, real cups of coffee just as I had brought to my own grandmother a long time ago. Afternoons, they napped together on the four-poster bed that once belonged to my father.

'Remember Ya Mama's feet . . .' My mother took care of her feet, soles as smooth as paper, nails dipped weekly in henna. When she could no longer bend to reach them Adama buffed the undersides with pumice.

We would sit for hours sharing memories: fleeting, brightly coloured, sometimes surrounded by darkness, passing them back and forth until I was no longer certain whose were whose. She lent me her own memories of childhood with which to remember my mother.

We had played the game the day before for the first time in a long while. Sorting reminiscences the way we had baby clothes.

Storing some and putting others aside for the new baby, creating space for new things. That afternoon, though, there was no game. We sat together in a sleepy silence, I watched her head sink, listened to her breathing come in slow sighs.

I stood up to fetch a cloth to fold under her head. On my way I reached for the plate of banana bread. Hali! The plate seemed suddenly as heavy as if it was made of iron. My arm dropped. The plate slipped from my fingers, clattered and spun on the stone floor. Adama, startled, leaped to her feet. The heaviness slid down the side of my body into my leg. I tried to take a step, but I couldn't pick my foot up off the floor. Falling, I felt myself falling. With my other hand I reached for the table and missed. Through the gathering darkness I saw Adama hurrying towards me as I toppled forward.

Later I realised it had been haunting me, stalking me all that day: the steel-grey light – I would forever see the world in shadowy twilight. A doctor was called, a quack who gave me headache pills. Then a proper doctor who had studied in China. And he told me I had had a stroke.

I still went to the store. Adama pushed me in a wheelbarrow. The roads were too rutted to allow a wheelchair to pass. Kadie wanted me to stay home and rest. But I missed the smell, the feel of the place. 'When did you ever see a mother sleep while her child was crying?' I told her. There was always work to do. On days when Kadie went to visit our other shops, I worked the till with my one good hand while Adama climbed the stepladder to bring down the cloths.

My sister Hawa came to see me. Looked at me with sad eyes and shook her head. 'Nothing happens for nothing,' she pronounced with hidden pleasure. I gave a wave of my good hand, dismissing her. There's a certain kind of person who can always find an explanation for things that happen. My sister was one of those. Something bad befalls somebody they don't like and they say that person must have brought it upon themselves. When precisely the same fate comes their own way, this time it's a spirit bringing bad luck. A person they envy prospers only because that person made a bargain with a powerful spirit. But when they lose their own business, is it because they didn't work hard enough or because they ate all the proceeds and failed to reinvest them? Of course not. It is a *moriman*'s curse, purchased by a rival!

The doctor had explained to me exactly how it happened. A blood clot stopped up one of my arteries so the blood couldn't reach my brain. Like a dam in a river. Even I could understand that. He wrapped a rubber tube around my arm and took my blood pressure, tested my pee for diabetes, wrote a prescription and ordered me to cook with less palm oil.

I took advantage of my state not to offer Hawa anything that might encourage her to stay. She only ever visited when there was something she needed. This time, though, she seemed to want to stay for ever. I peered into her shadowed face.

When had this secret war between us begun? I wondered.

Five months later, though, her words came back to me. Terrible things began to happen to all of us. It was as though the end of the world had come. The earth crumbled, the sky rained down, people fled for their lives. *Nothing happens for nothing*. I wanted to straighten my crooked body, I wanted to stamp the earth, raise both my fists and scream at the skies.

What in the world had we all done to deserve such a fate?

When I think back now, we kept the knowledge a secret, even from ourselves.

Lorries travelling roads in the South were held up by gunmen who hauled the driver down from his cab, thieved the goods from the back of his vehicle and carried them away into the forest. They set fire to the lorry, sometimes roping the driver to the wheel. Other times slicing off his ears and stealing his shoes before leaving him to walk home. A band of miners were marched away from their workplace and not sighted until months later when they appeared on the other side of the country. Their kidnappers never said who they were or what it was they wanted. There were rumours of tattooed strangers who arrived in towns and moved among the people, members of a secret clan, whose mark was worn by the women under one breast and by the men on the buttock. They looked just like you or I, it was said, some spoke in languages nobody could understand. They disappeared as quickly as they came. There were stories of young men and women who slipped away to join them. The youths' families claimed their children had been stolen and scoured the countryside. Then there were other stories, ones that made your eyes stretch. Of beings that could become invisible, that could fly, leap over houses, that gathered to dine on the hearts of their victims from whence they derived their supernatural powers. There came a time when everybody had heard these stories, some had even claimed to have witnessed them with their own eyes.

Yet who the strangers were, nobody could say.

Members of the ancient clans, the leopard and the crocodile, outlawed for many decades but still continuing their fearful practices, said some. Others insisted such feats were beyond the power of mortal man. And others still said everybody else was talking nonsense, these deeds were the acts of the Army, devious in their hunger for power.

On the radio a Government spokesman reassured us. Small groups of insurgents were at work in some parts of the country. The Army was involved in a series of mopping-up operations, they said. He made it sound as harmless as spilled milk.

What an insurgent was, nobody knew. Then somebody said it was another word for rebel. Rebel!

People whose children had vanished hid their faces. People reporting fresh disappearances had their homes turned over, the roofs torched. People fell silent, dared not open their mouths to speak. There was a stillness in the air. From the outside it looked like calm, but beneath the surface were turbulent, invisible currents: fear, suspicion, confusion.

Still, life continued, for none of us had the luxury of pausing. For many years that was the way we lived. Finding scapegoats. Turning our faces from the truth.

A rooster used to call false dawns all through the night. I remember because when I woke up his voice was the first sound I heard. By then I had begun to find myself more and more a stranger to sleep. I knew I'd be awake now until morning. It was age, of course, and an effect of my condition. I couldn't keep my eyes open after lunch, only to be awake in the early hours, lying on my back, alone and floating unhinged upon a tide of darkness. That particular morning I woke with a full bladder. Impossible to wait for morning and Adama to come and help me. I put out my hand, felt for my stick, knocking it to the floor. I groped, found it with my fingers and hauled myself up.

Outside the air was cool, damp. I made my way slowly, inching forward with my now sideways walk, like a crab across the ground.

I didn't bother to go all the way to the latrine. I urinated out of doors, something I liked to do: the feel of the air on my thighs, the breeze murmuring in the trees, the smell of damp grass, the sound of the night birds interrupted by the hiss of steaming piss. I pulled up my *lappa*. It amused me to think I was doing something possible only under the disguise of the night. What, I sometimes wondered, would happen if I were to do the same thing in the middle of the day? They would think I had finally gone mad, but men do it all the time, don't they?

Ah, my eyes, my twilight eyes. But for them I would have noticed sooner.

I urinated with my back to the house. I closed my eyes, savoured the weakness that follows the release. Finished, I opened my eyes and squatted there, in no hurry to go back inside, slowly generating the energy to stand up. My eyes rested on the horizon. I blinked. I squinted. Looked again. Brilliant dancing lights of orange, green and gold in the east. Not the warm glow of a bush fire, these were flashing lights, more like Chinese fireworks. I looked up at the night sky and saw the moon still high above me. I stood up, watched the shifting hues of this unearthly display. For a long time I was still, not knowing what to do.

Inside the house I shook Adama's shoulder, we were alone, the two of us. I showed her what I'd seen. We did not sleep that night, we kept a vigil on the back verandah, watching the lights on the horizon.

Early prayers and the mosque was full, my neighbour stopped by with this news – for I had long given up going. Afterwards everybody wanted to talk about the omens in the night sky. At ten o' clock my nephew came and pushed me to town in my barrow. Those days, the effort was far too much for Adama. Twice we had thought her labour was beginning, twice the birth attendant had been summoned. Both times it turned out to be a false alarm. Still, Kadie and Ansuman had delayed travelling to Guinea. In the end, though, Adama had urged her parents to go. Even if the baby came, we would manage.

Adama walked alongside me. The streets were quiet as we made our slow progress through them. In the square I noted half a dozen empty stalls among the regulars. No charcoal. Now, that was interesting. Charcoal was delivered from out of town first thing in the morning. I noticed one other thing, though I mentioned none of it to Adama – all the traders had already sold out of bread.

We opened up the shop, customers were scarce. A little after eleven Mr Wurie passed by with news of strangers sighted on the main road out of town. It was only a rumour, he told us quietly, but we ought to know. I thanked him for that and his offer to help us in any way he could.

At midday I closed up the shop. Other shop owners had already done the same. We spent a short time moving stock to the storeroom at the back. I took the money box and hid it under the stairs. Afterwards we pulled down the metal shutters and set off home.

Just two streets from the house, past the old railway station, there is a place where the wall of a house juts out and the road curves sharply around it. We turned the corner. On the road ahead of us I spotted Kamanda, the madman. He was wearing an old fisherman's sweater and a pair of trousers with the seat torn out. Around his neck hung a necklace of bottle tops and crumpled drink cans. Kamanda's face was running with sweat, he was babbling, spraying great gobs of spit. His calloused feet with their long, grey toenails stamped the earth as he marched up and down, up and down, swinging his arms.

'Kamanda! Kamanda!' I called. For he was a gentle soul. I had often given him the offcuts from reams of fabric, which he wrapped around his head or tucked into his belt like fluttering handkerchiefs. I had never seen him like this. I tried to calm him with my voice, but there was no reasoning with him at the best of times. For a few moments he seemed to settle, only to jump up, as if to attention, and begin striding up and down again.

At home I sent my nephew back to his house. 'Hurry! No shillyshallying,' I urged him. Then I busied Adama, telling her to bring the washing in, round up the chickens, and to light a fire.

While she was occupied I went around the house collecting up all my jewellery and precious things. From the suitcase under my bed I fetched the gifts I had bought for Adama's baby, a silver coin with a hole in the middle and a gold chain to hang around the baby's waist. Along with my most valuable pieces I tied them up in a cloth and dropped them into the water jar at the back door, then I sank a large stone on the top. The lesser pieces of jewellery I spread out on the table in the middle of the room.

Outside I loosened the tether of the goat and waved my stick at her until she bolted into the bushes. Afterwards I went to the yard and ordered Adama to bring the biggest of the cast iron pots and twelve cups of rice. Adama exclaimed upon the quantity, but did as she was told.

A lot of rice. Yes, indeed. I intended to cook enough to feed an army.

There was a town I used to visit. I had been there many times before. In that town was a factory which manufactured dyes and finishes. Every once in a while the owners produced a new range of colours and invited all their customers to view them. I always took the job of going to see the new range myself. Before I had my stroke it was something I liked to do. I liked the metallic tang in the air inside the main hall of the factory, the wooden vats of colour stirred by men with iron paddles, the smudges of colour on the walls. Mr Bangura, the foreman, was a cheerful fellow. A widower, whose wife had died of cholera, he had never remarried. On the third finger of his left hand he wore a ring. Not an ordinary wedding band, but a heavy gold signet ring engraved with two sets of initials. We always conducted our business upstairs in his office across a table holding many jars of pigment and glass tubes of colours. When our business was concluded he would serve me a cold drink out of the fridge behind his chair while we chatted about many things. Once he had joked that with our occupations we would make a good pair. And though I replied in a teasing voice that I was past all that, it occurred to me there was once a time when the idea would have not seemed such a bad one.

My visits to the factory also gave me a chance to see Alpha who worked nearby as a teacher's assistant in a boy's secondary school. He would cycle to meet me, carrying lunch for us both in aluminium pots wrapped up in cloths. We would share our meal, catch up on each other's news and after I had rested a little and Alpha run whatever errands he had in town, we would set off to the factory, Alpha walking his bicycle, me alongside him.

The last time I visited, the heat had been dazzling, the sun directly overhead. The grass was pale yellow and bone dry, rustling in what little breeze there was. The great, black boulders scattered at the bottom of the hills glistened in the sun. The sky was hazy, streaked with clouds. It was too hot even for the birds, who hid from the heat in the branches of the trees. The factory was some small distance from the town. Despite the heat Alpha and I walked without stopping, lost in the pleasure of each other's company.

There was no guard at the factory gate. We passed through, still chattering and we walked on up the empty drive. Mr Bangura didn't hurry down to welcome me, or wave from his office window as he usually did. I noticed, yes. But did I think it so very strange? I don't know, perhaps I only think so now.

The big factory door stood open. We stepped through. Inside the main hall, silent pools of colour. A paddle lying on the ground by my feet. Not a soul in sight.

For some reason we did not call out. We stood still and stared around us. Only a moment or two later did we open our ears and listen, and when we did we heard a sound that must have been there all along. A buzzing, like a faint whine, like an aeroplane engine high in the sky. We followed the sound across the factory floor towards the great, double doors that led out to the back, where deliveries came and went. On the opposite side was the storeroom where the tubs of pigment were kept.

One thing nobody ever mentions afterwards is the smell. The indignity of it, I suppose. Such a commonplace smell. One to make your mouth water and your stomach rumble. For the rest of your life at a family gathering, a festival, it will serve to bring back the nausea, return you to the horror.

What is it? It is the smell of roasted meat.

The roof of the storeroom was mostly gone, what remained had collapsed into the building. The windows were ringed with black, shards of darkened glass like broken teeth stuck out of the frames. On the ground below one window lay a tub, partly melted, the spilled violet powder a shock of colour. The door had turned to charcoal, and split apart as Alpha kicked it. The sound of buzzing soared. All around us briefly turned to black as we were engulfed by a great mass of flies. I covered my face and hit at them with my hands, and once the air cleared I saw what was inside.

They had been rounded up and herded inside at gunpoint. We know this because it happened later, to others. Those few who survived all told the same story. At first they imagine it is a robbery, they are being locked up to stop them from raising the alarm. From the window they watch carefully the movements of the armed men. Then they see the plastic containers, smell the petrol as it is splashed on the walls and roof of the store. Men with guns encircle the building. Those inside begin to shout and hammer at the door, frantic now. Somebody takes a tub of dye and throws it at the window, it smashes the glass. They scramble over one another to escape the stifling fume-filled air and the certainty of death. The first one to try to climb out is shot.

The screams of the men as they burned must have been terrible, must have filled the air, sent the birds and animals fleeing. And yet nobody hears them. Their killers are deaf to them. There is no one else for miles. And afterwards, when the gunmen are gone, have ransacked the office and made off with the vehicles, silence follows. A desperate, resilient, unbreakable silence.

Alpha and I uttered not a word, not even a gasp, except the grunt he gave at the effort of kicking in the door. We moved around the corpses, who stared up at us through melted eyes, reached out to us with charred and twisted limbs. Some lay alone. Others were fused together, so here a corpse which seemed to have too many limbs, there a pair in apparent embrace. Most of all I remember the hands, by which I tried for a short while to identify Mr Bangura, searching for his ring. Brittle, blackened sticks reaching out. For what? Curled claws, trying to hold on. To what? To life itself, I can only imagine.

So you see, on that day I believed I knew what was coming. I sat outside on my old stool and positioned myself where I could best see the road. I settled down to wait. Whatever was out there was on its way. On its way to us.

Adama sat next to me, I watched her hands as she unpicked the frayed edge of a basket and prepared to repair it. I saw how her usually nimble fingers stumbled over the repair, weaving and unpicking the same few inches over and over. At that moment she turned her unblinking gaze up at me.

'Let me fetch you something to eat.' She was concerned for me, as I was for her. Each one pretending for the other's benefit. I had no appetite, my mouth was dry as sand.

'Yes, please. I'm a little hungry.'

As she rose she pressed the heel of her hand into the small of her back and stood there for a moment. I watched her cross the yard and bend over the cooking pots. For a while she remained doubled over. When she straightened again I saw her features tremble with pain.

Dear God, I said to myself. Not now.

She saw me watching and tried to force her lips into a smile. 'Another false alarm.'

'With your mother it was just the same,'

We sat and waited, the cooling feast spread out in front of us. We saw nobody. No visitor come to pay respects, no neighbour to exchange the news of the day. Not even a single passer-by.

In the last part of the afternoon I sat up suddenly, cocked my head and listened. I could hear dogs barking. Not the snarling, yelping of a scrap. Nor the howling call and answer that went on through the night. Rather a relentless, monotonous barking that started and did not stop. I sat listening while I worked out where in the town it was coming from, tracing its progression through the streets towards us.

I stood up and went, quickly as I could manage, into the house, unlocked the storeroom and gathered up a few pieces of smoked fish, some dried cassava. I poured two cups of rice into a hand-kerchief and knotted it. I found a packet of matches, a little money and a tin cup, tied them all up in a *lappa*. By the time I had finished I was exhausted.

I thrust the bundle into Adama's hands. I told her what she must do. She shook her head: 'No!' she said. The baby might be on its way, I told her. I knew the pains had been coming all afternoon. I had seen her turn away from me every time it happened. The poor child began to cry, and, Oh, how I wanted to cry too, to clutch her and weep, for this wasn't how we had imagined it would be when she came home for the birth. Instead I reached out and gave her shoulder a shake. In the distance came the sound of gunfire. Somebody ran past in the street shouting a warning. I still had my hand on her shoulder, now I pushed her as hard as I could towards the door, telling her to find the neighbours and join them.

She went. She did as she was told. I said I would follow as soon as I could. Maybe the baby would come today, maybe it would come tonight. Maybe it would come next week. But it would come. I could only pray I would be with her when it happened. I kept sight of her as she walked through the banana groves. My ears followed her progress long after she was no longer visible. For several minutes I stood and listened to the clicking of her fingers fading as she walked into the arms of the forest. Only then did I turn to go inside.

When my mother died she left me her possessions, among them the great chest in which she once stored her belongings. It was empty now. I went over to it, dragging my bad foot along the floor. I opened the lid, laid my stick inside. With all the strength left in my one good arm, I hoisted myself up on to the edge. I balanced there for a moment, then I leaned forward and let myself topple in. I lay there, a little winded. Then I reached up and pulled the lid down over me. I curled up in the darkness and went on waiting.

I could hear nothing save a few muffled sounds. And all I could see was the narrow beam of light that came from the space between the lid and the box. For the first time I began to feel afraid. For a while I did nothing, just listened to the sound of my own breathing. In the closed space my breaths seemed raucous, as though they had transformed into vapours, clamorous with life, swirling around, searching for a way out.

I tried to make myself comfortable. I should have put down some cloths or sacking to line the inside. Too late now. I was lying on top of my stick and I squirmed until I managed to ease it out from under me. I turned on to my back and lay there with my knees bent. The temperature inside the box was rising, it would soon be as hot as a furnace. I loosened my clothing as best I could. I pulled off my head-wrap, bunched it up and put it under my head as a makeshift pillow. The effort made me thirsty, but I had no water. I didn't dare risk climbing back out, I would have to manage without.

After a bit I began to explore my surroundings. This had been my favourite hiding place when I was a child. I'd lie on top of my mother's belongings, waiting for someone to come and find me, as scared of being discovered as of not being found at all. When the lid finally opened above me, I screamed and screamed. Still, I went back, over and over, to hide in the same place. I didn't think anyone would imagine I would be so stupid as to choose such an obvious place. My double bluff never worked. I prayed it would work this time.

I ran my fingertips around the sides of the box. It was well made, solid and strong. We were more or less the same age, and yet I was the one who'd begun to sag and creak. The box on the other hand had only grown more handsome with the years: the richness of the patina, the worn-smooth surface. I had become so used to it over the years, I'd stopped seeing it, but it was a very elegant box.

I came across a knot in the wood and explored it with my fingers. It was grainy, at odds with the feel of the rest. I scratched it with my fingernail and felt it crumble. I reached up and took a pin from my hair and began to dig at the place. The knot wasn't wood at all, but some sort of plaster, probably where the carpenter had plugged the place where a knot had fallen through. I scratched away like a mouse until I had made myself a spyhole. It was a little high, I had to push myself up on one elbow, but it was better than nothing.

There was more light now, a circular beam coming in through the spyhole. I followed the beam to the other side of the box where it revealed a series of markings: vertical cuts, where somebody had scored the wood with a knife. Two rows of ten, one above, one below. A carpenter's trademark? Perhaps the box had been made using wood from something else. I ran my thumbnail across the rows, backwards and forwards, making a vibrating sound like a musical instrument.

Now I remembered. As a young girl, watching my mother. Every year, on the day we ate the first rice of the new harvest, going to her room where the great chest stood. With a sharp knife she would score the wood in the same place every year. Every year for ten years. Ten anniversaries. Ten birthdays. Asana and Alusani. Then Alusani died and stole her happiness to take with him back to the other world.

Rofathane. I had fought so hard to leave all that behind. And yet.

We had a herbalist, a carpenter, a blacksmith, a birth attendant and a boy who never grew old. Soothsayers prepared us for the unexpected. Teachers travelled to us, bringing the word from Futa Djallon. People who wanted to live in Rofathane had first to find a patron and then to ask permission to settle. There existed an order, an order in which everybody had their place. An imperfect order. An order we understood.

A lullaby came to me, one my mother used to sing:

> *Asana tey k' kulo,*
> *I thonto, thonto,*
> *K' m'ng dira.*

> Asana, don't you cry,
> I'll rock you, rock you,
> Until you sleep.

I hummed softly to myself, and as I did so I began to rock back and forth, growing sentimental, a wet-eyed, foolish old woman. I thought of my mother and father, sleeping safely in their graves. I thought of Osman, of Ngadie. I hoped Kadie and Ansuman were still in Guinea and that they would hear what was happening and not come back. I feared for Alpha.

Voices! Ugly, bold, challenging. They seemed to come from all directions. Voices and the sound of running feet. The feet were bare, I remember that because there was something oddly unthreatening in the way they patted the earth.

I put my eye to the spyhole, and looked left and right.

Two men and a woman came into view. Walking high on the balls of their feet. The woman and one of the men were carrying guns, resting them upright against their shoulders, fingers on the trigger. Just like they do in the cinema. The other man carried a machete and smoked a cigarette. They were looking this way and that, all around them, as they advanced.

Such strange garb, they were dressed like children who had found a dressing-up box. A pair of ladies' sunglasses. A military-style jacket with gold epaulettes. A red bra. Jeans. Camouflaged trousers. A T-shirt with the face of a dead American rapper. A necklace of bullets. Around their necks and wrists dangled charms on twisted strings. They were talking to others I couldn't see, but their talk was unintelligible to me. I thought at first it was some strange tongue, the kind we made up as children. But every now and again a fragment of the exchange occurred in my own language. Gradually I realised that I was listening to several languages being spoken at once.

I had left the back door to my house open. This was how I could see what was going on. I expected my neighbours had bolted theirs before they fled, and sure enough a moment later I heard the sound of wood splintering, of a door being broken from its hinges.

Beneath the cooking pot in the yard the embers of the fire throbbed faintly. One of the intruders raised the lid of the cooking pot. Good, I had wanted them to find the food. I saw him dip his fingers into the sauce, he made a joke to the others.

I pulled my eye back from the spyhole. The other man was wandering dangerously close to the house. I listened to his steps as he approached the door, heard him carefully cross the threshold, the click of his weapon. My heart thudded, my breaths came short and fast. Surely he could hear me, I thought. I cowered inside the box, waiting for the lid to open. They would kill me straight away, of that I was certain. An old, crippled woman, there was not much sport to be had with me. Softly, the footsteps came closer, inches now from my head. I held my breath.

He stopped, swivelled, turned. He had spotted the jewellery on the table. The chink of metal as he turned over the pieces and began pocketing them. The sounds must have alerted the others, I heard them coming to see what he was doing. I listened in the dark as they began to squabble over my possessions.

Somewhere in the distance a voice shouted orders. The three looters snatched up the remainder of the jewellery and began to move off. I put my eye to the spyhole, watched their backs as they disappeared. I lay back and breathed out.

I slept. I woke. I slept again. A serpentine dream wove its way through my mind. Dreams of discovery. Dreams of death. I slipped in and out of consciousness and woke struggling for air. My tongue was stuck to the roof of my mouth. For a moment I had forgotten where I was. My body was damp, pools of sweat had gathered on the floor of the box. Something had woken me. I could hear scattered gunfire. From outside came the smell of burning straw. I peeped out of my spyhole. Against the darkness, a halo of flickering light: fire from flaming houses

In the yard a stone ricocheted. A figure appeared carrying a burning brand. It lit up his features, turning his nostrils into black holes, his eyes into dark hollows. With silent steps he crossed the yard, making for my neighbour's house.

The hours passed. I must have lost track of time. The next I knew the three from before were back. I listened as they slit the throats of my chickens and roasted them over the fire. The contents of my cooking pots were passed around. More people came, bringing loot from the surrounding houses. Evidently they had broken into the bottle store. There was music and much rough laughter. Different smells drifted into the box: the sour smell of unwashed bodies, rum fumes and the scented smoke of marijuana.

Hamdillah, how I prayed. I don't deny it. Not at all. To the gods of Islam and Christianity, to every god in the skies plus any others I might not have thought of. Would they set fire to my house when they had taken what they wanted? Would I die of thirst trapped in my hiding place? Somewhere my fate was already cast in stones.

Have you ever wondered what it is that makes people do terrible things? I have. Since that day, I have set my mind to it many times. All the stories of supernatural beings and yet those men and women out there were not so different from me, only that something inside them had been unleashed. So, where does it come from, the fury? A thousand indignities, a thousand wrongs, like tiny knife wounds, shredding a person's humanity. In time only the tattered remnants are left. And in the end they ask themselves – what good is this to me? And they throw the last of it away.

At dawn, finally, they slept. I listened to the sound of their snoring. I didn't dare let myself fall asleep again in case I snored too, or cried out in my dreams. The sun was halfway up the sky and the temperature inside the box was rising rapidly by the time they had woken up. Through my circular window I watched them rouse themselves, collect up their weapons and as much of their stolen booty as they could carry, and stumble away like sleepwalkers.

I waited two hours more, then I opened the lid of the box and climbed out. I plunged my arm into the water jar and retrieved the bundle. I allowed myself a few sips of water before I picked my way across the yard, through the banana grove and into the trees. I kept on walking. I left the path. I crossed the boundary into the sacred forest. It was a forbidden place, but what did that matter now? Things had changed, perhaps for ever. The old order had gone, those rules no longer applied. I had to find Adama, to help bring her baby into this world.

With me I carried my gifts for the baby. But what would I say to her? How would I explain that her great-grandmother, who had lived for longer than eighty years, had learned nothing at all, had no knowledge to give? That she had arrived in a world where suddenly we were all lost, as helpless as newborns.

17

Mariama, 1999

Twelfth Night

KURU MASSABA MADE THE world and placed it upon the head of a great giant. This is what Pa Yamba told me once. Every day the giant turned himself slowly from east to west and then slowly turned himself back again. People lived on the earth and should have been happy, for everything they needed was there. But they fought among themselves and their anger caused pain to the giant in the form of terrible headaches. He shook his head to free himself of the torment and brought down great storms that only tormented him more. In time the pain became unbearable. The giant lay down, grew sick and died, the world became dark.

This is what we know happened to the world. I told Mr Lockheart this story. And this is the story I will tell you, the last one.

'Go on, Mary,' he said.

Kuru was angry. So angry he turned his face away. But when he heard the distress of the dying people on the darkened earth, his heart softened. He forgave them, he placed the world upon the head of another giant who turned from east to west every day. He pushed all the bad spirits into the underworld, and gave the rest of the world to human beings, because he loved them. But Kuru is disappointed again, because we will not love him the way he wishes to be loved.

Sometimes the giant stumbles. You can feel it. He is weakening. Every time he stumbles the earth is shaken, it crumbles and cracks. The spirits in the darkness down below are woken.

'What will happen then, Mary?' Mr Lockheart liked to use my

name a great deal, and to look me in the eye as he did so. I had expected this, I wasn't offended by it. I quite liked him.

I replied: 'If you would like to call me by my name, it is Mariama.'

'I will, if that's what you would like. I thought Mary was your Christian name. Why do you call yourself Mariama?'

Yes, Mary is my *Christian* name. That's exactly what it is. That's all it is.

Mariama was the name given to me. The nuns took it away and replaced it with something that sounded like my name, that I learned to answer to. It was easier to remember, they said. For whom? I might have asked. And why did I need a name that was easy to remember? Perhaps they thought we weren't worth the effort. Or that it was presumptuous of a little pagan baby to walk through life trailing a name of four syllables, flagrantly, like an ermine cloak or a silk scarf, something that should only be worn by the most important people. But Mary wasn't mine. It never had been. Mariama was the name my mother had chosen for me.

Some of this I said out loud. Some I kept to myself.

Mr Lockheart nodded: 'I see. Mariama it is. And you must call me Adrian.'

He glanced down at the desk, I could see he wanted to pick up his pen and make some notes about me. He wasn't sure. Now he was masking his hesitation by pretending to look like he was thinking about something. He was new, had only been here a few months. But he thought that if he was calling me by my first name, I should call him by his. They all did that, so they could feel they were treating us like equals.

As a matter of fact, if it were up to me I would tell him to call me *Aunty* Mariama. Because at his age he ought to show a little respect. That's if it were up to me. But it isn't.

I think of that giant turning slowly round. From east to west, from west to east. Endlessly revolving. I wonder if that is why our lives so often end up in the same place they began? Because life is not a straight line, just as the earth isn't flat. You don't walk and walk until you reach a place you know is the end. Like the Europeans once believed. They thought if they sailed their ships towards the horizon they would plummet off the end in a cascade of water. Then came Galileo. And after that they found us here, clinging on to the curve of the earth. What took them so long? I sometimes wonder. We knew the earth was round long before that.

No, life isn't a straight line. It is a circle, whose slow and gentle bend we fail to spot, until we realise we are back where we started. I don't know when I realised I knew this, but it was some time before I met Adrian Lockheart.

The next time, Adrian Lockheart asked: 'Do you believe in ghosts?'

'You mean like the Holy Ghost.'

'Are you teasing? It's OK if you are. I don't mind. And I take your point, Mary.'

'Mariama.'

'Mariama.' A pause. 'I mean ghosts, spirits, devils.'

He is trying to understand, and despite myself I would like to help him. He has read newspapers and scholarly reports about us. And he has been talking to the others who come here. He will have been out drinking with them, which I know is where he was last night. I saw him: leaning across the table, hovering above the pools of beer stretched out on the plastic. He is the new boy. The others enjoy the fact, they can pretend to be old Africa hands. Tales of cannibals and juju. If ever they see a shadow of scepticism on his face they shake their heads knowingly. 'I'm telling you. Just like that. Dead. Convinced someone had placed a curse on him, doesn't matter how educated. I've seen it before. Rwanda. The Congo.'

He thought he would be working with child soldiers. Or at the very least the limbless, the lipless, the eyeless, the tongueless. Instead he got me. But he was a good man, and determined to make the best of it.

I asked what his own opinion was, since he was the Spiritual Advisor.

'I'm really a counsellor, that's just a fancy title.' He smiled when he said that.

So I told him, no, I wasn't teasing.

March is the warmest month of the year, and this was the warmest March for many years to come.

We used to meet on Friday mornings, eleven o'clock. His office had bare walls and a concrete floor, a bare light bulb descended from the ceiling on a three-foot, brittle cord. Too low, so each time he passed it he was forced to duck slightly. A small pink burn showed on his forehead. A desk, five chairs, one of which was broken and pushed against the wall. One he sat on. The other three, of variable height, were placed in a row in front of his desk. The middle one was directly opposite him, soft but too low slung, it left you peering across the surface of the desk at him. Choosing either of the others meant you would be at eye level, but off-centre. I chose the one that was closest and sat down, looking at him sideways on.

He turned his chair to face me. My skin prickled under his gaze, so I stared straight ahead of me at the wall, or else out of the window. Sometimes he turned to see what I was looking at. But there was nothing to see. Just a badly built wall with dried concrete oozing out between the breeze blocks and a trail of withered bougainvillea.

He suffered in the heat, clawing at his collar; the back of his shirt was soaked with sweat and stuck to the plastic chair. Still, he refused to give in to it. Every day a tie, a long-sleeved shirt, and a jacket that hung uselessly over the back of his chair.

Our sessions ended when the day was at its hottest.

'Quick! What's the first thing that comes into your mind.' As if we were playing a game. So I told him about my niece, whose child had died. He asked me how I felt about that. I told him I was sorry for my sister's daughter, she had wanted this child very much.

'Some people believe these things are just God's will, Mariama.' Adrian said in his hushed voice.

I told him it was probably no such thing. It was the child's will.

She had changed her mind. For her one world was as good as the other. It is we who are so much attached to this one.

One morning, the sixth or seventh time we met, Mr Lockheart had another idea. He asked if he might visit my room, he had heard so much about it. I didn't like to let anybody inside, not even the houseboy who cleaned the bedrooms of the other staff. On Mondays I left my waste paper basket out for him. On Tuesdays he left a dustpan and brush leaning against my door. But he, Mr Lockheart, Adrian, was quite insistent. He said it would help him to understand me.

I pushed open the door of my room. I crossed in front of him towards the window, unhinged the shutters. A ray of sunlight lit up the opposite wall, bouncing off the shiny surface of the magazine pictures. I opened the window and pushed the shutters all the way back, until they hit the outside wall with a bang. The room glowed with light. I had never seen it like this, it pleased me. Sounds from outside entered the room, mingling with the dust that played in the air, and set the colours of the pictures shimmering. The images sparkled and came alive. A shark swam towards me with red, gaping jaws. A shoal of silver fish swam by. A red starfish flashed, on and off. A blue sea horse reared. A conger eel hid in the darkness of his cave. A sleepy eyed turtle with wrinkled features glided past. A setting sun glittered upon the waves. All around me the sound of water, crashing and foaming on to the shore, trickling back down the sand to the ocean. The sounds filled my ears, I shook my head.

Adrian stepped across the threshold, and stood with his back against the wall, slowly crossing his arms in front of him. He tilted his head upwards towards the painting on the ceiling. Kassila! Nacre teeth, glinting coral eyes, ears of fragile oyster shells, his great scaly tail coiled and flexed. He reached down to us with spiny fingers. Adrian swallowed. I saw his Adam's apple, hard and fragile, move up and down behind the translucent skin of his throat. The fingers of his right hand fluttered briefly against his arm.

I looked at Adrian and I looked around me. Before we came here I thought I was going to feel ashamed, but I didn't. Instead I felt proud. This was the first time anybody had seen my room, with my permission. A month before, the urgent matter of a bats' nest in the roof of the room next door had brought the caretaker over, he in turn called the matron, and she the principal. That's where this whole thing with Adrian Lockheart started, when the sessions began. They had not known quite what to do. It did not seem to occur to them just to leave me as I was.

He didn't speak for quite a long time, eventually he said: 'What is it?'

'It's my work,' I replied.

The pen Adrian Lockheart used to record our conversations was an old-fashioned fountain pen. A fine example, with a gold nib that made scratching sounds like the birds on the roof. One day, when he was called out of the room briefly, I picked it up and examined it. The shaft was made of marbled enamel, the nib engraved with the manufacturer's name. When he came back in he told me it had belonged to his grandfather, who had lived and worked in this country once. His grandfather's fondness for our country made Adrian want to see it for himself.

'Lockheart?' I asked.

'Silk. On my mother's side.'

The same name as the old District Commissioner. I replaced the pen on the table. I pretended the name meant nothing to me.

Adrian had something he wanted to talk about. He said we started but never did finish the discussion.

'The giant shakes his head and frees the spirits from underneath the earth, isn't that what you told me?'

I nodded. That's what Pa Yamba Mela had told me. When I was a child, growing up. A lot of people thought Pa Yamba was a fool. That his magic was nothing but trickery, that his prophecies were cleverly worded so as to mean anything. He couldn't pull thunder out of the sky any more than you or I. He claimed to have magic powers just to make people afraid of him. And many were. In that way he became powerful. You could say that was a kind of magic.

'The underworld will rise,' I replied.

'And when will that happen?' Adrian shifted in his seat.
'It already has.'

Once I lived among nuns. They told me stories of the lives of the saints, men and women who had visions, sometimes of God, Jesus or Mary. Other times these visions were premonitions.

Well, I had a vision of something that came to pass.

It was in the middle of the day, a market day. The sun was hot, bearing down on the top of my head. So bright it made me squint. The shadows were short and black, black, black. The air was heavy like glue, impossible to breathe, it wrapped itself around me. I made my way uphill, pushing against it all the time, my head bowed, my legs straining. Where the road was steep I stopped for a moment to catch my breath. I remember I looked up at the sky. Above me the sun and moon hovered on opposite sides of the blue, one indistinguishable from the other.

Suddenly I heard a great rush of wind, as though a whirlwind was racing towards me. I braced myself and waited. Nothing. The grass and trees stood straight. And yet the sound went on, becoming louder, filling my ears, rushing around my head. I felt myself becoming unsteady. I looked down at the ground and at my feet. I reached out for something to support myself, found a bollard and leaned against it.

There was a Creole graveyard below me, very old, at least one hundred years. I saw a crowd of mourners walking between the graves. They were carrying several coffins. It looked as though a whole family had died. But even though they were dressed as bereaved people, instead of weeping, the relatives appeared almost unconcerned. One or two were even laughing openly as they hoisted the boxes towards the waiting graves.

I looked and looked again. Something strange. I could see straight through the flimsy wood of the coffins. There were no bodies inside, only piles of sticks. The mourners were talking to each other, I could see their mouths opening and closing. I was too far off to hear what they were saying, though the calls of the market traders reached me. It was as though they were communicating soundlessly, like animals. And I alone seemed to see them. The people in the market went about their business, bargaining and bantering with one another. Other strangers walked between the stalls. A young woman buying sweet potatoes stood right next to one of them, who stared lasciviously at her breasts. When she turned around she brushed past him, but never so much as glanced his way.

A fist of fear squeezed my belly. Trailed its fingertips slowly across my scalp. Sapped the strength from my muscles. I gasped, choking on my own breath. Drops of moisture rose on my forehead. I let go of my load. The plastic bags tumbled down the hill, tearing open, all of my oranges bouncing away. A dread filled me, a dread unlike any I had ever felt. Not the terror of God, or his angels, but the sickly fear of man.

I saw them returning at night, moving between the headstones and the mausoleums, indistinguishable from the shadows, from the dark shapes of the statues. Great slabs of stone and marble were heaved aside, coffin lids swung open. I saw the graves open up, the spirits of the dead walk away from their resting place.

Then just as suddenly the vision disappeared. It was market day again. A little boy, naked but for a pair of shorts, was standing next to me holding my shopping bags. Another boy had climbed up the hill and was holding out the last of the runaway oranges. They were both smiling up at me, thinking of the coin I would give them, ignorant of everything I had just witnessed.

When I had finished speaking Adrian waited, as though I would go on. As though there was more. There was, but for the time being I was finished. I folded my hands in my lap. He was staring out of the window, flexing his long fingers. He didn't turn to me when he spoke, and when he did his words came quiet and slow:

'That was how they got into the city, wasn't it? The rebel army. They hid their weapons and their men in the graveyards. Collected them at night.'

Yes, I told him. That was how it happened. Nobody realised it until later. We awoke the next day to find them in our midst.

We were silent together for a while. Then he pushed back his chair and left the room. When he returned he was carrying a tray, upon which some tea things slid dangerously about. He set them down, stirred the tea to hasten the brew, poured two cups. Halfway to the top, the way Europeans do. He added milk to both cups, and pushed the sugar bowl towards me; the loose grains stuck to the underside of the bowl scratched the surface of the table.

'The starlight was blue. There was a patch of the night sky where the stars crowded together – astronomers call it a "butterfly cluster" – and in the middle a single pale, yellow star brighter than all the rest. I used to like to tell my class about the stars. For some reason they can imagine it, the night sky. Even the ones who were born blind. We would go outside and they would turn their faces upwards, like flowers to the sun. Somehow they could sense the vastness above.' I stopped. The sky had never looked so beautiful as it did that night.

'The next day was Twelfth Night. Did you know that? They came on the feast of the Epiphany.'

A fly had become trapped behind the window. The angry buzzing invaded the room, and an insistent tapping. Tap, tap. Tap, tap. As the fly hit the windowpane. The tapping punctuated our conversation.

'Do you still believe in God, Mariama?'

'I believe he exists.'

'What does that mean?'

'Just that. I believe he exists. I don't believe *in* him.'

Adrian folded his hands in front of him.

'Like you here,' I said. 'I believe you are sitting there. I can put out my hand and touch you. You exist, but that's all I know about you. I don't know whether you are good or bad. Whether I can trust you, or whether I would be a fool to do so.'

'You can trust me, Mariama.'

A pause. Tap, tap. Of course, we were talking about God.

'So what do you think about, when you think about God?'

'I think he doesn't like black people very much.'

★　　★　　★

Something happened here. A change. Stealthy, creeping, slow. Like the way the desert is gradually covering the plain, one grain of sand at a time. It took place without us even noticing, so that the moment when we might have resisted passed unremarked. Suddenly it was irreversible. The evil had been let loose. But it was no longer among us, it was within. Everybody became part of it.

In the city the animals grew fat while the humans starved. The dogs were sleek and fit, their coats glossy. Vultures gorged until they could barely take to the air. The abundance of food gave the dogs a new confidence, the only ones with the freedom of the city. Under the bridge the fish nibbled at the jetsam of human corpses jamming the bay where every night suspected insurgents were shot by the dozen, their bodies tossed over the railings.

From the East, which had fallen into the hands of the rebels, a cloud of smoke drifted across the river to the West, bringing with it the scent of blood and fear. And every night the stars formed the shape of a beautiful butterfly hovering over the city. We hid and waited for them to arrive. And waited, until in the end we were forced out by our hunger.

I was standing at a checkpoint, behind a queue of people. The checkpoint was manned by black soldiers from another country, sent by their government to fight our war. They were poor; they were afraid for their lives; they had no choice; they hated us for it. Nobody spoke. You could smell the perspiration on the people as they waited silently for their papers to be checked.

Then, suddenly, from behind me – a woman's voice, shrill and steely.

'Rebel!'

Again. 'Rebel!'

The soldiers' heads snapped up. One of them handed back the identity card he was holding, tightened his grip on his gun. Two of them began to move down the queue, towards the source of the outburst. I dared not look around. None of us did. The soldiers were heading straight towards me. Weapons at the ready, their faces arranged into expressions of hostility to cover the fear. Only when they had passed me did I dare turn around.

A woman was pointing at a younger woman further back in the queue. She stood with her legs apart, one hand on her hip, glaring fiercely. With her other hand she jabbed the air, shrieking the word repeatedly. 'Rebel! Rebel!'

Up until that moment the woman she had been pointing at had stood quite still, as though none of this had anything to do with her. The instant the soldiers seized her and pulled her out of the line of people, however, she came alive – struggling, begging and screaming. Her accuser, who was relentless, now released a torrent of accusations. She had seen the young woman with a pistol, had seen her in the east end of the city earlier in the month. A man, clearly the young woman's husband, came forward from the back of the line to his wife's defence. He approached the soldiers hesitantly, holding his hands out in front of him, the palms turned up. It was all a misunderstanding, he pleaded. But the soldiers didn't seem to want to listen. One of them slapped the man's wife, slapped her repeatedly, asking questions, demanding answers. Then they began to hit him, too. Both of them. He shielded himself by bending over double, but she had her arms pinned behind her back and took the full force of each blow. Their pleas, the sound of their voices, were lost in the flood of accusations.

And people knew the killers came in all guises: as men, as women, even in the form of sweet-faced children.

The officer in charge ordered them to be executed. There and then, in front of us. The soldiers stripped them, forced them to kneel. They shot her first. Then him. She was a pretty girl, flawless skin and angled cheekbones, I remember because I wondered, in that moment, if the soldiers who were away from home, away from their loved ones in this desperate, dark and ugly land were not somehow outraged by the way she looked. It made them want to kill her.

The bodies lay in the dirt. The rest of us shuffled through the checkpoint. On the other side a man in front of me told us that he knew her, the dead woman. Her accuser was a neighbour of his who had once lost a lover to her. Naasu. That was the murdered woman's name. He had only just realised who she was, now he was certain of it.

Soldiers loaded Naasu's body, and that of her husband, into the back of a lorry to be thrown over the bridge and into the bay. Much later, when it was dark, the people who lived among the rocks next to the water went out in their canoes, collected the corpses and buried them. The killers, the innocent, and those whose beauty offended, side by side in the same grave.

This was the story I told Adrian Lockheart. By the end he was leaning forward, his eyes glistening, the picture of professional caring. Not that he didn't care. He just wanted me to be in no doubt about it. But I could read Adrian Lockheart's mind. I could see the thoughts running behind his eyes. Beneath the still waters of sympathy was a great, heaving tide of relief. His mind was on his wife and his child in the place where he had left them, safe on another continent.

And this is what he was thinking. He was thanking God, thanking him over and over in all his merciful glory, that this would never be them. That he would never be me.

That was the last time I saw him. He wrote a report for my employers. In his opinion I was suffering from post-traumatic stress as a result of the war, the most notable manifestation of which appeared to be the habit of decorating my room in a manner that, while a little bizarre, was completely harmless. There was no reason I should not continue my work as a teacher.

The great Kuru Masaba, of course, the most powerful of them all. Creator of the earth, the skies, the rivers, the forests, the seas and every living creature. Kumba, the rain god who brings the rice harvest. Yaro, Anayaroli, whom they call Mammy Wata, goddess of wealth. Aronson, the hunter. Kassila, the sea god. Those are the only names that survive. The others are lost for ever. Don't you see? We have forgotten them.

Sometimes I still dream of them, like I used to. Adrian Lockheart taught me how to stop them from taking over my mind, to imagine a row of boxes and to put the things that disturbed me inside and close the lid. But they won't be contained.

Always it is Kassila who breaks out first and frees the others. Once I dreamed I saw them, strolling between the stars, surrounded by flashes of lightning and the roll of thunder. Cowrie shells and glass beads decorated their hair, gold rings and bracelets adorned their arms, they were wrapped in garments woven from rainbows and embroidered with sunbeams. They had their backs to us, they were walking away, headed to some other dimension.

Free from us, free from our foolishness, our fickleness and petty betrayals. They were arm in arm, laughing out loud. Without a care in the universe.

EPILOGUE

18

Abie, 2003

The Women's Gardens II

London, November 2003.

DURING THE LAST DAYS of my stay in Rofathane I decided I wanted
to bathe in the river. The morning was cool, a steaming bucket
stood outside my door. It was pleasant enough to stand in my palm
frond enclosure, and to pour hot water over myself, but that day I
wanted the sensation of water gliding over my body. I tied a *lappa*
around myself, searched for the nub of black soap. It was barely
light and I passed not a soul on the path through the old coffee
groves and the women's gardens, down to the river.

Slippery mud oozed between my toes, as I waded out into the
water. A little further out, where a bed of weeds like tattered
ribbons rippled in the current, the river bed turned to sand. Into the
deeper water now I released the knot of my cloth and let it float on
the surface. A tree, ebonised by time and the water, lay partly
submerged. The roots reached up into the air like a giant's hand. I
knotted the soap in a corner of the cloth and suspended it from a
limb. The water was cool, unexpectedly so. I shivered, raising tiny
goosebumps on my skin, took a deep breath and plunged below
the surface, coming up for air twenty yards on, where the river
parted around an island of mangrove. I kicked out down the
narrower of the tributaries, turned on to my back and floated for a
few minutes with my eyes closed, feeling the faint warmth of a new
sun on my face. I swam back to retrieve the cloth. I bathed,
lathering my body, watched the bubbles swirl away. And after-

wards, I climbed up on to the bank where I shook the river water out of my hair. I would tell Aunt Serah I no longer needed hot water in the mornings, I made up my mind to bathe in the river for the remaining days of my stay.

Wrapped in my sodden cloth I walked back to the village, passing the women on their way down to work in their gardens. Isatu, who gave birth to twins a few months ago, pressed an avocado into my hand and I walked on, tearing away the papery skin, biting into it like an apple. The scent of fruit, of damp earth, the 'touk touk touk' of a tinker bird, the women with their babies bound to their backs – there is nothing here that could not be a hundred years old, that could not have been exactly the same on the day Asana arrived here as a girl riding on her father's shoulders.

On my way through the village people called out little courtesies to one another and to me: 'Did you sleep well?' And I replied: '*Thanto Kuru.*' I was no longer a stranger. I knew just where into all of this I fitted. Because in this small world everybody had a place, meaning they all knew how they came to be here. A story of which every detail was cherished. And I had mine.

An hour later I left the house and set off in the opposite direction, past the last house in the village, down to the flat grassland on the edge of the forest. There I found Alpha, alone and kneeling in the dirt, surrounded by seedlings in black plastic bags. He was planting them, one by one, in a row in the ground, concentrating so hard he didn't hear me come up behind him. The sun was still low in the sky, my shadow trailed behind me. I stood behind Alpha for a few moments, watching him. When I saw him reach for the next seedling, I bent down and passed it to him. He took it without turning around and I wondered if he had known I was there all along.

'After tomorrow maybe we'll be finished planting out,' he said as he pressed the mud down around the roots. 'It shouldn't be too long until the rains come. Maybe two weeks, three weeks. We must keep them watered until then.'

I knelt down a few feet away, picked up a trowel and began digging, copying Alpha's actions.

'Am I doing this right?'

'Yes, Abie. That is quite all right.'

With my hands I moulded the earth into a miniature moat around the plant, feeling the dirt burying itself under my fingernails, then I poured water into it. The first three rows of trees had been staked, to save them from marauding porcupines and some kind of cane rat called a cutting grass. Alpha had supervised as the men set wire traps around the perimeter.

'I'm thinking we'll plant cassava as a cover crop. We can dry and store some of it.'

'Good idea.'

We had left the old plantation as it was and begun a new one on the other side of the village. The trees that lived on in the forest had survived the fire, but neglect had taken its toll. Their beans were a long way past their best. So we took cuttings and began to raise seedlings.

In the meantime a certain giddiness had come over my aunts as if the time spent remembering the girls and women they once had been had invigorated the spirits. They'd lifted the past from their own shoulders and handed it to me. I didn't see it as a burden, not at all. Rather a treasure trove of memories, of lives lived and lessons learned, of terrors faced and pleasures tasted.

Still today and every day those women appear to me in my mind's eye, my aunts in all their guises, often when I am least expecting it. Vibrant and noisy, tumbling through time, jostling for my attention, and always with something new to say about whatever it is I am doing. Superior by far to any box of disintegrating diaries and lifeless letters.

I passed Ya Namina's house, which is how I have come to think of it. A workman was knocking nails into the edges of the window frames. An evening a week earlier, as we all sat keeping company in front of the house, Asana had voiced her intention to move in, to live in her mother's house again. A moment later she eased herself slowly to her feet with the aid of her stick, saying she was on her way to bed. On the steps of the verandah she turned to Aunty Hawa, who that particular evening had scarcely shared in the talk, but sat silent as the chatter flew around her. 'And will you stay with me?' she asked. Aunty Hawa jumped up and ran over to her, and I saw her bend down and fleetingly touch her elder sister's feet.

They were all there on the day planting began. Serah poured a libation over the first seedling and uttered a short impromptu prayer. Then she told us she had something to say. She had decided to look for her mother. She and Mary planned a trip to the South, to the town where Serah's mother was last heard to be living. It was only a beginning, so many years and a war had intervened, but the women who made *gara* were full of information and all knew each other. They would carry with them the pieces of cloth from Serah's marriage box to show them. Every woman had her own designs like a trademark, somebody might remember. And afterwards Hawa sang a song, surprising me with a voice that was powerful and true. Gradually the others joined in, and I hummed along to the parts that were familiar, until after a few verses I had the confidence to sing out loud.

The day before I was due to return to the city to catch my flight to London the four of them decided to join me for my morning bath in the river. They were already there by the time I arrived, I heard the sound of their laughter and bickering bouncing across the water. I suppose, strictly speaking, Aunty Asana shouldn't have been there, but that was just a convention after all. And if I had learned one thing about my aunts, it is that they would not be bound by anything so flimsy.

Coming down the narrow path I saw them before they spotted me, Asana and Serah out in the dark water, beyond the fallen tree, their breasts bobbing round and high as young girls' breasts on the surface. Asana as lithe and whole as ever she had been. Hawa standing with her back to me, slim and straight, a sentinel waiting for her son to come home. Mariama in her element, shaking her head, a shower of crystal droplets like an elaborate crown.

Four African ladies having a bath, a group of water maidens basking in the river.

And later, when we had climbed out and were drying ourselves, Mariama called me over. She grasped one of my hands in both of hers and pressed an object into my palm, something heavy, warm and smooth. I opened my fingers and looked down. It was wet and glossy: a pure, black pebble.

That was three years ago, and every year since I have returned to Rofathane, taking with me my husband, my daughter and my son. The seedlings have taken root and now the young coffee trees stand taller than my children. And we have planted more: limes, almonds and cashew nuts, chillies and ginger, too. The first crop left the village, loaded into a truck in wooden boxes with the words 'Kholifa Estates' stamped on the side.

I am writing this at my desk in the den. In front of me sits a bowl of stones, a gift to me from Mariama along with the one she gave me in Rofathane. In the silver light of the morning they seem to glitter, sending out flickers of light and the occasional flash, like tiny shooting stars. Especially the crystals, the black stones and a grey one, the one that looks as though somebody has pressed their thumb into it. On summer days the corals and reds shimmer in the sun. And in the evening it is the pale stones, the smooth opaque cream pebble, the chalky rocks, which continue to glow in the dusk, long after the sun has gone.

My daughter loves to play with them while I write and she waits for a moment of my attention. In her hands they rustle and click against one another. Yesterday she came into my room.

'This is my favourite,' she said, holding up a stone roughly in the shape of a hexagon, smooth to the touch, but with a pattern of ripples. Then she gathered up all the stones, bent her head down over her cupped hands.

She remained that way for a long time until I asked: 'What are you doing?'

'Listen,' she beckoned me down.

I lowered my head to join her. 'What is it?'

'Listen to the noise they make,' she replied. 'It sounds like they're talking.'

ACKNOWLEDGEMENTS

Many women from among my family and friends spent hours sharing their memories with me of how it was to live as a woman in our country's past. They know who they are. I promised not to reveal their names. Instead I offer them my wholehearted thanks.

My stepmother Yabome Kanu devoted an entire summer to teaching me to speak Temne. She has patiently answered a myriad of enquiries and attended to many details of the novel on my behalf. Mother, muse, unpaid researcher. I am indebted to her.

In addition I owe my thanks to:

My cousin Morlai Forna for his assistance in researching in the village of Rogbonko and surroundings. My friend and agent David Godwin, for believing in me, for listening to my dreams and helping to make them real. At Bloomsbury, my editor Michael Fishwick for his passion for these stories, thoughtful editing and commitment to this book over three years. Alexandra Pringle for her advice on the manuscript and remarkable energy. Rosalind Hanson-Alp for lunch, laughter and advice relating to the fauna of Sierra Leone.

Above all to my husband, Simon Westcott, to whom I owe so much happiness.

ANCESTOR STONES

Aminetta Forna

A GROVE PRESS READING GUIDE
PREPARED BY LINDSEY TATE

QUESTIONS FOR DISCUSSION

1. In speaking of her marriage, Asana states "I learned about women—how we are made into the women we become, how we shape ourselves, how we shape each other" (p. 107). Using this quote as a springboard, begin your discussion by considering the central role of women in the patriarchal society portrayed in the novel. Is their crucial role something of a paradox? What are some of the specific roles that women undertake? Throughout the novel we learn much about the complex hierarchical system of marriage. How do the women support each other and how do they undermine one another? Note that the word "Ores" means both co-wife and rival.

2. At the beginning of the novel Abie returns to her childhood home of Rofathane from London and strains to hear the voices of the past "but the layers of years in between us were too many" (p. 10). What does she mean by this? What is Abie's role in the novel? Do you find her to be a satisfying and fully fleshed character? Are the stories

of the four aunts perhaps more accessible when filtered through Abie?

3. When Abie reads the letter she states that it is written in English "but the words, the sensibility, was African." (p. 8). How far could this statement apply to the whole novel? Think about the story that Abie tells at the beginning of the novel about different ways of seeing. Consider also cultural differences between the West and the African society depicted.

4. One of the striking images in the first pages of the novel is of Gibril Umaru Kholifa's iron four-poster bed being carried by eight men through the forest. How is the patriarch portrayed by the women in his family? What are their relationships, their memories of his public persona v. his private moments? Would you consider him a good father? How do the opinions of the aunts regarding their father change as they mature, and outside influences enter their lives?

5. What do the ancestor stones of the title represent? How do they fit in with Asana's statement that "there are many ways of looking at the same thing." (p. 236). Consider how important they are to Mary's mother. Explore the importance of names in connection with the stones, and throughout the rest of the novel, especially reflected in the character of Mary. What is Mary's given name and when is it changed, and changed back? Does she think of herself as Mary? What does it mean that the family seems to have referred to her as Mary the whole time Abie has known her?

6. Told as a series of stories, this novel celebrates the oral tradition. Whose work is the "guarding of stories" (p. 12) and why? Think of some of the different ways in which stories are told and used throughout the novel from the scare-tactic tales of Asana's grandmother to rumor mongering about Serah's mother. Discuss the place of truth and memory in the telling of stories. "What story shall I tell? The story of how it really was, or the one you want to hear?" (p. 15).

7. Consider the theme of silence as it runs through the stories. Recall why Mary was banished from going to the women's meetings once she learned how to talk. Can you think of instances in the novel where "words once uttered never die" (p. 62) and loose talk causes dramatic upheavals in the aunt's lives? What about later in the book during the dangers of the civil war? How does voting fit into the theme of silence? What is the role of Bobbio, the boy with no voice?

8. In many ways Asana, daughter of Ya Namina, represents the old way of life before the changes wrought by the twentieth century. What is her relationship with her mother? Why does she head so blindly into her disastrous marriage? How has Asana's opinion of her mother changed by the end of the novel? What profound realization occurs when she catches sight of her mother mourning, and what does it give Asana the strength to do?

9. Mary says "We deserted our gods . . . My mother would not yield. And to this day nobody has ever come to me and said she was noble and righteous to do so" (p. 36). In what ways does Mary's life reflect the seeming desertion of the gods of her childhood? In which ways does she find comfort in her early beliefs? Find examples of the blending of the old and the new in Mary's faith and practice of religion.

10. Hawa seems to attract bad luck and indeed her life is filled with unlucky events. In tracing the details of her misfortunes, do you see patterns beginning to occur? How much of her misery does she make herself? Think back to the best day of her life, "the day every one of my father's wives wished she was my mother. And every one of his daughters wanted to be me" (p. 68). What do these feelings show about her character? When she says about Khalil, "I loved him so much I sacrificed my own happiness" (p. 191) do you empathize with her or are you irritated by her actions? What about when she waits in vain for her soldier son to visit?

11. During her childhood, Serah rejects her mother when she is accused of adultery "I no longer wanted her for my mother" (p. 101). As Serah grows up and makes her own mistakes in life what is the irony of this rejection? At what point does she realize how much she owes her mother and how alike they are? Consider Serah's statement "I preferred to make my way alone than live with unhappiness" (p. 233) and discuss the ways she demonstrates this independence throughout her life.

12. Serah is one of the new generation who left their country without looking "back at the old, only forward to the vision of the new" (p. 214). To what extent is Serah able to leave her old way of life behind? How does she find herself caught between two worlds? Consider her relationships with Janneh and Ambrose. What do the red shoes represent? In the forty years that pass between her two experiences as a returning officer at a voting station how has Serah changed? How has Africa changed? Are there reflections of the world Serah knew from her childhood in the tense atmosphere of the voting station? Recall the women singing.

13. As Asana says about Rofathane, "change came slowly to this place" (p. 121). Talk about examples of the way in which the Western world started to infiltrate the society of the village, from Asana's stories of the moon-shadow man to the arrival of Mr. Blue and the mining companies. How did the creep of colonialism affect the lives of the aunts?

14. As the novel follows the aunts and they move beyond the reach of Rofathane their family history becomes entwined with the history of a nation. How has their childhood prepared them for this future? Do any of the aunts surprise you with their actions? How far do you agree with Asana's statement that her great-granddaughter "had arrived in a world where suddenly we were all lost, as helpless as newborns" (p. 297).

15. Consider the ways in which the author forces the aunts to confront and reflect on their own identities, and the ways in which they are viewed by others. Why is this especially important to Mary's story? Discuss her experience in England, the country with "so many mirrors" (p. 206) where "nobody looks me in the eye" (p. 206). What are her feelings when she returns home, and why? Why does she feel the need to communicate her story to Abie? How does her story mirror the story of Africa itself?

16. Toward the end of the novel Serah says "Sometimes I think this is what happened to our country. Nobody heeded the warnings, nobody smelled the rain coming . . . until we were all engulfed by it" (p. 264). Find instances from the lives of the four women of this constant refusal to admit the truth. The author often uses images of stopping up the senses to portray this smothering of the truth: "I plugged my ears with imaginary mud" (p. 64) and Serah covering the smells of poverty with the scent of flowers (p. 225). Discuss other examples.

17. "We were like a collection of differently coloured and shaped bottles," says Serah (p. 168) of the various children raised by her grandmother. How fitting a description of the aunts themselves is this? How are the aunts alike, how different? Do they become more or less alike as the novel progresses? Discuss the role of parenting in general in the novel, and that of the co-wife family structure.

18. At the end of the novel, Abie finds that she is no longer a stranger in Rofathane, and says that "in this small world everybody had a place" (p. 314). Asana states that at Rofathane there existed "an imperfect order. An order we understood" (p. 294). How far do you agree with this statement? What are your feelings about the order that existed?

19. How do the aunts make private acts of rebellion against the society of their childhood? Are these conscious acts, or

reflections of the changing times they live in? Why do you think they all end up at Rothafane again?

20. What is the effect of telling the stories with the added layer of hindsight after a long passage of time? How accurate do you think the details of the stories are, and does that matter to you? Can you think of examples of how the women grapple with the effort to remember, or even wonder whether they have the details right? What about clear images that bring back a whole scene?

21. Discuss the role of love and sexuality throughout the novel. Consider the importance of the theme of fertility from the constant references to the rainy season, to Hawa's tubal ligation. Asana describes her sexual initiation (removal of clitoris) as a special time in the company of women—are you able to support or understand her viewpoint?

22. Conclude your discussion of the novel by considering Asana's statement "I let it be known that I would consider relinquishing the birthright of womanhood in exchange for the liberty of a man" (p. 248). What does she mean by this, and how does it resonate throughout the novel? Look back at the question that started your discussion, perhaps, to fully understand the rich complexity of the birthright of women. Do you think that Asana's was a good decision to make?

SUGGESTIONS FOR FURTHER READING:

The Red Tent by Anita Diamant; *Falling Leaves* by Adeline Yen Mah; *Beasts of No Nation* by Uzodinma Iweala; *The Poisonwood Bible* by Barbara Kingsolver; *The Darling* by Russell Banks; *Season of Migration to the North* by Tayeb Salih; *Admiring Silence* by Abdulrazak Gurnah; *In the Eye of the Sun* by Ahdaf Soueif; *A Long Way Gone* by Ishmael Beah; *Half of a Yellow Sun* by Chimamanda Ngozi Adichie